EDGE OF *Falling*

ALSO BY SOPHIE HAMILTON

Pine Springs series

More Than Nothing

Every Reason Why

EDGE OF *Falling*

SOPHIE HAMILTON

This is a work of fiction. Names, characters, organizations, places, events, and incidents are either products of the author's imagination or used fictitiously. Any resemblance to actual persons, living or dead, or actual events is purely coincidental.

Published by Montlake, Seattle

www.apub.com

Amazon, the Amazon logo, and Montlake are trademarks of Amazon.com, Inc., or its affiliates.

EU product safety contact:
Amazon Media EU S. à r.l.
38, avenue John F. Kennedy, L-1855 Luxembourg
amazonpublishing-gpsr@amazon.com

ISBN-13: 9781662531361
eISBN: 9781662531354

Cover design by Allyse Karam
Cover image: © galacticus; © Nisachon Poompuang / Shutterstock; © Matt Champlin / Getty Images

Printed in the United States of America

For the girls who can manage
and the men who know it but say, "Let me help."

Prologue

One small lie was all it took to upend Avery Delgado's life.

OK, maybe it wasn't that small. Not the appetizer or dessert on the menu of lies, but nowhere near a seventy-two-ounce steak dinner either. It was a sizable side or small entree. The tater tot casserole of a lie.

And if she was strictly honest—which Avery usually tried to be—the lie that she chose to tell at seventeen years old was a bit of a "fuck you" to her parents.

To her dad, who seemed to have forgotten how to tell the truth.

And to her mom, who liked to judge other people for their poor decisions, when it was evidently so easy to make all the right choices. Like she had—by marrying Avery's father and securing herself a privileged lifestyle in one simple step.

If Avery hadn't seen Tanner Stone crash his truck that day in a rain-soaked school parking lot, she'd never have had to choose between truth or lie anyway.

If she'd been able to find her keys inside the messy jumble of her tote bag, she'd have unlocked her car, climbed in, and driven home. She may have cursed a little at the weather and reached out to flick on the heater, but her life would have carried on along the same narrow track as always. Generally blessed. Emotionally limited. Pretty standard.

Probably.

But sometimes it was the truth that hurt. And the truth had the power to steal dreams and destroy lives.

So Avery told the lie that would change everything.

Chapter 1
Avery

It wasn't the best start to the weekend.

"You promised you'd be ready," Bel complained from the doorway and, though her eye roll was indulgent, there was impatience in the tap of her foot. "We're going to be late!"

"I'm sorry. I was only—" Crouched on the floor and holding one sneaker with two upholstery tacks embedded in the sole, Avery cast her gaze over the rest of the tin's contents littered across her workshop floor.

Leo cut across her apology with his usual good humor. "Look, it's all easily sorted. Don't start explaining now or we'll be even later making it to the lake." He left Bel's side and plucked the shoe from Avery's grasp. "Give me that and I'll get the tacks out. You pick up the rest. Bel, message Gemma and tell her we'll text when we're on our way."

Avery shot him a grateful smile as Bel left them to it, mumbling about traffic flow, schedules, and herding cats.

In truth, the weekend ahead had Avery a little nervous. She'd tried to distract herself with a quick stock inventory and ended up making a mess, even though there was no reason to be edgy. What had Bel said? *"It'll be fun! A joint bachelor/bachelorette party and a whole weekend of hanging out with our friends and playing games!"* But Avery couldn't help the creeping niggle of tension at the base of her spine whenever she thought about the possibility . . .

Fumbling the upholstery tacks again, she dropped half the ones she'd gathered in her hand and let out a growl of frustration.

"What's up, Ave?" Leo's quick glance held curiosity. Solid and relaxed, he soothed her with his presence, as always. There was something so simple about their easy friendship and it helped her get a grip on her emotions.

She could do this; it was just two light-hearted days. What's the worst that could happen?

"Nothing at all," Avery assured him—and maybe herself—as she refocused on gathering the pins without getting stabbed. Together, they made short work of clearing up and headed back into the house to find Bel.

It was less than half an hour later when they pulled up outside a pretty yellow Craftsman-style bungalow one road back from Main Street. Peggy Winterburn stopped watering her lawn, just to make sure they weren't blocking her driveway, but Gemma, spilling out of her front door in a chaotic whirl, left the Pine Springs busybody no time to form a complaint if they were. Throwing a bulging travel bag into the trunk, she piled into the back seat, exuding excitement from the tips of her bouncing curls to the base of her ballet flats.

"How fun is this?! It's been so long since we went away for the weekend." Gemma dug into her purse, unearthing a pack of Twizzlers before they'd passed the town limits. She offered them forward to Leo and Bel, chucked one at Avery, and stuck the end of another into her mouth. "I've packed half my closet. The rest is in a heap on my bed." The confession was garbled around a mouthful of candy.

"Same." Leo shot Gemma a teasing glance from the passenger seat.

"You lie. I know you did Man Packing and only brought two tees and a couple of tighty whities, rolled up in a pair of shorts. But I'll be the one rocking it by the campfire." Gemma swept her hair back from her face and struck a pose.

"I don't wear tighty whities," Leo protested.

"If you're going commando on my front seat, I'm pulling over right now." Bel's finger hovered over her blinker.

"I've got pants on, for Chrissake. I'm not an animal." Leo chuckled when Bel's foot came off the accelerator. "OK, OK—and boxers. I'm one hundred percent decent. Keep driving!"

Avery sniggered. This kind of stupid bickering was exactly what she needed to get her mind off work and her mom. *And him.*

"Have Drew and Johnnie left yet?" Gemma looked between Bel and Avery for the answer.

"Yeah, they're an hour or so ahead of us. Johnnie said he wanted to be there early to help set up." Avery accepted another Twizzler. "He's taking his best man duties very seriously."

"Girlfriend of the best man is the worst role at weddings. You'll be lucky if you get to see him at all." There was sympathy in the dip of Gemma's shoulders.

With her Twizzler-free hand, Avery spun the small golden leaf that hung from the chain around her neck. "Won't be my problem. We're not seeing each other anymore."

"Since when?!" Gemma searched her face, head tilted as she tried to read Avery's level of emotion. It wasn't a struggle to reassure her.

"The other night, by mutual agreement. It was only ever casual anyway. Johnnie's busy with work and you know I don't date. Plus I think he quite likes Savannah's maid of honor."

"What will you do about pairing up for the activities?" Gemma asked with a troubled frown.

Avery's shrug was unconcerned. "We talked about that. We'll still do them together."

"That's what Drew said, too." Bel's eyes flicked up to the rear-view mirror. "So it'll be me and Drew, Avery and Johnnie, Gemma and Leo. Easy and neat."

Gemma tapped Leo on the shoulder. "Sad singles sticking together, right?"

He gave her an easy smile. "Fine by me."

"You should embrace being a sunny and serene single, living a happily unattached life," Avery said, twisting her hair into a ponytail and fixing it with the band on her wrist. "It's better than being made miserable by someone else."

Bel's glance held a well of understanding. "Not all relationships end in disaster, my little cynic. Just like not all singles are sad."

"Very true—and it's tempting to look on the positive side," agreed Avery, "but then I remember how that worked out for everyone who boarded the *Titanic* . . ." There was reluctant amusement in Bel's snort and Avery grinned. "Being single works best for me. I trust myself more than anyone else. Except you guys, of course."

"Goes without saying." Leo turned to smirk at her. "We're the best."

"Better than all the rest," Bel added dryly, reaching down to turn up the music.

And just like that the sing-a-thon began—loud, enthusiastic, and tuneful only on Leo's behalf. The playlist was a road-trip staple; they'd traveled together, belting out a selection of the same songs, for years now. As Avery leaned forward and gave her all to a slightly shrieky duet with Bel, she embraced the crazy pleasure of the carefree drive and the company of people who had her back.

Who else did she need when she had friends like these?

Stopping once for a bathroom break and again for coffee as they headed steadily north, the Twizzlers were long gone and they were all a little hoarse by the time Bel signaled to make the turn signposted "Shiverley Lake and Cabins." They weren't the first to arrive, and the parking lot was already half full. While Avery's bare arms had grown chilled from the air con in Bel's RAV4, the moment she threw open the door, the heat wrapped around her like a heavy woolen blanket.

Cozy log cabins nestled in the shade beneath a canopy of leaves. Through the gaps between tree trunks, sunshine dazzled off the surface of the lake. Naturally serene, quietly peaceful, the setting held a promised whisper of good times ahead.

They unloaded the car, splitting temporarily with Leo while he tracked down the cabin he was sharing with some of the guys, and found their own accommodation, which comprised two bedrooms off an open-plan central living area. In one corner, there was a miniature kitchen set up with a sink, some cupboards, a small fridge, a microwave, a toaster, and most importantly a decent-looking drip coffee maker. The rest of the room was given over to seating. Poking her head into the other bedroom, Avery noticed Drew had bagged the double for him and Bel already. His weekender was on the bed, zipper open and clothes spilling out like intestines from a fatal gutting.

Avery and Gemma's room was cute and compact. Matching quilted comforters covered twin beds, with simple wooden furniture filling the rest of the space. Dumping her duffel bag onto the floor by the window, Avery decided to unpack later.

Hearing male voices, she wandered into the living area again to find Drew sprawled in the armchair by the picture window and Leo handing out bottles of beer as Gemma pulled them from a cooler in the kitchen area.

When Bel emerged from the bathroom, Drew reached out and dragged her down onto his lap with a grin. As she cuddled in close, he murmured something into her ear and she laughed.

Her candy pink shorts and crochet tank top wiped any remaining traces of lawyer from her appearance and turned her into Weekend Bel, Avery's favorite version of her best friend. Teeth peeking through sinfully plump lips, she looked happy and relaxed as Drew's hand toyed affectionately with one of her neat afro puffs.

"Welcome to the party—took you long enough!" Drew's greeting was a tired drawl. He had bags under his eyes from the grueling shifts he pulled as an ER doctor but his smile still sparkled.

Avery tossed a pillow at his head in reply, then caught it when he chucked it straight back. "It's a nice day for a drive. Why hurry?" she said. "We had songs to sing."

"Leo said his ears were bleeding." Drew shot him a look of deepest sympathy.

"I didn't hear you complaining when we all nailed the bridge in 'Bad Romance.'" Avery turned, narrowing her eyes at Leo with a mock scowl.

"Did you nail it though?" he replied, stretching long legs out from his slumped position on a bright orange couch. "Or did it nail you?"

He'd pulled back his hair, twisting the long strands into a messy topknot, and his scruffy shorts and washed-out tee had him looking more like a teenager than a high-school teacher. Only the man bun and his neatly trimmed beard gave the nod that almost a decade had passed since their own schooldays. Back then, Principal Harris would have pulled him to one side with some strong words the moment his hair curled over his collar. But Avery didn't want to think about her right now.

Checking her phone, she was relieved to find no new messages waiting for her. No missed calls from her mom. So far, so good.

Maybe her luck would hold.

But, as Avery twisted the top off her beer, she had to admit she wasn't quite sure what she was hoping for—that he *would* be here or *wouldn't* be here?

At a guess, she probably had until the wedding to steel herself against seeing him again.

Tanner Stone was a success now. A household name—at least among sports fans. He was dating an influencer. Even though it was the off-season, she'd bet good money he had better things to do this weekend than rough it in a rustic cabin. He'd be traveling or training for sure.

Taking a cool, refreshing sip, Avery told herself to embrace the change of scenery. The cabin was comfortable, the weather was gorgeous, and the lake lay just a short walk away through the trees. It was Friday afternoon; the weekend stretched ahead. No responsibilities, no bar shifts in the Rusty Barrel.

Two full days of silliness and relaxation were hers for the taking.

Bring it on.

Chapter 2
Tanner

"Omigod, omigod—you made it! I didn't know if you would!" Savannah's arms were a vise around his neck as she bounced up and down.

His cousin's delighted smile made Tanner feel good that he'd prioritized coming home for this weekend. He let out a throaty laugh and hugged her back. "Wouldn't have missed it for the world."

"Cut it fine though, didn't you?!"

"I got in late last night. Had to hustle to get here. You know Mom—she found a million ways to hold me back, and Dex sends his apologies, but his flight is booked for the wedding." He'd spent the past month in the UK with his brother, coming down from the grueling NHL season by hitting the surf in Newquay—an annual tradition. This year, he'd needed the healing properties of the sea more than ever.

"Hey, man. Good to see you." Savannah's fiancé, Griffin, pushed a beer into his hand. "Welcome to Shiverley Cabins. Or 'Chaos on the Lake' as we like to call it!"

He wasn't far wrong by the looks of things. Running a thumb over the scar on his lower lip, Tanner's eyes roamed the clubhouse. He recognized about half of the guests and, guessing by the attention he was getting from the remainder, many of them recognized him, too. Music streamed from hidden speakers, amped-up chatter and high spirits rising above it. The scent of meat on the grill had him hoping the wait for food wouldn't be too long.

"Great choice for your . . . Damn—what are you calling this thing?" Tanner raised an eyebrow.

"Our Bach Bash!" Savannah threw out her arms, spilling Griff's beer down the front of his Henley.

"As in short for 'bachelor and bachelorette,' not the composer. We're not cultured enough for that." Griff licked the drink from his fingers. "I suggested the Final Single Mingle, but Sav wasn't keen."

"Maybe she's not willing to limit herself like that," Tanner said.

His cousin's punch had some real weight behind it. Luckily it fell on his good shoulder.

"Hey, no physical violence!" He held up his hands. "I'm an expensive commodity."

"Not here you're not, bro. You've come to the wrong place for fawning and flattery." Sam Archer's voice was dry as he appeared by Tanner's side. "We specialize in squashing egos and general abuse."

"With a side of we-remember-when-you-drank-puddle-water," Savannah added.

Tanner dragged his old school friend into a rough embrace. They'd not caught up in person since New Year's. "But you've missed me though, right?" He put more pressure than necessary into his grip on the back of Sam's neck.

"Well, the world kept turning but the days felt so long."

Shoving him away, Tanner held out his hand to Sam's partner, Kash. "Hey, buddy."

"I hope you're ready for this." Kash's dark eyes glittered with suppressed laughter. "You've not signed up for just any old single mingle. This one has an agenda."

"With organized activities," added Sam.

"And teams," Griff chipped in.

"It's a *Bach Bash* and it's going to be fun!" Savannah turned a stern eye on each of them in turn. "If I don't see everyone having fun, there will be hell to pay."

"I'm having fun already." Tanner summoned his winning smile and threw a casual arm around her shoulders. "So much fun. Just hanging out with you guys is a huge thrill for me."

"Understandable." Sam gave a sage nod.

"So how do the teams work?" Tanner took a gulp of his drink, enjoying the smooth slide of sweet malt down his throat. "Who's my plus-one?"

The look that Sam and Kash exchanged meant something but Tanner didn't know what. "Yeah, about that—" Sam said.

Savannah interrupted. "It wasn't easy because we weren't sure you were coming at all. I assumed, until you messaged this morning, that you'd bring Lily if you did."

Tanner ignored the veiled curiosity behind her words. "Sorry to screw with your arrangements."

"No apology needed. I'm not sure she'd have appreciated the patchy Wi-Fi anyway."

His cousin might have said more but she was cut off by Sam. "Surprised you didn't have a list of subs."

"I checked my spreadsheets," said Tanner. "There were so many offers but too little time to make the arrangements." With a grin, he took another long swallow of beer.

"Yeah, yeah," Savannah plowed on. "Anyway, most people are paired up already. I was going to put you with my maid of honor—Mia—even though she's going to be busy running all the games with Griff's best man . . ."

"Sounds promising." Tanner flashed his dimple, playing the part even as he continued to scan the busy bar area. "Is she cute?"

Kash chuckled and Savannah pursed her lips. "She's lovely but I've found a better solution. I've teamed you up with an old school friend of mine instead."

Tanner shrugged. "It's fine with me. I don't mind who I pair with." That look again. Just a quick glance but Sam was definitely fighting a smile now. "What? Why the sniggering?" Suspicion flared in his belly. "Do I know them?"

"I'm sure you'll recognize her," Savannah said. "Avery's dad used to be the mayor."

Tanner's beer froze midway to his mouth. He raised his eyes to the wooden ceiling while he processed the curveball he hadn't seen coming.

Of course it would be her.

Out of every possible ex-classmate of Savannah's, his partner for the weekend would turn out to be Avery Delgado.

His cousin's eyes were roaming the bar area. When they settled on someone on the other side of the room, she pointed and Tanner followed the direction of her finger. "There—over by the pinball machine. That's Avery."

Since the subject of their attention was blissfully unaware, it gave him a chance to study her, cataloging the differences in the woman he hadn't seen in a decade. The changes were subtle. Her hair was shorter, her curves a touch fuller in places. A square-necked floral sundress—simple, short, and cool—draped over bare thighs as she perched on a bar stool. Gripping a bottle in the pale fingers of one hand and a half-eaten hot dog in the other, she gestured with them alternately and joked with the people around her.

Just a glimpse of Avery's red hair used to have him smiling like an idiot. Tanner never knew why but she'd had that effect on him every time. Like a PB&J after shooting hoops or the opening guitar riff in "Sweet Child O' Mine," she'd plucked at a chord that vibrated deep in his stomach. His turbulent school years had been filled with watching and wanting.

But ten years was a hell of a long time.

More than a third of Tanner's life had passed since he'd last had a proper conversation with Avery Delgado, and they were very different people now.

"Tanner?"

"What?" His breath whooshed as Savannah's elbow caught him in the ribs.

"So that's OK then?"

They were all looking at him: his cousin, Griff, Sam, Kash. Tanner forced a smile. "I told you, it's fine. No problem at all. I remember her—it'll be good to catch up again."

Sam raised an eyebrow. He caught Tanner's eye and held it. *Really?* the look said.

Tanner had no reply for him. The Bach Bash was fast becoming an assault course, with the first obstacle constructed out of material from the past, and it'd be a lie to say he wasn't just a bit hesitant to tackle it.

"I'd better go say hi."

Pushing away from the bar, he crossed the floor. People moved out of his way. He drew interested glances from some, nods from others, and exchanged a few greetings as he kept moving. There'd be plenty of time for more chat over the weekend, but his feet had an agenda of their own at the moment.

The team physician, during Tanner's most recent medical, had recorded with approval his resting heart rate of forty-six beats per minute. Now, Tanner was piqued to find it spiking like it did after a shift on the ice.

She spotted him when he was a half dozen steps away, choked slightly on a bite of food, and hastily scrubbed a smear of ketchup from the corner of her lips. With a deep kink cutting a groove between her brows, Avery's hand reached for her necklace and he almost smiled then. So many years since he'd last seen her, yet such a familiar gesture.

The lack of standing room in the clubhouse had Tanner stopping a little closer to her than was comfortable, his thighs almost brushing Avery's knees. Someone clipped his shoulder, passing drinks from the bar into other eager hands, but he brushed off the apology; he'd taken harder hits from his own teammates in the locker room.

Spider threads of the past spun out between them—invisible, yet sticky. With guilt and gratitude churning inside Tanner's chest, he buried the fine residual strand of longing far enough down that he didn't need to acknowledge it.

"Hey, Stretch," he said. "It's been a while."

Chapter 3
Avery

That voice. Those eyes. That body! *Jesus Christ.* It all caught her completely off-guard, although it shouldn't have.

Avery had told herself that seeing him would be easy. She'd imagined they would only need to be polite from a distance in the large crowd of wedding guests. A nod. A wave, maybe. Only now, with Tanner right in her space and no warning, neither of those would meet the brief. He was so close she could reach out and lay her palm on his chest. Fit and fine, he was an unsettling wall of muscle, blocking her view of everyone around them.

"Hi." The single syllable was unsteady, so Avery shored it up with casual confidence and tried again. "I didn't think you were going to make it this weekend."

Tanner raised his bottle of beer, a careful twist to his mouth. "Surprise."

Yes. Yes, it was.

A surprise to be hit by a gallery of snapshots from high school.

A surprise to feel so floored by this man-version of the boy she'd once known.

A surprise to have that damn nickname snag her heart like a fishhook.

"Savannah must be thrilled you're here."

"Well, she squealed so loud my head is still ringing, so you could be right." Tanner picked at the label on his bottle, feet scuffing the floorboards and his tawny eyes never leaving her face.

"Right, guys! If I can have your attention . . ." When Johnnie banged a glass on the bar for quiet, her relief was immense.

Tanner turned to listen and, behind his back, Bel mouthed "Oh. My. God!" with exaggerated annunciation, black eyebrows scrambling in quivering arcs toward her hairline. While Avery smoothed her own expression into nonchalance, her stomach continued to fold in on itself like a sea anemone.

He stood so near, she could feel the heat from his body and it made her lightheaded. She watched Gemma check him out with huge, greedy eyes while trying to pretend she wasn't looking at him at all. And she wasn't the only one. That girl there was looking, too. Three out of four of the group in the corner. Those two near the window were even whispering together and fanning themselves. Avery didn't blame any of them.

She cataloged the similarities to younger Tanner even as she studied the tiny flowers on her dress with total concentration: the messy hair with a mind of its own, the amber eyes, the dimple, the height, the goddamn electricity. The differences centered mainly around his bulk. The guy was stacked now, his lean, lanky days firmly behind him. His olive cotton shirt hung loose over beige cargo shorts, sleeves rolled back to his elbows. The whole look was understated—casually, carelessly on point—and only someone who'd known both Tanners would be able to appreciate how far he'd come. How glossy he seemed.

The white Chucks that completed the outfit were a throwback to high school, but this pair, although not new, was in far better shape than the ones he used to wear.

Avery recalled those other sneakers, the soles flapping loose. The sharp crack of her head against the wall in the school hallway as Tanner had tripped and crashed into her, bowling her over like a set of pins. She'd had a bruise like an egg on the back of her head for days.

"Shit! I'm so sorry." His face had loomed over hers while she was still seeing stars. Scruffy hair, the color of wet sand, brushed his eyebrows and he pushed it back with agitated fingers.

"I'm OK." She wasn't sure she was.

Flicking at the toe of his tattered and filthy shoe, he'd glared at the broken rubber band that lay like a worm between them on the linoleum floor.

"Stupid thing snapped. I thought it'd hold out longer."

"Not really made for the job," she'd pointed out.

"Yeah, I guess so."

Thirteen-year-old Avery had pulled a hair tie from her wrist. "You can have this if you want. I always carry a spare. This one's pretty tough and it's got good stretch."

Tanner Stone's wide and irreverent smile had broken slowly across his face, revealing that one shallow dimple in his right cheek as he pulled the elastic over the toe of his sneaker and let it snap around his shoe. His eyes were two toffee candies. And Avery would have given him a dozen more hair ties if she'd had them.

"Concentrate, cupcake." The nudge from Bel caught her in the ribs. It was an effort to tune back into the present.

"Tonight is just for relaxing, but Savannah and Griff have given their approval for a little friendly competition this weekend. Nothing too demanding, so no need to worry!" Johnnie raised his voice to continue. "We've put you into pairs for some special activities, and points will be awarded for each one. Dig deep and try hard because the Bach Bash champions will be crowned on Sunday evening and you're going to want that trophy." A rowdy cheer went up before Johnnie calmed everyone again with the flat of his hand. "Listen carefully and I'll read out the teams of two."

Avery didn't listen carefully at all.

Does he want something, or is there another reason he's come over here now? Where's his girlfriend? Why does he still seem so familiar when so much has changed?

Tuning out ninety-five percent of what Johnnie was saying, Avery held a whole conversation with herself and picked at her thumbnail—right up until she heard their names.

"Avery and Tanner."

What? No!

Johnnie's expression was a touch apologetic. He shrugged, smiled, and moved on. Avery, horrified that her plans for a restful weekend had just gone up in smoke, registered the lack of surprise on Tanner's face.

Bel turned on Drew with a ferocious whisper. "Did you know he was going to do that?"

"He mentioned in the car that he might have to sit out of the games because of all the organizing." Drew scrubbed at his eyebrow. "I thought he'd told Avery."

"I don't mind sitting them out." She grabbed the solution with both hands.

Still Tanner said nothing, though his fingers snapped the clasp of his watch open and shut.

Bel pulled a face. "That'll be boring for you and it doesn't seem fair on Tanner." She eyed him shrewdly. "Nice to meet you, by the way. Please tell me you're carrying a non-career-threatening injury or something that'll give the rest of us an advantage along the way. Or we might be forced to mess you up!"

Drew snorted. "She's not joking. My girlfriend might be small but she's insanely competitive."

Avery wondered if that was a wince Tanner had smothered, but if he did it was gone in an instant, and he unleashed an infectious grin that sent her falling back through time with a sickening lurch. She tugged on the jagged edges of her composure while her friends absorbed him effortlessly into the group, her suggestion to sit out the activities left lying in the dust as they trampled all over it.

"Where's your girlfriend?" Avery interrupted, trying to get them back on track. "Why aren't you in a pair with her?"

Tanner shrugged, the small gesture evasive. "She's not here."

"Right." OK, that was unexpected, too. "Excuse me a moment." She slipped from her stool and threaded her way across the room.

Johnnie was chatting with Savannah's maid of honor, Mia, at the other end of the bar. Avery hesitated to interrupt until she remembered that he had tied her to Tanner for a whole weekend without a heads-up.

"Can I have a word?"

Looking over his shoulder, Johnnie pulled a face before he caught himself. "Sure. I've got a minute." They took half a step away from Mia but there was nowhere else to go without leaving the clubhouse.

Avery leaned in, keeping her voice low. "Some warning would have been nice."

Johnnie reached out to squeeze her wrist. "I'm sorry. I didn't think you'd mind and it's not going to work for me to join in—someone's got to be in charge of the judging."

"Please. There must be something else you can do." Avery was one step away from begging. "I don't mind tagging along with another team or swapping with someone else. Loads of people would like to pal up with Tanner."

"What's the big deal?" Johnnie glanced past her and held up an apologetic finger to Mia, his attention clearly divided. "Griff says he's a nice guy. And everyone else is happy in their teams. Plus, I've got no one who wants to change partners and no one to pair Tanner with if you back out, since he's turned up alone." He laughed and corrected himself. "That's not true. There are plenty of girls who'd swap in a heartbeat, but their boyfriends would kill me!" He tried a winning smile. "Come on—it's going to be fun. And the games are part of the weekend."

"Johnnie?" Mia rejoined them. "Did you say you'd put the scorecards with the packs of bottled water? If you did, I can't find them."

"No, I stashed them behind the bar. Over in the corner." He was moving away even as he spoke.

Mia shot her an apologetic glance. "Sorry, Avery—there's just so much to keep track of. If I'd known being maid of honor was this stressful, I'd have thought twice."

Avery gave her a weak grin. "No worries."

Johnnie took that as a sign he was off the hook. "Thanks, Ave. You're a star. I'll catch you later!"

And that was that. Her weekend spectacularly derailed, Avery turned on reluctant feet and headed back to her friends.

In her absence, Tanner had piled a plate high enough to feed a family and was tucking into a loaded hamburger. There was something fiercely elemental about the way he devoured his meal in enormous bites; it raised the hairs on the back of Avery's neck. Rocking lightly on his toes, constantly moving, he was charisma wrapped in a dazzling package, his smile flashing out between mouthfuls.

The infamous Tanner Appeal was clearly working overtime. Bel, Drew, and Gemma talked over each other, chatting as if they'd known him for years. Even Leo had a lazy half-smile as he sat back and observed. It was all too reminiscent of Avery's father and the way he became the center of every gathering he attended. It pushed uncomfortable buttons.

Avery's eyes narrowed on Gemma. Her last hope. She snuck a hand between Bel and Drew and tugged on Gemma's elbow, teasing her out of the group.

"Hey, babe! Get you with free access to the NHL beefcake this weekend . . ." Gemma murmured out of the corner of her mouth. "His muscles have muscles!"

Avery ducked her head close to Gemma's ear. "You want to be the lucky one? Just say the word and I'll pair up with Leo instead. Tanner's fun and you're single."

"Are you mad? You know how long I've been holding out for this weekend. This is my big chance." Gemma shot a sideways glance at the group and Avery's heart sank.

Gemma's torch for Leo had been carried for so long and with such a tight grip that the only person left, ironically, in the dark was Leo. Her friend's outwardly bubbly personality masked surprisingly low self-esteem. When awkward flirting and heavy hints had failed to make the impact Gemma craved in the early days of meeting Leo, she'd hesitated to be more obvious about her feelings. The result was an ongoing friendship that only Leo was entirely happy with, but Gemma lived in perpetual hope. And Avery didn't have the heart to take that hope away from her.

The clubhouse seemed to have shrunk since Tanner joined their group. The roof was lower, she could swear it was. If it had been warm before, now it was stifling—even with the doors thrown open to the evening air. Avery slid back into the group; the conversation ebbing and flowing around her. And just a few inches from her elbow, the boy she'd put her neck on the line to rescue—who'd turned into the man she'd tried her hardest to forget—devoured another hamburger, seeming as unperturbed as anyone would be if they had the world at their feet.

Tanner caught her eye and raised a brow.

Twisting a stray strand of hair, Avery pinned a smile to her lips. "Looks like I'm all yours, partner."

She wished she could take back the words the moment she said them. The frown that gripped Tanner's features as he cleared his throat made him look temporarily less assured, more distant. And he didn't come back with the smart response she'd expected. Instead the silence stretched.

At school, Avery had been the one with the world at her feet—a big, shiny fish in a small judgmental pool—while he'd struggled through each grade with poor marks and no lunch. Though she knew he'd heard the gossip, the disparaging comments about his shabby appearance and his family's straitened circumstances, Tanner ignored it all. And, like an iridescent beetle or the wind in the pines, he'd drawn Avery's attention. She'd found herself fascinated by his big wide smile because he used his whole body to express his happiness. Tanner smiled with his mouth, his eyes, his cheeks, even his hands. He made a person want to turn their face to him and soak up his joy like a sunflower under summer rays.

Serious had never looked right on Tanner Stone. Not then and not now.

Fortunately Bel, who had never met a silence she couldn't conquer, rallied the conversation like a trooper.

"I heard a sports reporter describe hockey as a cross between ballet and murder," she said. "Graceful but violent. It made me wish I'd taken it up."

"'Graceful but violent' is my go-to answer when anyone asks me how you are," snickered Drew, looping his arm around her neck.

Leo gave Bel a poke. "They haven't built a penalty box that could hold you. They'd need a shark cage."

As the banter swirled around them, Avery could have sworn Tanner's white Chucks shifted an inch closer to her stool. Putting it down to the number of people fighting for room in the enclosed space, she tried to ignore the fact that her pulse was beating at the base of her throat like the footsteps of an invading army.

And though she avoided his eyes, she was more than aware of the cautious glances he threw in her direction, as if he wasn't sure he liked what he saw. Avery told herself it didn't matter what Tanner thought of her. Any connection they'd ever had was ten years past its sell-by date and he had no solid place in her future.

It would be safest all round to focus on the present. The weekend looked like it was going to be challenging enough.

Chapter 4
Tanner

He'd always been a sucker for Avery Delgado.

Tanner remembered passing her on the sidewalk in town, several months after their collision in the school hallway.

"Hey, Stretch."

Avery's eyes were the palest of blue, framed by an indigo rim. She'd studied him carefully, a calm unveiled slide that held more honesty than when she was in the company of others. And the crashing waves of energy and jumbled thoughts inside Tanner had sighed and settled; the noise quieted. It was the damnedest feeling.

"Stretch?" She'd raised an eyebrow, and he'd gestured to his left foot, where the hair tie she'd given him had held his ruined sneaker together.

His latest pair were in better shape so far but not by much.

"You were right—it had good stretch. Lasted nearly a month."

Avery slipped an identical one from her wrist and held it out. "Might as well have a spare, just in case. Those look like they're going the same way."

There was no censure in her tone and that had surprised him, coming from the daughter of the local mayor, the girl who breezed through school with her small following of influential disciples.

Avery's friends back then had included the principal's daughter, the niece of Chief Roberts, and a handful of girls whose dads were big noises in the business guild. For all Tanner knew, she was still in touch with them now, although he couldn't see them here.

Her family name had clout.

His had none.

It made what she'd done for him even more extraordinary, and he'd never forgotten it.

"I'm talking to you!"

Tanner was wrenched from his thoughts by Savannah flicking his ear.

"Come with me. I want to introduce you around," his cousin urged and, more than ready for a distraction, he let himself be led away from Avery's circle.

As it turned out, the Bach Bash group was rowdy but fun. When the sun eventually dipped, the majority of guests headed outside to gather around a firepit where Savannah produced the necessary ingredients for s'mores like a rabbit from a hat. Grabbing a bottle of water from the bar, Tanner followed along, his mouth already watering in anticipation of the sugar rush.

He tried not to search Avery out but failed miserably.

Elbow to elbow with Kash, her hair flashed like flames in the evening sun, and when Sam's partner lost the marshmallow from his stick to the fire, her throaty giggle was infectious. Unaccountably envious that she'd given this first free burst of laughter to someone else, Tanner forced himself to maintain a healthy distance.

Maybe if he'd managed to find his voice inside the clubhouse, he could have said something more to break the ice. He had game, for fuck's sake. Where had it gone?

"I refuse to believe that Kash has done you dirty already."

"Huh?" With a grunt, Tanner turned to find Sam at his shoulder.

"Or maybe it's not him you're scowling at." Sam ran a thoughtful hand over his jaw.

"No, it is him," Tanner said, taking a casual swig from his bottle of water. "I was wondering what he sees in a goof-off like you."

"So many things—I couldn't possibly list them all." Sam gave a lazy grin. "But mainly he loves me for my brains and good looks."

"And self-effacing humility, too, I guess."

"Says the King of the Ice. Your modesty is the first thing to come across in interviews. You really need to work on your confidence." Sam grabbed the bottle from Tanner's hand and drained it in a couple mouthfuls. "I've missed you, bro. It's going to be good to have you home."

"'Bout time, I guess. I'm looking forward to it, too," he said.

"You must need extra closet space for all the team jerseys you've had over the years."

"There've been a few." More than a few. The turnover of teams, cities, and states had been exciting, exhilarating. Exhausting.

"Found somewhere to live yet?" Sam asked.

Tanner shook his head. Arlo, a college buddy who fulfilled the role of both manager and financial advisor, had sent him a few possible properties but he'd put off looking at them. There was just too much still up in the air. "There are people who'll sort that out for me once I know I'm staying."

Sam held a hand to his chest in a gesture of deep, mortal offense. "You don't need 'people,' jackass. You have me. I'm your people."

Tanner grinned. "Well, get on it then and earn your realtor's fee. I'd rather give you the money anyway."

"Already done." Sam looked smug. "I know just the place. I'll show you next week."

Kash parted from Avery and strolled over, bearing a gooey mess on a paper plate that he pushed into Sam's hands. "One for you. But mind, it's—"

"Fuck! That's hot!" Sam's eyes watered as he tried to extract the molten mouthful from his lips.

"Yeah, that's what I was going to say." Kash's voice was threaded with laughter. "Jeez-o-Pete, I can't take you anywhere."

Tanner wasn't listening, his eyes tracking Avery as she peeled away from the group and headed for the lakeside.

"I'll be back in a minute." Without waiting for a reply, he headed into the clubhouse to grab another couple of drinks, flipping Sam off over his shoulder for the knowing snigger he caught as he left.

She must have heard his footfalls on the wooden jetty—he wasn't anywhere near as stealthy on land as he was on the ice—but Avery kept her eyes fixed on the water in the slowly dimming light. Totally still, she was calm solitude in human form. It was something he'd been fascinated by at school—how she could appear so composed, even surrounded by people. He'd sometimes had the crazy thought that, if he rubbed himself all over her, some of Avery's poise would stick to him and seep into his bones. But he'd never gotten anywhere near to trying.

"Thought you might need something to wash away the charcoal." Lowering himself to the ground, Tanner passed her a bottle of water.

"It's not a proper s'more without a little ash."

He felt the low rasp of her voice like cool fingers down his spine. Peeling the label off his bottle, he screwed it up in his fist. "I went to a charity bash a while ago where they served savory s'mores. Salami, soft cheese, and olives. Not a hint of ash."

"Those aren't s'mores." Avery's sniff was laden with disapproval. "They're a crime against humanity."

The chatter from the Bach Bash, muffled and distant, became a backing track to the top branches twisting in the breeze, the waves lapping around the jetty posts, and the occasional mew of a gray catbird. Peace washed off the lake like steam from a bowl of soup. Tanner wished he could enjoy it, but his insides were all knotted and he didn't really know why. Flicking loose leaves and slivers of wood into the water, he cursed himself for the empty void where he usually stored his easy charm.

"It's so pretty here. Should be a nice weekend," Avery said eventually, and he made a noise of agreement.

It was going to be something, that was for sure. Whether he'd choose the word "nice" was up for debate.

She wrapped her arms around her knees as if she was cold, and Tanner almost moved a little closer—not so close they were touching but close enough that some of his warmth might make the leap from his body to hers—but he caught himself just in time.

Avery cleared her throat. "How's your family?"

Small talk. He could manage that. "They're all good, thanks. Dex is working in the UK. He turned into a nerd—I don't even understand what he does. It's something to do with designing software for security systems. Reid just started up a microbrewery in Traverse City."

He felt more than saw her nod. "I bumped into your mom in the diner a while back. She looked well."

"Yeah, she's great. Moving house made a big difference to her lungs and she takes her fitness pretty seriously now."

Getting his mom out of the shithole he'd grown up in had been his first priority. Although money couldn't buy good health, it was everything when it came to preventable illness. His mother's wheezing, whistling cough had woven through his childhood, filtering out from beneath her bedroom door with each fresh bout of bronchitis. And it was one of the reasons Tanner's bum shoulder scared the crap out of him. There was too much riding on his earning power to allow any physical weakness to put him out of action.

His left hand rising unconsciously to prod at the joint in question, he said, "She started dating again. Henry's a nice guy."

Avery's smile teased him with its brevity. "I heard that. He teaches at PS High, right? Leo's there, too—ninth grade."

"Yeah. He moved into town a couple years ago." There was another momentary silence. "How are your parents?" Tanner hesitated before asking, but it would have been a glaring omission to avoid the question.

She gazed out across the water. "They're fine."

"Your dad and Principal Harris still . . . together?"

Avery gave a tight nod and Tanner wouldn't have pressed any further if he'd been held at gunpoint. His knee bounced, his fingers tapped. Her sigh, softer than a whisper, escaped into the evening air.

"I'd better get back to the others. They'll be wondering where I am." Her voice was distant, a little stilted.

Stay a bit longer, Tanner wanted to say. *I have so many questions. Does this feel as weird for you as it does for me? And why is that?*

"Have you been dating Johnnie long?" he asked instead.

Avery's smile as she climbed to her feet was a glossy copy of her natural one. "We went out a couple times because he works with Drew and it was fun to hang as a foursome, but we're not together. I don't do commitment."

She turned to walk back along the jetty before Tanner could form a follow-up to her statement. Though he felt no impatience to return to the clubhouse, he stood up and fell in by her side.

"I've seen photos of you and your girlfriend online. She's very pretty," Avery said, sliding the charm on her necklace back and forth. "Will she be coming to the wedding?"

"Unlikely." Tanner's feet sank into the sand as they stepped off the jetty. "We've just split up."

She looked at him then, pale irises glittering in the half-light. "I'm sorry."

He didn't want to think about Lily. "It's no big deal."

"I'm sure the NHL's very own 'Ace Face' isn't short of offers."

Tanner smirked to hide the sharp tug of embarrassment. "You saw that headline?"

"And a handful of others."

"At least I get nicknames suitable for a sporting god now. Sam called me Doink for three years straight at school because our doorbell at home didn't ring properly."

"Nothing like old friends for keeping you grounded." Avery's mouth ticked up at one corner. "You're still close then—you and Sam?"

"I haven't seen enough of him recently but I'm hoping that's going to change now."

"Why now?" she asked and, when a few fiery strands of hair caught on the outside edge of her lashes, she pushed them away with delicate fingers.

He'd remembered her as far shorter than she was. In reality, the top of Avery's head sat level with Tanner's nose. He'd be able to press his lips to her forehead just by ducking his chin if he cared to. The thought did nothing for his focus.

"Uh . . ." Clearing his throat, Tanner looked away. "I'm signing with the Rapids. I'm moving back. Haven't you heard?"

Her small start told him she hadn't, and Avery's teeth caught on her lower lip. When her eyes searched his face, the pupils were tight dots in a sea of blue. Tanner examined her tiny gold nose ring, the spray of freckles over her cheekbones. The freckles had always been there; the piercing was new. He frowned at this proof of time gone by. She frowned at his frown.

"Where did you get to? I've been looking for you." Bel's call shattered their silent conversation as she approached them from the firepit area.

"Just talking tactics with my teammate." Avery jerked a thumb in Tanner's direction. "Tricks and treachery. That kind of thing."

"I'm so proud." Bel curled an arm around Avery's waist. "I like to think my scheming is a legacy that keeps on giving."

Outside the clubhouse, Leo Marsh and Avery's friend with the light brown hair loitered on a bench. Both turned speculative eyes toward him as Tanner drew closer. His memories of Marsh at school were vague because he'd been in the same grade as Avery—one below Tanner's own—and talented at music rather than sports. In Tanner's experience, the two didn't really mix. But he did remember Marsh had been smart. Way smarter than him.

His own schooldays had been filled with the stifling pressure to study and focus, the possibility of losing out on his college scholarship an ever-present specter lurking on every page. It taunted him each time Tanner opened his books, laughing at the grades that held him back as he tried to keep his head down and his GPA up. He knew his NHL dreams would scatter like smoke if he didn't.

"You're not helping yourself with all these careless mistakes."

"Have you tried being more organized?"

"If you'd take your studies seriously and pay attention, your grades wouldn't be such a concern."

He'd heard it all from his teachers. As if any of their comments were the least bit helpful.

He could still taste the frustration that came with being so easily distracted, the embarrassment of not being able to absorb and remember stuff everyone else found simple. The extra pressure had just made everything a hundred times worse. On the ice, focus wasn't an issue. Skating was instinct and pure joy combined. Thinking, planning, studying—that had taken everything he had. He'd needed the scholarship so badly.

Tanner rubbed a weary hand over his face. His head was heavy, his eyes gritty. It was around 3 a.m. UK time now and he hadn't slept well last night after napping on the plane. With the familiar effects of jetlag kicking in like a bitch, he decided against following Avery into the clubhouse and made his excuses instead.

Thirty-five minutes later, stretched out in a bed just a bit too short, Tanner folded his arms behind his head and stared up at the ceiling, chasing sleep that was now elusive.

He'd earned more money than he'd ever dreamed of and traveled the world in style when he had the time, but this weekend was stirring up issues he thought he'd dealt with. Insecurities that weren't welcome.

Because, much as he might try to forget it, he owed his success to the auburn-haired woman who still drew him in like iron filings to a magnet. And that debt was weighing heavy on his battered shoulders.

Chapter 5
Avery

It wasn't enough that Avery had to deal with a hand grenade chucked into her weekend in the shape of a six-foot-one blast from the past. Apparently, when it came to her life, there was always room for more pressure.

A couple of staff members had fired up the grill again this morning, cooking bacon and eggs in a skillet, drawing people out of their cabins with the rich and inviting scent. They handed out rough-cut breakfast sandwiches on a first-come, first-served basis, with cheery greetings and practiced efficiency. Avery was halfway through hers when she got her mother's first text.

Mom:

The shower's blocked.

Aww, hey, Mom. Yeah, I'm having a lovely time, thanks. Avery's spirits sank like a tissue paper flower in a pool of water.

I'll check it out when I'm home. Probably just full of hair and stuff.

Her mother took an inordinate amount of time to type her next message.

Mom:

It's going to be a long weekend. I haven't spoken to anyone since Wednesday.

I'm only away a couple of days and I called you before I left.

Mom:

A phone call isn't the same. But don't worry about me. I'm used to being alone.

Guilt was a solid ball in the pit of her gut as her mom's woeful instruction had the exact opposite effect. Juggling her phone to send another reply, Avery fumbled and dropped her sandwich.

"Crap!" The muttered word was smothered in frustration and laced with concern.

"Let's hope it's not a coordination task this morning." Leo crouched down before she could, his fingers closing around the remains of her sandwich. He examined it and wrinkled his nose. "You can't eat that—there's dirt in your egg. Want me to get you another?"

Shaking her head, Avery slid her cell into the pocket of her shorts. "I've had enough."

Leo lobbed the remnants into the trash like he was shooting a basket. Behind him, Tanner's eyes met hers as she backed away. He was leaning against the doorframe of the clubhouse, frowning slightly—or maybe just squinting into the sun. Avery wished he'd smile. She wished she didn't think everything was better when Tanner smiled.

As her phone buzzed again and then again, she also wished she didn't feel so burdened by pressure and duty.

She wished so many things.

Avery shook her head to clear it, suddenly out of sorts and needing some space. "I'm just gonna grab something from the cabin. I'll be back in a minute."

"No time for that, babe. We're on a schedule!" Gemma caught her by the waist from behind and spun her into a twirl, ignoring her resistance. Looking around, Avery realized people were already gathering for the first activity of the day.

Mia and Johnnie led them, like well-behaved schoolchildren, to a clearing away from the lake, where three staff members waited with smiles of welcome on their faces. Smiles that grew when they stared past Avery to the person behind her.

"Tanner Stone! Man, I can't believe it." The oldest of the trio, heavyset and bearded, was clearly delighted to recognize him. "I read about you maybe signing here—the Rapids are my team. We need someone with your speed, son!"

"Good to have your support, sir."

Avery watched as Tanner accepted the attention with understated grace, though his hand jiggled in his pocket. But the smile soon slid from his face when he spotted the harnesses rigged from the trees surrounding the clearing. He scratched uneasily at the scruff on his jaw, one sleeve of his t-shirt pulling back to reveal a landscape of pine trees spreading in dark ink over the expanse of his biceps. The tattoo was detailed and stunning. It reminded Avery of the pine stands that flanked Weller's Lake and the western outskirts of Pine Springs.

Pulling her eyes away, she faced front again as Johnnie blew a whistle. *What idiot gave him a whistle?*

"Welcome to day one of our Bach Bash Couples Competition. Find your partners, if you haven't already, and I'll hand over to Geoff here, who's going to introduce our first challenge—The Crate Stack!"

"Thank you, Johnnie." Geoff stepped forward, emitting geniality from every pore. "Right, this one is pretty simple. Each pair has to build a tower. You can only use two crates, side by side, for each level, and both members have to be on top for that layer to count." He gestured to a pile of molded plastic crates at the base of the trees. "We'll pass them up to you, one by one, but that's all we'll do. You have to position them, climb up, and balance. The attempt ends when the tower topples. You'll each wear a helmet and a full-body harness attached to the top rope setup when stacking and climbing, and every climber will be fully supported by what we call a 'belayer' down on the ground. It's the belayer's job to control the rope, and when you fall—which you will—they'll lower you slowly to the ground." Geoff looked straight at Tanner. "Whatever you weigh."

Tanner didn't seem reassured. His feet fidgeted in the dust. "I fucking hate heights," he murmured next to Avery, and she turned to see his throat constrict around an audible swallow.

"Sorry to hear that, big guy." Bel popped up next to them, and she rubbed her hands together, eyes sparkling.

"What the hell?" grumbled Tanner. "Has she got ears like a bat?"

"Yup." Avery nodded. "And the takedown skills of a tsetse fly. Don't expect sympathy."

It turned out that the pairs who did well were mainly those with smaller and lighter builds. Bel and Drew made it look easy, their coordination matched by their fearlessness as they led the pack with a climbing height of seventeen crates. Sam and Kash followed, giving them a run for their money. Leo and Gemma, not so much—although Avery doubted Gemma's full concentration was on the task. Savannah and Griff, exchanging wild kisses at each level without a care for the structural integrity of their stack, soon plummeted to the ground amid a sea of vomiting noises from their friends below.

Johnnie and Mia scribbled numbers officiously on clipboards which the couples could probably have remembered themselves but would have definitely exaggerated.

Watching the other teams, Avery embraced the distraction; it was compulsive viewing. Each time the towers tumbled with a crash, the rush of adrenaline forced a burst of laughter from her throat. With every fall, Tanner flinched.

Their own turn came somewhere around the middle. By the time she was being fitted into her harness, Avery had analyzed the issues and thought she might have worked out the best strategy. Tanner looked a little gray around the gills.

When he held out his hands so they could step up onto the first two crates, Avery hesitated.

"Don't leave me up here alone, Stretch." Though he smiled, the nervy twitch of his mouth was at odds with the playful words.

Avery gave a soft snort. "All eight inches off the ground? You're gonna have to dig deeper than that, Stone, or we'll be in trouble." But she stepped up, her hands drowning in the heat of his grip and a flush climbing her neck.

Damn, he was close. Avery pulled her fingers free and grabbed the straps of Tanner's harness instead. He grasped her elbows. She heard his sharp in-breath, felt the release brush her left ear. They both froze.

"Get a move on, you two, or we'll have to impose a time limit!" Bel heckled from a safe distance.

Keeping her chin down, Avery dragged her focus back to the task at hand.

Their first immediate problem was the size of Tanner's feet. When she stepped forward onto his crate to add another on top of her own, there was barely any room to stand. It wasn't so bad for the first half a dozen moves; they kept it quick, maintaining as much of a gap between them as they could. But as the tower grew higher, they were forced to grip each other tighter for stability and balance. Though Avery tried to pretend he was Leo, not a single molecule of her makeup was fooled for a second.

Nimble and flexible, she was far better than Tanner at crouching and turning in the limited space to fix each new level in place. He swore fluently every time he had to let go with one hand to reach down for another crate. By twelve high, the sway of the tower was clearly getting to him and his fingers bit into the bones of her hips until she could barely move. A swell of heat burned through Avery's chest, her breath coming in sharp and ragged gasps.

"I can't turn if you hold me that tight." She shot a glance up at his face. His jaw was clamped and way too close to her mouth. The slice of a short, vicious scar cut through the curve of his lower lip. Another edged one eyebrow. His nose had definitely been broken since their schooldays, possibly more than once. They were the marks of a man who lived a physical life, and he was no less attractive for them.

The proximity was way too much, way too soon. She'd barely got her head around Tanner's reappearance in her life and now she was plastered against him, breathing in his heat, swallowing his scent. She didn't want this.

She *maybe* did want this . . .

No, she did not want this.

"My fucking legs are shaking," he growled into her ear. "You're the only thing keeping me upright. And I have excellent balance."

Avery thought again that his face didn't suit a frown. The knotted eyebrows and tense mouth looked alien on Tanner; they reminded her of times she wanted to forget.

"One more crate and we can jump if you want. Bel can have this round."

"No, she fucking can't." Tanner's denial was immediate. "We're up here now so we climb until we fall. We're not quitting. Just . . . distract me somehow. Tell me something I don't know."

His hands relaxed enough for Avery to turn in his grasp, then he curled one corded forearm around her midriff and reached down to grip the crate being passed up to him on the end of a pole. Her heart clattered crazily as his stomach muscles trembled against her back.

Taking it from him, Avery edged the crate into place and they both shook with the effort of bracing themselves when the tower rocked beneath their feet.

"What do you want to know?" she asked, her voice strangled, as she stepped up and turned to face him again.

"Um." Tanner wobbled, paled, and gathered himself. "Who did you go to prom with?"

"Tyson Dax."

His double take nearly overbalanced them. Avery grabbed for his harness and missed, her fists closing around handfuls of damp cotton while Tanner's arms shot out to steady her. Her nose smashed against his neck, a narrow silver snake-link chain inhaled between her parted lips, warm and salty. Her stomach dipped and swooped as she spat it out. The tower wobbled, then settled. Down below, a chorus of "Oooooo's" escaped from the watching group. Unpeeling her fingers, Avery put a sliver of air between them.

"You're fucking kidding me!"

She wiggled free of his grip and stepped up onto the new level. Tanner groaned as she turned but followed as soon as she'd made space for his feet.

"Yeah, I am." Avery let the grin escape.

"Chrissake, Stretch," he wheezed. "Are you trying to kill us?"

Nope, but she had successfully manipulated the question so that was a win. There was a limit to how honest she was willing to be.

They managed another two crates.

"Tyson fucking Dax." Tanner grated the name into her ear, lips barely moving as sweat beaded on his ashen temples. "Like that psychopathic weasel would know a corsage from a Corvette."

He bent to reach for the next crate in slow motion, knees opening either side of Avery's legs, his quads bulging and quivering as he lowered. His hand ran the length of her spine. Searching for security, Tanner's fingers found the waistband of her shorts and fisted around the denim, his knuckles brushing bare skin. *Far* too intimate.

Avery pushed away without thinking, arms wheeling as she stepped back into empty space. Tanner, mid-crouch, had no chance to rise as the tower tumbled away beneath his feet. The stack of crates landed with a deafening clatter into the empty space at the center of the group below. Falling for what must have been milliseconds, but felt like eons, they were both caught by their ropes, harnesses pulling tight as they hovered in mid-air before being lowered slowly to the ground.

Thank God!

Unfastening her helmet, Avery waited to be unclipped from the webbing, her heart battering against her rib cage. Damp strands of hair clung to her neck and she was grateful for the soft breeze which swayed the branches of the trees around them. She needed to regain her composure. Needed some distance. Stepping out of the circle, she dodged the fallen crates and let another couple take their place.

"I think that was my fault." Tanner had followed her, wiping his face on the sleeve of his tee, the tense line of his jaw more relaxed now that his feet were planted back in the dirt. "Sorry if I grabbed you anywhere I shouldn't have."

"Crate-stacking legends in the making right here!" Bel appeared before she could answer, forcing Avery to take an unwilling step back into a mountain of muscle. "Future generations will marvel at our victory."

"Chill your beans—we haven't won yet, babe," Drew said with an easygoing drawl.

"There are more teams to go." Desperately grateful for the interruption, Avery struggled to sound casual as she made to move away from Tanner. She couldn't think when he was this close. "Don't be so cocky."

Bel just blew on her nails. "I think I'm gonna need a bigger trophy shelf."

Tanner's chuckle reverberated in Avery's sternum. She took a few hurried steps away from him.

"I'm going to . . ." She gestured vaguely toward the clubhouse in a way that could have meant she needed the washroom, a drink, or any number of other things. Weaving between bodies, her sneakers slapped against the grass as she jogged between the trees.

Out of sight of the others, Avery veered away from the main building and let herself into their cabin. Her knees still felt as if they were fighting the sway of the crates, her thoughts just as rattled and unsteady. All she needed was a shower, something to wash away the stickiness and the subtle fragrance of Tanner's cologne that was far too potent.

At school, the boy with the easy smile and secondhand hockey gear had spread mishap and mayhem in his wake. He'd gotten into fights, struggled in class, and was a regular fixture on one of the chairs outside Principal Harris's office—sometimes with

Sam Archer, sometimes alone. Tanner Stone wasn't someone Avery would have been allowed to hang out with.

She'd found it easier to let her dad choose the people she mixed with. There were expectations, he said, of the mayor's daughter and the company she kept. Sometimes those expectations felt like a collar around her neck. Back then, Avery's home life might have been a carefully controlled hothouse of intensity and pressure, but she'd tried not to let it show. She knew it was a small price to pay for reaping the benefits of a privileged lifestyle, and her parents reminded her frequently that she should be grateful. Mayhem was an extracurricular activity she didn't have time for.

But life has a way of laughing at high-minded plans. And exchanging her good fortune for Tanner's chaos that one night in the rainswept parking lot a few months before graduation must've given the universe the biggest laugh of all.

Leaning against the wall of the steamy bathroom, her glowing reflection stared back at her from the mirror. Even in the smeared glass, Avery could track the flutter of her heartbeat through her t-shirt. She drew in a shaky breath, and despite the shower Tanner's scent still teased her nose.

She'd dealt with all the disruption she could take. Any further chaos held no attraction at all. She needed to get a grip.

It was going to be a long weekend.

Chapter 6
Tanner

Heaping his plate with pasta salad, Tanner dropped onto a chair beside Sam and Kash.

"So, no Lily, huh," Sam mumbled around a mouthful. "Seemed to be going well at Christmas. What happened?"

"Subtle, dude. Very subtle." Flicking a torn-off crust of bread, Kash managed to clip the top of Sam's ear.

"Guys don't do subtle." Sam was unapologetic.

Kash frowned. "I do subtle."

"Yeah, but you're not most guys, babe. You're a one-off."

Tanner chuckled, chewed, and swallowed. "We had an argument when I didn't propose over the holidays. She wanted a big high-profile wedding this summer. She was pissed it wasn't going to happen."

"And she dumped you? Just like that?" Sam's fork hovered by his mouth.

"No." Tanner flipped a pebble he'd picked up in one hand. "She slept with the backup goalie, then ditched us both for a quarterback."

Kash choked on his food.

"Fuck." Keeping his eyes on Tanner, Sam pounded his partner between the shoulder blades. "The lengths some people will go to for a summer wedding."

Rubbing a hand over his chest, Tanner found only the leftover ache of bruised pride. "It's not that I didn't want to commit. But when it came down to it, I couldn't bring myself to commit to *her*."

"At least you recognized that she wasn't the right person in time," said Kash.

"And if you were the right person for her, she wouldn't have fucked the goalie or the QB." Sam's contribution was brutal but undeniably accurate.

Both statements were true. There had been an overriding sense of release with the end of their relationship. Although the lies had hurt. They still fucking hurt. "I gave her everything she asked for. A bit of honesty in return would have been nice."

"Ah, that's where you're going wrong, dude. Good relationships don't work on a bartering system." Uncharacteristically serious, Sam shoveled some more pasta into his mouth.

"Listen to you emerging from your blanket fort with some great advice," teased Kash, ruffling his partner's hair. "My boy's all grown up."

Tanner brushed aside a pang of envy at the casual gesture. "Well, it's a good time for a fresh start anyway." Above their heads, the ceiling fan droned, moving the humid air over his skin in pleasant relief. "I've been looking forward to coming home. There's stuff I need to sort out."

"And what's Arlo's opinion of the move?" Sam asked.

"Yeah, he wasn't exactly on board. He was pushing for a contract extension in Boston but that wasn't going to happen." Tanner buried the cringe of embarrassment before Sam sniffed it out. He wasn't ready to open that can of worms right now.

Taking another bite of his lunch, he found his attention wandering as Avery slipped into the clubhouse. Like the eleven-year-old he'd first met sitting side by side in the school infirmary with matching nosebleeds (his from a fight, hers from a basketball), she was all legs, eyes and fiery hair. Impossible to ignore. He'd been all too aware of her at Pine Springs High and it seemed nothing had changed.

She blended swiftly into her group of friends, laying her head against Leo Marsh's shoulder when he curled an arm around her waist.

Sam followed his gaze. "How're the two of you getting on?"

"Fine. It's good. But we haven't talked much yet." He dragged his eyes away. "She seems the same. But different."

Sam grinned. "We're all the same but different."

"And a lot more tired," added Kash.

"Remember when you pounded Tyson Dax for calling her 'Fanta Pants'?" Sam snickered.

"Funny—Avery mentioned him earlier," Tanner said, pushing aside his empty plate.

An anonymous tip and a random locker search less than a week after they'd fought had found two ounces of weed beneath Tanner's textbooks that he'd never seen before. It wasn't hard to join the dots since Tyson Dax supplied drugs to anyone who came asking, but with those in charge deaf to Tanner's protestations of innocence, he'd ended up with an out-of-school suspension for one day and an in-school suspension for the rest of the week. Even more serious, the incident went on his permanent record, confirming his place on Principal Harris's shit list.

"I don't regret smacking him one. He was asking for it," he said. "That little fucker was poisonous."

Griff and Savannah passed by on their way out of the door. "You've got fifteen minutes to change into swimwear and head to the lake for this afternoon's challenge," Savannah trilled.

"My mom says I shouldn't swim straight after eating." Tanner took a huge bite from an apple he'd pulled from his pocket.

"It's all part of my cunning plan." Savannah bopped him playfully on the nose. "I'm hoping you get taken out by cramp so I can use your body as a stepping stone to get to the finish line."

"That's cold, cuz."

"Brutal," Sam agreed.

"Is it wrong that I'm a little turned on right now?" asked Griff as he dragged Savannah toward the door with a grin.

Tanner, Sam, and Kash took less than five minutes to change clothes and were among the first to make it to the lake. The crowd gradually grew until everyone was gathered on the narrow strip of sand. With the sun beating down on his neck and a dribble of sweat running from the back of his hairline down between his shoulder blades, Tanner itched to get into the water.

Avery drifted closer to his side. She wore a dark blue bikini and her feet were bare, lavender nail polish on her toes, and all his senses went into overdrive like he'd taken a shot of adrenaline straight into a vein. Pulling back her hair into a russet ponytail which bared the soft column of her neck, she fixed it with a band from her wrist. A scrapbook of images from school playing in his memory, Tanner's fingers flexed by his sides.

While Johnnie and Mia ran through the rules of the paddleboard race, Bel planted her feet in the sand beside him, hands on her hips. "What did you say you were doing in the UK this last month?"

Tanner fought a smile and lost. "Swimming and surfing."

She jabbed a vicious finger at his stomach. "You and I are going to fall out soon."

Drew swooped in to steer Bel away. "Luckily, it's just a bit of fun, huh, babe? No need for physical violence. Not yet, anyway."

As it turned out, she shouldn't have worried because Tanner had never tried a tandem paddleboard before and it was far from easy. Getting the coordination right at the same time as mastering the steering was tough. His competitive spirit strained against its leash for the first five minutes but then melted away entirely against the backdrop of crystal-clear water, an azure sky, and Avery Delgado's laughter.

A smile that could light up downtown Pine Springs broke when she surfaced from her third dunking and Tanner couldn't hold back a matching one in response. Her teeth glistened white around that plush bottom lip, her body slick and shiny as she clambered back onto the board. Ahead of them, Sam toppled with a shout and a splash, while Kash fought valiantly to keep his balance, failed, and plunged into the lake with a bitten off "Son of a—!" and a fresh peal of laughter bent Avery double.

It was impossible to tell what was tears and what was lake water. The tiny gold hoop in Avery's nose glinted in the sunshine while the radiance on her face cracked Tanner's chest wide open in a way he hadn't realized was possible. The years disappeared and he was twelve again, wanting to keep talking to the girl with the matching bloody nose. He was seventeen and aching to kiss her. He was twenty-two and still wearing Avery's hairband around his wrist to bring him good luck.

The free fall through time ended with a lurch as reality hit him. He still wanted Avery Delgado.

He always had.

And Tanner wasn't sure what to do about it.

They finally paddled into the shallows in third place as Savannah and Griff celebrated a competent win. Sam and Kash, the runners-up, embraced with a whoop, tumbling into the lake still in each other's arms, and Avery dropped to her knees on their board, her chest rising and falling with a strained shudder.

"My arms are crying," she gasped, sucking in air. "That was so tough!"

Her navy bikini was threaded through with a narrow white stripe, the bottoms high-waisted, the fabric some kind of crinkled affair. Tanner, itching to know what it felt like, kept his hands to himself. He turned sideways on the wide paddleboard and carefully sat down, kicking water at Sam when he waded within reach.

Avery lifted her face to the sun as each new pair racing to the finish line caused their board to bobble. Her wet ponytail, terracotta dark, lay slick between her shoulder blades. Tanner studied her while her eyes were closed. Like a highlight reel of greatest goals, she was fascinating and absorbing at the same time. Her ears, the corner of her mouth, her elbows. He didn't think he'd ever noticed anyone's elbows before, but it seemed that no part of Avery was beyond his interest after all this time.

He cursed himself afterward for being so focused on her elbows.

A series of larger, choppy waves signaled the messy arrival of Leo and Gemma alongside them. Leo rocked precariously from side to side but Gemma, as solid as a newborn foal on a travelator, was even less steady. Fighting a losing battle with gravity, she tumbled backward, her paddle cutting through the air in a desperate bid for balance. Even as Tanner moved to intercept, the sharp edge of the blade caught Avery with a tooth-juddering blow on the side of her head. And she dropped like a stone into the water.

Chapter 7
Avery

"I am so, so sorry, Ave." Gemma fluttered and stammered beside her, still utterly wretched despite the passing of afternoon into evening. "Are you sure I can't get you anything? Another drink or . . . anything?"

"There's no need. I'm fine," Avery reassured her again, keeping the thrum of her headache and the burn in her cheekbone to herself.

Bel's silent comfort when she squeezed Avery's arm was more welcome than all the fussing.

"D'you do all your own stunts, Delgado? Or did you pull this one out for the special occasion?"

Avery turned her head slowly at the sound of Sam's voice as he walked into the clubhouse with Tanner, both freshly showered and casually dressed. And the memory of being carried from the water, her skin slippery in Tanner's grip as he held her tight to his chest, mangled the breath in her throat. Even as dazed as she was, she'd wanted to sink into his muscles, crawl inside his rib cage, and curl up there like a puppy in a kennel of bones. Weirdly peculiar and utterly unwise.

"Shut up, Sam." When Tanner ran golden eyes over her face, Avery looked away.

"It's alright. I'm fine," she repeated, "broken record" style.

Another squeeze from Bel. More guilty shuffling from Gemma. Avery hated the attention, and Bel, like any best friend worth her salt, knew it.

"So you all went to PS High, right? Ave, Tanner, Sam—" Bel's dark, clever eyes moved between them.

"And Savannah. And Leo," Sam added, with a nod at the doorway as Leo sauntered in, wearing an old Killers tour t-shirt that was one of Avery's favorites. She'd borrowed it more than once. Tried to keep it, in fact, but Leo was having none of that.

"How're you feeling?" he asked.

"She's fine," Bel, Drew and Gemma echoed in unison.

"Did you all hang out together?" Gemma asked.

"Hang out where?" Leo caught the eye of the guy behind the bar and asked for a beer.

"School," Avery murmured.

"Ah. Not so much, really. Ave and I only had a few classes together." Leo reached for his drink with a smile of thanks. "And Tanner and Sam were the grade above."

Avery could feel his watchful inspection of her injury. His and Tanner's. Drew had patched her up well, but the dressing was scratchy against her temple. The adhesive, tacky and tight, pulled at her skin. Three missed calls from her mom during the afternoon and the resulting callback she'd squeezed in before dinner had done nothing to lessen the pounding of her head.

"Bet she was a right little teacher's pet," Bel said fondly.

"She was popular with everyone but never a teacher's pet," Leo disagreed, loyal in his defense.

"Nah, I reckon I'm right. I can just imagine you getting away with murder, Ave." Bel swiped Drew's beer and took a mouthful.

Avery couldn't help it then. Her eyes slid to Tanner's face just as his fingers went to his wrist. They fidgeted a moment with the bare skin there and then dropped back to his side. It was a relief when Mia called the group to order for a scavenger hunt—the last challenge of the day.

This time the handouts, framed with cutesy hearts, took the form of a list of objects to be collected and brought back to the clubhouse.

"Points for completing the task and a bonus for the fastest pair home." Mia gave a yellow pencil to each team, then revealed a bunch of cotton scarves clutched in her other hand like a Machiavellian magician. "Oh, and you have to do it 'three-legged race' style!"

There was a kerfuffle as each team grabbed a scarf and anchored themselves together, debating if tight was better than loose and who should go on which side. Tanner settled onto the stool next to Avery, scarlet fabric wound between his fingers. Sliding his muscled calf against hers, he bent to tie it around their ankles and she had to force herself not to pull away when the hairs on his leg raised goosebumps on her skin.

"After two events, it's still tight at the top," Johnnie told them all with a grin. "Sam and Kash have the lead at the moment, but there's everything to play for."

"Yes!" Sam's fist pump was gleeful. "Winning in points *and* psychological damage."

"We should form an alliance and take them out," Savannah muttered behind Avery.

"Tempting." Bel's tone said differently as she shot Sav a glance through narrowed eyes. "But you're part of the competition, not a co-star in my victory montage."

"So every overly competitive weirdo for themselves then?" Despite her tension, Avery couldn't hold back a snigger and she felt Tanner's low laugh in the soft brush of his sleeve against her shoulder.

Johnnie dragged the whistle from his pocket, blew a swift, shrill blast, and the group dispersed with unsteady strides—good-natured trash talk floating behind them like the contrails of an airplane.

Avery and Tanner watched everyone leave, with Johnnie and Mia following along behind. Even the guy behind the bar disappeared somewhere, and the silence that settled over the clubhouse was a living, breathing entity. Tanner's body was as relaxed as hers was taut, though his knee jogged her own with its bouncing. Avery tried to channel some of his chill into her muscles. Tried not to fixate on his toned forearms a bare inch away on the bar, or the lower half of the tattoo edging out from beneath his shirtsleeve.

She wished she'd had the time to study his ink in more detail at the lake, but she hadn't wanted to be caught staring—or drooling. The cleverly etched Icarus on his ribs, wings outstretched and soaring toward the sun, was a charcoal-shaded work of art, even at a glance. As well as the pine trees, Tanner had three words written beneath his right collarbone in a cursive script and some lines of lyrics on the underside of the opposite arm. Avery was desperate to know what they said.

She was immune to the various charms of most guys she met. They could flirt themselves inside out and Avery felt nothing. Tanner merely existed in her vicinity and the urge to study him and document his idiomatic appeal tugged needily at her core. It was disconcerting.

"I'm fine with sitting this one out if you don't feel up to it," he said, breaking the silence.

Realizing she'd been quiet for too long, Avery reached for Mia's handout. "And give up on our shot at the trophy? No chance."

Tanner gestured to the door. "Shouldn't we get started then?"

Avery chewed on her lower lip as she examined the list. It was a relief to have something to focus on. "I'm thinking we need to work smarter, not harder."

He peered over her shoulder and they read through the items together.

SCAVENGER HUNT

- ○ *Something yellow*
- ○ *Something useful*
- ○ *Something that smells good*
- ○ *Something shorter than a toothbrush*
- ○ *Something soft*
- ○ *Something that tastes nice*
- ○ *Something loud*
- ○ *Something wet*
- ○ *Something round*
- ○ *Something sharp*
- ○ *Something light*
- ○ *Something you can fold*
- ○ *Something heavy*
- ○ *Something white*

○ *Something hot*

○ *Something that makes you happy*

○ *Something flat*

○ *Something only an adult would use*

○ *A keepsake*

○ *Something that starts with the first letter of one of your names*

"O . . . K . . ." Avery murmured finally. "I think we should be fine, if we just . . ."

Hiking her purse onto the bar, she tugged a Kleenex free from a small packet and placed it next to the pencil. From an inside pocket, she fished out a foil square between finger and thumb.

"Condom." Avery held it up. "Cherry flavored."

Tanner's eyebrows rose, along with one side of his mouth. "So it is, Stretch." The expression on his face sent a plume of heat spreading through her bones but she didn't let it show. "The ankle restraint will be an added novelty but I'm game if you are."

The teasing was obvious and gentle; it felt like intimate fingers tugging at her hair. When Avery held his gaze and the smile slid away from his lips, she wanted to call it back.

"Your face looks so sore." Tanner's eyes traced her cheekbone, then settled on the dressing at her temple. They turned steely as she opened her mouth. "Don't tell me you're fine. I'm not listening to that shit. I've taken enough hits to the head to know when something fucking hurts."

Avery found herself nodding instead. "Yeah, it's sore."

"There was a lot of blood."

"Good job it's fresh water. No sharks."

That wide, infectious grin tugged at his mouth. "I'd have sacrificed Sam to save you if it came to it."

"I won't tell him if you don't."

"Deal." He lifted a bottle of water to his lips and took a long swallow. "Your friends seem like a cool bunch. When they're not trying to kill you."

Avery gave a small snort. "Yeah, Gemma's as clumsy as she is sweet. She can fall over in the middle of a flat field but she's literally the nicest person I know. She teaches kindergarten."

"And Bel?"

"No one could call Bel nice or sweet—and expect to live." Avery smiled at the thought. "She's amazing. A total queen."

"Amazing, how?" Having Tanner's whole focus was a heady feeling.

"She has a mind like a bear trap—she qualified as a lawyer last year. She's terrifyingly ambitious, a total badass, and really funny." Avery rolled the yellow pencil back and forth on the bar. "Her parents live in Chicago and she has four brothers—all lawyers, all obsessed with their work. They're kind of humorless. You know, 'time is money' and all that. Next to them, Bel's like a firework in an ash cloud."

"Sounds like you're lucky to have her." Tanner's knee bounced. "But you've always had a lot of friends. You were popular at school with all the right people."

Avery gave a dismissive snort as she assessed the items in front of her, playing for time. "I'm not sure any of us actually enjoyed each other's company. It was more about teenage networking and maintaining an image back then."

"What changed?"

Not wanting to go there, she straightened on the bar stool and brushed the question off. "Everything changed. I found my crew. I grew up and met Bel through an apartment share. She helped me care less about who my parents considered suitable friends."

Tanner gave a low hum. "And Leo? The two of you seem close."

Avery didn't know if Johnnie and Mia's return at that moment was a relief or a disappointment. She set the scavenger list down over the Kleenex and the condom.

"That was fast! And with an injury, too. Very impressive." Mia gave Tanner a high-five, blotches of color highlighting her cheekbones as she looked side to side. "Where's your haul?"

"We've got it sorted," Avery answered noncommittally.

"We do?" Tanner asked out of the corner of his mouth.

"We do."

She bent her head to run him through her plan. With her lips a fraction from his ear, it was hard to ignore the close-up detail of the stubble on his jaw and the clean, soapy scent of his skin. Even the cotton of Tanner's t-shirt against her arm gave her a sensory shiver. And the curve of his smile grew wider as she whispered.

Other pairs were coming back now, laden with random objects—some big, some small. The first few were out of breath, having taken the task seriously. Bel and Drew barged alongside Savannah and Griff in the doorway, creating a plug of bodies in the narrow space.

"You're gonna break my ankle if you keep shoving, babe!" Drew's plea was pained.

"First place has gone already so you're playing for runners-up positions," Johnnie called from the end of the bar.

Avery and Tanner gave the couples a smug little wave.

"Dammit, Ave—what the fuck!" Blinking between them, Bel was clearly torn between pouting and punching.

When the room was full again, the group formed a ragged semicircle around the bar, Avery and Tanner in the middle. Mia stepped forward to join them.

"Care to explain exactly how you've completed the list?" she asked skeptically, her brow a perfect furrow.

Avery moved the scavenger hunt checklist to one side. Underneath it, neatly placed, lay the yellow pencil, the Kleenex, and the condom. Tanner gave her a smirky chin lift and she plucked the tissue from the middle.

"This is flat, white, useful, soft, and I can fold it. It also starts with a T."

"You've got to be freakin' kidding me," Bel groused, without heat. Others let out groans.

Avery hid a grin as she picked up the pencil and waved it. "Yellow, light, sharp, shorter than a toothbrush." She licked along the length of it. "And wet."

"Gross," said Gemma.

"Pretty sure that's not shorter than my toothbrush." Griff tried to get picky.

Tanner plucked the pencil from Avery's hands and snapped it effortlessly in half. "It is now."

Reaching for the foil packet, Avery held up the condom. "This is something an adult would use and it makes you happy."

"Makes me happier not using one," Drew chimed in.

"Makes me happier than having a baby," countered Bel.

"It's round—well, inside the packet, it's round," Avery continued, "and it's flavored so it should taste nice." Her face expressed doubts about that. "Anyway, I'd like to give it to Tanner."

He took it from her hand with a grin. "Thanks, Stretch. I'll treasure it."

"Now it's a keepsake." She was beginning to enjoy herself.

The heckling grew from a few lone voices to a rumble, but everyone was smiling, even as they complained.

"Tanner's hot and heavy." Avery reached for her glass and took a few sips. She couldn't look at him when she said that.

"And Avery smells good." He tipped his head toward her, his nose less than an inch from her hair. She steeled herself to sit still.

"So, that's it, I believe." She shrugged. "We've covered everything on the list."

Mia was ticking each point off the sheet of paper in her hands. "Wait—you forgot something loud."

Avery wrapped her free ankle around the leg of the barstool beside her and tugged. It hit the floor with a crash, narrowly missing Mia's toes.

"Alright, Phineas and Ferb, that's a wrap." Sam shook his head.

Chuckling beside him, Kash kicked at the pile of stuff by his feet. "I can't believe we have to put all this shit away now."

Johnnie conferred with Mia and then announced, "Delgado and Stone get full marks for the scavenger hunt."

"And lateral thinking," drawled Griff.

Leaning closer, Tanner bumped her elbow with his. "Nice one, Stretch. You say Bel's smart but that was fucking clever."

Avery smiled. And just for a little while, the pain in her head receded and the weight of responsibility on her shoulders felt lighter. She sipped her drink, leaned into the warmth of Bel's arms when they threaded around her neck, and made no mention of the fact that her ankle stayed bound with Tanner's as the chatter rolled on around them.

Chapter 8
Tanner

He stepped outside to take Arlo's call.

"I've tried you twice already this evening." There was an irritable edge to his friend's words that wasn't uncommon when Arlo had to wait for something.

"It's the weekend," Tanner answered simply. "And you know I'm at Savannah's pre-wedding thing."

"I don't understand why you couldn't all just go out and get wasted. None of this dragging it out for a whole weekend shit."

Tanner stifled a snort. "Yeah, cos you're famously one to cut a party short. Did you want me for something?"

"I've got the paperwork through from Rapids management." On the other end of the line, Tanner heard the rattle as Arlo popped the lid on a plastic pot of gum. "Still not sure about this move, dude. You had better offers and Boston wanted to keep you."

Tanner rubbed at the uncomfortable hitch in his chest as his feet led him down toward the lake. "We've been over this, I've considered all the pros and cons. Last season was brutal, with Mats's accident and my shoulder causing me trouble. There was . . . that other stuff, too." Things he was mortified to think about.

Arlo scoffed. "Must suck to be you with women just throwing themselves—"

Cutting across him, Tanner said, "Staying in Boston is out. I want to see how it feels to be nearer home again while I give it another season to see if I'm gonna need surgery."

The words stuck in his throat. Trying to outrun the toll that hockey was taking on his body gave him more nightmares than he was ready to admit.

"I'll tell you how it'll feel. Quiet. There's fuck all going on in Pine Springs. Unless you want to spend your days talking about potholes and the weather." Arlo chewed as he grumbled.

"You've never been here." Just steps away from the toes of Tanner's sneakers, the water rippled seamlessly in a coral-tinted glow as the sun dipped below the trees. "Come visit and you might not be so keen to rush back to your traffic pollution and high-rises."

"It's more likely *you'll* miss the nightlife, restaurants, and women, and then you'll kick yourself. Can't be much variety in a town with a population under three thousand."

"Maybe I don't want variety," Tanner said softly.

Arlo's laugh echoed in his ear. "Sure you don't. Remind me how well you got on settling down with Lily again."

"Fuck off."

"Casual is the way to go, dude. You'd be stupid to tie yourself down at this stage of your career—to a woman or a second-rate team."

Happily single, Arlo embraced both his lack of emotional ties and the role he'd awarded himself in Tanner's life, doling out sage advice as if they weren't exactly the same age. Only, some of his words of wisdom weren't ringing quite as true these days.

"I'd tie myself down to the right person without a second thought," Tanner admitted, his mind sliding all too easily to blue eyes and freckles.

There was a long pause on the other end of the line. "Fuck me, bro," Arlo groaned. "What have you done?"

"Nothing—yet," he said, then paused for a moment. "But Avery Delgado is here."

"Who?"

"The girl who saved my scholarship." Tanner dug the heel of his shoe into the sand.

"The high school princess?" Arlo asked.

"Yeah, her."

His friend scoffed. "Keep your distance from that one, dude. You jump in with your 'I owe you' shit and she'll be after payback before you know it."

"You're wrong," Tanner said. "She's never reached out before." Not even when he'd wanted her to. He chose to ignore Arlo's quiet grunt of disagreement. "I'm going to sign the Rapids contract as soon as I'm home. I'll call you on Monday and we'll run through the details, OK?" Winding up the call, Tanner shoved his phone into his pocket and took another minute to stand and stare, while old memories twined like ground fog around his feet.

By the time he wandered back to the clubhouse, some of the group had dragged folding chairs from a stack near the grill and settled in a circle around the firepit. Savannah and Griff, as rightful guests of honor, had secured the comfort of the swinging bench seat with actual cushions, firelight dancing over their faces in the dusk. Johnnie and Drew handed out fresh beers and Tanner took one even though he didn't really want it.

"Nice work on the scavenger hunt, you two," said Savannah.

"I had very little to do with it." Shrugging off the praise, Tanner met Avery's gaze on the other side of the firepit. "Avery's the brains in our team. She's always been smart."

"Not sure I ever worked as hard as you did, though. I was just lucky it came a bit easier."

The glow of the flames flickered across her face, blending with the red of her hair, and the generosity in Avery's reply was as sweet as warm syrup on his tongue. He'd always found her kind. She had seemed to look deeper than anyone else—past the lanky fidget with worn shoes who couldn't stay away from trouble if it took out a restraining order on him and left the country. Despite her dad being the mayor, Avery had never treated Tanner any differently because his mother worked in the local laundromat.

"I'm picking up vibes." Leaning forward, Gemma wiggled a finger. "Were you two a thing back in the day? Are we talking high school crushes?"

"No, I'd have known if you were." Savannah fixed Tanner with eagle eyes. "Right?"

Avery, flushing fiercely, opened her mouth—and he didn't want to hear her deny it, so he gave a careless shrug, the beer bottle loose in his hand, and said, "You saw her at school. I never stood a chance."

It was an answer and not an answer at the same time.

Leo got up to throw another log onto the fire, shifting his chair closer to Avery to avoid a wispy plume of smoke. When her eyes remained on Tanner, bright and steady over the rim of her glass, he wished he could read her expression.

"I know—let's play Truth or Dare!" Savannah bounced in her chair and everyone groaned.

"Just because we're at a camp doesn't mean we're actually still fourteen, Sav," Sam groused without heat.

"She could have picked Spin the Bottle," Kash pointed out.

"Exactly! And it's my special weekend so you don't have any choice." Unmoved by the moans or Sam's complaint, Tanner's cousin jumped up to stand in the circle and began to spin with her eyes shut.

"Mind the firepit!" at least four people shouted in unison.

Her pointed finger was on Kash when she stopped and opened her eyes. "Kash gets to start. Truth or dare?" Savannah asked, her eyebrows dancing with evil intent.

He gave a gusty sigh. "I'll go with truth and hope I don't regret it."

The game turned out to be pretty damn funny because Savannah chose to keep the questions just the right side of savage.

Kash admitted that his guilty pleasure was watching either of the first two *Despicable Me* movies with a packet of dried mango slices. ("Embarrassingly wholesome," griped Bel.)

Leo had to do one of the TikTok dances on his "for you" page.

Sav was roasted for rating her own looks as a ten out of ten.

Gemma read out the last five things in her search history—one of which was "do ducks have accents?"

Drew managed to fit all the toes on one foot in his own mouth.

Griff admitted to having performed a striptease—fortunately it had been for Savannah.

Sam ate a stick of chalk from Gemma's purse and said it tasted like a whitewashed cookie.

And, while Johnnie had to watch the trailer for The Exorcist without looking away, everyone got temporarily sidetracked and decided that Bel was who they'd want on their side during a zombie apocalypse.

"Honored," she responded simply.

As the temperature began to dip, Avery dragged a hoodie from the back of her chair and tugged it over her head. Stretching the soft cotton right over her folded knees, she huddled in a bundled heap, a smile playing over her lips as she listened. When Drew dared her to let the person opposite draw a tattoo on her body with a permanent marker, Tanner walked over to crouch by her knees. His hands, so deft with a wrist shot on the ice, felt clumsy as he held Avery's smooth skin taut and tried to ignore the scent of her shampoo in his nose. He sketched a hockey stick on the outside of her thigh that Bel said looked more like a dead snake. He'd never been great at art.

He chose truth when it came to his turn because no way was he letting Sam dare him to do anything.

"What's your biggest regret?" Savannah asked.

Ouch. His cousin landed a direct hit with that one. He should have gone with a dare after all.

Running his tongue over teeth that were suddenly dry, Tanner tried to think of something humorous so he wouldn't shatter the vibe, but nothing came to him. In the end, there was only one thing he could say. "That's pretty easy. It was me who smashed up Principal Harris's car in the school parking lot—the other two, as well. And I regret letting Avery take the blame."

He felt her jolt of surprise like jumper cables to his chest even from a distance, and there was a moment of absolute silence.

"You didn't!" Gemma's mouth was an open "O." Leo stared, his heavy eyebrows pulling into a scowl.

"But Avery owned up. It made the *Pine Springs Observer,*" Savannah stated, as if that last fact alone was intrinsic proof of his innocence.

Tanner noticed Bel was quiet for once.

"Only a small paragraph. No photo." Avery's voice was husky as she neither confirmed nor denied. "My dad had connections at the paper."

His family had no connections.

And if that didn't sum the situation up in a nutshell.

It was the most selfless thing anyone had ever done for him. But he wasn't the same scared teenager anymore and there was no reason to keep this secret any longer.

"It's true," he said simply. "It was a filthy night and pouring with rain. I caused the accident."

"No way!" Savannah's jaw was gaping.

"Tell us more," begged Gemma from across the firepit.

The flames crackled, sending orange sparks spiraling into the night sky. Avery picked at the cuff of her sleeve, ignoring everyone's stares.

A grin split Drew's lips. "You sly dog." He reached around Bel to give Avery a shove. "You kept that one quiet!"

"Details." Savannah aimed a kick at Tanner's ankle. "I want details."

"It was when they were installing outdoor lighting and the new CCTV system in the PS High parking lot."

"And there was that single floodlight hooked up to a temporary generator," Sam added. "Right in the middle."

Tanner nodded as his fingers drummed against his thigh, beating a similar patter to the rain that night. "My mom had another chest infection and we couldn't afford the medication she needed." He remembered the terror of feeling so fucking helpless. "It was playing on my mind and I was angry. I wasn't concentrating. I'd no idea Avery was even there." Across the firepit, he met her eyes and they were soft. A small shower of sparks burst from a log as it split.

"What happened?" His cousin was hanging on his words.

"I had my battered old Chevy truck then. It was a solid beast, but the tires were worn and I stepped too hard on the gas. There was so much surface water the back end lost its grip."

He'd hit the brakes and fought to straighten up as the truck fishtailed.

"I sideswiped the generator. The floodlight fell. The principal's car and two others were underneath it."

Simple words; an incomplete description. Avery's exhale carried a multitude of clearer memories known only to the two of them.

There had been a moment when the floodlight almost regained its balance and he'd thought he might get away with it. But gravity was a bitch. The whole top-heavy structure had teetered then fallen, the aluminum tower crashing down across the hoods of three parked cars—one of them belonging to Principal Harris. Six huge LED light heads exploded in a shower of glass and sparks, the car windshields shattering beneath them. And a sudden backwash of darkness had swallowed up the devastation.

Like the swinging pendulum in a longcase clock, everyone turned to Avery.

"Why did you take the blame?" Savannah asked.

Avery hugged her knees, half of the new wobbly tattoo peeking out from beneath the hem of her hoodie. "Tanner was already on a final warning after sticking up for me with Tyson Dax. I didn't want him to risk his scholarship when I might be able to get away with it."

Tanner noticed the subtle movement as Bel threaded her fingers between Avery's.

"How did you carry it off?" Griff asked.

Avery gave a small, careless shrug. "After Tanner left, there was no one else around. I reversed my car into the fallen floodlight, hard enough to bash a crater into the bodywork. And I went to see the principal."

Tanner had thought he might throw up when he recognized Avery's VW Golf the next morning. The site of the accident looked so much worse in the unforgiving light of day, cordoned off as it was with red and white tape—and Avery's car right in the middle of it.

"I thought maybe she'd hit the fallen floodlight in the dark after I'd gone. When I tried to own up to Principal Harris, she wouldn't listen. She told me she 'wasn't in the mood for misguided chivalry.' I was so damn confused," Tanner said.

He'd found himself back in the hallway, with the principal's office door shut firmly behind him and not a single idea what in the hell was going on.

"As it turned out, everyone took Avery's confession as gospel because who would make up something like that?" Tanner watched her lips quirk when she met his eyes.

"Did you get into trouble with your parents?" Gemma asked, leaning forward.

"Not really, because they accepted it was an accident, although it gave Aunt Delia a new way to yank my mom's chain for a while. She made out it was the start of a slippery slope to delinquency."

Everyone in Pine Springs knew Avery's aunt. She was the fearsome owner of Diner 43, the best place in town for a hearty breakfast if you didn't mind it coming with a generous helping of sarcasm and scowls.

"Must have been devastated you didn't double down on it, babe. Delia would have been so smug if you'd embraced a life of crime." Bel gave Avery's hand another squeeze.

Propping one foot over the opposite knee, Tanner fiddled with the laces of his shoe. The moment the floodlight had toppled was seared so deeply into his brain he would never be free of it. He'd seen it falling over and over again for months, the shower of sparks lighting the inside of his eyelids every night when he tried to sleep. He'd heard the crash and the explosion of glass on repeat, could still taste his panic and despair.

"Avery—" Savannah broke the silence, but her voice choked and she didn't continue. Tanner saw Avery flash her a self-conscious smile that acknowledged everything his cousin couldn't quite manage to say.

"Hockey was the only thing I knew I could do to make money," he said to take the heat off her again. "I had to get that scholarship to take care of my mom and my brothers, and Avery handed it to me on a plate. There's not been a day since when I haven't been grateful for that. She was a miracle."

Tanner's throat felt raw from the memories. Drafted to the NHL at the end of his freshman year of college, he'd had the opportunity to stay on and continue his education while playing for his school, but his need for the salary and signing bonus had driven him to pursue his professional hockey career as soon as possible instead. Within a year, he'd moved his mom into the neat and clean little three-bedroom house that she still refused to sell today. Even better, he'd been able to afford all the medical care she needed.

Sam, as usual, was the one to break the lingering moment of intensity.

"Dude, you're such an attention seeker," he complained, flipping the cap off another bottle of beer. "I'll be picking bits of chalk out of my teeth for days, and you win everyone over with some crappy driving and a sob story."

As laughter dispersed the light layer of solemnity that had fallen over the group, the chatter moved on to other subjects. And Tanner took a long, deep breath, relieved to have finally taken ownership of that niggly splinter from the past.

But when he risked a glance over the firepit, he found Avery staring at him in a way that made him wonder if he'd done the right thing.

Now that their secret was no longer a secret, had he unwittingly released her from the only tie that connected them together?

Chapter 9
Avery

"Got a minute?"

Bel hugged the frame of the bedroom door. She was already dressed for the day but barefooted, her cheeks glowing from the slick of face cream Avery knew, if she stepped closer, would smell of peaches.

"For sure." Avery tied a knot in the front of her oversize tee and reached up to pull back her hair.

Bel came further into the room. "Your face looks awful."

Avery glanced over at a mirror on the wall as she wound a hairband around her ponytail. The swelling on her cheekbone was tight and hot, the bruising around the cut on her forehead darkening. "Thanks. It feels worse," she quipped. Especially since she kept prodding it. "What's up?"

Bel sat down heavily on the edge of Gemma's bed. She rolled her full lips and sucked her teeth. "Here's the thing. Drew and I found something we weren't looking for when we were doing the scavenger hunt last night." There was watchful concern on her face. "We found Johnnie and Mia. Near Mia's cabin. They were . . . very close together."

"How close?" Avery raised an eyebrow.

Bel picked at a thread on the patchwork comforter. "'Lip locked' close. 'Jump apart when you're spotted' close."

"OK." Avery opened a tube of sunscreen and dotted it over the bridge of her nose.

Standing up, Bel wrapped her arms around Avery's waist. Her chin only slotted neatly onto Avery's shoulder because she stood on tiptoe. "I know you're not seeing each other anymore but I didn't want it to catch you unprepared."

Avery gave herself up to Bel's hug even though she genuinely didn't need it. "I don't have feelings for Johnnie—he can lip-lock whoever he likes and I wish Mia good luck with his hideous shift pattern. You know I choose not to date because I'm happier this way."

"One day, you'll meet someone who makes you want to take a chance."

"Unlikely." Never would she let herself be broken the way her mom had been shattered by her dad. No one was worth that. Not even a ridiculously toned hockey player with a dimple to drown in. "I'm not willing to give up a part of myself to someone else who won't take care of it."

"Not all guys are like that," said Bel without heat.

"No." Drew seemed to be one of the good ones. For now. "Not all guys, maybe."

Bel knew her well enough to read Avery's thoughts. "This isn't the time for me to reassure you, Tessie Trust-Issues. But my wisdom will become crystal-clear in the future."

"What are you being wise about this time?" Gemma swept into the room, ducking down to fish her sneakers out from under the bed.

"It's hard to narrow it down." Bel nudged Gemma's butt with the ball of her foot. "But right now we're talking about the true joys of a good relationship."

"No, we aren't," said Avery. "Bel put forward the proposal and I was countering on the grounds that solitude and fulfillment are not mutually exclusive."

"They say being in a healthy relationship increases your life expectancy," Gemma grunted as she pulled on her shoes.

"They also say that the benefits of being able to sleep like a starfish in your own bed make you less likely to kill someone for snoring." Avery dug in her pocket for a ChapStick.

"Not sure I caught that TED Talk," murmured Bel.

When Drew interrupted to ask if anyone had seen his glasses, Avery took a walk to the jetty before breakfast and sat down, legs dangling over the edge, and called her mom. She'd had four texts from her already—two requests for help with an online order for a doormat, and two complaining about the weather.

"Hey, it's me. Thought I'd catch up quickly while I had the chance."

"Thank you, darling." Her mother's voice lacked color and Avery found herself, as always, trying to evaluate her mood from those initial three words.

"I've ordered the doormat for you. You should have it Tuesday. How's your weekend going?" she asked, even though she was the one who was away and her mom's Saturday had likely followed exactly the same pattern as most other days.

"Fine. Quiet. I decided not to use the shower until you're back."

Avery hid a sigh. "Probably best. I'll pop in sometime tomorrow."

"You'll stay for dinner?"

"Sure." Tucking a loose strand of hair behind her ear, Avery stared out over the lake. "Did you give any more thought to the meet-up group I found? It would be worth finding out what activities they offer. You might make some new friends."

Please lean on someone else, Mom. I'm getting so tired . . .

"Maybe I'll call next week," her mom said. They both heard the lie. "Have you spoken to your father?"

"Not this week. I'll catch up with him soon." Avery knew her dad was in Italy on holiday but it would take physical torture before she'd spill that nugget of information to her mother. "Look, I only have a few minutes before things get busy again here so I'm going to have to cut this short. But I'll see you tomorrow."

Her mother was unwilling to let her go so it took a little longer to tie up the call. When they finally said goodbye, Avery had dug half-moons into her palm with the nails on her free hand.

"And how's your weekend, sweetie?" she murmured to herself. "Oh, running smoothly, Mom. Thanks for asking. It's just your average Bach Bash—nowhere near as exciting as your shower problems."

"I don't know about 'average,' Stretch. For all we know, Savannah's planned a dance-off in fancy dress tonight."

Raising one hand to shield her eyes from the sun, Avery looked over her shoulder. A glow surrounded Tanner as he loomed on the jetty in the morning light. From her position on the wooden planks, he took on the proportions of a golden god—at once improbably muscular, smoothly at ease, and achingly appealing. Like someone who had it all and took it for granted.

She swung back to the water. "Bel will be in her element if she does."

There was a shuffle of shoes behind her and then Tanner lowered himself onto the edge at her side. His hand lay between them, palm down on the jetty. When his little finger brushed Avery's thigh, she was achingly aware of the contact.

He said nothing more and they sat for another few minutes. He wasn't still. She'd never known Tanner to be still. One of his ankles swung back and forth above the water as he flicked a stone off the jetty. Every part of him was animated, from his eyebrows to his fidgety feet, and somehow his solid presence added an extra sparkle to the beautiful surroundings.

He made her feel things she didn't want to feel and it was dangerous.

"I suppose we should go see how they're planning to abuse us this morning." Avery swept a loose strand of hair out of her eyes, sucking in a breath when she caught the bruise on her cheekbone and Tanner's brow pinched.

"It's an obstacle course. With blindfolds. I read my itinerary like a good sheep."

"And sheep are famous for their reading," she snickered despite herself.

"It figures they'd need some way to get off to sleep. Counting themselves jumping over a fence is just weird."

"Pretty sure the whole counting-sheep thing is a fallacy. I've tried and I get hung up on how there are so many different shapes and sizes of sheep. I can never make mine identical enough to be restful. It ends up keeping me awake."

The light in Tanner's eyes sparkled like polished bronze and a rueful smile spread over his lips. "Trust you to tackle it with that level of commitment."

Avery climbed reluctantly to her feet. Tanner was slow to follow, his eyes fixed on the cut at her temple.

"That still looks pretty sore."

She lifted a hand to touch it. "It's not so bad."

"Yeah, I think it is."

"No, it's—"

"I'd imagine it would really hurt to put a blindfold over it. It's probably *way* too tender for that." Tanner's grin was calculating. "I'm guessing it wouldn't be a bad thing for you to sit this activity out and find someone who's willing to help you play hooky instead."

Last night's uncovered truth hung between them in the cool morning air. The group had continued to chew over Tanner's revelation until people drifted off to bed. Avery wasn't looking forward to it being brought up again today—with all the painful buttons it pressed. She'd already considered bailing on the morning but had given herself a firm lecture about being a coward.

Escaping . . . now, that was tempting. With Tanner? Risky.

Avery seesawed between the options for several long moments, and just the fact that he gave her the time she needed helped her come to a decision.

Raising her fingers to her temple again, she faked an exaggerated wince. "Ow."

Tanner's grin widened. "Yeah, I thought so. Let's go make our excuses."

Chapter 10
Tanner

They found a roadside deli which didn't look much on the outside but smelled like heaven when they walked through the door. Taking a table by the window, Tanner ordered a Cuban sandwich, baked fresh in-house and oozing with melted cheese. Avery tucked into French toast made with a cinnamon roll, and when the first bite brought a tiny smile to her face, he thought it was like the bright outline of the sun beaming along the edge of a cloud.

Crap, he needed to focus. He'd sought her out this morning, tugged toward her by that link of theirs—the one that had survived a decade of no contact—and a burning need to get to know her better. With the benefit of maturity and not in front of a crowd of his cousin's friends this time. But now he finally had his chance, all he could do was stare at her, thinking she'd grown even prettier than she'd been back then, regardless of the black eye and the passing years.

Sitting across from Avery Delgado was an experience he hadn't quite prepared himself for. His teenage self was freaking out and the words he'd wanted to say for so many years died in his throat. So, he gave himself over to enjoying it. This might be his last chance to be alone with her this weekend. He'd enjoy it while he could.

At least he'd won their lighthearted scrap over who would pay the bill. Picking up the check for breakfast soothed some of the burning need inside him to even out their debt and, if payback had to start with a roadside platter of French toast, so be it. He could take her to any number of five-star establishments later.

"I'll be back on my diet plan tomorrow, but it feels good to let loose a little here and there." He swiped at a string of cheese that looped from the sandwich to his lips.

"You watch what you eat even in the off-season?" Avery asked, her eyebrows kinking.

She'd been so quiet on the ride up he'd wondered if she regretted their escape plan, but she was finally looking more comfortable again. Maybe it was the food.

"Yeah, I don't like to give myself too much work to get back in shape before training camp starts." Tanner noticed his knee bouncing and he made the conscious effort to still it. "Dex is a veggie. So I ate well while I was in the UK and the surfing was great for my fitness." Flashing her a grin, he took another giant bite. "I'd say I've earned myself some wiggle room."

Toying with her fork, Avery pinned him with those blue eyes that seemed to reach into his chest and urge his heart to two-step. "You've filled out a bit since school. You'd have mashed me like a truck if you were built like this when we collided in the hallway."

Tanner threw back his head and laughed. A few customers looked their way. "That was barely a tap. When you spend your working hours getting slammed into the boards, you need all the bulk you can get."

She winced, spearing another piece of French toast. "Doesn't make you indestructible, though."

Damn, he wished it did. Unwilling to dwell on his worst fears, he chose to keep things light. "Sadly no, but I've still got all my teeth. And there's not many players who can say that."

"You've had a lot of injuries recently."

Rolling his right shoulder, Tanner felt the now-familiar grind of unstable tendons. "Yeah, it was one thing after another last season."

"Well, we wouldn't have met if it wasn't for those two bloody noses."

He couldn't tell how Avery felt about that since her eyes dipped to her plate as she scraped it clean. He itched to ask what shape the years since school had taken for her. Did she regret that their paths had ever crossed at all? As far as Tanner could tell, he'd been the only one to benefit, and the discomfort of that thought sat heavy on his chest.

They ordered toasted marshmallow lattes to go (Sam would have teased him for it) and followed a sign for an out-and-back riverside trail along a pedestrian boardwalk that wound through willows and oaks. If this had been a date, he'd have reached for her hand as they began to walk—there was an overwhelming itch in his fingers to touch her—but everything in Avery's body language screamed "friends." And it made Tanner's skin feel too tight.

"Will you miss your old teammates now you're signing somewhere else?" Her sneakers made a hollow echo against the wooden planks.

"Maybe a little." He knew one thing for sure that he wasn't going to miss and, with the sudden clenching of the muscles along his jaw, Tanner made a careful sidestep away from what had really driven him from Boston. "But I wasn't there long and I'm used to pulling on a different jersey, although it's always daunting to settle into a new team. No one likes being the new guy."

He grabbed at a spindly branch, which bent like a bow as Avery passed it and threatened to bitch-slap him in the throat.

"Will you stay in touch with Mats Dahlin?"

"Mats? For sure. He's a good friend." Tanner drained the last of his drink.

Her feet slowing, Avery came to a halt and squinted up at him. "The accident sounded horrific."

He suppressed a shudder. "Honestly, I've never been so fucking terrified in all my life." The memory of blood-red ice was all too clear in his mind again—the slick of Mats's neck beneath his hands as Tanner tried to keep the lifeforce from running through his fingers. "I was next to him when it happened. I saw Cote go down, headfirst. His feet flew up and one blade caught Mats across the neck. It happened in seconds. I knew it was bad. I didn't even think. I just grabbed him."

"He wasn't wearing a neck guard?"

He shrugged. "Not many of us do."

"They said if you hadn't put pressure on his neck immediately and gotten him off the ice, he'd have bled out."

Tanner crushed the takeout cup in his fist. "Yeah, they said that. But the trainer and the team doctor were amazing. They took over from me as soon as we reached the bench. Mats made it because of them."

The blue of Avery's eyes was warm. "How is he doing now?"

"He missed the end of the season but he'll be back next year." Tanner huffed. "The fucker took years off my life and only spent three days in the ICU."

She searched his face a little longer, before taking the crumpled cup from his grip and throwing both his and hers into a nearby trash can. Again, he noticed the smattering of freckles on each of her elbows.

"I guess it hasn't all been plain sailing—" Avery broke off, chewing at her lip. He wondered if it tasted of marshmallows.

"What hasn't, Stretch?"

"Your career. The upward trajectory of Tanner Stone after leaving Pine Springs."

He almost snorted. If only she knew how much of a struggle it had been. How much of a struggle it still was as he battled injury and age alongside the aftermath of Mats's horrific accident. His career path might have looked smooth, but to Tanner it had felt like a dizzying journey as he ricocheted through the world of pro hockey, bouncing off the sides like a pinball with nothing to slow him down, no one to ground him or give him an anchor. Always hoping the next team, the next base, would be the one to hold him. Always somewhere in between where he'd come from and where he wanted to be.

Tanner cleared his throat. "No one's life is all roses. I've been lucky—I know that more than anyone. And I've done what I set out to do with making a difference to my mom's life and her health. But everyone has good days and crappy days. Times when things run smoothly and times when it all feels like a shitshow. Doesn't matter who you are or how golden things look from the outside."

Avery turned to face him. She was so close he could see the navy ring around the outside of her irises, and fresh freckles brought out by the sun smattering across her nose. "You sound tired. Even now, after your surfing break."

Tanner was surprised. He thought he'd hidden it better than that. "I'm fucking exhausted, Stretch," he admitted. "I don't know what's wrong with me. I feel like I'm running on empty."

There was a moment of silence between them before Avery started to walk again.

"I guess there's no real reason for feeling so tired," she said finally, and there was a deliberately dry edge to her words that pricked the bubble of tension hovering between them. "Apart from maybe the trauma of your friend's injury, the constant strain on your body, and the pressure to perform, intense training and media attention. No reason at all."

He couldn't hold back a snort at the summary. Her candor, the teasing, was refreshing. Avery's unsentimental insight eased the knot in his chest. "You're right. I should quit whining and suck it up."

"Who do you whine to usually?" she asked as they fell into step together. "You've got friends, right? People who support you? The ex-girlfriend before she was an ex?"

In all honesty, he couldn't remember the last time a girlfriend had asked him for more than his credit card. Sure he had his mom and his brothers, but Tanner liked to put on a solid front for them. This kind of sharing felt new, edgy, and vulnerable. "I've got Arlo. We both took a business class together at college and thought that made us experts." He gave a self-deprecating laugh. "Well, him more than me—at least he came out of it with a degree. He's been my manager and financial advisor ever since. It works for us."

And you? he wanted to add. *What are my chances of spending more time like this with you?*

"And now you'll have your family and old friends around you, too," Avery filled in with a casual shrug. "Lots of people to help you find out who you are."

When the boardwalk became a dirt trail and the trees fell away to reveal a shallow portion of river stretched out to their left, he instinctively stood back to let Avery step over a fallen tree. Her long legs flexed and stretched, drawing his eyes like magnets. Remembering the chill of her thighs in his hands when he'd carried her out of the lake, a zap of electricity traveled the length of Tanner's spine, flipping the bird at his resolve to keep things light and easy. He hadn't felt this kind of attraction in ages.

In fact, maybe since high school.

"Did you go to college?" he asked hoarsely, grasping for the first thing that came to mind.

Avery's fingers went to toy with her necklace, as her mouth ticked up at the corner. "I studied interior design at CMU for a year, but I didn't have the right eye for it. Turned out I was more drawn to the practical skills—I loved making things. So, I dropped out when I got an internship with an upholstery shop in Vicksburg. My dad wasn't impressed."

Tanner could imagine. From what he remembered of Joseph Delgado, Avery's father was the type to have pretty rigid aspirations and expectations. "Upholstery? Like, fabric and furniture, right?"

"Yes, in a nutshell," she said, looking out over the river. "I set up on my own, just over three years ago. I've got a workshop in the backyard, and I juggle repairs and restorations with thrifting and renovating my own finds."

"That sounds cool. I'd like to see some of the results."

Avery shrugged him off. "It's not as exciting as hockey."

"I might disagree."

She shot him a sideways glance. "Well, it doesn't pay well enough just yet to make it my sole income, so I boost it with regular shifts in the Rusty Barrel. I think my dad hates that even more."

"Not his kind of place, huh?"

"Not *our* kind of work," Avery corrected him with lofty emphasis, a mocking half-smile revealing her contrary opinion.

In the calm quiet of the sultry Sunday morning, the scent of wildflowers and fresh leaves filled Tanner's airways, and he suspected he could spend endless time like this with Avery. There was still something about the steady parts of her that soothed the edgy parts of him. The parts that never shut up.

"I'm glad we skipped the obstacle course, Stretch. You're a pretty easy person to talk to."

The careful smile that flickered on her lips made him wish again that they'd had more time between the floodlight smash and him leaving Pine Springs. If only he'd been able to get to know her properly back then, things might have been different. But he'd tried to stay in touch and she'd disappeared on him. The memory stung like a jellyfish burn.

Tanner eyed her surreptitiously, taking in the way Avery's hair shone a dozen different shades of red in the sunlight. Even with the array of colors across her bruised cheekbone and the cut knitting together on her forehead, she called to him like none of the models, influencers, or puck bunnies had in the last ten years. Not Lily, not anyone.

"So, what's with the 'no dating' rule then?"

Oh, smooth, you big dumbass. That was very smooth.

Avery wrinkled her nose. "I date here and there, though it's rarely worth the effort. I just don't *do* relationships."

"Why not?"

She shrugged. "I have trust issues."

Tanner kicked a pebble down the path. "Any particular reason?"

The laugh that forced its way from her lips sounded more bitter than humorous. "Yeah. Because men can be dicks. Women, too. Especially to the person they're supposed to love." Beneath the grin Tanner could just see a hint of weariness and disillusion behind Avery's eyes, both so fleeting you could miss them if you weren't paying attention. "Let's just say things were . . . difficult . . . after my dad left. My mom needs a lot of support. I don't have time to look after a partner as well."

"Someone else could look after you," he suggested.

"Someone else could make everything worse," she countered with a single raised brow. "So you're safe from me hitting on you, Ace Face. I'm immune to your considerable charms."

Smothering a swell of disappointment that he felt right to the base of his stomach, Tanner flashed her a cocky grin. "But you agree they are considerable, right?"

Avery rolled her eyes. "We should head back," was all she said in reply. "It's getting late."

The Escalade he'd rented at the airport screamed luxury, from its leather finish to the all-in-one screen system. It was probably just as well that the center console, with its built-in cooler, was so damn wide. Tanner might have been tempted to casually brush her fingers if he could reach and, straight after Avery's candid knockback, that was far from the smartest of moves.

When they pulled up in the gravel lot near the cabins, he reluctantly killed the engine, unwilling to call time on their morning together. And, as Avery released her seat belt and reached for the door handle, the question that had been on his tongue all morning spilled from his lips.

"Nothing will ever mean more to me than what you did at school—it was the start of everything good. But you said you'd keep in touch, Stretch."

Tanner could hear the raw edge of hurt that charred his words in the silence.

"How come you broke your promise?"

Chapter 11
Avery

The day before Tanner had left for college, he'd caught her halfway along Main Street and pulled his truck up to the curb.

"Hold up!" he'd called through a part-open window, and Avery had corralled the butterflies in her chest as he slammed the door of the Chevy behind him and loped around the hood to join her on the sidewalk.

"No car yet?" Tanner had asked with a wince, pushing a few scruffy strands of hair out of his eyes.

She'd shaken her head. "I have to pay for half of the repairs, so I'll pick up some shifts in the diner over the summer break."

Avery remembered the way that guilt had twisted his mouth as he shoved both hands into the pockets of his jeans. "I'll send you the money, I swear. I don't have it now, but I'll pay you back as soon as I can."

"It's fine," she said, brushing him off. "I don't mind the work. It keeps me busy and my friends will come in to see me."

"Let me know if you have any trouble with Tyson Dax. I'll find a way to kick his ass from a distance." Then he'd given her that dimpled grin, no less appealing for its hesitance.

And Avery had pushed her own lips into a smile. "Maybe you could take a contract out on him when you earn your first million."

"Oh, please—I could get a contract on Ty for a chewed mouthguard and a packet of peanuts. I'm not wasting my millions on him." She could still hear Tanner's chuckle now.

Unwinding the band from her hair, she'd held out the elastic. "Take this. You might need another one before I see you again."

Snaking it through his fingers, he'd pulled in a shallow breath, the smile sliding slowly from his lips. There was a rip in the neck of his t-shirt and Avery could see a sliver of paler skin where it gaped. "Thanks. I owe you."

"No, you don't. Not for anything." She'd answered him seriously. "This is your chance. It's what you've worked for. Go out there and make it count."

He'd nodded, almost said something, but stayed silent instead. So many lost *maybes* hung in the air between them—things that could have been and never were, chances not taken. Avery felt an emptiness take root in the space Tanner was about to vacate.

"Hey, you—this ain't no parking spot for delinquents!" The irate interruption from Chief Roberts shattered the moment as he slowed his SUV to a crawl and bellowed through the window. "Move your goddamn truck!"

"Sorry, sir." Tanner had raised a hand in apology, his eyes sliding back to Avery's face as the chief of police drove on. And there was no time for more chat. "Stay in touch, Stretch," he'd said as he backed away.

And she'd promised him she would, already knowing that Pine Springs was going to be a less colorful place without him.

That second lie, unlike the first, was unintentional—and the snapshot of Tanner's answering smile had played on repeat in her memory for so much longer than she'd ever imagined it might.

Tap, tap, tap.

Avery turned to find Gemma wiggling her fingers in an apologetic wave. She swung back to Tanner but he shook his head and laid one large, heavy hand over the top of hers. It felt like a balm on her nervous system, as if he'd tucked a weighted blanket around her shoulders.

"You know what? It doesn't matter right now." His lips tipped into the hint of a smile. "Let's leave further confessionals for another time. Our next escape."

She wondered if he meant that or if they were just easy words. Maybe he didn't actually care what had happened after he'd left town. Why should he? He'd moved on to better things, changed in a multitude of different ways. And her experiences weren't likely to interest him after all these years.

Sliding her hand out from under Tanner's, Avery just nodded and climbed out of the car.

"How are you feeling?" Gemma stroked her arm cautiously as she eyed the blossoming bruise. "Is your head OK? You missed a fun morning!"

"Lots better, thanks." Waiting for Tanner to join them, Avery arched an eyebrow. "Tell me you and Leo gave Bel a run for her money."

Gemma grinned, sweeping a curl out of her face. "We did our best, but Leo's legs got tangled up in the crawling net. Sam and Kash were on fire though. They smashed it."

"Faster than Bel and Drew?"

"Not sure. Johnnie and Mia wouldn't give out the times," said Gemma, peeling off toward Bel's car. "I came to grab my sliders. I'll see you two back at the clubhouse."

"Ready, Stretch?" Tanner's voice, when he rounded the hood, was casual and Avery seized the return to safer ground with gratitude. A sideways glance caught him rolling his shoulder the way she'd seen him do at breakfast and she wondered if it was painful.

"I guess we should go see what the plan is for the afternoon." She turned reluctant feet toward the cabins, suddenly less than eager to rejoin the chaos. But also not really willing to delve deeper into her broken promises . . .

"Well, I'm starving again," he admitted with a dimpled smile, "so unless we're fencing with Taylor Swift on unicorns within the next half hour, they'll need to fucking feed me first."

"Jeez, Taylor *and* unicorns? Anything else is going to be a huge disappointment now."

"One thing first, though." Tanner crooked a finger through one of her jean loops. "Come here."

Avery's breath stuttered and stilled as he pulled her into a no-nonsense embrace. Unbidden, her hands curled instinctively around his back to the curve of his shoulders, where their breadth stretched out his t-shirt, and her heart leaped into her throat, strangling any protest she might have mustered with the biological impossibility of having organs where they didn't belong.

They'd never hugged before, but Tanner's body felt familiar and utterly unfamiliar at the same time. Stomach-swoopingly disturbing. Blissfully terrifying.

Her pulse thrashed at the base of her throat like debris caught on a wire fence.

What . . . ? Why?

"This is a 'thank you' hug, Stretch," Tanner said, reading her mind, and his smooth exhale slid across the rough words like seaweed over barnacles. "Thank you for seeing more than the screw-up with the missing shirt buttons at school. Thank you for my scholarship. Thank you for what you did for me and my family."

Avery felt the sincerity in the clench of his jaw against her temple, heard it in the low timbre of his voice reverberating through her sternum, but she couldn't look up. He was way too close. Too tempting. She'd want to study the scar on his lower lip, pick out the flare in his amber eyes. She already knew she wouldn't want to look away.

Letting her head fall onto Tanner's shoulder, Avery tucked her face into his neck, overwhelmed and struggling for control. The bruise on her cheek twinged but she didn't care. His scent, soporific and sexy, warmed her through to her core—salt and mint and cotton and coffee.

"You didn't have to send the money." Her voice was shaky against the softness of his tee. "I'd already paid off the repairs when Sam gave it to me."

Tanner's gruff laugh echoed beneath her ear. "It wasn't your debt, Stretch. I told you I'd send it as soon as I could."

Her hands traveled of their own accord to press flat against his chest, absorbing the rise and fall of his breaths as his thumbs traced the delicate skin on the outside of each arm, halfway between tickly and sensual.

If she *did* do relationships, she'd want a hug like this one every day.

Maybe multiple times.

Hauling her common sense back from its temporary vacation, Avery scraped together her scattered resolve and decided that two minutes was an acceptable amount of time for a gratitude hug. She enjoyed all one hundred and twenty seconds way too much, before disentangling herself with a desperate reluctance that bordered on misery.

"Thank you for the thank you." She was glad he couldn't see the tremor in her knees. "And for breakfast, too."

"No problem. I'm your partner this weekend, here for all needs—getaway driver, paddleboard rescue, sunscreen application. You name it." Tanner accompanied the husky offer with a winning smile as they started across the parking lot.

But Avery was already steeling herself to resist needing him at all. Pretty words were easily spoken and, in her experience, people were quick to say all kinds of things they didn't really mean.

* * *

The afternoon featured no Taylor, no unicorns—just a far too energetic game of volleyball in which no one paid much attention to the rules and Bel moaned constantly about the "goddamn frickin' height" of the opposing team. She was less than impressed that it didn't count toward the Bach Bash Championship points.

Once they were a sweaty, exhausted mess, everyone cooled off in the lake.

By the evening, there was an end-of-semester feel to the celebrations and a wildness hung in the air. As Avery filled her plate from a table laden with side dishes, Bel gestured to the grill with a dangerously careless fork and a greedy moan.

"You've outdone yourself with the organizing, Sav," she said. "Great place, great food. Good job."

Savannah beamed.

"Have you left any for us?" Bel scrutinized Tanner's plate, which was heaped with corn, coleslaw, and two hot dogs so loaded he had to secure each of them with a thumb apiece to stop the toppings from escaping.

"I think there might be a pickle to split between you, if you're lucky." He took an extravagant bite of one hot dog and flipped a wink at Avery that should have come with a health warning.

After their hug, she was still struggling to meet his eye.

Someone cranked up the music. Gemma shimmied over from the bar, holding three bottles of Peroni above her head. She pushed one toward Bel, another at Avery. Her hips were swinging and there was a wide, sloppy curve to her painted lips.

"She's been on the shots," Avery murmured in explanation when Tanner raised an eyebrow. "Got the party started early at the cabin."

Bel stepped closer and he bent his head to hear her. "Dutch courage. It could get messy. Gem can't hold her alcohol."

That soon became a literal statement when Gemma spun happily on the spot and a jet of beer sprayed in an arc from the neck of her bottle. Covering her food to protect it, Bel rolled her eyes.

Whoever was in charge of the playlist had done a great job of lining up all the best songs from their high school days. It didn't take Bel long to dump their plates and grab Avery by the hand, pulling her into the thrum of people already dancing. Within minutes, Gemma had joined them, towing Leo in her wake.

As Tanner chatted with Drew, Avery gave herself up to the music, achingly aware of his proximity with her every move. He was impossible to ignore. Warning bells rang in her ears, even as the sparks of unwelcome electricity fizzed in her rib cage.

Physical attraction. That's all it was.

And who could blame her?

"I Gotta Feeling" sang the Black Eyed Peas, as if they could read her mind, and Gemma joined in at the top of her voice. Reaching for Avery's hand, Leo spun her fast, letting go again when her hair whipped his face, and she stepped back into a solid wall of steel, her head connecting sharply with Tanner's chin. He caught her hips in a strong grip before his fingers gentled.

"Careful, Stretch. My jaw can take it but your head's been through enough already."

The words vibrated like the low growl of an idling motorbike into the shell of Avery's ear, giving her a full-body shiver, and she knew he felt it. When she turned to face him, Gemma slipped into the gap she left, twirling around Leo with carefree abandon, and Tanner tugged Avery smoothly out of the way.

His lips curved, his hair was mussed. White t-shirt, silver chain, denim shorts. How could such a simple outfit look so damn hot? She'd just seen him demolish three plates of food yet there wasn't an ounce of spare fat on him. It honestly wasn't her fault he seized her breath. It was all him. She was only human.

Although, it turned out Tanner couldn't dance. So maybe life was fair, after all.

On the ice and in the water, he had fluid moves to spare. Avery watched his games more often than she'd ever admit. He'd once said in a magazine interview that skating was like harnessing sheet lightning and surfing like riding a bird. But on the dance floor, the bird escaped and the lightning was a liability. Free and unselfconscious, he was a dancing disaster. It was a mystery because Avery knew he could play the guitar, too.

Where was his rhythm now? Where had his famous coordination gone?

She couldn't help herself. The smile grew, tugging her lips wide. She covered it with her hand until Tanner took out Sam's beer with his elbow and then the laugh burst between her fingers; she couldn't stop it.

Even as Sam griped, Tanner's tawny eyes turned molten. His face lit up, powered by her own giggles. He was wonderfully, gloriously unconcerned that she was laughing at him and it increased his sexiness by one hundred percent.

Tanner was the most compelling guy she'd ever known. Nothing had changed there. Avery's heartbeat, already thrumming from the dancing, raced even faster, driving her blood like river rapids through her veins. The breeze from the open doors blew his scent into her nose and she wondered if the makers of his cologne had insider knowledge of everything that made her mouth water.

Since when had breathing become something she had to concentrate on doing? Just dragging the air in through her throat was a challenge when he was this close. The need scrabbling in her gut was frightening. It defied all the emotional blockades she'd put in place, every pledge she'd made to protect her heart.

Avery had a feeling Bel might be right: things could get messy. Especially if she stayed right here, within reach of temptation.

Dancing was fun, but running was what she did best.

She needed some air.

Chapter 12
Tanner

The swinging bench seat gave a metallic squeak when Avery sank onto the cushions. It groaned louder at Tanner's weight a few moments later as he settled beside her. She spared him a brief sideways glance that held none of the easy joy of the past half hour and he had instant regrets about following her.

Fuck. Maybe she doesn't want my company. Or any company.

"It was getting hot in there," he said awkwardly and she hummed a vague agreement. "But I'll leave you alone if you came out here for some peace."

He went to push himself to his feet again, a flush already climbing the back of his neck, but Avery halted him with a slow shake of her head. "No, you can stay."

Beneath his sneakers, a few scrubby tufts of grass blended into the dirt, and Tanner dug his heels in to start them rocking. The sky was a blush of indigo, peppered with stars and offering an apologetic illusion of romance when there was none to be had here. The rapport he'd built with Avery over breakfast felt suddenly intangible. The simple embrace that had twisted all his nerve endings into a burning tangle, even the dancing of just a few minutes ago—it was as if they had involved two other people and he had no idea why.

Half of Avery's face was in shadow, the other half curved with the hint of a distant smile. Tanner saw her eyes drop to where a scar ran in a half-moon across his kneecap.

"Reid threw a lamp at me." He traced the raised line with a careless thumb. "I was supposed to catch it but he forgot to check I was looking."

Avery gave a light snort. "And I used to wish for siblings."

"Rookie mistake."

She curled her fingers into the sleeves of her hoodie, fiddling with the cuffs. It was the same one she'd worn last night and clearly an old favorite, the lettering across the chest cracked and faded from repeated washing.

"I would never have wished my parents on a brother or sister, though. At least, not the fallout from their split."

Tanner was surprised by the openness of her confession. Avery looked just as taken aback to have said it.

"Did you see it coming?" he asked hesitantly. "The breakup, I mean."

Knowing just the surface of Avery didn't feel like enough, and he itched to uncover the things that really mattered to her. But she took so long to answer that Tanner kicked himself for making another wrong move.

"Not really," she said at last, lifting her chin to stare up at the sky, her head resting against the bench cushions. "I knew there was something going on. I'd heard my dad on the phone in his office, late at night, when he thought he was alone. The sound of his voice was way too intimate for a casual conversation." Letting out a hiss of air through her teeth, she shifted slightly, her eyebrows clamping into a frown. "But it wasn't the first time—he'd done it before. I knew it. My mom knew it. It was still a shock when the thing with Ottoline Harris lasted and he decided to leave us."

Tanner stretched an arm along the backrest, his thumb only a puck's width away from her neck, her hair tempting his fingers. "I wondered sometimes. At school, your smile was so bright when you were surrounded by your friends. But it faded when they weren't watching."

Avery's one-shouldered shrug was self-mocking. "Appearances matter. And no one else ever spotted it, so you must have been the exception."

He ached to touch her, wanted to ask more, but they were interrupted by a sudden wave of people spilling noisily from the clubhouse.

Bringing the portable speaker with her, Savannah lowered the volume to a comfortable background level as the others grabbed chairs or just flopped down on the ground.

With no regard for the lack of room, Bel squeezed herself next to Avery on the bench seat, wiggling her butt to steal all the space she could. "Shift over," she directed and Avery was suddenly plastered to Tanner's side by her friend's hefty shove.

His skin sizzled everywhere they touched.

"Dammit, Bel—this is a two-seater! You're not that tiny." Embarrassment highlighted Avery's cheeks as she unpeeled herself from Tanner's arm and, even though he couldn't stop his muscles clenching beneath her touch, he offered an easy grin to soothe her agitation.

"Nonsense. I'm a particle of dust." Utterly unconcerned, Bel made herself comfortable.

"So, you two live together, right?" he asked huskily, just for something to say.

"We do at the moment," said Avery, her body taut beside him, "but Drew keeps asking Bel to move in with him."

"I'll give in one day, but I like living with Ave." Bel smothered a yawn. "She smells nicer—ER docs are all hand sanitizer and disinfectant. Plus, sometimes when he's gaming, Drew eats dry tortellini straight out of the bag. I'm gonna need him to take a psych eval before I move in."

Johnnie and Mia emerged from the clubhouse with a handful of items and two self-satisfied smirks.

"I'm going to feed him that damn whistle if he blows it at me when I'm all chilled out and sleepy," Bel threatened darkly.

Clapping his hands, Johnnie called for silence. "We've added in the placings for the obstacle course and it's time to announce the Bach Bash champions!"

"Surely we're all winners?" Sam suggested lazily from over on Tanner's right-hand side.

"Sounds like something a loser would say," said Bel, leaning forward to flutter her eyelashes at him, and Tanner couldn't hold back a grin.

Avery relaxed enough to snigger, too. "Remember, it's the taking part that matters."

"Oh, my sweet child." Bel shook her head in mock sorrow, patting Avery's thigh with tender sympathy. "How naive you are."

"As it happens, after allocating points to the top three places in each couples game," continued Johnnie, doing a solid job of ignoring all the heckling, "we have ourselves a three-way tie-break situation!"

"And that's between Savannah and Griff, Bel and Drew, and Sam and Kash," added Mia with a flourish.

"So, we literally *are* all winners," Kash laughed, clinking beers with Sam.

"Not us, though." Tanner leaned closer to Avery's ear, his stomach clenching as her hair danced tantalizingly close to his lips.

"Sorry we're out of the running, Stretch. I should have checked how badly you wanted it before I talked you into playing hooky."

Her shrug wrinkled the sleeve of his tee and heated his skin another few degrees. "The French toast was worth it."

"But you said there's a trophy." Gemma pouted, her gaze wobbling from Johnnie to Mia and back again. "Someone has to win the trophy."

Johnnie held it up—plastic, tacky, and all of four inches tall. "Which is why we are going to settle the Bach Bash Championship with a riddle."

"What the fuck?" It seemed Bel wasn't entirely on board.

Tanner felt Avery huff out a laugh and, when she lifted cornflower blue eyes that crinkled at the edges to his face, he couldn't hold back a grin to match the curve of her lips. The tension between them drained away, fading into the night on the shared moment of humor.

"The first person to answer correctly will secure the win for their team," said Mia. "So are you all ready?"

"Let 'er rip, 'tater chip!" Rubbing his hands together, Griff braced himself in eager anticipation.

"Here we go." Johnnie readied them with an officious clearing of his throat. "Tell me something you can hold in your right hand but never in your left."

"Urgh!" Bel's growl of frustration rocked the bench seat, but Drew, sitting on the ground by her feet, jerked upright with a shit-eating grin.

"Leave it to me, babe—I've got you," he said, holding a clenched fist aloft in preemptive victory. "The answer is your left elbow!"

Drowned out by Bel's squeal, Johnnie's confirmation was hardly heard and barely needed as Drew found himself knocked sideways by the five-feet-nothing of his feral lawyer girlfriend.

"My medical genius!" she crowed, peppering him with kisses as they rolled on the grass.

The pair were crowned Bach Bash champions but no one really cared other than Bel, who flaunted the trophy like it was the Stanley Cup. Sav, Griff, Sam, and Kash all agreed to share the runner-up prizes, passing the two bags of Reese's Pieces and Peanut Butter Cups around the group.

In the sudden peace, a fresh log split and spat on the fire, sending a stray spark leaping through the air to land on Avery's sleeve. Tanner, whipping his hand out to flick it away, wasn't fast enough to stop the scalding ember burning through the material.

"Dammit—you love that hoodie!" Bel sat up and eyed the rounded scorch mark with sympathy.

"I guess it's had its time now." Picking at the burnt edges of the hole, Avery was pragmatic. "Nothing lasts forever."

"Love, hope, and faith are eternal," Savannah chipped in, snuggling closer to Griff on the other side of the firepit, and it was only because she was still so near that Tanner heard the tiny sound of disagreement that Avery made deep in her throat.

"And glitter," said Gemma, out of the blue, her words slurring gently. "You can never get rid of that shit."

Bel's giggle was contagious. Soon Avery was laughing, too. And as Tanner's grin spread over his face and the whole of his left side tingled with the pressure from Avery's body, he sent up a prayer of thanks that he'd decided to come home for Savannah's Bach Bash.

He wouldn't have missed this for the world.

Chapter 13
Avery

"I've got the plates ready," her mom said, as Avery stepped over the threshold with the Malaysian takeout she'd collected on her way over. Though her mom's auburn bob was glossy and her makeup immaculately done, the eyes behind her pastel glasses were tired.

She wasn't the only one.

The usual concern piled on top of a general layer of irritation as Avery trailed her mom through to the spotlessly clean kitchen, trying to shake off the fog of too little sleep and a day that had tested her from the very start.

Violet took an open bottle of wine from the fridge and topped up her own glass. "Will you join me?" She tipped it in Avery's direction.

God, could I use one. "Yeah, but make it small."

They dished up the food and Avery dug into her purse for the small bottle of hot sauce she'd brought with her.

"I don't know how you eat that stuff." Her mom pulled a face, but there was something close to a smile on her lips. "It must overpower the flavor of anything you put it on."

"I think it's an addiction," Avery admitted, giving the bottle a shake. "Nothing tastes as good without it anymore. Bel says I need therapy."

There was an awkward lull as they sat down at the table and Avery cast around for a suitable conversation starter that wouldn't involve the jumbled tangle of things she had no desire to discuss.

I had a great time at the lake! Got right up close and personal with the only guy who could tempt me to break my dating ban and then said goodbye with a weird nod from a distance and no actual words after a rowdy breakfast. Plus Gemma threw herself at Leo in a drunken stupor, was sick all night, and is now swearing off men and alcohol. Oh, and to top it off I've had a ton of trolling comments on a livestream I posted on Friday and it's pissing me off . . .

Who the hell gave someone abuse for deconstructing a footstool?

It made no sense.

But none of this was worth mentioning to her mom. Asking about her mother's weekend would also be a bust. Any plans for the week were a similar minefield. Her parents' social lives had been seamlessly intertwined until Avery told the lie that made the paths of Joseph Delgado and Ottoline Harris collide. In the fallout, her mom had retreated from it all, cutting herself off from everyone but Avery. She rarely went out, and the lack of exercise, fresh air or stimulation meant she slept poorly, too. It was far from healthy.

"Watched any good TV recently?" Avery fell back on a regular query that often saw satisfactory results, but even that was the wrong choice.

Her mom drew her bottom lip between her teeth. "I pressed something on the remote by accident and set the subtitles to Spanish."

"I'll take a look after dinner," Avery promised, swallowing a sigh and summoning up a smile instead. "It'll be an easy fix."

"Nothing's easy when you live on your own and you don't have anyone to ask." Her mother pushed a forkful of char kway teow around her plate.

"You have me," Avery said firmly. "I'll sort it. And I'll check out the shower, too."

"Your father used to be so good at all the household maintenance."

"Dad used to be good at calling other people who knew what to do," she pointed out. "He wasn't handy himself."

"He was a very busy man." Her mom's statement was a reprimand. Clandestine affairs and a messy divorce had failed to knock Joseph Delgado from the pedestal Violet had placed him on.

Yeah, he'd been busy. It took time juggling other women alongside a mayoral role. And after he'd left them he'd certainly been too busy to pick up any of the pieces. That had been Avery's job.

She shook off the weighted memories and tried to step out from under the gray cloud that often seemed to hang over her mom's orderly house. "Luckily for you, I'm pretty handy around the house, too. There's not much I can't do with the help of YouTube."

It was on the tip of her tongue to point out that she'd also be living alone when Drew finally managed to talk Bel into moving in with him—something Avery was resigned to and dreaded in equal proportions. Even more terrifying, though, was the very real prospect that her mom would see this as the perfect opportunity to pressure Avery into living with her. And that was never going to happen.

They discussed the food as they ate, debating their favorite dishes, and Avery took it as a win when she got her mother to try the tiniest drop of hot sauce.

"Oh, Avery—that's burning my lips!" Violet reached for her wine glass and the atmosphere lightened just a little.

Sliding her empty plate to one side, Avery pushed to her feet. "Right. TV first. Then I'll look at the shower."

* * *

The next few days followed the regular weekday pattern and the online abuse seemed to take hold and grow. Having never had a problem with it before, Avery couldn't understand why it had started now.

"As fast as I block them, I get a new one," she complained to Bel as she fixed her a dirty martini—*heavy on the dirty*—during her next bar shift. "How can there be this many people out there with a passionate hatred of upholstery?"

"Babe, keyboard warriors don't need a reason to lash out. They jet poison like a human water cannon and love every minute of it." Bel rolled her eyes and took an appreciative sip of her cocktail. "You just have to ignore the shit out of their pitiful existence and they'll move onto someone else soon."

Avery hoped she was right. The derogatory comments about her hair, her voice, her boobs, and her ass were mortifying. The ones about her professional skills—or lack thereof—were plain infuriating.

"It's the Greater Internet Fuckwad Theory," Leo drawled, pushing his empty glass toward her across the bar. He ran a hand over his beard, the blue of his t-shirt a shade darker than his eyes. "Normal Person plus Anonymity plus Audience equals Total Fuckwad. Just keep blocking and deleting, Ave."

"Yeah, I guess." She moved to the beer tap. "You having another?"

The Rusty Barrel hadn't gotten busy yet, and Bel and Leo, both dropping in for an early drink on their way home from work, were taking advantage of the lull before the storm.

"Please." Leo nodded. He could walk to his place in ten minutes at an easy stroll and pick up his car in the morning.

"Don't look now, but it wouldn't be the biggest shocker if my top troll suspect has just walked through the door." Avery murmured the words without moving her lips, only to have Bel and Leo both immediately swing their heads in *the* most obvious, choreographed arc. "Great, guys. Well done."

"Urgh, Paige 'the human lightning rod for grudges' Harris." Bel wrinkled her nose. "You could be right there."

Of course Paige spotted them in the nearly empty bar. Of course Kai, the only other bartender, was in the middle of serving the only other group in the place. Of course that meant Paige and Mandy Roberts headed their way.

"Hey." Avery greeted Ottoline Harris's daughter—her stepsister, her ex-friend—with a neutral expression. Mandy, the niece of the town's old chief of police, and another school friend to position herself in Paige's camp during the aftermath of the wreckage created by Avery's father and Principal Harris, gave her a frosty nod. "What can I get for you both?"

The two girls placed their order without acknowledging either Bel or Leo.

"Still pulling the bar shifts, then." Paige's smile stalked Avery as she reached for clean glasses.

"I love how you state the obvious with such a sense of discovery," Bel said with a delicate sip of her drink.

Paige didn't spare her so much as a glance. "I wasn't talking to your attack dog, Ave, so you can call it off."

"Yes, I'm still here. At your service and loving life." Spooning ice from the bucket, Avery chose to ignore the comment, the way she'd trained herself to ignore ninety percent of what came out of Paige's mouth. "How are things with you?"

"Very busy. The hours are long, but helping people is so rewarding." Paige swept her bangs off her face.

"I know what you mean. I feel the same," said Avery, placing the two gin and lemonades in front of the girls. "Enjoy. That'll be twelve dollars, please."

There was a pitying smile on Paige's lips when she ran her eyes around the bar. "I don't think our careers are comparable. I literally save lives on a daily basis."

"You work in pharmaceutical dispensing, Paige. Not humanitarian aid." Avery's reply was droll as Mandy pushed her card into the chip slot.

"And yet your father is so invested in everything I do. I'm not sure you can say the same." Saccharine dripped from the carefully delivered jab as Paige picked up her drink, already turning away from the bar. "Have a lovely evening. Don't work too hard."

"Off to save the world, one corn cushion at a time," said Leo, just loud enough for her to hear, and Bel snickered as Paige's shoulders visibly tightened.

Avery tried not to let her barb take root. Though they'd been close at school, there was too much murky water under the bridge now to expect any kindness from Paige. The collateral damage was so much worse when friendships went bad and newfound enemies knew all your weakest spots.

That reminded her. "Have you managed to smooth things over with Gem?" she asked Leo.

Faceplanting into his hands, he gave a prolonged groan. "I've done my best but she's just not getting it. Tell me, am I the asshole here? I don't know how to make it any plainer without being cruel. I just don't like Gemma the way she wants me to."

Avery passed him his beer. "It's not your fault and you're not an asshole. I've met enough to know."

"She'll get over it," Bel said baldly. "She'll have to. You can't force these things—you either feel it or you don't."

"I wish I did," Leo grunted. "It'd be so much simpler."

It already seemed as if the Bach Bash had happened ages ago.

"Did you end up giving Tanner your number?" Bel asked, her dark eyes sharp and searching.

"No point." Avery shrugged. "And he didn't ask for it."

"Would you have if he had?" Leo raised an eyebrow.

Propping both elbows on the bar, she rested her chin on the heel of one hand. "He didn't," she said again.

Avery had been telling herself that it was better for Tanner Stone to slide out of her life as easily as he had slid back into it. By Savannah's wedding, he'd probably be dating someone new and any temptation would be tempered by his unavailability.

The thought curdled in Avery's stomach even as she forced herself to acknowledge the truth of it. Tanner was far too hot a commodity to stay single for long. Over the years, she'd caught glimpses of his dates in the tabloids or on social media; they'd all been as gorgeous as him, most of them in the public eye. He wouldn't struggle to find the next candidate, another eager admirer.

"What if he had?" prompted Bel, and Avery had sympathy for the clients who found themselves on the other end of her friend's unwavering persistence.

"He's a celebrity, wealthy, popular, busy, in demand." Avery ticked each point off on her fingers. "He's sex-on-legs, with endless opportunity to screw around, and I am so not up for that."

"But *you* don't want a relationship," Bel pointed out with uncompromising accuracy. "So what does any of that matter? If you wanted a short-term fling with anyone, he sounds like the perfect person to do it with."

And Avery, desperate to refute that, found herself scrabbling for a response.

Chapter 14
Tanner

Staying in his mom's house, after so many years away from Pine Springs, was like trying to push his feet into a new pair of skates. A tight fit.

Neither the reception nor the individuals were the problem, even though it had been strange to get his head around Henry's presence here and there. But Tanner liked the guy and he could see how good he was for his mom. There wasn't much he wouldn't put up with to see her so happy and, with Reid promising to visit at the weekend, he looked forward to catching up with his brother, too.

No, the main problem with staying there was a size issue. Something Sam or Arlo would kill themselves to crack a dirty joke about.

He was just too damn big for his mom's compact house.

With every shower, Tanner smacked his elbows against the tiles, his head against the fittings. The ceilings were low and his feet hung over the end of the bed in the spare room. He felt like a full-sized human in a hobbit house.

Thank God he'd bought this place for his mom—the childhood home he'd grown up in had been far smaller.

And since when had his mother started to shrink?

Tanner was sure she was shorter than before. She definitely had a few more lines on her face, although most of them were happy ones. And even the odd thread of gray among the blonde. He found this proof of time passing disturbing. It pulled on emotional threads that were already taut in his chest and made him want to reach for his wallet.

"You ready to replace your car yet, Mom?" He kept the question as casual as he could.

Cassidy gave a dismissive snort. "Nope."

"The new Range Rover Evoque looks nice."

"I'm happy with the CR-V."

Glancing over, Henry gave him a kind, knowing smile before continuing to slice the vegetables. "I'm sure your mom'll let you know if she needs anything."

Cassidy leaned over Tanner's shoulder and wrapped her arms around him, her chin on the top of his head. The kitchen chair let out a worrying creak. "It's so good to have you here. I can't believe I get to keep you close by for a while."

"I'm happy to be home, Mom." With the ink still drying on the Rapids contract, it was a relief to know that the decision was made. He just needed to sort out his own place now. "Sam's got a house to show me later. He's just about to complete a renovation on a Victorian farmhouse. He sent me the link and it looks good."

His mom beamed. "I love that boy! Haven't seen him recently. Bring him around soon, will you? Kash, too."

"Why not ask them to join us for lunch on Sunday, when Reid's down?" Henry suggested.

Tanner looked around. "You might need a bigger table, Ma. We could go shopping for one?"

Cassidy pinched his earlobe but she laughed as she did it. "I like my table just as much as I like my car. I don't need a new one."

Her eyes danced, forcing Tanner to smile with her. It was so damn good to see his mom looking so well. He'd never take her health for granted, but the memory of scary days when she'd dragged herself to the laundromat with a gray pallor and a cough that left her sweating were fading to a grim blur. His success had given her the option of where and how much she wanted to work.

A muscle jumped in Tanner's cheek. What if he couldn't always make sure that she had that choice? What if he had to have surgery on his shoulder and he couldn't get it back to full strength?

"You make it so difficult for me to show off," he grumbled, trying to force a grin to his lips. "How's a guy supposed to tell you he loves you if you won't let him buy stuff?"

"Sweetie, I have a spoiler alert for you and I want you to listen good." His mom clasped her hands to either side of his cheeks. "It's not love if you have to buy it."

Yeah, nope. Tanner wasn't falling for that one. He'd slogged his guts out to get to this point purely to look after his family—and anyone in his circle who needed it. The pressure and the responsibility were downsides he bore willingly. After all, there were firefighters out there taking risks every day. Scientists pushing the boundaries of knowledge. Frickin' astronauts exploring the outer reaches of space. He was hardly going to whine about being paid a ridiculous amount of money because he could shoot a puck.

Things had fallen into place for him ever since Avery had made that sacrifice in the PS High parking lot. He hadn't deserved his good fortune then, and he didn't really deserve it now. His money should at least do some good where it could. While it could.

With her on his mind, Tanner took a conversational swerve to change the subject. "Avery Delgado was at the lake for Sav's Bach Bash."

"Avery?" His mother's smile was warm. "I haven't seen her in a while either. How's she doing?"

"She's fine." Those would have been Avery's own words. He knew it.

"Such a popular little thing when you were at school. Has she changed much?"

"Not really. She's just taller. Her friends are a cool bunch and it was good to catch up—although she took a helluva hit to the head from a paddleboard paddle."

Henry looked over from the stove. "Putting the literal 'bash' into Bach Bash."

His mom spared Henry an eye roll for his awful joke before sitting down at the table. "Poor Avery."

"Does her dad still live in town?" Tanner, greedy for any information he could get, took advantage of his mom's attention while he had it.

"He moved out to Muskegon with Ottoline a couple years after they got together. I've not seen either of them since." His mother shook her head. "He always looked and sounded too good to be true. So smooth and so sincere. I wasn't surprised he did what he did but I was surprised by her."

Tanner pictured Principal Harris at her desk on the morning he went to own up about the floodlight. It had surprised him, too. It must have taken Avery's feet out from underneath her. He rubbed at his chest.

"And Avery's mom?" he prompted. "She's still local?"

"She found herself a place just outside of Pine Springs. Not that far. I haven't seen her in years, though. I guess the memories keep her away and, Lord knows, Delia isn't much of a draw to bring her into town." Rising to her feet again, his mom rummaged in one of the cupboards for a plastic bowl. She swept the peelings into it from the chopping board, always happier to tidy than do the actual cooking. "Violet wasn't in a good place after Joseph left her. I don't think she coped well—there were some worrying rumors floating about for a while."

Henry winced as he took a package of chicken from the fridge. They both hated gossip.

"That poor child. She's really been through it," his mom added.

Tanner felt sick.

He'd moved on, living the dream—filling his off-season taking luxury trips with family and friends, sampling the perks that came with his new salary instead of spending time in Pine Springs—while Avery had been suffering.

A couple of sporadic texts, a few months, and he'd given up on her because he was busy and his feelings were hurt. No wonder she hadn't kept in touch.

* * *

So much space. Tanner's shoulders dropped and he let out a long, easy breath.

"I could get a pool table in here." He ran his eyes around the foyer of the farmhouse. It was certainly big enough.

"Only if you want me to whip your ass every time I visit." Sam shrugged.

"Oh, please. You play like a one-armed weasel."

"Hate to break it to you, bro, but weasels famously have legs, not arms."

"If they did have arms and there was a single, poor little limb-challenged specimen, he'd play like you."

In the doorway, Jackson Hale raised an eyebrow. He was a tall guy with fierce blue eyes and an even fiercer scowl, who was apparently responsible for the stunning renovation of the farmhouse. "Christ on a bike. There's two of them," he muttered in a "give me strength" kind of tone.

"Let them have their fun, Jax." Kash grinned. "Then we can play grown-ups and get this signed off."

Tanner could feel his smile growing as they continued the tour. The property ticked every box he didn't know he had. The renovation was fantastic. Period features had been retained throughout, but they were paired with modern fittings in the huge open-plan kitchen and all the bathrooms for a touch of luxury living and maximum wow factor. The spacious first-floor rooms boasted eleven-foot ceilings, with four large bedrooms upstairs. There was a large barn in the grounds and a swimming pool.

The whole place was grand without being flash.

"The last bit of tiling will be finished in the next week or so and there's still some landscaping work to be done," said Kash, as they circled back around to the kitchen.

"We weren't planning on opening the house up to viewings this early but I thought it might suit you." Sam was grinning. He knew he'd sunk the putt.

"I was going to rent first. There are a few things I need to sort out before I buy." Tanner raised his main concern.

The other three exchanged a look.

"Yeah, that makes it tricky because we want to use the capital from the sale for our next purchase. But I'm sure we can come up with a plan." Sam didn't seem concerned. Kash nodded.

"How about if I rent for a couple months, get settled in, and invest some capital into the business as an interest-free loan in the meantime?" Tanner had thought this out on the drive over. "I can get Arlo on the numbers and have him give you a call."

"I'm good with that." Jackson Hale pushed away from the doorframe.

"Let's head to the office and go through the details while we've got you dangling on the hook." Sam's eyes were sparkling as he rubbed his hands together. "And maybe I can talk you into a few optional extras—like gold-leafed ceilings or a helipad? Or you could just hand over your wallet and I'll take care of it all."

"Funny, but that's what Arlo says, too." Tanner grabbed the back of Sam's neck, trapping him in a headlock for old times' sake. "And I want his and hers helipads. One for me and one for your mom."

They grappled for a while until they realized that Kash and Jackson had left them to it and gone back outside.

In the event, Tanner was thankful he'd had the foresight to tell the guys to kick him out no later than 2 p.m. so he wouldn't fall foul of his tendency toward time-blindness. Nerves had him sweating beneath the collar of his shirt on the forty-five-minute drive to the rink, and his neck was tight as he pulled into a parking spot at Ludlow Heights Arena.

Harrison Fisher stood up to greet him with an approachable smile on his lips that sat at odds with his bulldog-like build. The Rapids coach sported more hair on his chin than his head. A thick-rimmed pair of glasses were pushed firmly onto his nose, and his neck was a wide slab on top of beefy shoulders. His office had the faint whiff of stale sweat and coffee but Tanner, well-used to the reek of countless locker rooms, barely registered it.

"Welcome to the team and thanks for meeting me here." Fisher held out his hand. "I've got back-to-back meetings today so you've helped me out."

They covered general topics for a little while—his summer, the weather—and Tanner, grateful for the quiet office space, tried to stop his mind wandering. Fortunately, the coach wasn't a guy for extended small talk.

Fisher fixed him with an eagle eye. "So, getting down to business, your skills are just what we need. You play on the edge, but you're effective and, since the rest of your fitness is beyond question, the pluses outweigh any concerns we may have about your shoulder. However . . ." Fiddling with the mouse to wake his computer, Fisher squinted at the screen and Tanner braced himself. "I want to talk about the reports I've had through from your last two coaches. I'm not impressed."

"I—" Shit, what could he say to that?

"Reading between the lines, it looks to me like they've let you down—unless you're more of a dick behind the scenes than I'm realizing." Leaning back in his chair, Fisher cracked his knuckles. "So can you clarify the situation for me?"

Tanner forced himself to lay his cards on the table. "I'm hyperfocused on the ice, sir, but I've had problems with timekeeping and organization. Moving teams has meant changes in my routine and I've struggled a bit with that. There were some clashes with upper management, too. When I kept running into the same issues, I started questioning myself and stopped pushing through—another failing of mine."

"I see." Observing him over steepled fingers, Fisher nodded. "And what kind of help did they offer you?"

"Well . . ." Tanner flicked the catch on his watch strap open and shut.

"Let me guess." Raising his eyes to the ceiling, the coach sighed. "You were told there are a million other guys who'd die to be in your position and, if you didn't pull your finger out, they'd move you on and fill your space with someone else instead."

Tanner's voice was husky when he answered. "Pretty much."

"And your last coach . . . Boston may have wanted to keep you, but it's obvious from his emails that he's not your biggest fan. Why did he have such a problem with you?"

Embarrassment heated Tanner's neck and he had to struggle to force the words out. "There was an issue between me and his wife, sir."

Fisher's eyebrows rose above the frames of his glasses. "You slept with—"

"No!" He rushed to interrupt. Fuck, this was mortifying. "She . . . was up for it. I wasn't. I had a girlfriend then, although we've split up since. But the coach's wife didn't want to take no for an answer. She was really . . . persistent, and it made things seriously awkward."

"Well, that's an understatement." Fisher regarded him steadily as Tanner fidgeted and twitched.

"I didn't want to stay after that," he added, forcing himself to hold eye contact and praying the man opposite believed him.

"I can see why." Leaning back in his chair, the Rapids coach rubbed at his bearded jawline, one corner of his mouth twitching into something that hinted at a smile. "Fortunately for both of us, my wife left me some time ago. That leaves me free to work all the hours under the sun, and you free to play your part without being sexually harassed."

Tanner let out a tight breath, but his relief was short-lived as Fisher continued in the same blunt fashion.

"You'd be a shoo-in for a top-six role, but your injury complicates things. I've looked over your medical records and it's unclear if we should be looking at surgical or non-operative treatment for your shoulder. Once the team doc has given you a full assessment, management will be able to make a more measured decision."

Tanner's heart sank and his stomach rolled. It was nothing he didn't know already, but hearing it out loud was like a blow to the back of his head. There was no guarantee that he would come back as strong if he had to have surgery. He'd been trying to convince himself that this injury was just a hiccup in his career, but what if it was the beginning of the end?

"Look, control what you can, and let the rest go for now," said Fisher, picking up on Tanner's spiraling anxiety. "Let's talk more after the physical. Someone will be in touch with the arrangements."

The coach stood up and they shook hands again. Fisher was reaching for his phone before Tanner had made it back out into the hallway.

Walking slowly to his car, he tried to rub at the burning in his chest but it made no difference. He felt like the high school screw-up all over again, watching his scholarship chances collapse in an explosion of glass.

I've worked so fucking hard for this and now it could be over.

Sickness churned in his gut.

So many people were counting on him. Was he going to let them all down after all?

Chapter 15
Avery

Gemma joined Avery and Bel for a girls' movie night. She'd recovered most of her usual bounce, though it looked a little forced. They changed into pajamas, argued for a while over what to watch, and eventually curled up on the couch with blankets, popcorn, and *The Hating Game*.

Bel's cell pinged before Joshua had uttered his first "Shortcake."

"It's girls' night, Drew!" Avery and Gemma shouted in unison, each throwing popcorn in Bel's direction.

Bel studied her phone. "It's not Drew. It's Tanner."

Avery's hand stilled in the popcorn bowl. "Yeah?"

"Why's he messaging you?" Gemma looked confused.

"He says he got my number from Sam because Sam doesn't have Avery's." Bel glanced up. "He wants to know if you'll meet him for coffee tomorrow. Any time."

Blinking far too many times, Avery swallowed hard around a kernel of popcorn that seemed to have grown in size. There were damselflies in her chest that didn't belong there. She was a fortress of solitude, goddammit. She didn't do emotional angst.

"O . . . K . . ." Her voice hitched on the drawn-out word as temptation won out over common sense. "Why not?"

One of Bel's eyebrows climbed into a teasing arch. "Don't want to refer back to your list of all the ways that he's no good for your health?"

"Even breathing is bad for you if you do it underwater," Avery mumbled defensively.

"And we're talking about coffee, not a lifetime commitment." Bel smiled, neat white teeth showing her approval. "So shall I give him your number then?"

Avery hesitated for another second, then shrugged. There had been a time, years ago, when Tanner had been in her contacts, and her in his. But numbers could be deleted. She'd done it before. "OK."

Gemma gave a dramatic sigh. "Leave it to you to hook the NHL hottie without even trying, while I get friend-zoned by the love of my life."

"Don't be dramatic." Bel spoke as she typed, her admonishment kinder than the words implied. "Leo's not the love of your life. He's just a guy who is incapable of hanging up a towel and sneezes like the world is ending. There's someone better out there for you."

"There's no one better than Leo." When Gemma faceplanted into a cushion, Bel and Avery exchanged eye rolls. It looked like Leo's continued attempt to avoid cruelty had worked against him.

Avery's cell pinged.

Unknown number:

Hope it's OK Bel gave me your number? Can delete if not.

Another notification. The second message brought a shadow of a smile to her lips.

Unknown number:

This is Tanner btw!

Avery added his name back into her contacts and did what she'd wanted to do so badly ten years ago. She answered him, keeping the message light.

Glad you cleared that up. Thought it was someone looking for foot pics.

Tanner:

Well, I won't turn them down if you're offering.

Even you couldn't afford my feet, Ace Face.

Tanner:

I bet that's not something you imagined yourself typing tonight.

Avery fought a chuckle.

"When you've quite finished your flirt-fest over there, we'd like to carry on with the movie," Bel nudged, but her tone was indulgent.

"That's fine—I can multitask." Avery passed her the remote as another text came through. "I'll be done in a minute."

Tanner:

So, coffee tomorrow?

I could meet you in the morning. 11 at the diner?

Tanner:

Looking forward to it already 😉

"All done." Avery set her phone down beside her and Bel pressed play.

But the movie wasn't enough to hold her attention anymore. It faded out entirely as Avery's memory rolled back ten years to the worst night of her life and the very last message she'd had from Tanner.

The soft cord fabric of the couch disappeared, replaced by the coarse material of the stained gray chair that had scratched her thighs in the relatives' room at the hospital. Avery could still remember how the exhaustion had permeated her bones, while the clock above the door had done nothing to break the 4 a.m. silence, frozen as it was at quarter past eight.

She'd tried so hard to push her mother toward anger after her dad left, desperate to witness anything other than the endless well of grief, but without success. Her mom had made Joseph Delgado her whole life. Without friends to turn to or enough of herself that wasn't just an extension of him, Violet had descended into a despair that was frightening. She wouldn't get out of bed, wouldn't eat, wouldn't talk, and Avery couldn't keep her afloat.

An overworked doctor said they'd pumped her mom's stomach and she was resting comfortably. He'd laid a kindly hand on Avery's shoulder before immediately answering a pager call and hurrying away again. Avery had known she'd have to phone her father once the night was over but she wasn't sure he'd come. It was part of the reason she'd put off contacting him until she knew her mom was going to be OK.

To pass the time, she'd reread each one of Tanner's first few texts from college. They were full of sunshine and positivity. There were scouts at the training sessions. More scouts at the games. His teammates were cool. His coach was impressed. The frat parties were crazy. *Message me back!* he wrote. *Don't leave me hanging.*

But Avery's life was spinning out of control, and she had no reply to send him. When she'd left him on read, Tanner's subsequent texts grew steadily more stilted.

The last one was brief. He'd said he was sorry to hear that her mom and dad had split up. He hoped things were OK. She should let him know if there was anything he could do.

But there was nothing anyone could do. And Avery was left grappling with the feeling that something very special had slipped beyond her grasp.

She gave an involuntary shiver as the featherlight reach of the past trailed a finger up her spine.

If she'd realized in the parking lot that stepping in to help Tanner would lead to her father's affair with Principal Harris and the downward spiral of her life as she knew it, would she still have lied for him?

Despite all the heartache between then and now, Avery suspected she knew the answer to that.

"You OK, babe?" Bel poked her with her foot.

"I'm all good." Avery summoned a smile. "Just old ghosts and popcorn deficiency. Hand the bowl over . . ."

* * *

Tanner was ten minutes late getting to the diner so she got to witness the full impact of his arrival.

You'd think he was a gladiator, striding into the Colosseum.

Heads turned, smiles fluttered, conversations died and resumed in whispers behind hands. There was much metaphorical swooning.

In a movie, he'd have crossed the floor in slow motion to the swell of an instrumental soundtrack.

Again, there was nothing flashy about him. He wore faded jeans and a khaki t-shirt. Avery suspected his boots had a designer label, but they were scuffed and well-worn. Obviously old favorites. One hand scrunched the top of a paper shopping bag, the other juggled his key fob. Nothing about his appearance shouted "Do you know who I am?" And still, he was as mouthwatering as a hot, buttered waffle.

Drizzled in maple syrup.

With blueberries on top.

Tanner slid onto the bench seat opposite her, a ready grin on his lips, and she snorted.

"Jeez. Could you make any more of an entrance?"

"I was only walking, Stretch. Same way I get most places when I'm not driving." Tanner ran his eyes around the diner and everyone who was staring turned away in a unified wave. Apart from one old lady with startling blue eyes at the table behind him. She caught Avery's eye and winked.

Avery plucked the menu from between the condiments, even though she knew every item on it.

"You used to be the one getting all the attention." There was a smile in Tanner's voice.

"I did not."

"You didn't see what I saw. People always noticed you."

"You're wrong." She kept reading the menu.

"I noticed you."

He had a way of stealing her breath even when she tried to stay unmoved. Avery's eyes bounced to his face and hung there. No wonder everyone looked. Tanner was magnetic.

"Your hair's wet." *Last of the great conversational gambits.*

He swept at some messy strands that were the color of biscuit crumbs. His biceps bunched, the tattooed pine trees rippling, and for a moment he looked tired again, inside and out. "I got in a workout this morning. Is it OK if I order food? I'm starved."

Avery guessed that explained the weariness. "You're always starved, but it's fine by me. I skipped breakfast."

Ducking his head, Tanner examined the wound on her temple. "That looks better."

She wrinkled her nose. The bruise had now turned an unflattering shade of yellow but the cut was healing well. "It's getting there. I mend quickly."

"Tanner Stone. As I live and breathe."

Avery blinked. Aunt Delia did not wait on tables unless she'd exhausted every avenue of local youngsters to terrorize. Or the universe was ending.

Was she— Eww . . . Was she—simpering?

Tanner flashed a grin. "Hey, Ms. Feeney. How're you doing?"

"Very well, thank you. It's been a while since we've seen you in here." Avery's aunt stretched her mouth into a smile that must have hurt, and there was lipstick on her teeth.

"I've not been home for a bit. It's good to be back."

Avery caught the eye of the same lady over Tanner's shoulder. Her eyebrows were as raised as Avery's own and she whispered something into the ear of the gentleman beside her. He sent Avery a charming salute, his lined face filled with a gentle mirth, as if they were all sharing a joke. Recognizing them both as regular customers, Avery turned a snicker into a cough before refocusing on Tanner and her aunt.

"How's your mother?" Delia wasn't smiling any longer. She pinned Avery with the unblinking gaze of a gecko. If she'd swept her tongue out and over one eyeball, it wouldn't have been a surprise. Disgusting, yes. Unexpected, no.

"Uh, she's well, thanks."

Her mother and her aunt weren't close. She suspected there had always been black-hearted envy on Delia's side, quiet superiority on her mom's. Neither warranted, neither dealt with. Her mother could have lorded it over Aunt Delia less when she became the wife of the local mayor. Her aunt could have been kinder when everything went to shit. Maybe there were some advantages to being an only child after all.

Delia sniffed, taking Tanner's order with another brief smile. She scribbled Avery's down without looking at her again and schlepped off to the kitchen.

"I'm guessing the two of you don't make friendship bracelets together." Tanner watched her go.

"Not often."

"I bought you something." Reaching for the bag next to him, he passed it over the table.

Avery eyed him suspiciously. "Why?"

Tanner's lips lifted again; the scar on the lower one pulled a little. He drummed lightly on the tabletop. "I wanted to."

She closed her fingers around the bag but made no move to open it.

"It's a 'no strings attached' gift to make up for us not winning the Bach Bash trophy. From one old friend to another." His voice was casual, but his eyes were strained. As if it really mattered to him that she liked whatever was inside.

Keeping her eyes on Tanner all the while, Avery stuck her hand into the bag and drew out a heather gray hoodie, the material as soft as a cloud in her fingers. It was the sort of hoodie you couldn't wait to pull on at the end of a long day. The sort of hoodie you would wear to death and then wear some more.

"I thought you could maybe use a new favorite because of the burn mark on your other one." Beneath the table, Tanner's knee bounced, knocking against hers. She was taken aback he'd even remembered the incident.

"It's perfect." A smile broke through her husky words and his face lit up like a sparkler. "Thank you."

Unfortunately, she then couldn't think of anything to follow up with. The fractured silence that followed as they waited for their food had Avery instantly overthinking her decision to meet up. But Tanner soon eased into a description of the farmhouse he was renting from Sam and the edgy discomfort was kicked into touch by her interest in his plans.

When Aunt Delia crashed a tray down between them, Avery snatched up the new, precious hoodie before anything splattered on it.

"Breakfast stack. Pancakes with bacon. One cappuccino. One water." Delia spared Tanner a nod, then left again.

They dug into their food.

"I wonder how many people in Pine Springs have had their first date here," he mused aloud.

Avery's knife stilled, mid-cut through a slice of bacon. "This isn't a date."

"I realize that." His eyes darkened as he looked away. "I should have asked you to join me for a milkshake when we were at school. My job at Jerry's Pizza didn't pay well enough to run to much more." Tanner's words were loaded with self-deprecation, his thumb rubbed the bone on his opposite wrist.

Did he mean that he'd wanted to? Or was it just an off-hand comment? She'd never imagined that he'd considered asking her out on a date, and the thought brought a fresh swell of regret.

"Look at you now, though." Deciding that deflection was probably her friend in this instance, Avery sipped her cappuccino. "You could probably buy everything off the menu in Jerry's Pizza and the diner combined."

"How times change, huh?"

Wasn't that the truth.

"Not just for you either," Avery said, searching for more stable ground. "Did you know Tyson Dax got locked up? His dad, too."

Tanner leaned back and grinned, as the sliver of tension drained away again. "Yeah, my mom told me. I was shocked."

She allowed herself a giggle. "No, you weren't. None of us were."

"So Chief Roberts finally pulled his finger out of his ass, huh?"

"Not likely," Avery scoffed. "It didn't happen until after he retired."

"Useless schmuck."

Avery swiped a jagged square of pancake through the swirl of syrup on her plate. "The new chief married Elenie Dax. They put Tyson, Dean, and Frank Dax away between them. She gathered the information, he backed her up. And he's done a lot to crack down on local drug problems, too."

Tanner's knee bounced beneath the table. "I like the sound of this guy."

"Yeah, Chief Martinez is cool." Avery nodded. "Cool *and* hot."

He choked on a sip of water. "Say that again."

"He's a good-looking guy."

"I'm gonna pretend you didn't say that, Stretch." Tanner's brow clouded with a mock scowl as he slouched on the bench seat. "It's bad form to rate the hotness of another man when I'm buying you pancakes."

A smile tickled its way up through Avery's rib cage; she was comfortable with his teasing. It felt safer when their conversation stayed light. "Objectively speaking, I suppose you're hotter, but the police chief is pretty attractive."

Tanner brightened. "How much hotter am I?"

"Don't be needy." Pressing her lips together, she kept a straight face.

"Are we talking so hot I redefine perfection?"

"Is that what the puck bunnies tell you?"

"So hot you'd drink my bathwater?"

"That's gross."

"So hot you want to bake cookies on me?" Tanner leaned back, a wide, cocky smile splitting his lips, and Avery suspected he could carry on like this forever.

She rolled her eyes. "I'm good, thanks. But Aunt Delia might."

"So hot you'd eat soup out of my armpits?"

That did it. She spluttered, coughed, lost the battle with her mouth, and threw her hands up to catch the laugh that spilled out; it drew the attention of Brody McAlpine, owner of the local gun shop, and Nathan Reyes, from the liquor store. "You did not . . . just say that!"

Tanner's grin grew, as if it was powered by his satisfaction in making her crack. His laugh was infectious, his company as easy as it had been when they'd played hooky at the Bach Bash.

And Avery continued to turn a blind eye to her strict rules on dating, because this absolutely wasn't a date.

Chapter 16
Tanner

Taking advantage of the chink in her defenses, Tanner talked Avery into showing him her workshop, following her back to her house when they were done in the diner. He wanted to find out more about what she did, and it was an added bonus that it distracted him from the morning's less-than-satisfactory workout session.

"You're a neat freak, Stretch." It wasn't a surprise.

His eyes trailed around the benches and shelves. Everything was tidy, ordered, and surprisingly fascinating. A floor-to-ceiling storage unit held bolts of fabric, strapping, springs, and stuffing, along with power tools he couldn't even identify. An Anglepoise lamp on the workbench stretched over a sewing machine, an array of smaller tools hanging on the wall behind. The bare bones of an old armchair sat on a small, raised platform in the center of the room.

Tanner ran his eyes over the suspended tools.

"What's that one for?"

Avery followed his finger. "It's a ripping chisel for removing old material."

"That one?"

"It's a tack lifter."

"Cool. Looks evil. And just the right shape to get up each side of Tyson Dax's nostrils."

She snorted. "Scary to know that was your first thought."

"You have a lot of chalk." Tanner peered into a tub on the workbench. "Better make sure you don't ask Sam over."

Avery's low chuckle warmed his chest again. Her laugh had never been directed his way at school, but it'd always had the power to turn his head when he heard it. It sounded even better all these years later, made him want things he couldn't have.

He stooped to study the gutted armchair, fascinated by the process of her work.

"That belongs to a woman in town. It's an old favorite and she wants it to match a redecorated room," she said from behind him. "It's rewarding to take something that's seen better days and give it a new life."

"I can imagine." Running the edge of a swathe of velvet through his fingers as he continued to wander, Tanner jerked his chin toward the chair. "I can't wait to see what you do with it. Always knew you were smart. Now it turns out you're smart and creative. I'm impressed."

Avery looked quietly pleased at the compliment. Maybe even a little surprised.

They sauntered back to the rented Escalade.

"You haven't had to give this back yet?" she asked.

"Suited me to keep it for now." Tanner hit the unlock button. "Mats is visiting sometime soon—probably after the wedding. He's gonna drive my car up and fly back."

"Nice."

"Wait until you see my G-Wagon. She's a beast." He eyed Avery's old Honda Element. Scraped, rusted, and one of the ugliest cars he'd ever seen, it set off a twitch in his right eye. "More than I can say for that."

Avery shrugged. "It might be time for a change soon—the air con's broken and it's not worth replacing. But I don't do a lot of mileage and I can fit furniture in the back."

"You can get furniture in the back of a school bus and it'd probably beat that old junker for speed."

This time, the mention of school brought shadows to her eyes; they cast clouds faster than Tanner could think of a smart comment to banish them. Avery twisted a hand in her hair and the sunlight picked out threads of gold in the burnished autumn strands.

"I'm sorry I didn't answer your messages from college. There was stuff going on here. I had nothing worth sharing with you." She swallowed hard. The fading bruise on her cheekbone and the scabbed cut on her temple added an air of fragility to her discomfort. "You needed to move forward. Your life was exciting and I was stuck. But I'm sorry I just dropped out of touch."

"What kind of stuff was going on?" Tanner wanted her to tell him herself.

It took a visible effort for Avery to tip her lips upward. "Just my parents screwing with my life. A mortifying meet-cute between my dad and Principal Harris that I got to sit in on after the parking lot incident. I'm still recovering from that one, by the way. And then, you know, divorce, depression, desertion. Nothing much." She gave an empty laugh that hurt his chest.

"That smile doesn't work on me, Stretch," Tanner said, pushing his hands into his pockets so he couldn't reach for her. "I could see through it at school and I can see through it now."

"I didn't go to prom with Tyson Dax—obviously. I didn't go to prom at all." Avery wiped at a smear on the front fender of his car. "My mom was in a facility for a while. Things were . . . difficult."

"How long?" he asked, his throat keyed rough with sympathy.

"Three months. Not long."

Long enough. And, dammit, she'd been alone all that time.

"All the best people skip prom, anyway. I didn't go either." He'd had no money for a suit.

The pasted smile that held no depth flickered and died on Avery's face as she met his eyes. "It was tough back then but it's all in the past. And it wasn't stuff I wanted to bore you with at college. I didn't really know you that well."

That hurt. Even though it was true.

"I wouldn't have been bored. I wish you'd told me. But maybe we could get to know each other better now." Tanner was treading on eggshells, caught in unfamiliar territory. It had been a long time since he'd had to work to get someone to spend time with him. "I told my mom you were at Savannah's bash. She asked me to bring you over for lunch. Reid's visiting on Sunday. Come and join us?"

Avery looked away with a frown, opened her mouth to say no. He knew it.

Tanner added some pressure. "She asked Sam and Kash too but they're busy. Don't make it a clean sweep. My mom would love to see you."

They were interrupted by the noise of an engine as a car pulled up behind the Escalade. The driver's door opened and a lanky pair of legs got out with Leo Marsh at the top of them.

"Hey." He strolled over to pull Avery in for a hug, leaving his arm around her shoulders. "I was hoping you'd make me coffee and listen to me moan about my summer school kids." He nodded in Tanner's direction. "Hi, bud. How're things?"

Tanner watched Avery relax in a way that sent a restive ache through the marrow of his bones. When she wrapped her arm around Leo's waist and leaned into his side, a muscle pulsed in Tanner's jaw. He tried to rub it away.

Lean on me, he wanted to tell her, and the thought came from an alien place. *I'm here. Lean on me.*

"All good, thanks." Forcing a grin, Tanner tossed his keys from hand to hand. "Just heading out, though."

"Thanks for brunch." Avery's blue eyes glittered. "And my hoodie."

Tugging on the car door, he took a chance. "Lunch," he said. "Sunday. I'll pick you up around midday. How does that sound?"

Avery hesitated for a few seconds before she gave in. "I can drive. Send me the address and I'll see you there."

Tanner knew when to quit. It would have to be enough.

* * *

She was on time to the minute, holding a bottle of wine and a small potted plant. He didn't know enough about horticulture to know what it was, but it was pretty.

Avery, though—she was gorgeous.

"Come in." Tanner stood back, trying to temper the smile that grew on his lips as he held the door open.

"Wow, it smells good in here," she said, following him through the entryway into the kitchen, where his mom, Henry, and Reid all turned as one.

His mother beamed. "That'll be the spices. I hope you're OK with hot food. Henry's made his specialty—Hungarian chicken paprikash."

"My friend Gemma won't eat gingerbread cookies because they're too spicy, but I'll eat pretty much anything." Avery held the plant out to his mom. "This is for you."

"That's so kind. Thank you, honey." His mother waved them further into the kitchen; the double doors to the backyard were wide open. "It's wonderful to see you! Come in and get a drink."

"What would you like?" Tanner asked. "We've got beer, wine, pop, and some White Claw left over from mom's book club."

"I'm driving so I'll take the pop, please." Avery's fingers toyed with the charm on the chain around her neck.

"Hey, Avery." Unfolding himself from one of the kitchen chairs, his brother crossed the room and bent to kiss Avery on the cheek. Tanner cursed himself for missing his chance to do the same. He stepped hard onto the toe of Reid's sneaker as he turned toward the fridge. "Ow—fuck! Seriously, dude. Haven't seen you in years, Ave! How're you doing?" Reid rambled through the string of sentences, the welcoming grin never sliding from his face. His brother was a charming sonofabitch.

As they settled at the table, Avery met the avalanche of questions from his mom and Reid with composure, delighting Henry with her enthusiastic appetite when they all tucked in.

"Me and my housemate don't really cook," Avery admitted. "I forget mealtimes and Bel works long hours. At the weekends, we're both too lazy to bother."

"I'm a terrible cook!" His mom laughed. "Henry takes over whenever he's here and, believe me, it's better that way. Even the boys make nicer food than I can. They all learned to cook when they were younger because I was ill so often."

Avery swallowed her mouthful. "I'm glad you're better now, Mrs. Stone."

His mother lifted her glass to her lips. "Me too, Avery. And please, call me Cassidy."

As the conversation rolled on around him, Tanner tapped his fingers on the label of his IPA, wondering why Avery's presence in his mom's house released the same cocktail of feel-good chemicals in his body that he felt when he was riding a wave.

He couldn't stop sneaking glances at her. The curve of her neck drew his attention like a magnet, although he tried not to look too often. The freckle on the tip of her left ear was just too tempting. Even her fingers, delicate on her cutlery, made him want to hold and examine them. She smelled of something feminine he couldn't identify. He just knew it fucking turned him on.

Avery turned him on.

Even knocking elbows at a too-small table and surrounded by family, she turned him on.

But she was skittish and had already stated her lack of interest in a relationship. And somehow the idea of a casual hook-up with her felt scratchy against his skin.

It left Tanner at a bit of a loss.

Arlo would die laughing to hear that Avery Delgado, girl and woman, was the only person Tanner had ever wanted who hadn't thrown herself at him. He'd never hear the last of it.

"Did you know you've got a smashed taillight, Reid?" Henry took another scoop of potatoes.

Tanner's brother grunted. "My own stupid fault. I backed into a parking spot and clipped a metal post. Didn't see it." He raised teasing eyes to Avery and, before Reid could open his mouth again, Tanner guessed what was coming. "Bet you can relate."

"Reid." His mom's reprimand wasn't enough to shut his brother's mouth.

"Been jumped by any floodlights recently, Avery?" Reid grinned. There was a wicked light in his eyes.

"That's enough," Tanner growled. He'd never told his mom or his brothers the truth about the crash. Even with his family, he was ashamed of what he'd let Avery do on his behalf. For their benefit.

She raised her chin, caught his eye. "No more floodlights, but a mailbox swerved into my lane the other day." When Avery smiled, he felt the jolt right through to his core. It humbled him that she still had his back after all these years. "I hate when that happens."

Reid snickered and, for want of the opportunity to pummel him or express his gratitude to Avery, Tanner flicked a pea at his brother's face.

His mom gave them both *that* look as she changed the subject. "How was training this morning, Tan?"

"Uh, it was cool. Went well." He wished she hadn't asked. The memory of how his shoulder had crunched and popped like Rice Krispies as he'd pushed it through a brutal workout made him antsy.

"So the new coach is happy with your fitness?" his mom pressed, waiting on his reply with keen interest.

Tanner snapped the catch on his watch a couple times. "I'll be having a full physical in the next couple weeks, but it's just routine." Downplaying the situation to his family was his go-to response.

Shuffling a forkful of chicken around his plate, he tried to stop his knee bouncing. He couldn't admit to any of them how anxious he was, how panicked he felt at the possibility of losing his ability to provide. He'd taken on that responsibility willingly and his family counted on him. They needed him at peak fitness; anything less and he'd be letting them down. And that, Tanner refused to do, even if he had to push his body past screaming point.

Feeling Avery's eyes on the side of his face, he flashed her an easy smile, shoving the worries and doubts deep down in his belly. When a frown flickered briefly across her brow, he wondered if she'd seen more than he meant to reveal.

"What do you do for work, Avery?" his mom asked, offering her the salad bowl.

"I'm an upholsterer and I do a bit of bar work in between."

"What fun to have such a mix—creative by day and social by night." She gave Avery a keen look. "I've got an old button back chair I've been meaning to get re-covered. Is that the sort of thing you do?"

"Exactly the sort of thing," Avery said, flushing a little as she promised to take a look at it while she was there. She looked so delighted by his mom's interest that Tanner's fingers crept to her thigh and gave it a brief squeeze. He would have loved to leave his hand there, but he made himself pull back.

"Tanner says you live near the fire station." Taking off his glasses, Henry cleaned them on the front of his shirt.

"I do. On Ellen Street."

"With a friend, you said?" His mom again, chipping back in like she was finishing a tic-tac-toe passing play.

"Yes, I rent with Bel for now, although I'm not sure her boyfriend will let me keep her for long." Avery placed her knife and fork neatly on her plate. "She's a corporate lawyer."

"Impressive." His mother reached over to smooth Reid's hair. "Just look at you all! So grown-up now, even my baby. It makes me proud. I feel old, but I'm proud."

His brother ribbed his mom for her sentimentality and Avery's lips tilted. That small, half-smile packed a punch, and Tanner shifted in his chair as her bare arm brushed his elbow, her skin pale against his ink. Why did she mess him up like this?

He wanted to trace a finger from shoulder to thumb and see if she broke out in goosebumps.

He wanted to press his mouth to the blue veins at her wrist and make her pulse leap, pull her hand back onto his thigh and trail it higher . . .

He *needed* to stop thinking things that were going to get him in trouble at a family lunch.

Chapter 17
Avery

The huge fallen limb from the beech tree carved a splintered crater through the roof of Avery's workshop.

On the plus side, the damage had happened overnight, so she wasn't in there at the time. But it wasn't super easy to focus on the positives as she stood a safe distance away with Bel and took in the devastation.

"Holy frickballs," murmured Bel.

Avery couldn't muster any words at all.

Up until now, the old thirty-foot tree had put on a good show of being a healthy specimen, but the jagged bough currently bisecting her workshop showed clear signs to the contrary. Wood and glass surrounded the crushed exterior and Avery couldn't get close enough to see if anything inside was salvageable.

It took the whole day for a hurriedly summoned arborist to clear the wreckage. By the time he packed up and left, Avery knew more than she'd ever wanted to about the phenomenon of "summer branch drop" and the need for routine tree inspections.

All very helpful. All too late.

How was she going to work now? She had orders, commitments. Bills to pay. Her head throbbed. Her stomach swirled.

Dumbass tree. Fucking summer branch drop.

YouTube videos could only get a person so far. She was going to have to do what her dad did best and call in the experts.

A quick call to Sam Archer gave her the number for a local building contractor. When Luke Farley arrived at the end of the afternoon to assess the damage, Avery recognized him immediately as the brother-in-law of the police chief and a regular at the Rusty Barrel.

"We're going to need to take the whole thing down. It'd be far harder to repair it than rebuild it. More expensive, too," Luke said, unloading some steel props from the back of his pickup. "I'll put these up to temporarily support the ceiling so you can get it stripped out, and then we'll make a plan from there."

With a promise to put together a quote for a new workshop, he left just in time for Avery to grab her keys and hightail it over to the Barrel for her evening shift, the wretched balance of her bank account running on a loop in her head throughout the brief drive.

Her phone rang as she pulled into the lot and Avery winced when she saw it was her mom.

"I tried you earlier and got your voicemail." Her mother's words tumbled over each other as soon as Avery picked up. "Why didn't you answer? Where have you been? You didn't tell me you'd be out of touch."

"Just busy, Mom. Nothing to worry about. My workshop got—"

"Only, you always answer and then I started to think something might have happened. And I didn't know who to call to check if you were OK."

Avery sighed as she climbed out of her car. "That's why you have Bel's number, just in case I'm not available." Which barely ever happened. "You can always try her, but you have to remember she might not be able to answer either if she's working."

"Oh, I wouldn't like to bother Bel," her mother said quickly. "She has a proper job."

Yeah, that hurts a little. Avery rolled her shoulders against the slight that her mom hadn't realized she'd delivered. "Talking of work, I'm just about to start my shift so I can't chat now. What did you need me for?"

"Oh." There was a brief pause as her mother searched her memory. "Well, I can't really recall what it was right now, but I know it was important."

Avery bit back a sharper retort, saying instead, "I'm sure it was. Jot it down if it comes back to you and I'll call first thing tomorrow for a longer chat. Got to go now, though. Bye, Mom." Jogging the rest of the distance to the main door of the Rusty Barrel, she called out "Sorry, sorry, sorry!" to Kai as she stepped inside, though she was barely five minutes late. Dumping her purse onto a shelf beneath the bar, Avery shoved the worries of the day aside and jumped straight into work.

It was a live music night so she knew it would be a busy one. For the next hour and a half, there was no break in the throng of customers who swarmed the bar. It was hot, noisy, and frantic and, though Avery still felt queasy whenever she thought about her workshop, there was no time to dwell on it.

The band was four songs into their set when she looked up to find that the next trio waiting for drinks were Tanner, Sam, and Jackson.

Three good-looking men, and Avery was alarmed to find she only had eyes for one of them.

Wiping a sheen of sweat from her forehead, aware of how the lank strands of her bangs were sticking to her face, she drew on her shallow reserves of resilience to greet them with a friendly smile.

"Hey, guys. What can I get you?"

Their order was simple—beers all around—and, though there was a brief argument when Jackson and Sam wouldn't let Tanner pay, none of their comical insults packed any heat.

"Did you get hold of Luke?" Sam shouted to be heard above the tumult of music and chatter.

"I did. Thanks for giving me his number. All sorted." Shooting him a grateful smile, Avery moved straight on to serve another group of customers.

Out of the corner of her eye as she pulled beers and poured mixers, she watched the boys take seats at the end of the bar. Tanner's head bent close to Sam's, and Avery guessed from the frown that pulled at his eyebrows that he was hearing about her workshop disaster. *Dammit, Sam.* The phone number had been helpful but couldn't a girl keep her fight with nature to herself?

The steady stampede of patrons gave Avery no time to stop. The noise level increased as people continued to swarm into the bar and one order blended straight into the next. She only remembered when her stomach started grumbling and her head swam a little that she hadn't taken any time to eat since that morning. Her t-shirt grew damp, her neck even more so.

Avery refixed her ponytail and pushed on.

As she collected some empties between customers, grabbing a handful of glasses from near Tanner's elbow, he turned away from his conversation and leaned over the bar.

"Sorry about your workshop," he said. "Anything I can do to help?"

His mouth brushed her ear and Avery found herself recoiling from Tanner's fresh cleanliness like a vampire from a crucifix.

Urgh, why did he have to smell so good when she was so sweaty!

"No, I don't think so. It's beyond life support. There's just the burial to go and I'm handling it."

She tried for flippancy but Tanner's mouth tightened where that scar bisected his lip. "No need to do it alone."

Avery forced a smile. "Thanks, but I've got it. It'll be fine." And she moved away to take another order.

An hour went by with no letup in the swell of customers. It was so damn airless in the bar and the music was making her head pound. Chugging water in an attempt to cool down, Avery kept on moving, serving drinks with careful concentration and a fixed curve to her lips. More than once, as the evening crawled forward in slow motion, she was aware of Tanner's tawny eyes on her face while Sam and Jackson talked across him.

Eventually, when she made one more pass close by the end of the bar where the boys were sitting, he called her over.

"More drinks?" Avery asked, dragging her sticky top away from her stomach in a surreptitious movement.

"Yes, please." Tanner's sneakers bounced on the footrest of his stool as he leaned closer. "You look washed out. Have you eaten?"

"Washed out" was probably kind. Avery tried not to take offense.

"I ran out of time." She pulled them another three beers and rang the sale into the cash register. "It's been a day."

Handing over some crumpled bills with one hand, Tanner dragged his phone from his pocket with the other as she moved on again.

Eventually the evening began to wind down.

The band played their last couple of songs and set about packing up their equipment. As Kai switched to the speaker system for more chilled background music, the crowd thinned a little and the frantic pace slowed. And Avery found a chance to breathe as the bar slowly emptied.

"Sorry it's been so mad." Kai wiped his brow with the swipe of a wrist and grimaced. "Got let down at the last minute—Nina was sick and no one else could cover. You've been great tonight."

"No problem." His appreciation went a long way to making up for the hectic shift.

Giving a wave to Tanner, Sam, and Jackson as they headed for the door, Avery continued to clear up until the bar was orderly again and the last load of glasses was in the dishwasher. She was grateful that the restock and sticky surfaces were a problem for tomorrow's cleaning crew and not her.

With a final goodbye to Kai, she grabbed her purse and turned exhausted feet toward the door.

In the darkened lot, her car sat among a scarce handful of others left by conscientious patrons. It stood out only because of the hefty hockey player leaning against the fender with his bulky arms crossed, and Avery's stride faltered.

"I thought you'd gone," she said, though the evidence to the contrary was right in front of her.

Tanner smiled and gestured at two pizza boxes propped on the hood of her Honda. "Found these and thought I'd stick around to share."

"You found them?" She would have raised an eyebrow if she'd had the energy.

"I know. What are the chances?" When he opened the top box, the scent of herbs and dough had her stomach growling and Avery's feet carried her forward of their own volition. She found herself with a slice of pepperoni-laden pizza in her hand before she could blink.

God, she was hungry!

"Eat," Tanner encouraged, his eyes a golden gleam in the blanket of night. "That was a crazy shift. You didn't stop all evening. And it sounds like your day sucked, too."

With no energy or desire to argue, Avery took a huge bite with a heartfelt moan. It was heavenly, even without her usual dollop of hot sauce. She'd resigned herself to having a quick grilled cheese at home before falling into bed, but this was so much better—and so much faster. With the hefty clean-up mission awaiting her tomorrow, she'd need all the strength she could get.

"Thanks, Tan," Avery mumbled around a mouthful of cheese and carb heaven. His thoughtfulness plucked at an unfamiliar cord in her chest and some of the tension went out of her shoulders.

"My pleasure, Stretch." Tanner's dimple deepened as he snagged a slice of his own from the box. "Got to be some perks of a lifetime loyalty card for Jerry's Pizza."

As they stood side by side in the dark, Avery wasn't sure anything had ever tasted quite so good as this unexpected midnight feast in the lot of the Rusty Barrel.

Chapter 18
Tanner

He suffered through a morning training session in the gym that was both low-impact *and* grueling, followed by an extensive physical. Poked and prodded to within an inch of his life, Tanner gritted his teeth until it was over and tried not to let the creeping dread overpower him at every "hmmm" and huff from the team doc.

The moment it was over, he jogged out to the parking lot without stopping to shower or change, desperate for an instant diversion from his spiraling thoughts. He knew where he could find it, too.

Throwing his gym bag into the trunk of the Escalade, he climbed into the driver's seat, his quads protesting from the workout, his shoulder from the rigorous testing. And as he headed for Pine Springs, Tanner brooded over the message he'd found in his DMs earlier—an intrusion that was one hundred percent unwelcome.

> Boston isn't the same without you. Will you make it back for a visit any time soon? xoxo

He rarely checked his social media accounts in the off-season, and only used them sporadically at other times to duty-post enough to pacify the relevant comms team. Damn, he wished he hadn't looked now.

On the surface, the message seemed innocuous, but Bethany Jenner was shameless. She'd put Tanner in a horrible position with her suggestive flirting and unwelcome touches at any and every social occasion before his move. Polite knockbacks, gentle disinterest, and outright avoidance had failed to keep her at a distance, while the power imbalance had hamstrung him from a stronger protest.

Her husband was a great coach, a good leader and mentor—to others, at least. But watching his wife chase after his player had done nothing to endear Tanner to Laurie Jenner.

Flexing his fingers and tugging at the neck of his tee where it suddenly felt infuriatingly fucking restrictive, Tanner shifted behind the steering wheel. He was deeply relieved to have escaped that mess; no way in hell would he be answering Bethany's message.

Pulling up at Avery's address within the hour, Tanner bypassed the house and headed around the back, footsteps faltering as he turned the corner and took in the destruction. Held up by steel props, her workshop looked more like a collection of parts than a solid structure.

Drawn forward by movement inside, Tanner paused in the open doorway and watched for several silent minutes as Avery packed fabric and other materials into boxes, his eyes bouncing around the interior. The space had already been partially gutted. Her peaceful, orderly working area was a war zone, utterly trashed by a missile in the shape of a fallen bough.

No wonder she'd looked so wiped last night.

"Where's the armchair?"

Shooting a glance over her shoulder, she jerked her head toward three heavy-duty flexi tubs filled with detritus. "Mostly in there—the roof timbers crushed it. Mrs. Alberty is going to give me so much grief." Her face was shadowed with fatigue, her blue eyes dull. She looked no more rested than she had last night. "My sewing machine is toast, too."

"Thank fuck you weren't inside when it happened." A chill inched its way up Tanner's spine at the thought. "Mrs. Alberty will understand it was an accident." Surely no one would hold something like this against her.

Avery snorted. "You've been out of Pine Springs too long. Elfrida Alberty isn't really your understanding sort."

"Avery—"

"But you're right—it could all have been worse. It's only a shed, some work stuff. It's not important." She shook the debris off another swathe of fabric.

"It is important. It's your personal space."

She just shrugged, and he didn't know what else he could say to make things better.

"Sorry I couldn't make it sooner. I came straight from a training session."

"I didn't expect you at all. And Bel, Drew, Leo, and Gemma said they'd help later." Avery's folding and packing took on a more intense edge, her fingers clenching so tightly around the materials that her knuckles were the color of bone.

"Just stop for a minute . . ."

"There's a lot to do."

It killed him when a rebellious tear made it past all her willpower and trickled from the outside corner of one eye. Tanner couldn't stand to watch her crumble.

Spanning Avery's waist with his hands, he turned her toward him. Her protest ended in a wet choke as she sagged in his grip, fisting her fingers against his chest.

"I've got you, Stretch." His arms were tight bands of support that held her up, held her together as her shoulders shook.

Everywhere inside him, parts he couldn't even name ached. "Let it out."

"I'm sorry." The apology was muffled by his tee.

Tanner felt the judder of her breath against his chest. "You're allowed to be upset."

"I'm not usually a crier." Avery's voice was little more than a raspy whisper. "It's just been a strange week. I'm a bit on edge."

She felt both fragile and solid in the circle of his arms, and Tanner's heart rattled against the cage of his ribs like a stick on a rickety fence.

"Your mom?" he asked.

"Yes, her—always her—and some other things. It's nothing."

"Tell me." He was going to prize this out of her if it took all day.

Avery shrugged. "I've been getting nuisance calls and someone's booking Lyft rides in my name—it's ruining my rating. Plus, a load of weird shit keeps getting delivered and I've no idea where it's all coming from. It's pissing me off."

Drawing back, Tanner eyed her curiously. "What kind of deliveries?"

"A stuffed fish, a box of straws with dicks on them, and a bulk bag of manure." She pushed her bangs off her face with a weak huff. "Kinda funny, right?"

"Not really." He frowned down at her.

"I was home for the last one, so at least they didn't just drop it and leave." Avery attempted a smile. "Don't need any more crap to deal with right now."

Tanner took the fabric from her hands and folded it as neatly as he could, running through the possibilities of what might help the most.

"I'm probably just tired," Avery muttered, scrubbing at her eyes. "Last night was a late one."

"You need a break." Tucking her hand inside his, Tanner led her out of the ruined workshop and toward the house. It was a testament to her weariness that Avery followed without protest.

The back door handle turned easily in his grasp. "Are you hungry?"

She wrinkled her nose. "I don't think so."

"Right. Maybe later then. You could use a nap first anyway."

She pulled back. "There's no need. I'm just—"

"Tired, Stretch. You said it yourself. Plus naps are the best. I highly recommend them." He made a swift decision. "*I* need a nap, even if you don't." Tanner conjured up a wide, fake yawn. "I did the power yoga session from hell this morning and I'm wiped."

"Wait—you do yoga?"

He grinned and pulled her further into the house, assuming he'd stumble across a living area. Yep, and there it was. The couch looked big enough.

"I do. Not well, but I give it my best shot. Helps to loosen up all the bits that get too tight during the season." He slumped onto the cushions and kicked off his sneakers. "Sit down. We're having a nap."

"Oh, make yourself comfortable, why don't you?" Avery groused, but there was no bite to the snark as her fingers reached for her necklace. She chewed her lip when Tanner patted the space beside him. "I'm a mess."

"So am I. I didn't shower after my workout."

She shifted her feet and let out a long exhale. "There's more to do outside. I can clean up later."

"Good call." Sprawling lengthwise on the couch, his feet hanging over the end, Tanner dared her with a cocky eyebrow raise. "Half an hour. Then we'll get back to it."

He wondered if she'd give in, and his pulse skipped in anticipation. His mind might have gotten the memo that Avery wanted to keep things casual but the dumbass had forgotten to make sure his body understood; they were on two completely different pages. And even as he steeled himself to keep any physical contact as impersonal as possible, his fingers twitched with the need to touch her again, the urge to comfort and soothe her while she was struggling.

After a moment, Avery lowered herself to the cushions. Tanner closed his eyes and tried to look like he was on the verge of sleep. When she slowly stretched out, he slung a deliberately casual arm around her waist and drew her against him, his heart in his throat as he did so.

Avery's body softened in infinitesimal stages, the tension leaking from her like an ebbing wave. Tanner kept his breathing steady and deep. She pillowed her head on the palm of one hand and settled, her midriff damp beneath his fingers. The scent of hard work and feminine warmth eased into his nostrils. His heartbeat reached for hers, checked out its rhythm and, he could swear, started to keep the same time. Around Avery, it was almost as if he lost his restlessness and found a purpose.

Even knowing he had hours of torture in his not-too-distant future when he would replay how good she felt in his arms, relaxation soaked into Tanner's bones and his talent for falling asleep anywhere and anytime he was horizontal worked in his favor. The sofa was comfy, the morning's training session had been tough. With Avery's hair brushing his jaw and the sweep of her hip beneath his arm, he soon lost the battle and drifted off.

* * *

"Aw, how cute are they!" (Gemma.)

"Adorable." (Leo, with dry agreement.)

"Just like Rose and Jack floating away from the *Titanic* wreckage, if Rose had just shifted over a bit." (Bel.)

"There wasn't room on the door!" (Gemma again.)

"Even Kate Winslet said there was room." (Bel.)

Tanner opened one eye. "There was definitely room."

"See?" Bel said, as if his word was enough to settle the debate.

Avery's friends stood just inside the doorway. At some point while he'd slept, Tanner had shifted onto his back and Avery was now draped over his chest, still dead to the world. He couldn't sit up without waking her.

"She needed to stop," he offered as an explanation.

"I'm sure she did," Bel agreed with an understanding smile.

Leo's eyebrows knotted. "We've come to help."

Tanner gave Avery a small squeeze and she burrowed into his armpit with a grumbled protest.

Gemma giggled. Leo grinned.

Bel decided to make coffee.

Tanner lowered his chin until his mouth was right by Avery's ear. "Nap time's over, Stretch," he murmured, although everything in him wanted to stay right where he was.

Chapter 19
Avery

She watched him while they worked. It was impossible not to. Tanner burned brighter than everyone else. He might be a celebrity, but he didn't act like one—he got stuck in, lifted the mood, teased, hummed, and buzzed with energy.

He might look a little different these days, but from everything she'd seen since they'd reconnected, the old Tanner was still very much there on the inside—the goofy kid she'd first gotten to know with his shoes falling apart. Kind, funny, sweet. Boundless charisma.

But now he had muscles, too.

And though Avery was pretty sure she wasn't a shallow person, she couldn't take her eyes off them. Or his tattoos. Or his face.

She secretly wanted back on that couch so badly it was hard to concentrate on the clean-up.

Tanner made her forget things like trashed workshops and self-imposed dating bans. He brought the sunshine and the sex appeal. And Avery cursed that she had been too tired, too worn down, to make the most of their embrace on the couch before good sense kicked back in.

She didn't want to be sensible.

Hold me again.

Let me breathe you in.

Could I maybe, possibly, nibble on your neck?

She suspected the shambles of the past twenty-four hours had made her delirious.

Bel caught her staring as Tanner hefted the heaviest of the storage boxes against his stomach, forearms corded and shoulders bunching. The ink of his tattoos rippled over his biceps.

"That guy could cause a global heatwave," Bel muttered out of the corner of her mouth. "You should let him melt you like a popsicle."

Avery could feel it happening already.

"Do you know how many germs are exchanged with every kiss?" she murmured in response. "Eighty million. Eighty. No one needs to take that kind of risk on the regular."

Sniggering openly, Bel patted her shoulder. "You keep telling yourself that, hon. One of these times it'll sound convincing."

"Where do you want this?" Tanner asked as he passed them in the doorway.

"It can be stacked in the living room for now," Avery told him.

Leo followed with the chair from her workbench.

The space was nearly empty. Opening her desktop filing cabinet, Avery started to remove her folders of invoices, orders, and receipts, but Tanner stopped her with a hand on her arm having returned from the house.

"Leave it as it is and I'll take the whole thing out," he said. "It'll be easier for you."

"Let Leo help—" she began to protest but he brushed her off.

"It's just another workout, Stretch. I'm all good." There was a clipped edge to his reassurance that had Avery frowning, but he lifted the filing cabinet without so much as a grunt and turned for the doorway.

"I was thinking of putting it in my car rather than the house. There's so much stuff everywhere already."

Following her out to the driveway, he waited patiently while she unlocked the battered Honda and shunted the cabinet into the trunk. Once his arms were empty again, Tanner shot her a sideways glance.

"Have you got anywhere else you can work? Maybe your mom's house or something?"

Avery shook her head. "She doesn't have the room. I'll look for somewhere to rent tomorrow. I have to track down a replacement armchair for Mrs. Alberty as soon as possible."

And re-cover it for free. She almost groaned at the thought of the lost hours, the dip in her earnings, the setback to her plans for tailing off her shifts at the Rusty Barrel.

Tanner blocked out the sun, a halo of light surrounding his frame like a nimbus, and there was a smile on his face when he shrugged. "Lucky for you I'm moving into a big-ass farmhouse this week with way more space than I need."

She opened her mouth but his eyes begged her to hear him out.

"There's an outbuilding I'm not planning to use and, since your workshop's all packed up as it is, we can easily move everything—lock, stock, and barrel—over to my place. It'll give you time to get something sorted here." Tanner leaned a hip against her car and crossed his arms. "Training camp doesn't start until September so I can help you set everything up, but I swear I won't get under your feet."

"I'd get under yours." Avery scrubbed a dusty hand across her forehead. "It's very kind of you, but I'll work something else out."

"You don't need to." He shrugged. "Let me help."

Damn, she was tempted to accept, knowing she couldn't afford to fall too far behind with the orders she had and how much a rental unit was likely to set her back. But it went against the grain to let someone else solve her problems. She'd learned that relying on someone else was a fast track to disappointment.

Avery shook her head. "I really appreciate the offer—"

Tanner lifted a hand to tug at her ponytail—such a schoolyard gesture, it had the frown sliding from her face. "Not only do I not need the outbuilding right now, but I also wouldn't have my new house without you. I wouldn't have gotten into college. I wouldn't have a place on the team or a fuck-ton of money without you. So, for Chrissake, let me pay back some of that unbearable burden. It's driving me crazy."

His words teased but Tanner's eyes were serious, and Avery was struck by the strange novelty of having any man offer her just what was needed at the moment she needed it.

"Please." He pulled on her hair again. "It'll be fun to have you around. I don't know many people around here anymore."

A ragged laugh escaped her throat, and relief was a rising bubble of air that made her head spin. Avery couldn't bring herself to say no when his offer would solve her biggest worry right now.

"Plus, having you on the property will help keep me safe from all the ladies. I could do with a bodyguard." Tanner pushed with the humor, a grin spreading slowly over his lips. Dammit, he knew he had her.

But who will keep me safe from you? This arrangement could prove to be a double-edged sword and Avery sensed she might be the one in danger.

She rolled her eyes. "I suppose I could help fend them off. I'll tell them you collect Barbies."

"You're mixing me up with Sam." Slinging a casual arm around Avery's shoulders, Tanner squeezed. The weight and the warmth were more intoxicating than anything else she could remember. "And they'll never believe you anyway. I'm too much of a catch."

* * *

When Drew joined them, they got stuck into Mexican takeout in the living room, with a Marvel movie Bel bullied them into watching in the background. The warmth and spice hit the spot, filling Avery's stomach and making everything seem less desperate. The nap hadn't hurt either.

She'd showered and pulled on clean shorts and a fresh t-shirt. Over the top, Avery layered the hoodie Tanner had given her and his mouth ticked upward when he saw it.

He'd taken a spot on the floor, circling Avery's ankle with a casual loop of his fingers when her foot trailed by his side from her position on the sofa, his fidgety hands needing something to toy with. The light scrape of his thumb over her ankle bone was both soothing and unreasonably sensual. It felt irresistibly intimate, though she wasn't even sure he knew he was touching her.

Drew and Bel snuggled on the single armchair and tried to explain the purpose of an Infinity Stone to Gemma.

"But why don't they just teleport?"

"Different stone, babe. This one doesn't open portals." Bel gave a lazy stretch.

"I'd give it back," Tanner murmured. "Who wants a stone that won't open a portal?"

It was strange and yet not strange having him here with her friends. Content to blend into the group without any flexing of his ego, Tanner was undemanding company, more like a long-time acquaintance than a popular figure in the public eye.

A similar thought must have crossed Bel's mind because she suddenly said, "So, fame's a weird thing. How do you cope with it?"

He shrugged. "I'm not that well known outside of the hockey world so I have it easier than most. I've got the money and opportunities without too many restrictions."

"You make it sound simple." Bel smiled.

"Money makes everything simple." Drumming his fingers on his thigh, Tanner's mouth tensed and Avery wondered why. "I've had none and things were shit. Now I have loads and they're better. I can spoil my mom and my brothers, buy whatever I need, travel wherever I want. People respect people with money. It greases all the wheels."

"But it can't buy happiness," chipped in Gemma, wafting a quesadilla.

"It can buy a lot of the things that make people happy," he countered.

"But is it the *things* that make people happy?" Avery mused aloud. "Or is it all the intangibles? The feelings, good friends, freedom. Support."

When he tilted his head to look up, Tanner's eyes locked on hers and she felt the impact of them ripple through her bones.

"So deep, Stretch," he said with a grin, "but misguided. It's definitely the things."

Avery flicked his ear. She disagreed, but she could understand why he thought the way he did.

Turning to Drew, Bel asked, "If you had all the money in the world, what would you buy, babe?"

"Probably a garage full of supercars. I'm a sucker for something flashy."

"Don't I know it." Bel rubbed her nose against his cheek. "That's how I landed you in the first place. Leo?"

He thought for a moment. "I'm not sure. Concert tickets, I guess. With VIP seating."

"I'd have a slide put in to replace the stairs."

They all turned to eye Gemma.

"You live in a bungalow," Avery pointed out.

"But I wouldn't if I was rich. I'd have a four-story brownstone and I'd need that slide." Gemma drained her can of Coke.

"If you kept the stairs and got in your step count, you'd have glutes of steel instead of a wobbly butt from sliding and too much good living," Bel suggested.

"That'll be my personal trainer's problem, not mine."

"I think it might involve you, too," Avery countered.

Tanner tugged on her foot. "What would you buy, Stretch?"

Snuggling deeper into her hoodie, she considered the matter. "Right now, a new workshop sounds good. With a roof."

"That's boring! Be creative," Bel urged. "How can I rest easy in my haunted Scottish castle if you're being all frugal and restrained?"

Avery laughed but the question was too big. She could think of a ton of things she wanted and not a single one of them involved money. She'd like her mom to be happy. She'd like her to have other people in her life other than just Avery. She'd like her parents to act like parents. She'd like someone to take on just a little of the strain of keeping everything running smoothly. She'd like someone to share some of the responsibility.

"I'd like a pair of Red Wing boots with a stacked heel and laces. They're really pretty." It was all she could think of. "And a cloak of invisibility, obviously—because imagine how useful that would be for avoiding Paige."

They came up with more and more outlandish suggestions until the movie came to an end and everyone began to talk about heading home. Avery's cell rang as she gathered up the takeout boxes.

"Hey, Dad." Hands full, Avery tucked her phone under her chin but Tanner swept the cardboard from her grasp.

"Avery." As he did most other things, Joseph Delgado spoke unhurriedly with smoothness and grace. "How are things?"

"Oh, not so bad. Pretty standard." She caught the twitch of Tanner's eyebrow in her peripheral vision.

"Work OK?"

"Um—" So maybe she should tell him. "Well, not the best, to be honest. A branch from the beech tree wiped out my workshop yesterday."

"Do you need money?" She could hear the frown in her dad's voice.

Avery pushed down a sigh, told herself it was a kind offer. "No, thanks. I'm alright for money," she lied, as Tanner followed her out to the kitchen with the trash.

Her dad grunted. "We're going to bed now, but come for dinner on Friday and we can talk more."

She hesitated but couldn't think of a good excuse. "OK. I'll see you then."

"Great. Bye, sweetie." He hung up without waiting for a reply.

Avery dropped her phone onto the countertop.

"Good chat, huh?" Tanner cracked a smile.

"The best."

"He's making time to see you, though." The tilt of his head recognized her lack of enthusiasm at the prospect.

"Yeah. Dinner on Friday at his place. He'll call again on Thursday and either change it to a restaurant or cancel."

Lounging against the narrow breakfast bar, Tanner shoved his hands deep into his jean pockets and his teeth flashed. "Lucky for you, I'm free on Friday."

She stepped around his legs. "Like I said, it probably won't happen."

He shrugged. "I'll come if it does and we can do something else if it doesn't."

"You don't want to have dinner with my father."

"Who says I don't?" Tanner grinned again. "Always a pleasure to catch up with the mayor."

Avery forced the pizza boxes into the recycling. "He hasn't been mayor for years."

"Ah, come on. It'll be fun."

"It most certainly won't be fun. Even Bel limits herself to a few dinners a year with my father for the sake of her blood pressure."

Tanner bumped her arm. "Sounds like you could use some company then."

She had to admit he had a point. "Come if you want, but it won't be as chilled as lunch at your mom's house. I'm not going to hold you to it if something better crops up."

Well-used to empty words and unmet promises, Avery pushed Tanner's offer to the back of her mind, steeling herself for another awkward dinner in the brief time slot her father would allocate. It was usually best to suck it up and go alone anyway. Who else wanted to put up with her family drama?

Chapter 20
Tanner

Even nearing sixty, Joseph Delgado was smoother than silk bedsheets. He charmed the waitress who showed them to their table, steering Principal Harris—now Ottoline Delgado—in front of him with a gentle palm on the small of her back. He drew his wife's chair out for her from the table, smiled warmly across the room at someone he recognized, and flicked his shirt cuffs when he finally sat down with a flourish.

Avery's prediction had been spot on, with the venue changing from the Delgados' home to this restaurant. From the way the ex-mayor ran his eyes over the other diners, Tanner guessed Joseph enjoyed the social scene more than the pleasures of a quiet family dinner.

Ottoline's daughter, Paige, had joined them, too. Tanner remembered her face from school but it seemed altogether less friendly these days. At least it did when she looked in Avery's direction. There was bored disinterest in her greeting and dismissal in her studied lack of eye contact, yet he was sure they'd hung out together back then.

"Lovely to see you, Paige," said Avery. And he could tell she didn't mean it.

The dynamics around the table were fascinating.

In an initial moment of awkwardness, Tanner's less-than-sterling teenage reputation sat between them all like a birthday cake at a funeral, but Avery's father was far too charming a host to let the tension build. He asked Tanner a steady stream of questions about his career, his decision to play for the Rapids, and his return to Pine Springs. And all the while, he ran his thumb over the back of his wife's hand and twinkled chocolate-colored bedroom eyes at the all-female waitstaff. He somehow managed to be both a man's man and a ladies' man at the same time.

What he wasn't was a daughter's man.

Tanner watched Avery turn into a two-dimensional cardboard cutout of herself with every minute that passed by. Her father didn't ignore her. He'd kissed her on the top of her head when they arrived, poured her a glass of water with a smile, and let her place her food order first.

Other than that, he didn't seem to know what to say to her.

Avery, who'd been puzzled, then outwardly surprised, when Tanner had followed up on his offer to accompany her for the evening, shone less brightly than usual, as if she'd deliberately turned down the dial on her personality to fit into this gathering.

It was Ottoline who finally brought up Avery's workshop.

The barest hint of a frown ticked Joseph Delgado's forehead as Avery explained what had happened—and Tanner, toying with his knife, wondered idly if he'd had Botox. Ottoline asked most of the questions, listening intently to the answers with pursed coral lips.

"But your homeowner's insurance will cover it?" The ex-mayor topped up his wine and offered the bottle to Tanner.

"I called them today and they said they would." Avery plucked at the napkin on her lap.

"Good."

"Do you have somewhere to work in the meantime?" Ottoline asked.

"It would be such a shame to disappoint your customer," added Paige, and her choice of the singular noun wasn't in any way a careless one.

Ignoring her completely, Avery flicked him a glance. "Well, Tanner's offered—"

"Maybe it's time to look for a more mainstream career?" Tanner watched Avery's shoulders tighten at her father's interruption. "One with a bit more earning power. It would give you a chance to jack in the bar work."

Delgado gave "bar work" the same inflection other people might have given "cannibalism," and Tanner decided it was time to interject.

"Lots of people are either creative or practical. Being both is a hell of a talent." He would have continued, but Avery's father acted as if he hadn't spoken and steamed onward.

"You could learn something from Paige. She's done the smart thing and got herself a job with health insurance and a retirement plan." There was a tic at the corner of Delgado's mouth. "Unlike you, it seems she actually listens to me."

"I could always put my feelers out and see if there's anything available with my company," suggested Paige, all sugar-sweetness. "I know there are no vacancies in my team but I think we'd both find it uncomfortable for you to work beneath me anyway."

"You can save your feelers the effort, thanks. I like my job." Avery's smile was bright and brittle. "Both of them."

Fuck. No wonder she didn't look forward to these meals. Simmering from her discomfort, Tanner rolled his right shoulder and bit back the knee-jerk defense he wanted to launch on her behalf.

Joseph rolled his wine glass in his fingers, disapproval in the flare of his nostrils. "Lucky you've got Bel to help out with the rent then. How is she? Been made partner yet?" A rich thread of admiration decorated the humorous question.

Avery chewed her mouthful before she answered. "Too busy with world domination right now."

"Of course she is. The girl's on a fast track to success." Joseph smoothed the napkin on his lap. "And she knows it, too. Not short of confidence, that one."

"No, but it's all warranted," Avery agreed.

"Forging a proper career will do that to a person. Gives you belief in your own value. And makes other people want you." He leaned forward as if he was imparting a great secret. "It's all about making other people want you."

From everything he'd heard, Tanner suspected Joseph Delgado had struggled to limit that maxim to his business dealings. When her father's smoky advice set Avery's left eye twitching and her fork paused in front of her lips, he wondered if she was thinking the same thing.

"I thought it was all about the money?" Tanner dropped the question into the mix with a deliberately lazy drawl. "Or did I miss something?"

Avery wiped her mouth on her napkin but not so fast he didn't spot the tiny smile she was trying to hide, and satisfaction bloomed in his chest.

"Were the pre-wedding celebrations fun?" Ottoline did them all a favor by changing the subject. "Savannah is your cousin, isn't she, Tanner?"

"She is. And the weekend was great. Avery made a cutthroat partner for the activities and she put me to shame in the crate stack challenge. She's fearless."

They chatted briefly about the lakeside venue but Tanner could tell from the way Joseph's gaze began to roam the restaurant that they were losing his interest.

"It's nice the two of you have had a chance to reconnect." Ottoline's head tipped in a birdlike fashion, her eyes skating from Avery to Tanner and back again. "I wasn't aware of you spending much time together at school."

"We barely knew each other then," Avery said, bruising him with the simplicity of her words.

"But we're working on changing that now," Tanner added.

Joseph was back in the game. "You could do worse, Avery," he twinkled. "Tanner's career has had quite the trajectory. The boy's done well. It would be foolish not to appreciate that."

Even with the compliment, Delgado made Tanner feel like a commodity rather than a person. Since his approval when Tanner was at school with his daughter would have been non-existent, it meant less than nothing to him now. His stomach gave a queasy roll as he took a wild stab in the dark as to how far he'd slide from grace again as a washed-up has-been if he crashed out with this damn fucking injury.

Avery hauled him back from his downward spiral with a calm reply to her father's advice. "Oh, there's a lot to appreciate. I like to start with Tanner's humor, generosity, and family values, and finish with his biceps. His bank balance is probably the least appealing thing about him. Well, that and he plays golf, but it would be unfair if he ticked all the boxes."

For once Joseph Delgado had no answer. A chuckle fought its way past the unexpected tightness in Tanner's chest and Avery's blue eyes glittered, dew-on-a-spiderweb pretty, when she smiled back at him.

"I was never one of the girls who swooned over the jocks at school," said Paige dismissively. "I like brains."

"On toast or served cold?" Tanner asked, injecting a little bite into the casual question.

"With eye of newt, probably," Avery murmured, blocking her words from her dad and Ottoline by raising her glass of water to take an unhurried sip.

"You're both so funny." Paige's retort was withering.

"We think so," said Avery, bathing Tanner in a conspiratorial smile. "Fancy splitting a dessert? The chocolate cherry cheesecake here is the best."

"You're on." Tanner leaned back in his chair and shot her a wink. "But you're the only person I'd share chocolate cherry anything with."

Dinner didn't get any less painful after that and they cut it as short as they could. There was a palpable edge to Avery's relief as they left the restaurant after exchanging stilted goodbyes. The evening sun was low and sharp. Flicking down the sun visor, Tanner pulled out of the parking lot and headed for home.

He shot a sideways look at Avery. "So you've noticed my biceps, huh?"

"Oh, I'm not like Paige. I'm superficial to my core."

Tanner huffed. "I think you're the least superficial person I've ever met."

When she just flicked him an indecipherable look and turned to gaze out of the window, Tanner found it impossible to tell what she was thinking.

"So, I'm guessing your friendship with Principal Harris's daughter went south somewhere around graduation," he ventured. "Paige seems to be nursing some hostility."

Avery snorted at the understatement. He wished she came with instructions that would tell him when to push and when he should leave well alone. But he was still playing catch-up on information when it came to the missing years between them, and now seemed as good a time as any to fill in some of the blanks.

"What's her beef with you? I thought you were close at school."

Her face still averted, Avery let out a low sigh and he saw her fingers flex on her thigh before she spoke. "I lost myself for a while after my dad left us to be with her mom. And my mother . . . wasn't coping." She chose her words carefully, her voice small. "I guess there was some twisted pleasure in that for Paige, because she was hurting from her parents' divorce, too. But when things began to smooth out a little and I made more friends, that didn't feel like the right kind of justice to her when she really wanted her parents back together."

"But you're adults now and it's all in the past. Surely it's time to move on." Tanner frowned.

"You'd think, wouldn't you?" said Avery, nibbling on her thumbnail. "But Paige doesn't see her dad much anymore so she's kind of adopted mine instead. She meets his expectations and he builds her up. It's all pretty surface level, but it suits them both."

Tanner heard the sense of betrayal buried in her words, and he respected Paige and Joseph Delgado all the less for being so casually cruel. "Your dad and Principal Harris seem pretty happy together."

"Yeah, somehow it works. And long may it continue." Avery sounded doubtful.

"Maybe your mom's better off without him."

She took a while to consider his words. "I just wish she would either get angry or get over it. She's been stuck in a holding pattern of sadness that's kept her as trapped as Paige."

Tanner tapped on the steering wheel, and a quick sideways glance showed him how the light played across Avery's face through the windshield, bathing her freckles in dappled orange. "And you? How do you feel?"

"Disillusioned," she said, eventually. "And let down. But resigned."

He hummed an acknowledgment, fighting the urge to touch her in some way, offer comfort that was long overdue.

"He told us he was moving out the same day I got your first text from college. It was one of the reasons I didn't answer." Avery's fingers twisted the charm on her necklace and Tanner winced at the timing. "He came home with takeout and we all had a lovely, relaxed meal together before he said that he'd fallen in love with Ottoline."

For a while, he thought Avery might leave it at that and the silence drew out between them. But finally, she found more words and they spilled from her like too much wine poured into a glass.

"My father always played fast and loose with the truth. He'd say things with such style and conviction, it felt rude not to believe him. He wasn't cruel or unkind. Just a master of subterfuge and self-interest. And I remember thinking, when he finally said he was leaving, how strange it was to actually believe the words that were coming from his mouth." She huffed out a sound of empty amusement. "Mainly because his suitcase was by the door and it was already packed."

"And your mom didn't see it coming?"

"She'd known for years that he had other women. We both did." Avery rubbed at a non-existent mark on her skirt. "But she had status and security, a beautiful house, a nice car—all the trappings. Plus a job she enjoyed in human resources. And they worked together, carpooled sometimes. You probably didn't know, but alongside being mayor, he was a part-time consultant at the same company she worked for. They were so intertwined she didn't know where he stopped and she started. And she loved him."

"Fuck."

No wonder Avery was so against relationships, so slow to trust; the fallout from her parents' split must have been seismic. The icy realization dawned on Tanner that telling her about the whole Bethany Jenner shitshow would be unwise in the extreme unless he wanted her to run for the hills.

"When he finished his goodbye speech, he opened the floor up for questions," Avery continued, injecting some humor into the memory. "I had so many I didn't know what to ask first, so I said nothing. My mother wouldn't even look at him. And when he left, he told me to remember he was only ever a phone call away if I needed him. But that was crap." Her voice lowered and Tanner had to strain to hear the last part. "I needed him plenty but he was never there."

"I'm sorry, Stretch." Not for the first time, he wished he was better with words. She deserved so much more than the bare minimum. "I can't even imagine how tough that must have been."

"It was." Avery looked out of the window again. "And now we're best if we keep things light. I don't rely on him. He doesn't expect much from me. We have dinner every couple months and it suits us both."

"You don't seem to argue."

"You have to care to argue. And neither of us really care. He's always been caught up in his own world and his own plans. He's not that interested in mine."

Tanner found it hard to relate. Even when he'd lived hours away, he'd called his mom twice a week and her support had always been invaluable. He was holding back about his shoulder only to save her from worrying, not because she wouldn't listen if he needed her to.

"I love him but I don't respect him. He loves me but he loves himself more." There was zero self-pity in Avery's voice, just a weary acceptance.

His admiration for her resilience swelling like a rolling wave, Tanner was hit by a dogged urge to do something nice for her that wouldn't encroach on her boundaries. Give her a reason to smile.

"You know what we should do?" A spontaneous thought burst into his head before he had time to consider its value.

"What's that?"

"We should throw me a housewarming party. Tomorrow."

"You're kidding, right?" Avery blinked. "Why tomorrow?"

Genius idea, Stone. Pull out a fucking Band-Aid to cover a decade of emotional trauma and have yourself a get-together. Tanner gave an internal cringe but pushed onward.

"Why not? The first load of my stuff arrives in the morning. I can pick up some food and drink, ask some people over, and we'll make the rest up as we go."

Avery's face lost some of its tension. "You make it sound so simple."

"It is simple, Stretch."

"You've barely moved in. You're not even settled."

He shrugged. "No one will care."

"Who would you ask?" Avery studied him with interest, as if he was suggesting something so extraordinary it fascinated her.

"No idea." Tanner tapped an idle tattoo on the wheel. "We could start with your crowd. Get Sam and Kash over, plus anyone they want to ask—they know a ton of people. Savannah and Griff would probably come, too. I'll message the guys on my new team. It'll be a good way to get to know them better."

"There's not much time to sort it out." Avery straightened the shoulder strap of her dress, a smile spreading over her lips. With effervescent bubbles fizzing in his chest, Tanner had to struggle to keep his focus.

"All we need is food, drink, and pool floats. How hard can it be?"

* * *

It turned out it wasn't that hard at all.

Sam embraced Tanner's request for guests with enthusiasm, and the kitchen and yard were filled with people, only some of whom he recognized. Everyone brought food with them, and most brought alcohol too—especially his new teammates. Bowls, bottles, cans, and dishes covered the surfaces in the kitchen, and no one raised an eyebrow at the unpacked boxes piled high in the foyer.

Bel and Drew concocted a wicked punch recipe, adorned with chunks of floating pineapple and liberally laced with gin. With every new batch they made, the alcohol content went up.

Patting himself on the back for his impulsive stroke of genius, Tanner left some of the Rapids guys to a heated discussion on skiing versus snowboarding and meandered from the kitchen out into the sunshine.

"Tan, my man!" It was hard to tell if Sam was quite literally punch-drunk or just high on life as he waved Tanner over to a small, disparate group on the pool deck. "Come meet some more people."

Spotting Avery's red hair among them, Tanner slid willingly into a gap beside her and, when his fingers accidentally brushed the band of warm, bare skin just above the waistband of her denim shorts, he felt the jolt in his groin.

"You know Jackson, but this is his far better half, Leah." Sam draped his arm across the shoulders of a diminutive pixie with clouds of dark hair. When Jackson growled and pulled her away, Leah just laughed, raising a hand in greeting. "And then we have Florence and Liam, Luke and Thea, Dougie and Summer and, finally, Hazel and Otto."

"It was Luke who came round to prop up my workshop," Avery told Tanner.

"We've already met." Tanner nodded at the tall blond guy whose joinery outfit had been finishing off Sam's snagging list in the house over the past week.

"My brother's on duty, else he and Elenie would have joined us," Thea said.

"Your brother?" Tanner squinted against the brilliant blue of the summer sky.

"Roman Martinez—Pine Springs' chief of police. We're twins," Thea explained with a smile. "Florence is the baby of the family."

"Ah, I see. I've heard a lot about him already. It's a shame he couldn't make it." Reminded of their conversation in the diner, Tanner snaked a glance at Avery, who fluttered innocent eyelashes, making his lips twitch.

"I know all these guys already from the Rusty Barrel," she said. "Apart from Hazel and Otto who are diner regulars. You won't remember because you had your back to them, but they were sitting behind us when we were there last week." Her gesture took in the elderly couple.

"Gotta love small-town living." Tanner grinned, shaking hands with Otto.

"Gorgeous house you've got here." Hazel swirled the ice in her punch. "The boys have done you well, haven't they? Clever lads." She twinkled at Sam, Kash, and Jackson, her British accent instantly charming. "I've had a few tours during the renovation and I call dibs on the guest bedroom with the cast-iron fireplace."

"You'll have to get in line with the other jersey chasers, my love." Otto raised a calm eyebrow. "If I'm using the correct terminology?"

Sam and Jackson both coughed into their drinks.

Taking the old lady's hand, Tanner gave it a gentle squeeze. "Consider it yours. I like a woman who knows what she wants."

"Don't encourage her," Leah warned. "She has no concept of boundaries as it is."

Hazel didn't even try to look affronted. "Not true at all," she said candidly. "I merely find them inconvenient and unnecessary.

If you let them, boundaries get in the way of all the things that are most interesting to find out."

"That's a fair point," Sam agreed.

"You're welcome any time you like." Tanner tipped his head toward Avery. "The only jersey chaser you'll have to contend with is this one. She'll be using my outbuilding for a workshop."

Avery jabbed him in the side but her scowl was soft. Her hair smelled of something sharp and fresh—maybe lemon, maybe mint. He had not the first fucking clue, but it was delicious. "It bothers him that there's not more chasing on my part," she said drily.

She wasn't wrong.

He would kill for a little more chasing.

A trickle of sweat ran the length of Tanner's spine as the sun sent shards of light reflecting off the surface of the pool. His t-shirt was sticky against his shoulders.

"I'll give you a call about the rebuild as soon as I get the insurance sorted," Avery told Luke.

"Whenever you're ready." Luke's shoulder hitched by an infinitesimal degree. Tanner had already discovered that he was so laidback he bordered on horizontal. "I don't need the full payment upfront anyway. And I can fit you in from the middle of next month."

"What do you do?" Leah asked Avery, her eyes alive with interest.

"I'm an upholsterer and I usually work from home." Avery pushed a few stray strands of hair out of her face.

"She had some damage to her workshop," Tanner volunteered.

Leah and Hazel exchanged a glance.

"Been there, done that. Showed the arsonists who's boss." Leah spun a hammered silver ring on her thumb.

With an unamused glower, Jackson grunted, "Too soon, Raven. Way too soon for jokes."

Tanner took a swig of his beer. That sounded like a story he'd have to extract from Sam later.

"It was just a tree branch through the roof. Nothing as serious as arson." Avery brushed it off.

"Any chance you restore vintage or antique furniture?" Jackson asked.

"I do—and I can source it, too. A lot of the pieces I repair are thrifted or from house clearances."

Sam and Kash exchanged a glance. "Why didn't we think of this already?" Kash said.

"Think of what?" Avery looked between them.

"We need old furniture for staging our renovations. It'd be good to have some pieces to move between houses for photographs," Jackson explained, his eyes keen. "Sometimes people ask for them to be included in the sale, too. Can't promise it'll be much but I've got a list of things I could use straight off, if you'd be up for it."

It was the most Tanner had heard Jackson say in one go, and Avery's face lit up. She looked radiant, excited. So beautiful it made his heart hurt. He wanted to squeeze her hand but didn't. And it suddenly felt even warmer out here in the sun.

"Absolutely," she said earnestly. "I'll give you my details and we can work something out."

"Think you'll buy this place?" Thea's question drew Tanner's attention back to the group.

"Not sure at the moment but I'm considering it. I'm not in a hurry to decide."

"You could even see what we take on next and then choose between the two," Sam suggested. "We might—"

A chorus of yells interrupted him, followed almost immediately by a huge splash, as half of Tanner's team took flying leaps into the pool.

"There goes my plan for a peaceful float in the sun," sighed Florence.

Dougie, Liam, and Sam were already tugging off their shirts. Kash dragged Jackson with him in pursuit.

"Give us ten minutes to noodle-joust and I'll make sure the pool is all yours." Throwing the promise over his shoulder as he backed away, Tanner followed the others, the lure of the water too great to resist with the dial on his internal temperature set so high by Avery's proximity.

"Boys," he heard Hazel murmur behind him. "Less drama than girls but so much harder to keep alive."

Chapter 21
Avery

They drifted side by side, pool floats barely bobbing on the flat calm of the water. The heat from the day hung on with its fingertips and Avery, only just beginning to feel the drape of night against her skin, couldn't be bothered to move.

Everyone else had gone home and the yard was an oasis of peace. Bel and Drew seemed to have forgotten they'd given Avery a ride to Tanner's house, disappearing without so much as a goodbye. In fact, all her friends had gradually melted away until she'd found herself here, alone in the dark with Tanner, trying to convince herself that it was only because someone had to help him clean up.

"The stars are so pretty," she murmured.

Tanner turned his head and the sloppy grin that curved his lips had an unruly effect on her heart. "Not as pretty as you."

"Oh, puh-leeeze." Avery snorted, even as the compliment brushed like warm fingers up her arms. "You must have better lines than that."

"I have all the best lines. You'd be putty in my hands if I hit you with any of them."

She rolled her eyes and gazed back up at the sky, her thoughts pleasantly fuzzy around the edges, courtesy of Bel's punch. "Let's not ruin a perfect night."

"It's not quite perfect."

Avery glanced at him again.

"You're too far away." Linking his little finger around hers, Tanner tugged her nearer. His eyes, softly unfocused, never moved from her face.

Cast out of marble in the moonlight, he was all masculine planes and edges—just the chisel-slip of the scar through his lip to tether him to the realm of mortality. The silver chain around his neck rested in the water-filled dip at the base of his throat, and his tattoos, over the framework of hard muscle, were art sketched upon art.

Her chest hitched. The lightest of shudders danced over Avery's skin. "I think you're a bit drunk," she said and was flustered to hear a breathless pitch to her words.

"Just buzzed." Tanner's face was half in shadow as that grin flared again like a dangerous weapon. "It'd be irresponsible to be drunk in charge of a pool float."

"Glad I don't have to call Chief Martinez."

"Stretch, you and me are going to have words if you keep bringing up that guy. Especially when I'm just about to kiss you."

The night ground to a halt around them. The only movement was the water slapping gently against one of the filter traps. A dog barked twice. And some distance away, the trill of an eastern screech owl bounced through the air.

"I don't date." Was she reminding him or was she reminding herself?

"I didn't ask you for a date. I asked you for a kiss."

"Strictly speaking, you didn't ask," Avery pointed out, buying herself time to deal with her internal meltdown.

"I didn't want to risk you turning me down." Tanner's pool float bumped hers, their fingers still intertwined. His confession was soft but intense.

Swirls of heat tangled in her belly as Avery fought the battle between alarm and desire. It was so damn hard to resist the words, the setting, the effects of the alcohol—and the magnetic draw that reeled her closer and closer to Tanner.

"I suppose you could always ask and see," she suggested finally, her voice catching.

Buzzed or not, Tanner rolled from the inflatable with all the easy coordination of a surfer and shook the water from his hair. It was one of the sexiest moves Avery had ever seen. With stars blinking through the strands, he looked like the romantic lead in an epic love story, the physical manifestation of all her filthiest dreams. Tall and fit, he'd be anyone's hero in a heartbeat. But there was so much more to Tanner than that. Funny, sweet, confident, thoughtful. As she'd told her dad, he had an unfair mountain of positive attributes, alongside his pretty, pretty face.

"Wait—" Avery panicked and Tanner froze, shoulder-deep in the water. "We'll still be friends after this, right?" She wasn't sure she could bear to risk something that was already proving so special.

Placing his hand over his heart, he vowed with solemnity, "Even if we're hideously incompatible in the making-out department, I promise you'll still be my friend."

"OK." She gave a shaky laugh and heard the nerves around the edge of it.

Wading slowly to her side, Tanner loomed over her in the dark, his mouth uncommonly serious and incredibly tempting. "Avery Delgado. Please can I kiss you?"

Maybe she was still giddy from Jackson Hale's offer of more work. Maybe she'd had enough punch to dull the edges of her common sense. Maybe the electricity bouncing off Tanner's skin had short-circuited her brain. Whatever the reason, Avery found herself blinking slowly before saying, "Go on, then."

The twin flames that flared in his tawny eyes turned her bones to liquid, but it turned out she didn't need a reliable musculoskeletal system of her own. She yelped when Tanner scooped her up from the pool float, his shoulders slick beneath her grip as he strode into the shallows.

He lowered Avery to her feet against the side of the pool, the water lapping at her breasts as goosebumps pinpricked her skin, despite the lava-hot swirl in her stomach. A half-step closer and he trapped her, chest to chest, thigh to thigh, between his body and the wall. It was too much. He was too much. Flustered, she studied the Icarus tattoo on his ribs, just visible below the surface.

His index finger raised her chin. "Eyes on me, Stretch," Tanner whispered.

And then he dipped his head and his mouth covered hers.

Tanner's lips were cool but his tongue was warm. It slid between her teeth like hot coffee and Avery drank him in. His taste was unfamiliar and vividly fresh. Fruit punch and pheromones—savory, potent, and utterly addictive. Beneath the palms of her hands, his heart pounded an insistent rhythm that echoed her own. One arm slid around her waist, pulling her closer. His fingers fisted in her hair and he kissed her with utter focus.

Immersed in Tanner, she never wanted to find her way out. Avery stole shallow breaths that didn't belong to her and pushed all conscious thought aside. There was a lot to be said for living in the moment.

"So fucking delicious." His growl in her ear sent a sensitive shudder through her limbs. "Better than chocolate-covered cherries."

Avery's snicker died on her lips as Tanner's fingers tracked the length of her back, curled around her hips, and lifted her feet from the floor.

"Put your legs around me."

She followed his instructions blindly, her calves closing on the concrete curve of his butt. Tanner's rigid length flexed, hot and heavy, against her core. The feeling was indescribable. A moan mingled with a sigh and spilled from her mouth. When Avery tilted her pelvis, his tortured groan vibrated on her lips.

The water washed around them and she was surprised it didn't steam where it licked at her fevered skin. Huge hands spanning her thighs, Tanner's mouth drifted to her neck, his teeth grazing a path from her collarbone to her ear. When his fingers brushed the edge of her bikini bottoms, idly tracing the crease at the top of one leg for several long seconds, an ache began to build low down in her abdomen as need piled on top of desire.

But Tanner paused. "Can I?" He murmured the strained question against her skin.

Avery gave the slightest, jerky nod of her head, her body strung as tight as a zipwire, stomach quivering, poised for the freefall. And when his fingers stole beneath her bikini into the flood of warmth and moisture between her thighs, they sent a starburst of sensation licking through her center.

His breath rasping, Tanner trailed his thumb back and forth, tantalizingly slow, tension coiling tighter in every muscle of his body with each sensual sweep. He returned to her mouth as if he couldn't stay away, and his tongue teased hers, playing the sexiest game of tag she'd ever known. And all the while his hand moved between her legs, making her long for more.

"Yes . . . there." Did she mean his touch or his mouth? Avery had no idea. She clung to his shoulders; she burned everywhere. "Tanner—"

He slid his hand out of her bikini bottoms with a grunt and she protested at the loss of it. Protested again when he boosted her out of the water and onto the pool deck. Heaving himself up on straight arms beside her, Tanner grabbed Avery's hand and tugged her to her feet. He adjusted himself in his trunks with a feral grin, tipping his head toward the house.

"Shall we?" And there was a hint of uncertainty behind the swagger.

He was too close to think sensibly. Too overwhelming. Even in the semi-dark, it was like being blinded by the sun. Tanner shone. He always had. He was all she could see.

"I want you, but I don't want to want you." The jumbled sentence was all Avery could manage while this desperate need for him pulsed through her veins.

"I know," he said, and she heard the depth of understanding in his voice. "You're scared—I get that. But maybe we could have just one night?" He was as still as she'd ever seen him. "One perfect night."

His eyes never shifting from hers, Tanner hung on her reply. Droplets of water clumped his lashes.

"Just one night?" Avery repeated, so tempted. "And it won't ruin things between us?"

Tanner moved his hands to frame her face and his thumbs burned a path along her cheekbones. With his breath on her lips just before he placed the softest of kisses there, Avery felt her rules and resolution crumbling to dust.

"We won't let it." He smiled and it was beautiful.

In the dark, the pool filter gurgled, crickets chirped. And Avery caved.

"OK," she said with the tiniest dip of her chin. "Just one night."

She heard the breath escape from Tanner's chest. The honey of his irises glowed as he grabbed her hand again, and Avery knew she'd have more luck stopping the sunrise than her feet from following him across the patio.

At the back door, a sugar spoon of common sense had her pointing out, "We left the towels by the pool."

"It's fine." Tanner towed her inside.

"We should dry off."

"Nope." He shut and locked the door behind them, then swept her up into his arms. Avery squealed.

"You'll slip!"

"I won't." Sure-footed and determined, Tanner strode into the foyer without even reaching for the light switch.

"Your floors will be soaked!"

"I don't care," Tanner rumbled.

"Your carpet—" They were on the stairs now.

"Fuck the carpet."

His teeth flashed white in the gloom, and there was something about the fact that he could pick her up and carry her without breaking a sweat that sent any further sensible thought leaking from Avery's ears. She melted into him, her fingers curling around his thick traps as she leaned in to catch a droplet of water with her tongue that was trickling down his neck. Tanner rebounded heavily off one of the walls with a stifled curse.

He turned into an open doorway, saw it was the bathroom and reversed, muttering about still finding his way around. They struck lucky with the next one.

"Tanner, no! Your bed—"

He dropped her onto the mattress and knelt above her, silhouetted in the dark. His eyes raked her body; Avery wished she could read his expression. Was it the alcohol fizzing in her system or could she actually feel the desire pulsing in her veins? She was grateful for the combination because they drowned out any voice of reason that might have stilled her hand as she reached for him.

Her fingers brushed Tanner's abs and they rippled. He tipped back his head, his throat bunching around a rough swallow as he palmed the front of his shorts where they jutted over his erection. Carnal sin personified, he was the definition of raw sensuality. The physical embodiment of way too many of Avery's secret fantasies. She wanted time to study him. Time to learn his masculine angles and curves after all these years of wishing and wanting. Time to press her mouth against the many knicks, bumps, and scars he'd gotten on the ice.

But Tanner decided she'd had all the time she needed.

Climbing from the bed, he dragged his trunks down his legs, the wet fabric clinging and resisting. Utterly unselfconscious, he finally discarded them on the floor—and now it was Avery's turn to swallow as she untied her top with shaky fingers. Taking it from her, Tanner threw it in the direction of his trunks without turning to look. He ran a hand through his hair as she shimmied out of her bikini bottoms, mindless of sheets already damp from their bodies and her hair. When she reached for him, aching and desperate, he turned away instead.

Avery twisted on the bed, following his movements with a frown. "Tanner?"

Crossing the room, he grabbed a canvas bag and upended it. With a frantic shake, Tanner sent the contents spilling onto the carpet, kicking at the mess with his foot. "Where the fuck are they?"

"What are—" She suddenly realized what he was looking for and his frustration broke her tension, a giggle escaping as she cupped her chin with the palm of one hand. He shot Avery a wild-eyed glance as she said, "We should have kept hold of the one from the scavenger hunt."

Responding with just a growl, Tanner bent suddenly to grab a singular foil square from the middle of a tangle of socks. "No need—we're all good."

He threw the condom onto the nightstand and stalked to the end of the bed.

Prowling onto the mattress, Tanner braced himself over her body, hands planted either side of her shoulders, and Avery thrilled at the unswerving intent on his striking face. Noses just inches apart, lips too, he stared down at her like she was his faceoff opponent and they were waiting for the puck to drop. But with less clothes.

"So you can hold a plank." Avery's voice was a croak. "Color me impressed, Ace Face."

The smile started in his eyes and flared as his mouth parted in a grin that was sex and fire and all Tanner. She raised her finger to trace the arc but was beaten to it when his lips met hers, his body lowering inch by electric inch until he covered her like a blanket. Avery moaned at the heat. His weight, his hardness, was consuming. Even as she explored the scar near the corner of his mouth with her tongue, her legs were parting, urging him closer.

Then he was the one groaning.

In a fluent maneuver that caught her by surprise, Tanner pushed up to kneeling, sitting back on his heels above her and reaching for the foil packet. He opened it with his teeth, his eyes on Avery's all the time. Wordlessly, she sat up and stole the condom from his fingers, unwilling to give up her chance to touch him so intimately. He jerked within the circle of her hand, thick and hot as she rolled the protection over his length, and Tanner grabbed her wrist when she tightened her grip around him.

"You're gonna embarrass me soon." Laughter wrapped in sandpaper rasped from his throat, and Avery's stomach clenched as he pushed her flat again.

Tugging at her hair, he sucked on an earlobe and she shivered as the cool silver chain around his neck slid over her skin. Grasping his biceps, she closed her teeth on his shoulder and he rocked between her thighs, his cock settling, steel on silk, against her groin. Their movements were disorderly, desperate, a little unhinged. Maybe it was all the alcohol. Maybe it wasn't.

"This is not going to be my best work, Stretch." Tanner grunted as she licked at a spot in the crook of his neck which made him shudder. "I've wanted you for too long."

Avery wasn't listening. She continued her exploration, found one of his nipples and became obsessed with the feel of it pebbling between her fingers. He tasted like chlorine and sunshine. She loved how he jerked and twitched beneath her tongue and hands.

When he lowered his head to sweep his mouth over her breast, she felt his needy rumble against her sensitive skin.

"Fucking gorgeous. These have been driving me mad since the Bach Bash. I've had a lot of dreams about your tits." Tanner drew her nipple between his lips and the warm drag of his tongue tugged at her core.

Smoothing a hand over her stomach, he traced downward from her navel, his fingers dipping between her legs. Without hesitation Tanner's thumb found her clit, already needy from his attention in the pool, and Avery lifted her hips from the sheets to deepen his touch. They both moaned as his broad index finger slid inside her.

"So fucking wet. So fucking tight. You're killing me, babe."

His words pushed her closer to the edge as his thumb matched the circles that his tongue mapped around her nipple, and Avery's eyelashes fluttered and closed against her will. He played her body until she was all sensation, no thought. The release started in her toes, traveling beneath her skin. When Tanner slid a second finger in to join the first, sucking harder on her breast, she bowed and broke. His name was a thing with jagged edges when it escaped on a shattered cry.

He caught Avery's mouth again as she trembled and shook, dipping his tongue into the warmth and eating her sighs straight off her lips. She pulled him even closer. Fixing satisfied, hungry eyes on her face, Tanner hooked a hand around the back of one knee, drawing it up and out. He rolled his hips. Avery felt his hard length right there, where she needed him most, and he pushed slowly into her against the tail end of her orgasm.

The stretch was blissful. His pained growl even better. Tanner's eyelids flickered; she was sure her own did, too. And then he was deep inside her, pinning her to the bedsheets with his body, branding her from the inside out with each thrust. She couldn't hold him tight enough.

He felt like heaven.

She felt like crying.

It felt like belonging.

"Yeah, that's it. Christ, you feel fucking fantastic." A light sheen of sweat slicked between Tanner's shoulder blades. His arms shook and his forehead dropped down to hers. "Just like that, just like that." He was almost chanting.

Avery reveled in the bunching of his inked muscles, his sheer mass pressing her into the mattress. Her head spun, their gasps growing louder in unison. Quicker than she could comprehend, everything went fabulously, deliciously taut once more.

"Oh, yes. Yes, Tanner. I . . ." The words were indecipherable. They came from the back of her throat as another wave of pleasure flung her through the air and she lost herself in a blanket of stars.

Tanner came hard and fast inside her and Avery relished every pulse of his release, clasping him tightly to her until they both finally stilled.

"Don't move. Stay there," she mumbled into the dip at the base of his throat when he shifted, and he gave a breathless laugh.

"I'm not going anywhere, Stretch."

His promise glowed like a sparkler in the darkened room.

Chapter 22
Tanner

Fuck. This feeling.

Forearms against the sheets, either side of Avery's shoulders, Tanner supported most of his weight with trembling biceps. He pressed his lips to her temple, aftershocks of sensitivity still thrilling through his system.

Unlike every other sexual experience he'd had before, he wasn't eager to either crash out or jump up and leave. He ached to stay joined with Avery forever, soaking in the calm that flooded from her body to his. It was a revelation.

Mine. It was all he could think, running in a loop through his head. *Mine.*

Except she wasn't.

"If you were a color, you'd be blue." Tanner was embarrassed by the words as soon as they left his mouth.

Avery opened her eyes and the exact pools of blue he was trying to find the words to explain mainlined feel-good hormones straight into his bloodstream. His cock twitched inside her but Tanner made himself slowly withdraw, delighting in the way she caught her breath as they separated. He rolled onto his back, threading his fingers through Avery's and pulling her hand to his chest.

"I love the ocean," he said. "There's something about the waves that steadies me. The huge expanse of water, the endless push and pull. I don't know what it is, but being surrounded by all that blue is my happy place. I can just be." Tanner lifted her hand and kissed the base of her thumb. "That's the kind of blue you are."

He watched her throat bobble. Had to smile when Avery's eyebrows kinked, as if she needed to study his words to make sense of them. She wasn't one to take a compliment lightly.

"When did you get your nose pierced?" He changed the subject to let her off the hook, his butterfly brain distracted by the glint of the small gold hoop in the half-light.

"Just before I dropped out of college." She turned her head to stare up at the ceiling. "I wanted to do something just for me. It seemed like an added bonus that both my parents would hate it."

He chuckled. "You didn't fancy getting a tattoo, then?"

Avery turned onto her side to face him. "Not yet. I like yours, though." Raising herself up on one elbow, she ran her eyes over his arms and torso. "The pine trees are fantastic. And this is stunning." Her finger traced one of Icarus's wings.

Pride swelled in Tanner's stomach. He bunched his muscles beneath her gaze and delighted in the roll of her eyes. "I like to think it represents strength over adversity rather than the dangers of carelessness. I'm almost a blank sheet compared to a lot of the other hockey guys. Some of them are covered."

Lifting their joined hands, Avery read the lyrics inked on the underside of his biceps: *Rolling waves and midnight kisses, reckless truths and desperate wishes.*

"Where's this quote from?" she asked.

"Dex plays in a band—they're lyrics from a song his buddy wrote. I just liked them."

"And this one?" Avery traced the three words on his collarbone, her fingertip cool against the sweeping curve of script that was intertwined with foliage. "The leaves look just like the charm on my necklace."

Tanner wanted her to draw over every inch of his body, but this was going to be harder to say. It felt like laying himself bare.

"They're as close as I could remember anyway." Avery's eyes shot to his face. "You've probably forgotten what you said to me when I left for college—"

She caught her breath and he saw the moment that it registered. "I said 'Make it count.' And you tattooed it on your body. With my leaf."

His mouth curved in a slow smile. "I've always listened to what you say, Stretch."

When Avery dropped her gaze to study his tattoo for a few more seconds, he wondered if he'd freaked her out. Then, dipping her head, she pressed a kiss to the words in a gesture that squeezed at Tanner's heart.

"I'm really proud of you." Her voice lowered to a whisper. He caught his breath as she laid her head on his chest, his hand curling automatically into her hair. "You did exactly what you said you were going to do. I always knew you would."

Tanner's eyes burned; he rubbed silky strands between his finger and thumb. The punch-induced buzz of earlier had all but worn off and he was thankful for the crystal clarity of this moment. "Couldn't have done it without you."

Slanted shafts of moonlight cast faint shadows across the bed; he still needed to sort out curtains. But the grind of tendons in his shoulder as his hand drifted to the petal-soft line of Avery's neck reminded him that curtains were the least of his worries.

"Sometimes I wonder if I even know who I am without hockey," Tanner admitted into the dark. "It scares me to death that I might have to find out."

Avery propped her chin on one hand and he could feel her searching his face even as he avoided her eyes. "What makes you say that?"

Clearing his throat, he forced himself to continue now he'd started. "My right shoulder's not great." When she instantly tried to move off him, he tightened his grip with a huff. "You're not hurting it by lying there."

"What's wrong with it?" Her voice was soft.

"Instability from all the hits over the years. Dislocates far too easily these days and it's affecting my range of movement, no matter how I adapt my workouts."

Avery winced. "What has the doctor said?"

It was easier than Tanner had expected to share his biggest fear with her. "He thinks it's likely I'll need surgery at some point."

"And that would sort it?"

"If everything goes right."

"Which it will." Avery sounded as sure as if she had a direct line to all the shoulder surgeons in Michigan state. "And then you'll be back on the ice before you know it."

Desperately grateful for her quiet confidence, Tanner closed his eyes, his chest rising and falling on a sigh. "I don't know how to do anything else, Stretch. I've been poor before and I don't want to go back there again. Too many people are counting on me."

Avery toyed with his silver chain. "There's no reason you'd be poor, even if you had to stop skating tomorrow. You must have earned a ton of money. As long as you're smart with it, you'll have enough of a cushion to work out what you want to do in the future."

"Arlo's my money man. He looks after that side of things for me."

"If it was my money," Avery gave him a prod, "I'd want to make sure I was on top of it, too. Don't be too trusting." She lowered her head to his chest again. "And you're not a one-trick pony.

You can do loads of things. You just haven't had to find out what those are yet."

Her faith in him glowed in the dark, driving his fears into the shadows, and Tanner's arms tightened reflexively. They lay quietly for several long minutes, a restful calm bleeding back in through the silence.

"Tanner?"

"Yes, babe?"

"These sheets are really clammy."

He gave a lazy snort. "Yeah, they are."

"I told you we should have dried off," she grumbled. Neither of them moved.

"You can lie on top of me if you're cold," he offered, laughter purring beneath his ribs. "I'm here to serve."

Avery stuck two chilly feet between his calves instead and shifted closer. "Don't make offers you'll live to regret."

Maybe it made him weird, but knowing that he could keep her warm satisfied a basic need in Tanner's gut. "I have heat to spare, Stretch."

"Too right you do. You're like a human wood stove," she mumbled, but she pressed even closer, her breath tickling his collarbone.

With one hand cushioned beneath her cheek on the pillow, Avery was still for so long he thought she'd drifted off. Eventually, Tanner extracted himself carefully, drawing the sheets over her slim, pale legs. He grabbed a pair of boxers and padded quietly to the door.

"Yellow." Drowsiness had turned her voice husky.

"Huh?" Tanner turned in the doorway.

"That's what color you are." Her eyes stayed closed. "Yellow. Like the sun."

He visited the bathroom, examined his reflection in the mirror, and rubbed a hand over his heart. It was several minutes before he could make himself move again.

Thirst drove him to the kitchen, where the tiles were still damp underfoot. Filling a glass from the tap, Tanner raised it to his mouth and drained it. Returning to the bedroom, the light from the landing fell over Avery's face before he clicked it off. Twitching and blinking, she half opened her eyes and the sleepy relaxation gradually melted away. Sitting up, she swung her legs over the edge of the mattress.

"Where are you going?" he asked.

"Home. I just need to find my clothes." She studied the wet heap of her bikini on the floor. "Hmm, maybe yours will have to do."

Scooping up a white t-shirt from the heap he'd tipped onto the floor, Avery dragged the soft material over her head, her hair spilling through the round neck like flames burning through paper. The image distracted Tanner from her words and it was several seconds before they registered.

Fuck that.

He sank down on the mattress and pulled her onto his lap. "You're not going home, babe. Not at this time of night."

Avery tried to stand up, her voice taking on a harder edge. "Don't make this something it isn't."

Loosening his arms even as the hurt bloomed painfully in his chest, Tanner murmured against her ear, "Definitely not doing that, Stretch."

She eyed him suspiciously. "We agreed on one night. I'm not up for dating or a relationship—especially with you."

He couldn't prevent the flinch and Avery's face softened immediately, apology twisting the plush lines of her mouth.

"That sounded wrong. I'm sorry." She curled her fingers around his biceps. "I just meant that you, with your job and your lifestyle, have even more temptation and opportunity to cheat than the average guy. And I don't trust the average guy further than I can throw him."

Tanner smiled, though it was more of an effort than usual. "So presumptuous. As if I'd want to date you either—with your smart mouth, beautiful face, and irritating intelligence. Yuck."

Avery frowned at his teasing. "I just—"

"Yeah, yeah. You're just warning me off and restating your boundaries. I get it and that's cool." He lifted her gently from his lap. "Message received, loud and clear. I'll obviously take you home if you want to go. But you're very welcome to stay so we can get some sleep."

She looked torn but tempted.

"Just one night, no strings attached. That's what we agreed," he promised. "And tomorrow we'll move all your work stuff into my outbuilding if you still want to. I'm not pushing—I'm gonna be guided by you. You want to work from here for now until your workshop gets rebuilt, then the offer is there. If not, that's fine, too."

When Avery didn't move, Tanner pushed to his feet.

"OK, Stretch. Let's go."

She gave him another long look and then turned back to the bed instead. Sliding under the sheets, Avery stretched out on the mattress. A tingle ran over his skin, relief warming his blood, as Tanner smiled at her in the dark and copied her actions. Not daring to pull her close, he reached for her hand instead and threaded his fingers through hers.

"If it was anyone, it would be you," Avery said eventually.

And although her words were the furthest thing from an encouragement, Tanner found himself balanced on the very edge of falling, in the same way he'd almost fallen before, scrabbling for handholds in an attempt to slow the inexorable slide.

Way too fast. Way too soon.

Lacking the chill or self-preservation of any other twenty-eight-year-old with a plethora of opportunities at his feet and a hefty bank balance at his disposal.

Arlo would kick his ass, but he couldn't find it in himself to care.

And Tanner rubbed his thumb over the same inch of her soft skin until long after Avery had fallen asleep.

Chapter 23
Avery

She lay in the unfamiliar bed and watched the watery bands of daylight inch across the ceiling as the morning approached. The alcoholic haze was long gone, sacked in her own end zone by the terrifyingly momentous experience of sex with Tanner Stone.

Avery dipped her chin to the left.

He slept like a bear in winter, out for the count, a heap of warm muscle. She could still feel him between her thighs, his stickiness coating her skin. The sheets smelled of sex, pool water, and Tanner. Avery wished she could sink into the mattress and have his scent surround her but, now that she was awake, her body wouldn't relax. She half wanted to nudge him from sleep, so that he would touch her again and make her forget all her self-imposed rules. It was as much as she could do to keep her hands and her restless, spiraling thoughts to herself.

Eventually, she had to get up. It was impossible to live inside her own head any longer.

Stealing quietly from the bed, Avery grabbed her phone and crept downstairs, without bothering to search for any other clothing, Tanner's t-shirt brushing her hips with each step. The clock on the stove read 05.54. A hint of sweetness from the leftover punch still hung in the air. Scraped-clean dishes and empty bowls teetered in haphazard piles near the sink, and there were glasses everywhere. She could swear they had multiplied overnight like unwanted emails in an inbox. Surely Tanner didn't own this many glasses. Where had they even come from?

Checking her phone, Avery found three texts and four missed calls from her mom, but the voicemail she'd left didn't sound too concerning. Apparently, she wanted to buy a milk frother and wondered if Avery had any recommendations. It was too early to ring her back just yet.

Casting a dubious eye over the shiny new coffee machine on the counter, Avery considered the benefits of a long glass of water.

Yeah, fuck that.

The need for caffeine had her reaching for an unopened box of pods and the instruction manual.

With the mug warming her hands and coffee yelling in the face of her weariness, Avery gazed sightlessly out of the bifold doors, her head thrumming. In the glass, her reflection stared back, a little pale, a whole lot ruffled. She looked as conflicted as she felt.

How could the best night of her life have left her feeling this bad?

Well, she knew the answer to that.

It was because she could never afford to go there again, and the one night she'd allowed herself with Tanner was over.

Avery's stomach cramped.

She protected her heart for a reason, and her "no relationship" rule was in place to do just that. Tanner—the biggest threat yet to her emotional stability—not only had the means to smash that fragile organ with a hammer, but the charm to talk her into visiting the hardware store herself and handing him the tool in a gift bag.

She couldn't let him be her downfall. The ongoing blowback from her parents' divorce had taught her better than that.

Draining the last of her coffee, Avery carried the mug to the sink and ran a bowl full of hot soapy water, reaching for the nearest glasses. The only way she knew how to handle this was to shut down her feelings before they grew any bigger. Retreat, regroup, and shore up her reserve.

Remember that passion doesn't last. Good sex doesn't equal commitment.

As she rinsed, scrubbed, and wiped, then moved on to drying, sorting, and stacking, Avery lectured herself with every item of glassware and crockery she cleaned.

Don't think of slippery kisses in a moonlit pool.

Don't think of warm, strong hands or tawny eyes burning in the dark.

Don't think of blues and yellows, tattooed words, and whispered confessions.

Easy.

Closing her eyes, Avery leaned on the edge of the countertop.

Not easy.

"You didn't have to do that."

Tanner gripped the top of the doorframe with both hands and flexed, as if an ancient oath required him to assert his dominance over the doorway in order to pass through. His plain gray tee rode up to expose a few inches of toned skin. Tousled hair and bleary eyes hinted that he'd rolled straight out of bed and reached for his clothes.

Avery reeled her tongue back into her mouth. Great. Less than fifteen seconds and her new reserve was under fire.

"I know. But it was here. And so was I." So smooth, so slick. So stupid.

"I like you being here." She could hear the smile in his rusty voice.

He filled the doorway—90+ kilos of pure muscle and sweetness. The combination of the two crooked a cocky finger and begged for her attention. Avery concentrated very hard on drying the glass in her hand. She placed it on the kitchen island, reached for another.

"You got the coffee maker working." Tanner padded into the room. "You goddess."

Avery raised an eyebrow at that. "I read the manual."

He stretched. "Yeah, guys don't do that. We press buttons and hope for the best."

"And how does that work for you?"

Tanner eyed the machine warily. "I'll let you know in a minute. Want another one?"

"No, I'm good, thanks." She watched him with reluctant amusement as she carried on drying glasses. Damned if she'd do it for him. He was a grown man with the brains to master his own coffee maker.

"Sam's got a van we can borrow to pick up your stuff later. Him and Kash are going to meet us at your house this afternoon."

"Look, it's really kind—"

"I have the space, Stretch. And you can't work without a base." Tanner shot her a sideways glance. "It's no big deal to me."

But it was to Avery. Turning to anyone else for help went against every brutal lesson she'd had to learn.

Opening her mouth to firmly turn him down, she was hit by the sharp recollection of the chaos at home, with her supplies littering the first floor of their house. Bel was being good about it so far, but there was no space to work and Mrs. Alberty had not been understanding about the loss of her armchair. Avery needed to track down and re-cover a replacement as soon as possible, and she had other orders waiting, too. Realizing she'd be stupid to refuse Tanner's offer, she bit back the words on the tip of her tongue.

"It'll give us the chance to get to know each other again," he said lightly, still studying the coffee machine.

"Hmm." Avery chewed on her thumbnail.

"As friends, if that's what you want." Tanner gave a grunt of satisfaction as he finally found the button that had coffee spilling into the mug below.

She didn't want it at all.

She wanted him to take her hand and lead her straight back to bed.

She wanted him to weigh her down against the sheets with those inked-up muscles and make her forget all the reasons why it was a bad idea.

Avery folded the dishtowel into a neat rectangle, something elusive pressing heavily on her chest. "Yes. I think that's best. Last night was probably all about the alcohol anyway."

Tanner gave her a searching look as he crossed to the fridge, and his fingers drummed on the handle of the door while he reached for the cream.

"God knows how much gin Bel and Drew put in that punch." A flush crawled up the back of her neck as she struggled to put up the roadblocks she knew were needed. "It would be ideal if I could use your outbuilding, as long as it's honestly not an inconvenience. I don't want things to be awkward between us."

He poured a glug of cream into his coffee and nodded. "Let's just decide they won't be. We'll be super mature about the whole thing. I'd like to have you as a friend, Stretch."

"That sounds good." Avery felt relieved, deflated, pleased, and disappointed all within the space of three syllables. She needed to get a grip.

"OK, then. Let me just grab a quick shower and throw on some clothes. Then I'll drop you home and see you later when I've picked up the van." Skirting the kitchen island, Tanner paused as he passed behind her, bringing his mouth close to Avery's ear. The scent of coffee and sex flooded her senses, curling her toes against the unforgiving floor tiles. "Just so you know, it wasn't the alcohol. Not on my part, anyway."

And then she was left alone in the kitchen, one hand to her heart, as Tanner disappeared into the foyer and jogged up the stairs.

* * *

"They're a handy bunch to know when it comes to getting stuff done." Bel jerked her chin at the Ford Transit by the curb, where Tanner and Kash were manhandling Avery's bulky workbench in through the rear double doors.

While Avery couldn't disagree, there were other things on her mind that she needed to confess to her friend.

"I messed up." The words spilled from her lips with a groan.

Cocking her head, Bel eyed her with interest. "Related or unrelated to the fact you didn't come home last night?"

"Related."

"And you stayed at Tanner's?"

"I did." The gust of air escaped slowly from Avery's chest.

"But you didn't jump his bones?" Bel guessed with a frown.

"I did."

Two black eyebrows shot sky-high. "But he was a disappointment?"

"No, the opposite."

"*You* were a disappointment?" Now Bel was frowning again.

"No!" said Avery in frustration.

"If you tell me you forgot to use protection, I'll kick your ass."

"And if you don't let me get a word in soon, I'll kick yours," Avery growled.

A broad smile plumped Bel's pretty, rounded cheekbones. "Sorry, babe. I'm all ears."

Avery sighed. "Now I don't know what I was even trying to say."

Sliding an arm around Avery's waist, Bel leaned into her. "Can I guess?" she said. "You were probably going to say that you slept with him and it was amazing, because of course it was—I've seen the guy. And now you're freaking out because you refuse to date anyone, especially a super-sexy dude in the public eye with herds of available women at his literal fingertips, but you also can't stand the fact that he's now in the 'look, don't touch' zone. Forever. How am I doing so far?"

Avery turned to rest her chin against the cushion of Bel's hair. "Nailed it."

"And what was his reaction when you hightailed it from his bed like he was a chainsaw-wielding maniac?"

"He took it really well. He wants to stay friends." The thought tasted sour on Avery's tongue when it shouldn't.

"Hon, if that guy wants to be friends with you then you can paint me red and call me a barn." Bel dug her fingers into Avery's side.

They watched Sam amble over to the van with Avery's desk lamp, which had somehow managed to avoid being crushed. Chuckling at something Kash said, Tanner shoved Sam against the fender and a play fight began in earnest.

"He could do me some damage, Bel," Avery admitted in a low murmur as misery took hold of her vocal cords and gave them a twist.

"Or he could be the someone wonderful you deserve."

"I don't trust him with my heart." She fiddled with her necklace but the charm in her fingers only reminded Avery of the leaves Tanner had tattooed on his collarbone.

Bel pulled a pair of sunglasses from the V-neck of her top and dropped them onto her nose. "You don't trust him with your heart *yet*," she corrected. "Give it time."

"It'll take more than time. It'll take a miracle. I refuse to end up like my mom." Even the thought made Avery shudder.

"But you are not your mom. And, from what I can tell, Ace Face doesn't have a lot in common with the great Joseph Delgado. Don't just assume he has low morals because he plays sports and has more than his fair share of testosterone."

Her eyes following Tanner as he shifted some of the contents around the inside of the open van, Avery didn't answer.

Maybe he *was* one of the good ones, but she didn't intend to take the risk. No man was ever going to get the chance to crumble her like a stale cookie.

Chapter 24
Tanner

"You can redirect all my mail now I'm settled." Tanner shifted his phone to the opposite hand as he squinted out of the bifold doors at the yard beyond.

"It's no bother for me to keep forwarding it on from here." He heard the shrug in Arlo's voice.

"I'd rather we changed everything over. It'll make it easier for me to keep track of stuff. I've done the USPS change of address form online and sent confirmation letters to the bank, the IRS, my credit cards, and insurance."

Tanner had taken Avery's advice to heart, ashamed of how hands-off he'd been with his finances in recent years. As long as he'd had money in his checking account, he'd paid next to no attention to the bigger picture or put much thought into future-proofing his earnings. And that needed to change.

"It's just going to be a ball-ache when you move on again." Tanner could hear Arlo flicking his pen against his teeth. "Would have been simpler to leave everything how it was."

"I'm planning to be here a while if everything goes to plan." Turning away from the glass doors, he meandered across the kitchen. "I love the house. Fisher's cool and I'm getting to know the Rapids guys. The team doc says he'll have my tests back this week."

"But you sound more upbeat already. What's made you so perky if you're still waiting on the results?" Arlo sounded suspicious. "Has Lily been in touch?"

Plucking an apple from the fruit bowl, Tanner tossed it from hand to hand, his cell tucked between shoulder and ear. "That would have the opposite effect, believe me. Lily and I were done a long time ago. I'm just enjoying reconnecting with the friends I have here."

Arlo let the silence drag out for a few moments. "You've met someone, haven't you?"

"Maybe I have." The temptation to bring Avery into the conversation was irresistible. "But not in the way you mean. Not yet anyway."

"She turned you down?"

"She's . . . not quite on the same page as me just yet." Admitting it made Tanner's stomach tight as he took a bite out of the apple and crunched it.

"Tell me we're not talking about your high school crush," Arlo groaned.

"Avery's more than a crush."

"It's just not worth it, bro. If she's playing hard to get, throw her back in and reel in another one." Arlo was a true romantic.

"I'm playing the long game with this one. She's definitely worth it." Through the bifolds, Tanner saw Avery leaving the outbuilding, picking her way across the backyard and heading for the kitchen. A smile spread upward from his toes. "Gotta go now. Change over my mailing address on anything you can think of and we'll catch up again soon."

He hung up just as Avery stepped in through the open doors.

"Is it OK if I make a coffee?" she asked.

"Help yourself. I told you to take anything you need." He'd considered buying her a coffee machine to put in her workshop but decided against it when he realized it would keep her out of the house. That was the only act of selfishness he'd allowed himself; otherwise Tanner was giving her space. But he got a buzz from knowing she was out there, either working away on the neat two-seater couch she'd picked up mid-week or putting together the proposal that she'd promised Jackson.

He had, however, ordered a heavy-duty, industrial-grade sewing machine to replace Avery's damaged one. And she'd been so horrified by his extravagance, he'd had to agree that she could pay him back over time.

Like he had any intention of taking her money.

"Comfortable temperature out there?"

"It's perfect. With the fans going and the doors open, there's a nice cross-breeze. Air con would have been a mistake unless you want to pay to cool the whole of Pine Springs." Avery flicked him a grin over her shoulder as she clipped the coffee pod in place. "It'll be ideal for your gym equipment once you've got rid of me again."

He'd gotten Jackson's electrician to check the wiring in the outbuilding and install two large ceiling fans. With all the extra rooms he had going spare inside the farmhouse, Tanner doubted he'd ever use the space for working out, but that's what he'd told Avery so she wouldn't suggest paying him back for the fans as well.

"What are you up to today?" she asked as she shoveled sugar into her coffee.

"Meeting some of the Rapids guys for golf soon."

"You getting on well with them?"

Tanner passed her the cream from the fridge. "Yeah, they're a great bunch."

Her smile did things to him that were almost unbearable. It was relaxed and open, mirrored in her eyes, and Tanner's fingers ached to reach for her hair, her neck, and pull her closer. His mouth wanted her mouth, the press of her lips. He was desperate to touch her anywhere. Avery's light perfume mingled with the scent of coffee and went straight to his dick.

Fuck, this distance between them was killing him. He had it bad.

He'd explored her body, mapped the contours of her curves, learned the sounds she made beneath his fingers, and sunk into her like he was coming home. And now he had to respect her wishes and slide from lovers back to friends as if none of that had happened. Or risk driving her away.

No way in hell was he going to do that.

"I'd better go get changed," he said, tugging lightly on the chain around his neck. "Don't work too hard."

And he left Avery in the kitchen, before he could press her up against the counter and kiss her until she couldn't remember why he wasn't worth taking a chance on.

* * *

Not his finest round of golf, Tanner had to admit as they played the last hole. Did he care? Yeah, a little bit. Guys were competitive creatures; it was in his DNA. He had a smile on his face, though, and his shoulders were loose for once.

Sitting on top of a broad ridge, the course was hard with long rough but the scenery was stunning. In addition, the banter throughout the afternoon had been gold.

Tanner had learned that Cam (right defenseman) had gotten married last year, and he and his wife were expecting a baby in the fall. Karl (goaltender and the owner of an exceptionally bushy beard) was celebrating his tenth wedding anniversary the following weekend, while Olli (center, originally from Finland) was more than happy being single.

"Thank fuck for Google," grunted Karl. "Diamonds for ten years, it said. Made choosing a gift easy for once. I might have got it right this time."

"If in doubt, you can't go wrong with a purse," said Cam. "The more expensive the better. My wife has a dozen. I'm never sure if women carry so much shit because it gives them an excuse to buy another purse, or if they need so many purses because they carry so much shit."

"Helps to keep your own pockets empty though, doesn't it?" Olli chipped in as they walked down the fairway. "In between girlfriends, I have to carry my own keys when I go out and it ruins the line of my pants."

"Yeah, that's literally the reason I got married." Cam's tone was drole. "Fuck carrying my own keys, I thought."

Tanner grinned. He didn't remember seeing Avery with any particular purse, now he came to think of it—just a selection of fabric totes. Maybe she'd like a new one. After all, Lily had gathered together a collection in almost every color over the eighteen months they'd dated, and they seemed to make her happy.

"How do you pick them out?" he asked Cam, who spluttered in response.

"Me, pick them? Are you nuts? She'd never let that happen." Cam's smile was broad, even as he rolled his eyes. "I get told what to buy. Sometimes she sends me direct links. Occasionally, she orders them herself in my name. The guesswork is minimal. It's safer that way."

Damn. That didn't help. "Does she have a favorite brand?"

Cam shrugged. "Fuck knows. I don't remember shit like that. It's why my lovely lady gives me so much help in the first place."

"Can't go wrong with Prada, Gucci, or Balenciaga. And Givenchy have a great slouchy shoulder bag," suggested Olli, and they all turned to look at him. "Hey, don't hate me—I have four sisters and I know my designers."

Karl's hefty shove sent him flying into the rough.

As Cam lined up his shot on the green, Tanner's phone vibrated in his pocket and he fished it out to see who was calling.

Shit. No way was he answering that. He declined and blocked with a few quick swipes of his thumb, the summer breeze suddenly sharper than before.

"Everything OK?" Karl asked. "You look like someone pissed in your Wheaties."

The frustration spilled over, smothering Tanner's embarrassment. "One of the reasons I wasn't sorry to leave Boston," he admitted with a grimace. "A little too much personal attention from the coach's wife."

Karl's heavy brows drew together. "Unwanted?"

"Yeah, completely."

"That's out of order." The goalie folded his bulky arms. "Must have put you in a crappy position."

"She hit on you?" Olli joined the conversation as Cam sank his putt.

"Multiple times," said Tanner, fiddling with the Velcro on his glove, knuckles tight.

"And you knocked her back?" Cam retrieved his ball and moved out of the way for Karl.

"Multiple times," Tanner repeated grimly.

"What the fuck. That sucks, dude." Olli scowled, as Cam nodded in agreement. And Tanner, more used to Arlo's assertion that he should be flattered and quit complaining, experienced a warm flood of gratitude for their understanding that went a little way toward easing his agitation.

Strolling in off the course, they were met in the clubhouse by the general manager who gave them a hard sell on membership; it took several minutes of polite conversation before they could excuse themselves. The small group eventually headed out to the parking lot with a branded golf towel each and four complimentary tee times.

Karl read the embroidered lettering on his towel out loud. "'May The Course Be With You.' That's genius, dude. Look at me LOL-ing."

Tanner grinned as Karl opened the driver's door of his Maserati. "Mine's better." He screwed it into a ball and chucked it, hitting the goalie full in the face.

Peeling the towel off his beard, Karl held it up.

The three words etched in classy gold thread read: "Kiss My Putt."

Chapter 25
Avery

Bel had just taken delivery of two pizzas at the front door when Avery's mom rang her in a state because she could hear footsteps upstairs in her house. It took a while to work out what she was saying because she was so hysterical.

"Have you dialed 911?" Avery asked, grabbing her keys while her stomach made a leap into her throat.

"No, I rang you!" her mother sobbed. "I'm in the downstairs bathroom with the door locked."

"Can't you get out and go to a neighbor?"

"I haven't got any makeup on!" Violet's wail sounded as if she'd smothered it behind her hand.

"Call it in and then ring me straight back. I'm on my way."

Bel plucked the keys from Avery's hand and chucked them onto the table, pushing the pizzas at her instead. "I'll drive. You'll need to speak to your mom and you're not going on your own."

Still clutching the boxes as she slid into the passenger seat of Bel's car, Avery answered her mother's call when she rang back and tried to keep her calm as they peeled away from the curb.

"I can't hear anything now," Violet whispered after nearly ten minutes had gone by. "I think they must have gone." And she let out a stifled shriek as Avery heard the sound of a knock at her mother's front door echoing clearly over the connection.

"Mrs. Delgado—this is the police. Can you open up?"

"Go let them in," Avery instructed. "We'll be there soon."

Her mom's front door was open and all the lights were on inside the house when Bel pulled up behind a black Interceptor and Avery scrabbled to release her seat belt.

Roman Martinez met them halfway up the path.

The police chief was an intimidating figure with his stony demeanor and reluctant smile. He'd quickly become a familiar presence around town after his move from Detroit, and Avery often served him in the Rusty Barrel when he was off-duty. Underneath his serious exterior was a genuinely decent core. Martinez had turned out to be everything Pine Springs needed, especially after the horror of his predecessor.

"False alarm." When the chief rubbed at the hint of scruff on his jawline, a wide silver band on his ring finger caught the light. "The door was locked when we got here and there are no signs of a break-in anywhere. We've done a thorough sweep of the house." His brows pinched together. "My best guess would be that your mother heard the pipes knocking under the upstairs floorboards. It happens sometimes when the hot water makes them expand. They rub against the fittings and it can sound a little like footsteps."

Avery's breath gusted from her chest; she clenched her hands to stop them from shaking. "Thank you. I'm so sorry we bothered you."

The hint of a smile ghosted one corner of the chief's lips. "It's what I'm paid for," he said easily. "Better a false alarm than an actual break-in. Saved me a mountain of paperwork."

Dougie Taggart jogged down the steps from her mom's front door, leaving Violet standing behind him like an anxious wraith on the stoop. "Hey, Avery, Bel. All clear but she'll be pleased to see you. Think it shook her up a bit."

Avery thanked them again and the two men headed for the police cruiser.

"Chief Martinez can take my particulars any time he likes," murmured Bel as she watched them drive away.

"That man looks at his wife like she's a freshly baked snickerdoodle," Avery said as she headed for the house, "so you can keep your greedy eyes to yourself."

"I know it. She's a lucky woman." Bel gave an insouciant shrug. "And I'm more than happy to nibble on Drew so I'm no threat. It just needed saying."

"Grab the pizzas from the car before you come in, would you?" Avery turned on the path, sagging as the adrenaline began to leave her body. "We might as well have something to eat. And Bel?"

"Yes?"

"Thanks for coming with me."

Her friend's grin was fast and sassy. "Love a bit of high drama and uniform. Beats another night in with *The Bachelor*."

Avery's mom grabbed her hands as she met her in the doorway. Her breath still choppy, Violet tugged her inside. "I called your father but he didn't answer. I didn't know what else to do."

Of course he didn't answer. He never had in the months following their split. Not even when her mother had been hospitalized. Why would he pick up her call now, when they hadn't spoken in years? Resentment burned in Avery's throat.

Joseph Delgado had amputated himself neatly from Violet's life, and any pleas for support from Avery as her mom floundered and sank had been brushed firmly to one side, leaving her with the sole responsibility of keeping her mother's head above water. Her father was not a fan of anything emotionally awkward. And a spiraling ex-wife with fragile mental health was the epitome of awkward.

Bel's arrival with the pizza saved Avery from having to answer her mother.

"We've brought dinner to share, Mrs. Delgado. I hope you like it spicy." Bel held the boxes aloft like Olympic medals made of cardboard and breezed past them into the house.

"Let's go eat," said Avery and she shepherded her mom in front of her, following the scent of cooling pizza toward the kitchen.

* * *

Tanner, leaning against the doorframe of her temporary workshop, casual as anything, took one look at her face the next morning and asked if there was any chance she could rearrange her schedule to join him for an outing.

"I shouldn't," Avery said weakly. "I have Mrs. Alberty's new armchair to finish."

And a fake Facebook page to report.

Why the hell would anyone bother to set up a malicious account for her business? Avery scrubbed at the headache that had started throbbing in her temples when Leo called to say he'd stumbled on the profile under his "People you may know" suggestions. Checking it out, she'd found a handful of one-star reviews and a post saying she was closing down.

"A couple hours couldn't hurt, could it?" Tanner wheedled, and Avery wondered how he knew that she needed a distraction.

And, however much she reminded herself that she was an island, better off on her own and at the whim of no one else's moods or changeability, he *was* a distraction. Even knowing what leaning on someone else had done to her mother, Avery found herself craving Tanner's company with a strength that scared her.

Inexplicably, when she opened her mouth to say a firm "Thanks, but no," she found herself agreeing instead.

Clearly delighted to have won the battle with such ease, Tanner moved fast and, within the hour, they were walking into an Open Skate session at one of the three ice rinks in Kalamazoo.

The arena hummed with activity. Kids of all ages littered the ice, with the occasional adult dotted among them, and the outing was so unexpected, so *public,* that Avery felt a complete absence of tension or regret, the heaviness in her spirit getting a welcome lift.

Dumping a huge bag on the floor, Tanner tugged at the zip. "Sit down and kick off your shoes," he said.

When she did as she was told, he helped Avery slide her feet into a pristine pair of black and white skates. Gazing down at the top of his head while he laced her boots, she itched to weave her fingers into his messy hair and smooth the sandy strands. Having him so near was too tempting, his grip on her foot between his knees unreasonably sexy. There was something about the assurance in Tanner's movements that made her want to climb him like a tree.

Keeping her hands to herself, Avery redirected her traitorous attention to the skates.

"These are so comfy. Whose are they?"

"Yours." His eyes flicked up and down again.

"Pretty sure I'd recognize them if they were."

"Well, they are now." Tanner flashed her the irrepressible grin that did so much damage to her resolve.

"I don't need skates," Avery said.

"Maybe I think you do."

She couldn't find an answer to that right now so she let him continue until the laces were secure and Tanner pulled her to her feet.

The air temperature was frigid. When Avery rubbed at her arms to chase off the chill, Tanner frowned.

"Damn—I should have gotten you to wear something warmer." She could tell he was frustrated by the oversight.

“I’ll be fine . . .” She didn’t get any further before he stripped off his hoodie and pulled it over her head, engulfing her in a sensory swamp of residual heat and the spicy, masculine scent that was all Tanner. Avery slid her hands into the sleeves. “Now you’ll be cold.”

His grin made a sneaky return. “I’m a human wood stove, remember.”

The reminder of their night together closed a fist around Avery’s lungs. She felt the press of his body against hers as clearly as if she were still curled around him. A visceral need to experience it again raced through her veins like meltwater through a narrow rock gorge, stealing some of the strength from her knees.

She’d have been so much safer in her workshop.

Swiping his baseball cap from the bench, Tanner jammed it onto his head, pulling the peak down low over his eyes in an attempt to avoid attracting attention. And her pulse thrummed again.

Would it kill him to be just a little less aesthetic, for Chrissake?

“Let’s go, Stretch.”

Holding out his hands, he drew Avery to her feet and led her to the ice. A boisterous babble and the grating scrape of blades hit them like a wall of noise, music pulsing in the background. It was surprisingly easy to push everything else aside as the first tendrils of excitement tugged at the corners of her mouth.

Baseball cap or not, Tanner’s casual confidence attracted attention the moment he stepped onto the ice; he was kidding himself if he thought he could stay under the radar for long. He skated as naturally as he walked, with a similar swagger to his movements—something that watching him onscreen had never quite captured—and his looks, his build, his ability, all blended into a spotlight on his shoulders.

Pushing hesitantly away from the boards, Avery took the hand he offered, and the rough heat of Tanner’s calloused palm against hers felt infinitely more dangerous than the prospect of taking a fall.

"Hey, you're not bad!" A delighted smile lit up his face. "You've done this before."

"Not many times," she warned as he tugged her faster.

Thigh muscles bunching as his feet moved with fluid ease, Tanner spun to skate backward, fingers still linked with hers. His balance and control were effortless, the hours and hours of practice apparent in every smooth glide as he towed her around a small boy with a penguin-shaped skate aid.

It was sexy as fuck. And distracting.

Misjudging her next push, Avery stumbled and Tanner caught her elbow before she went down.

"Steady there!" he warned. "Just keep it loose and easy."

"Not helpful." Avery took a double handful of the front of his t-shirt, buzzing all over from his closeness. "I could have said that when we were stacking crates. You weren't so 'loose and easy' then."

When Tanner threw back his head and laughed, he drew the eyes of everyone close by. Releasing him reluctantly, she picked up her stride again and they skated a few circuits of the ice.

"Give me another half hour and I'll be ready for beer league," she bragged as her steps became more fluid with repetition. "Sign me up and stick me on the first line."

Tanner winced. "We might have to bulk you up a bit, or you'd get annihilated."

"Nah, I'd let them underestimate me and then I'd surprise them."

"Surprise them how?" His dimple grew deeper.

Avery fixed him with as steady a look as she could manage on two blades. "I am the storm, Tanner."

He spluttered and choked, the overhead lights burnishing gold flecks in his eyes that singed like sparks in her chest. "Oh, they should be very afraid. No one is safe when Avery 'The Storm' Delgado is on the ice."

"You can talk," she said. "Seems you're always in the middle when everything kicks off. D'you enjoy the fighting?"

"Maybe less so these days but it's still a rush. Although the bruises I get during the season are something else," he admitted. "Growing up, the fights were a great way to let off steam. I've toned it down some as I've got older. There's only so many times I want to reset my own thumb in the penalty box."

Avery flinched at the thought. "You had a lot to be frustrated about back then." More than most.

"Yeah. No dad, no money, crappy grades, Tyson Dax, fucking expensive hobby. I was always fighting." Tanner's grin made light of it all.

Since he'd brought it up, she ventured to ask, "Have you ever tracked down your dad?"

"Dex did—he's in the UK now. They spoke a couple times on the phone and then we both went to see him a few years back." Tanner spun her out of the way of a group of teenagers.

"What was it like?"

His face lost its ready smile. "He's kind of weird. Not a people person. Lives alone on a smallholding in Wales with a ton of animals and a compostable toilet. Didn't seem to bother him that he left us high and dry for a bunch of sheep." Tanner's grip on her fingers was almost painful. "All I could think of, when I was looking at him, was how sick my mom had been and how much she struggled to provide for the three of us. And all the while, this guy was messing about in his rows of carrots and fucking onions without sparing us a thought. I wanted to push over his water butts."

"Have you stayed in touch?" Avery asked carefully, seeing the hurt in the bitter twist of his mouth.

Tanner's lopsided shrug was an answer in itself. "Didn't seem any point. We left him with our numbers and I even offered him money, fuck knows why. I don't think he wanted either. In the end, he took the contacts but that was all. We've not heard from him since."

"I'm sorry," she said, clasping his hand a little tighter, and her heart ached for him.

"Don't be. I'm OK with it." The lie showed in the way his eyes stayed stormy. "He's never been in our lives and my mom is amazing. I'm sorry for her that she had to struggle so much without him, but we don't need anything from him now. I've handled everything he should have. Shouldn't have looked him up in the first place."

They skated in silence for a few minutes before Tanner made a deliberate attempt to change the subject.

"Want to talk about that look on your face this morning?"

"What look?" Concentrating on her footwork, Avery hoped he'd let it go.

"The one that held the weight of the world." He glided easily next to her. "The one that was guilty and exhausted at the same time."

It was scary how he managed to read her so well.

"Late night," was all she said, her eyes dropping to her feet. Her mom had clung to both Bel and herself until nearly midnight, making it impossible to leave.

"Look up or you'll end up on the ice," Tanner instructed gently, and Avery could feel his fixed attention on the side of her face. "I didn't think you had a bar shift."

"No, not working. There was a bit of an issue with my mom."

"She leans on you a lot, doesn't she?"

Trapped by years of keeping her feelings to herself, Avery tried to sketch a description of her mom that would be the least revealing. "Oh, she just gets a bit lonely and needs some help with simple stuff around the house. She doesn't really have anyone else to call."

"You know you can ask me, if you need some extra backup, right?" Tanner slowed his strides to take both of Avery's hands. "I'd like to help if I can."

"I had Bel," she said, choosing to avoid his question rather than consider it, although her throat tightened at his offer.

Tanner had told her himself how much he moved around. He wasn't someone to rely on. Like a bright day in the middle of winter, it was tempting to trust the sunshine, but for all she knew he'd be gone soon. Avery had no intention of putting her faith in him only to regret it later.

"I'm glad you did. But if ever you need me, I want you to call," Tanner pressed, his eyes fixing hers with earnest intensity. "That's what friends do, Stretch. They support each other."

There was a strange prickle in her nose and the nod Avery gave him was jerky, as if her puppet master's attention had failed for a moment, letting the tension in her strings go slack.

"Not sure if this breaks the code we have going on here," Tanner said casually, giving her a sideways smile, as his thumbs swept rough strokes over the backs of both hands, making it hard to concentrate, "but I thought of you over the years, Stretch. Not all the time, mind. Sometimes not for a while, and then I'd see someone who looked a little like you, see an abandoned hairband on the sidewalk. Or I'd remember something from our schooldays and realize even though we didn't get to hang out much, you were present in all of my memories. And sometimes I'd wonder what things might have been like if I'd taken a different path."

Avery swallowed hard and cleared her throat. "I guess everyone wonders that at some point or another. But there's no such thing as a do-over." She gave him a quick look, steeling her heart against a stab of regret as his bright eyes seemed to shutter. "I guess we live the life we're meant for and learn our lessons along the way."

Tanner began to slow, almost coming to a halt, with Avery's fingers twined so tightly with his that she wasn't sure where she stopped and he began. Hooked by the unreadable expression on his face, she dangled helplessly, unable to tear her eyes away as the ten years since school disappeared and this current highly charged moment took over everything.

When Tanner's breath left his lips in a visible cloud, like iced cotton candy, Avery's traitorous senses wanted to spear it on a stick and nibble at its edges.

"Excuse me?" The scrape of skates on the ice came to a stop as a young girl pulled up beside them, twirling a blonde braid between gloved fingers. "Are you Tanner Stone?"

"I am." He pulled away to smile down at the pint-sized interruption and Avery's exhale was shuddery. *That was close, too close.* "And you are . . . ?"

"Ella-Jane Wilson. I'm here with my sister and she said it was you." The child's snub nose wrinkled when she smiled and her top teeth were slightly crooked.

"Where's your sister now?" Tanner asked, looking around.

"She's a better skater than me and she was too embarrassed to talk to you." The small girl pointed out a young teenager in a purple puffer jacket on the opposite side of the rink.

"Are you a hockey fan?" Tanner crouched so that he was no longer towering over the youngster.

"I love it! I've just started in the hockey program and I'm gonna play pro when I grow up."

"I don't doubt it," he said with a grin, offering his hand for a high-five. "I did all my youth skating here, so you're in good hands."

Another couple of children drifted over, gazing up at Tanner with curious eyes, and Avery shuffled gratefully out of the way so they could get closer. This was what she needed between herself and Tanner—a bit of distance, a TV screen, hordes of small children . . . any buffer to stop her throwing her very real and reasonable rules out the window.

"You're not my favorite player," chipped in a small boy with brutal honesty, his black, springy curls hugging close to his scalp. "I'm a Blackhawks fan."

Tanner's eyes danced when they met Avery's over the boy's head and she couldn't hold back a snicker.

"Good choice," he said wryly. "They're a great team."

With a winning smile that could have stopped wars, Ella-Jane tugged on his sleeve. "Can you help me with my crossovers?"

Tanner glanced back at Avery. "Well now, I'm here with a friend of mine—"

She waved him away with a sweep of her hand, cutting him off before he could finish. No way was she giving up the chance to let their conversation slide, and part of her was desperate to see how he handled this. "Don't you worry about me. I'm fine right here, sticking close to the edge. You guys go and show off somewhere else."

And of course, Tanner tackled it like he did everything else—with enthusiasm, charm, and bucketloads of charisma. Resembling a frosty Pied Piper of Hamelin, he led a ragtag group of small children around the ice for the next half hour, while Avery watched him with her rebellious heart in danger of melting like butter on a hotplate.

Before they left the rink, he signed all the baseball caps they had at the concession stand and promised to return as a guest coach for one of Ella-Jane's youth Stick & Puck sessions.

Avery wondered if he was just trying to impress her.

For all she knew, the season would start and none of them would see Tanner for dust. Not her, not his Pine Springs friends, and not Ella-Jane. He'd be traveling again, living the dream, rubbing shoulders with puck bunnies and fans. And he wouldn't spare a thought for promises made or offers of help.

Slick words meant nothing on their own. And no one knew that better than her.

Chapter 26
Tanner

Avery had friend-zoned him completely again after their skate, keeping Tanner at a distance that was driving him nuts.

One step forward, five steps back.

At a loss as to how to win her over, he resorted to old measures and reached for his credit card.

"I bought you something," he said, as casually as he could manage, when Avery entered the kitchen after another long morning in her workshop. He was desperate to see what she was working on out there but knew he couldn't handle being in that small a space without touching her. It was becoming a problem.

"What is it?" Crossing the room to fill her glass from the faucet, she shot him a suspicious glance and leaned a hip against the nearest cupboard.

Tanner jerked a thumb toward a neat, cloth-wrapped package on the table and tried not to fidget. "Take a look."

Avery's steps across the kitchen were measured and a little reluctant. With careful deliberation, she unwrapped the soft suede purse as he eyed her eagerly for her reaction.

"I thought the color would suit you—I guess it's a kind of rust, right? And it's called a hobo bag, apparently." He knew he was babbling.

"Why?" Avery asked, her face blank.

"Fuck knows. They all had weird names."

"No, not why is it called a hobo bag. Why have you bought me a purse?"

Dammit. He should have thought of an answer to that. "It was on sale."

Her fingers stroked the leather even as the warmth in her voice dipped dangerously close to freezing. "You know you can't lie for shit, right?"

Tanner took another desperate slug from his own glass of water. This wasn't going the way he'd expected. Lily would've lapped it up. "I bought the purse because I wanted to. Because I thought you'd like it."

"It's designer." Avery touched the metal lettering on the handle.

"Could be a knock-off."

She fixed him with a cool stare. "Is it?"

"No." He'd dropped nearly $2k on the tote but she didn't need to know the details. The minute he'd seen it, he'd known it was perfect for her.

Avery set the purse down firmly on the table.

"You don't like it?" Fuck. He'd made a mistake. Tanner rubbed at the back of his neck.

"It's beautiful." Her glare sat at odds with her words.

"So . . . ?" He was floundering here.

"I've told you before, with the sewing machine and the skates, I'm not that person. The one who's impressed by big gestures and expensive gifts. I don't need that from my friends." Avery's mouth was a stubborn line.

Frustration made Tanner's voice sharper than he intended. "What do you need, Stretch? Because it seems to me that you don't let yourself need very much at all. You've forgotten how to expect anything from anyone."

Avery's blue eyes flicked up to his face and away again, searing a hole through his heart with the depth of misery they contained. "And you need to remember that there's more to life than money, so I guess we're both a little defective."

She was stubborn, infuriating, entrancing. Wounded and untouchable. Tanner was embarrassed by the effect she had on him; it was pitiful. But his flash of anger faded and died right there, in the shadow of her pain. He reminded himself daily that it'd taken ten years to get to this point. He'd already played the long game. A little longer wouldn't kill him.

"I might be defective, Stretch. But you're not. Whatever you think."

"I need to get back to work." Seemingly intent on avoiding his words, Avery drained the glass of water, catching the last stray drop on the rim with her tongue, and Tanner forgot to breathe for a second.

Correction. It might very well kill him.

Looking for something else to focus on, he picked up the top letter from a pile of mail on the table and opened it. A rental contract for an office space in Boston. Tanner frowned and set it aside to discuss with Arlo. "You got a bar shift tonight?"

"I have."

"I'm meeting Sam and Kash for a drink later."

"I think my friends are going out, too," was all she said in reply, the careful reserve still in place. "Should be a fun night."

He forced a crooked smirk. "I always bring the fun. It's what I'm known for."

Avery scoffed and Tanner welcomed the thaw now they were back on safer ground. "Please. We both know that's Bel."

She made a move toward the door, but Tanner didn't want to let her go. "What are you working on today?"

He was rewarded by the small smile that relaxed Avery's face. "I found a couple antique wingback chairs that look perfect for one of Jackson's projects. I'm just about to head out and pick them up."

"What will you do with them?" As someone who was now more likely to throw away and replace anything broken, he was fascinated by the process of Avery's work. Wished he could find a reason to wander outside more often, just to watch her repair, shape, staple, and stitch from a distance. It was a painstaking and surprisingly physical craft. She was so talented.

"I have some blue velvet I want to use for these two. It'll be a big change because they're pretty trashed right now."

Avery's nose twitched, the gold hoop catching the light, and Tanner's gut clenched. Ever since the night of the party, his body had craved hers with a need that was electric. Everything she did set it off, from a nose wrinkle to a shrug. His mouth burned with the memory of her lips against his, the warmth of her tongue, the sharp edge of her teeth. His recollection of the feel of her skin frequently left him aching. He'd lost whole minutes having to talk his cock into submission and it was only getting tougher.

The worst pain.

The best pain.

He didn't care. He just wanted her close.

Avery was still talking and Tanner yanked his attention back from its wishful crawl to the bedroom.

"I'd better get on, anyway. I told the guy I'd be with him by mid-morning." She took a double handful of her hair and swept it back into a ponytail, tugging a band from her wrist to fix it in place. Distracted as he was, Tanner still smiled at the memory of another time, another hairband.

"Want a hand?" He struggled to keep his voice neutral, knew she'd resist if she felt pressured. "I've got nothing on and it would give me a free workout."

"You want to come pick up old furniture?" Avery paused in front of him on her way out of the kitchen, wary confusion warring with something far more intense on her face.

Tanner shot her a cocky grin, designed to inflame, and it was as if their casual conversation was nothing more than tissue paper over another deeper layer. "Can't think of anything I'd rather do."

Those fucking lips, the color of wet clay, parted a little as she stared up at him, and a plume of hunger flared in her eyes. Tanner recognized the look because, damn, if it didn't reflect everything that was starving and needy inside himself.

Suddenly infuriated that she was denying them both the chance to quench this goddam *burn*, Tanner took a step toward her, backing Avery up against the kitchen island. With only a few inches between them, the heat from her body sent his own temperature climbing. Her chin jerked upward as she stared him down, unflinching and watchful.

There was a tremble in his hands as he clenched them, keeping just enough of a distance.

"Kissing isn't dating, right? Do you have rules about kissing?" He knew he sounded desperate and he didn't care. The flames that snapped to life in Avery's eyes turned his restraint to piles of ash.

"Not that I can think of right now," she said slowly, and her voice was hot steam over fiery coals.

His gaze dipped to the flush coloring Avery's delicate collarbones, the straps of her sundress so narrow, so slight, he could snap them with one firm tug. His length flexed at the thought as

Tanner trailed his eyes higher and watched the pulse jump at the base of her neck.

"Good." And then he shifted closer, so close that his lips were a breath away from hers, the temptation to close the distance almost overwhelming. But he waited, keeping a stranglehold on his desire as tawny eyes met blue and threw down a challenge.

The move was hers to make.

The suspense was agony.

And then Avery closed the gap.

Denial melding into passion, the kiss started out hard and hot, a little desperate on both sides. Their mouths clashed, tongues swept, bodies pressed. Tanner's hands were on her hips as a groan wrenched from his throat and his heart threatened to combust inside his chest.

But he forced himself to slow the pace, easing off until Avery softened in his grip, the tension easing from her muscles like water draining from a sponge. The pliant give of her tongue against his had Tanner's eyes fluttering closed. He explored her mouth gently, his fingers bunching the cotton of her dress as she clutched at his biceps, neither pulling him nearer nor pushing him away.

He sucked on her lower lip, catching it whisper-light in his teeth and delighting in her shaky exhale. Her breath was sugar and seduction. He kissed her and kissed her and kissed her, until his legs shook and his throat was parched.

The realization that if he didn't stop now he likely never would, forced him to step back. It made his soul cry. His dick, too.

Beneath the curtain of Avery's bangs, her pupils were blown, narrowing the blue of her irises to skinny rings. Tanner's voice was rough when he spoke. "Let me know when you want to leave and I'll be ready."

Her nod was an uncoordinated bobble. The swollen curve of her lips filled him with territorial pride and he forced himself to move to the sink, where he filled another glass from the faucet and chugged it down. His erection pulsed, hot and insistent, in his shorts.

"I'll see you in a bit," she said, heading for the patio doors. Tanner pretended not to notice when she bounced off the corner of the table on her way past.

"Stretch," he called after her.

"Yes?" Avery spun a little too quickly to face him.

"Take the purse with you or I'll give it to Bel."

For a moment he wasn't sure if she'd take the bait, and a scowl returned to scrunch her eyebrows. "You wouldn't."

With a one-shouldered shrug, Tanner winked. "Try me."

Though she clamped her lips, Avery's mouth quivered and she snagged the tote bag from the middle of the table.

"She's not having my purse," she said darkly, sweeping toward the bifold doors.

Bracing his arms against the front edge of the sink with a hoarse laugh, Tanner dragged in a deep breath. The champagne bubbles in his lungs went straight to his head.

He'd been right before. Being *friends* with Avery was likely gonna kill him.

But what a way to go.

* * *

Tanner wasn't the only one invested in the situation.

"Any progress with the 'Wooing of Avery Delgado,' dude?"

When Tanner stopped by to pick up Sam and Kash on his way to the bar, Sam didn't even wait to pull the door of the Escalade closed behind him before he launched in. And his use of quotation marks was irrefutable.

"Maybe a small hint of some," Tanner said, "but I'm fumbling around like an idiot. She's different than the women I've dated before."

In the passenger seat, Kash stretched out his legs. "Perhaps that's not a bad thing."

"She's got major trust issues."

Sam snorted. "With a father like Joseph Delgado, who'd blame her. My dad says he slept with the female half of the town council when he was mayor. That's gonna leave scars."

"They say trust is built with consistency," said Kash sagely. "If you're serious about a relationship with Avery, your best bet is to keep showing up. Keep proving that you're trustworthy."

"I'd listen to him if I were you. He reads all the good magazines," Sam quipped, leaning forward in his seat to fix Tanner with a stare. "You are serious, aren't you? Because if you're not, you should leave her alone and do casual with someone else."

Tanner pulled into the parking lot of the Rusty Barrel and rubbed at his chest. "I've never been more fucking serious in my life," he admitted.

They found Avery chatting with Bel and Gemma—both perched on stools and already clutching drinks. Drew and Leo, away over the other side of a surprisingly quiet bar area, were playing pool.

"Easy night for you," said Sam, looking around. "Don't often see it this empty in here."

"With any luck it'll stay that way." Avery met Tanner's eyes and there were heated coils of turbulence twisting through the blue.

"It's not down to luck. I asked the Bar Fairy to keep it chilled tonight." Swirling the ice in her drink with satisfaction, Bel took a sizable gulp of something vibrantly red. "I'm not in the mood for screaming to make myself heard."

"The Bar Fairy?" Tanner raised a quizzical eyebrow.

"She's like the Stop Light Fairy and the Parking Lot Fairy but less car-focused," Bel said.

"What . . . ?" He paused, not even sure how to continue.

With a half-smile, Avery shook her head. "I wouldn't even go there," she advised. "Her brain does some weird shit in her out-of-work hours. Just think of it as a form of manifestation."

Since Sam and Kash insisted on buying the first round, Tanner pulled up a stool next to Bel. Avery served their drinks and then went to help another customer further along the bar.

"I know something happened at her mom's the other night," he said quietly, close to Bel's ear, while the guys fell into conversation with another Pine Springs local. "Is everything alright there?"

Blowing out a sigh, Bel wrinkled her nose. "Poor Violet—she freaked herself out so bad." Flicking a quick glance to make sure Avery was still busy down the other end of the bar, she leaned in a little closer. "Look, Avery probably won't tell you herself, but this kind of thing happens regularly. Except this time it involved the police—although it turned out to be no big deal. Usually it's a more low-key 'emergency' that *needs* Avery's help almost every week. Often just maintenance. Small things here and there. Her mom has too much time on her hands and no one else to call. Really, she just wants the company."

Tanner's stomach tightened. This wasn't what he'd imagined when Avery had mentioned some trouble at her mom's. Casting about for the right next question, he asked, "Doesn't she have friends?"

"Avery's pushed until she's blue in the face, but her mom won't put herself out there. It would make a huge difference if she got out more. Instead, she shuts herself up in the house and wallows in the past." Bel grimaced. "It would drive anyone nuts."

They broke off then because Avery returned and Tanner lost himself in watching the ease of her movements as she dried and replaced clean glasses, wiped down surfaces, and changed one of the optics. Even with the central air conditioning, it was humid inside the Barrel. And the outfit she'd chosen to work in—denim shorts and a yellow tee, with her fiery hair pulled up into a ponytail—had Tanner almost swallowing his tongue. The whole look was such a throwback to the girl he'd known at Pine Springs High and fantasized about every night for a whole year.

Fuck, how had this happened? He'd never been this gone for a woman before.

She was honest about her feelings and upfront about her boundaries—however much he might wish he could breach them. There was no messing around, no pretense.

She'd always seen him exactly as he was—not a kid with no money or status when they were young, not just a famous face or a money bank now. Her acceptance had always been golden.

He realized there wasn't much he wouldn't do for her in return.

If he hadn't been watching so closely, Tanner might have missed Avery's reaction to the message she got on her phone. She was between customers when he saw her dig in her back pocket and pull out her cell. There was curiosity on her face as she swiped with her finger but it shuttered into something far harder to read.

Surprise? Not a good one, if so.

Was that concern? Tanner couldn't tell.

Maybe there was another problem with her mom.

Avery scrolled with a few jerky flicks of her thumb, and he was just about to push to his feet and ask her if things were OK when Dougie Taggart and Luke Farley caught her attention at the other end of the bar. Putting her phone away, she reached for a glass and he reminded himself that she had a right to privacy.

Sam's elbow in his ribs was Tanner's first hint that he'd missed something. They were all watching him watch Avery; he felt the flush climb the back of his neck.

"Gemma asked if you're looking forward to the wedding." His buddy's grin hinted that the question might have come a handful of times.

"What's not to love about a wedding?" Tanner raised the bottle of beer to his mouth. In all honesty, he'd barely remembered it was less than two weeks away. That meant Dex would be flying over soon. It would be good to catch up with his brother again, even though it hadn't been long since his own UK trip. He knew his mom would love that, too.

Joined first by Leo and Drew, who'd finished up their pool game, and then Avery during a lull in orders, they continued to chat about the wedding.

"Sav's found a good one there. I think Griff's even more excited about getting married than she is." When Bel drained her glass, Avery reached for it automatically. "We were exchanging monster smut recommendations at the Bach Bash—"

Leo choked on his beer. "You and Griff?"

"Me and *Sav*. The boy's enlightened but not quite that enlightened," said Bel. "Anyway, Johnnie asked Griff if he minded Savannah reading that sort of shit and Griff said there's nothing sexier than a woman who knows what she likes."

Tanner watched a gentle smile curve Avery's lips, temporarily banishing the frown from her brow.

"He's not wrong," Drew chipped in as he reached for his beer. "It's all about having confidence in your relationship. Why should I care who bangs in Bel's books if I'm the one she wants to bang at home?"

"So beautifully said." Bel pretended to wipe away a tear. "My boyfriend, the poet."

Avery's eyes met Tanner's and she snorted.

"So, what I'm hearing is that the secret to a happy relationship is monster smut," said Leo. "That's really good to know."

Her body angled toward him, Gemma seemed to hang on Leo's words and Tanner could almost hear her wondering if she should put in a request at the library.

"Monster smut *and* only fight when you're naked," suggested Sam with total sincerity.

"Separate tubes of toothpaste aren't a bad idea either," added Kash.

"And no swiping the batteries from the gamepad," said Drew. "That's fucking annoying."

"Monster smut, nudity, toothpaste, and no stealing, unless you think you can get away with it." Bel ticked each one off on her fingers. "And they say relationship counseling is hard."

"Maybe we could bracket the above under 'open communication and understanding'?" Avery sighed. "That way we could stop saying 'monster smut' and sound like we're having an emotionally mature discussion."

Flashing her a wicked grin, Tanner leaned closer. "Now where would be the fun in that?"

The dusting of freckles on her cheekbones was so pretty that it did no good at all for the tightness of his pants—and replaying their kiss in his head didn't help much either. He was only vaguely aware of the footsteps behind him, and that made it all the more of a shock when Paige Harris's voice cut through the background music with shrill venom.

"Good to know you're as much of a disruptive little bitch as always, Avery."

Chapter 27
Avery

Paige's accusation drew the attention of everyone in their half of the bar and a wave of embarrassment swamped Avery right up to her hairline. She saw Bel visibly gearing up to tear into her stepsister and shook her head to stave off a full-blown catfight.

"I have no idea what you're talking about," Avery snapped instead, stalking out from behind the bar. "So don't come in here, laying into me when I'm working." She was so over taking this shit from Paige. Sick of taking shit in general. "Don't fucking lay into me at all."

The five texts she'd gotten earlier had already unsettled her. So juvenile, so unimaginative. So vicious! Dealing with Paige's long-held grudge was one thing. Knowing she'd pissed off someone else enough to attack her anonymously was something completely different.

Unknown:

I wrote a poem for you. Want to hear it?

Unknown:

Roses are red

Unknown:

Violets are blue

Unknown:

Life not going to plan?

Unknown:

Well, boo-fucking-hoo

With instant regrets for listing her contact details on her website, Avery had considered showing either Bel or Tanner for a few moments, but she hadn't wanted everyone else to hear; it wasn't like they could do anything about it either. It was much easier to block and delete.

And wait for another drama to take her mind off things.

"My mom bought those tickets months ago. It was supposed to be a special night out for them both." Paige quivered with self-righteous anger. "Thanks to you, she ended up going on her own. She was crushed!"

Avery turned to eye Mandy Roberts, who was hovering by Paige's elbow and sporting an equally belligerent expression. "Do you have anything to add to this? Because I'm still lost."

"Look, why don't—" Leo didn't get to finish his sentence.

"You and your fucking workshop," interrupted Paige, cutting him off rudely with the flat of her hand, her glare still fixed on Avery. "What was so important you had to talk to your dad about the details last night? It's a pile of firewood as it is. It's not going anywhere!"

Avery's heart sank into the depths of her stomach as she finally understood where this was heading. Watching the same realization dawn on Bel's expressive face, she couldn't bring herself to look in Tanner's direction. Instead, she checked automatically for any waiting customers, praying for someone in desperate need of a beer to save her from this hell. But, such was her luck, everyone seemed to have a full glass.

"I didn't see him last night," she said gruffly. "Whatever he told your mom, my dad wasn't with me."

Paige floundered like a trout on a line, her eyes snapping. "Well, where was he then?"

"You're going to have to ask him that." Avery ran a weary hand over the back of her neck. "I don't keep his diary."

She saw the doubt on Paige's face turn to suspicion, understanding, dismay, and then right back around to fury again.

"Maybe there's a simple explanation . . ." Mandy proffered doubtfully, and Avery remembered all the times she'd hoped for that very same thing.

Paige seemed to read the skepticism in her eyes. "This is all your fault!" she hissed, jabbing a finger at Avery's chest, right over the knot of shame that had begun to pulse in her breast.

"That's enough." Tanner took a quick step forward, his eyebrows a heavy, forbidding line Avery hadn't seen before, the corners of his mouth tight. "You can't blame Avery for something she's had no part in."

"Just watch me," spat Paige, her nostrils flaring. "If it weren't for her, my parents would still be together."

"That's ludicrous," Bel scoffed. "Your mom and Avery's dad fucked up their marriages between them. It had nothing to do with Ave."

Her stomach churning with humiliation and the resurrection of old wounds, Avery barely knew where to look. "You need to leave, Paige. I'm supposed to be working right now. I can't be getting into this with you."

"I hope you lose your stupid job." Angry tears flooded Paige's eyes and threatened to fall. "And if your father hurts my mother, I will never forgive you!"

She planted both hands against Avery's chest and shoved her hard. As Avery stumbled over her own feet and fell back a few steps—quickly steadied by Leo—Tanner spun Paige around by her shoulder. "Lay off!" he growled, his tawny eyes flashing dangerously as his usual easy charm melted away. And Avery caught a glimpse of the leashed temper and deadly intent that made him such a force to be reckoned with on the ice. "You need to take a breath and calm down."

Paige chose to do the opposite.

"Don't tell me to calm down!" Fronting up to Tanner with total disregard for their size difference, she took a wild swing at him.

"Paige, no!" Avery scrambled to get between them, but Paige was too fast.

Tanner caught her wrist in mid-air, just before it connected with his face. "Christ, Paige—I don't want to hurt you!"

"You can go fuck yourself," Paige cried, utterly enraged, and she used all of her strength to wrench her hand down and out of his grip.

Perhaps she caught him by surprise, or perhaps it was just the angle, but either way her sudden twist was accompanied by a sickeningly hollow pop that echoed in a second of silence, and Tanner let out an involuntary grunt of pain. Avery's blood turned to ice as he clutched at his right shoulder, an instant clammy sheen rising to coat the sickly pallor of his face.

Mandy Roberts squealed and Bel clutched at Drew. Sam slammed his beer down onto the bar. "Fuck, man!"

Her mouth falling open in a horrified gape, Paige stepped away. "I didn't . . . I'm sorry—"

Shoving her to one side, Avery caught her breath at the visible deformity of Tanner's shoulder beneath the tight cotton of his tee. Arm dangling strangely at his side, jaw clamped, he'd screwed his eyes shut to drag in a couple of deep and ragged breaths. His nostrils flared.

"Tell me what to do."

The words lurching from her lips rough with distress, Avery's heart hammered a frantic, helpless beat in the shadow of this new car crash.

Chapter 28
Tanner

With agony radiating from his shoulder in fiery pulses and a swell of despair threatening to cut him off at the knees, Tanner couldn't immediately answer.

"Give me a minute," he rasped eventually as the nerves screamed down his arm.

He was vaguely aware of Paige running from the bar, her friend hurrying behind. There was a babble of voices as everyone started to formulate a plan of action, but Drew pushed them all aside and took control.

"You probably know as much about dislocations as I do, so I don't need to tell you the drill," he said easily, grabbing Bel's cardigan from her lap and using it to immobilize Tanner's arm against his body in a few swift movements. "And I'm not touching this here—I can't afford a lawsuit from an NHL team."

"I'll take him to the ER." Avery's voice was shaky but decisive.

"Your car, babe . . ." Bel butted in. "I gave you a ride to work."

That registered through the tunnel of pain and muscle spasms, dragging Tanner out of his ruinous mental spiral. "What's wrong with your car?" he ground out between gritted teeth.

Avery's eyes swung back to him, rounded in disbelief and luminous in a face so pale that her freckles stood out in stark relief. "*That* gets your attention, when your damn shoulder is hanging loose?"

Tanner dug for a smile to reassure her but couldn't find one. *Fuck.* Every time, he forgot how much this hurt for the first few minutes. He just needed the adrenaline to kick in and it would subside to something more manageable.

"It's still attached, Stretch. Won't fall off yet," he muttered.

"Grab some ice, Ave," Drew instructed. "It'll help keep the swelling down."

"If you're OK with us taking your car, Sam and I will drive you," Kash offered. "I've only had one beer."

"Thanks, buddy—I appreciate it," Tanner grunted, flexing his fist to dispel the buzzing numbness creeping down to his fingers.

Within minutes, Avery was back with a half-dozen handfuls of ice encased in a Rusty Barrel staff t-shirt, and Drew positioned the bundle gently against Tanner's shoulder as she hovered anxiously beside them. "Keep that on there for as long as you can stand it."

"It'll be fine." He tried to set Avery's mind at ease, though the words sounded hollow to his own ears. She'd already taken a pummeling from Paige; Tanner didn't want to add to her worries. "Shouldn't take long to get it put back in place. This ain't my first rodeo."

The cocky humor he tried to inject into his voice fell flat and Avery didn't crack so much as a smile as Tanner turned for the door, flanked by Sam and Kash. Bracing his arm carefully against his chest, he supported the ice pack as best he could, while each footfall sparked a flare of pain through the abused joint.

No, it wasn't his first rodeo. Nor second, nor third.

But would it be his last?

* * *

The next week was a whirl of x-rays, check-ups, and discussions. With the dislocation realigned by a simple reduction maneuver, Tanner had been in and out of the ER in a couple hours with some muscle relaxants to numb the pain and a sling to support his arm.

Coach Fisher didn't bother to mince his words.

"If your shoulder pops in a bar fight with a girl, I think it's time to schedule the surgery," he said bluntly when Tanner rang to get him up to speed. "I don't think there's any choice since your hand's been forced, if you'll forgive the godawful pun."

Tanner felt his heart plunge down to his sneakers and stay there. He'd suspected Fisher would say that, but it made it no easier to hear.

"Leave it with us. The team doc'll get it sorted and come back to you with the details. Just rest up for now. Likely it'll be a couple weeks before we can get you booked in," Fisher said as he hung up.

Fuck, fuck, and double fuck.

What if he didn't come back from the surgery stronger? What if he just wasn't as good? What if this was the beginning of the end?

The possibilities rolled around and around Tanner's head until he didn't know which way was up.

He withdrew from everyone. Didn't answer his mom's calls, turned down Sam's offer of company and Reid's invitation to use his home as a bolthole while Tanner recuperated. And as for Avery—well, his feelings there were even more complicated.

Though everything in him rebelled at the idea of agreeing with Joseph Delgado, Tanner knew she deserved someone who could offer stability and prospects. Not a washed-up has-been who didn't know how to do anything but skate.

"I'm so sorry that happened," she'd said, the day after he had his shoulder reset, her eyes dark-rimmed with guilt, her hands gripping each other so tight that her knuckles were white. "I don't know what the hell got into Paige."

And then Avery had flushed and looked away because they both knew what had gotten into Paige. It was the result of her father leaving his characteristic brand of disruption in his wake, creating residual waves of devastation as he strode his own path.

"Not your fault," Tanner had answered gruffly, shifting the strap on his sling to take the pressure off his neck. "It was an unfortunate accident, that's all."

And he'd turned away from her when she'd gone to say more.

Since then, Tanner had made a point of staying out of the kitchen as much as he could. Especially during the times Avery often came in to grab a drink. She took to bringing him groceries so there was always something easy for him to eat in the fridge, and left notes offering to run errands if he needed anything. But he didn't want to be just another responsibility on her list of people to look after. He wanted to make her life easier, not harder.

And so Tanner took the mature approach of avoiding her. Just for now. To give himself a little breathing room.

He knew he was being a jerk, but it pressed every button he had to find himself poised on the edge of losing what he'd worked so hard for. Alone out of choice, and in pain through no fault of his own, he fought a constant battle with feeling sickeningly and scarily unworthy.

Chapter 29
Avery

If Savannah had been manifesting perfect weather, she'd done a great job. The wedding fell on a beautiful day, when the sky was the color of cornflowers and the heat stopped just shy of sweltering.

Squeezed into Drew's car, with Leo up front and Gemma and Bel alongside her, Avery linked her arm through Bel's on the back seat as they drove to the venue. She wasn't a toucher in general but the past couple of weeks had left her craving some comfort, and she only ever really felt this way with her friends. And, more recently, Tanner.

But thinking about touching Tanner was not allowed.

Even thinking about thinking about touching Tanner was hazardous.

God! If only her body would get the memo that Tanner Stone was not for her.

She'd barely seen him since his injury, and they'd never discussed—or revisited—that kiss in the kitchen. He'd pushed her away just as she'd been tempted to take a step closer, and it was messing with Avery's brain until she didn't know how to feel anymore. She missed his easy company with a strength that scared her more than taxes or tarantulas.

For such a walking green flag, Tanner had danger written all over him.

More and more, he invaded almost every one of her thoughts. Their connection was too addictive, his offers of support too enticing. She was scared she might never sleep with anyone else who could make her feel so good, and guilt-stricken that her messed-up family situation had forced him into the surgery he dreaded. The suspicion that she could fall for Tanner in a big way terrified her. And if she did, Avery wasn't sure she'd ever find her way out again. Just like her mom.

In short, she was a seething mess of worry and panic, and it was exhausting.

"Those colors are absolute fire on you," Bel said as she unthreaded her arm to reapply her lipstick in her compact. With a grateful smile, Avery ran her hands across the satin material spread over her knees.

It was a bit of a splurge purchase, but she'd not been able to resist the sleeveless multi-toned dress with the low, softly draping neckline. It skimmed her hips and fell to mid-calf, with a long side slit which flashed her legs. Blending from a deep plum at the top into pink just below her breasts, the color shifted again in a subtle wash to teal as it hugged her butt. Darker and darker to the hem. She'd fallen in love with it online and placed the order with a squeal.

"Someone's gonna love it," Bel whispered in her ear now, eyebrows comically waggling.

"Babe, let me remind you of our mantra." Avery adopted a stern tone. "'We dress for ourselves. If we dressed for guys, we'd spend most of our time naked.'"

She wasn't wearing this for Tanner, it was all for her. It had been a long time since she'd felt like buying herself something pretty, especially with the workshop to rebuild and the vindictive comments still targeting her online videos, and she needed the injection of confidence. Avery hoped it would all settle soon.

But as it turned out, someone did love it.

Tanner's confident stride faltered as they came face to face for the first time in days.

"You clean up good, Stretch," he drawled huskily, that dimple setting Avery's heart knocking in her chest. His left hand rose to fiddle with his strapped-up shoulder.

"You don't look so bad yourself," she replied, a little breathless, a little shy, and her greedy eyes took delight in ignoring all cautionary warnings, devouring him from his head to his shoes.

In a pale gray check suit and white dress shirt, Tanner was the image of cool, sharp elegance, and the navy sling did nothing to counteract it. He made Avery's mouth water. It'd been the same at school, back when he had nothing to offer but that damn grin. And now, with adulthood bringing adult feelings, his smile stoked such an instant fire deep in her belly she had to check each time that her clothes hadn't melted straight off.

How on earth was she supposed to resist him when he looked like this?

"Oh, listen to the two of you. Utterly adorable." Bel clutched at her heart, her best "Proud Mama" look on her face. "You're the loveliest. No, *you're* the loveliest! It's too cute for words."

"Pull yourself together, man. You're showing the rest of us up." Drew gave Tanner a friendly shove as he walked by, but it was with twenty percent of his usual force.

Left alone as the others wandered off, they both gave a half-laugh. Time was a fluid concept within the circle of Tanner's presence and Avery fought an overwhelming urge to step forward and press against his chest, lift her lips to find his mouth. She could almost taste him from here. Her body knew the fit of him now, and it didn't recognize the need for reins.

It was a big problem.

"How's your arm?" she asked, hearing the nerves when her voice cracked on the question.

"Much better." He glanced down. "Only wore the sling for sympathy. Might lose it later."

Avery, examining his face, saw the remnants of stress behind his smile. God knows he had a right to be concerned.

"I'm sorry I've been a dick this past week," Tanner said roughly, and his throat constricted as he swallowed. "I just needed some space."

She'd known that. Had even told herself to try to use it to distance *herself* a little. But it hadn't worked for shit.

"That's OK." Avery shrugged. "I get it."

"No hard feelings?"

She grimaced. "Hey, you're talking to the girl who dragged you into the bar scrap in the first place. I should be asking you that."

Shaking his head, Tanner took a step closer. "No hard feelings on my part, Stretch. Not a single one." He offered her the crook of his left arm. "How about we put all this aside for today and just enjoy ourselves?"

With only the smallest of hesitations, Avery slotted her hand through his elbow, her heart thrilling in secret delight at the opportunity to touch him so publicly. After all, appropriate contact was practically compulsory at weddings, right? It would be rude not to.

Only, this contact felt less appropriate than it might look.

The heat of Tanner's body through the sleeve of his jacket had Avery's fingers clenching as her palm burned, and his thigh brushed her hip with each stride. His natural scent mingled with his cologne—a mixture of wood and something peppery that tickled the back of her nose—triggering a mini firework display in her brain. It was a good job the venue went some way toward a distraction or she would have been toast before the ceremony even started.

When Tanner led her into the rustic barn, Avery's jaw dropped at the vast space, exposed beams, and tastefully decked-out interior. "Wow—this is stunning!"

"It's over one hundred years old. Savannah was bending my ear about it."

"I'm not surprised."

"You have to cross a little bridge to get to where they hold the ceremony. It's this way." Tanner guided her across the timber flooring and out through a huge sliding door at the rear.

Guests milled with drinks in hand, laughter and uplifted voices layering over one another like a serving of lasagna made from buoyant feelings and happiness. Avery couldn't see Bel, Drew, or Gemma in the swathe of people but spotted Leo chatting with Johnnie and Mia nearby.

A young guy with a practiced smile offered them drinks from a table set up on the grass, and Avery gave up Tanner's arm so he had a free hand to take one.

"Come say hi to Dex," Tanner said, threading his way between groups of people until Avery spotted his mom, Henry, and two brothers in conversation with an older couple. "He got in late Thursday so he's just about over the jetlag."

They were greeted with smiles of welcome.

"Avery, this is Griff's mom and dad. Avery's an old school friend." Tanner made the introduction without fuss, raising his glass to his mouth left-handed when he'd finished.

"What a gorgeous dress!" said Cassidy.

"Thank you. You look beautiful, too." Warmed by the compliment, Avery might have given Tanner's mom a kiss on the cheek if Dex, taller than she remembered and wearing black-rimmed glasses, hadn't stepped forward to drag her into a friendly embrace. They'd been in the same grade at school, even teamed up in Debate

Club once. But Dex had been smarter than her and a math nerd, so their contact had been limited.

"Hey, stranger." His grin was softer than Tanner's. "Good to see you!"

Tanner gave his brother two seconds before nudging his arm firmly from Avery's shoulders.

"You too," said Avery, taking a sip of her drink. "Love the glasses, but where's the British accent? I thought you might sound like Jude Law by now."

"I didn't realize that's what the single ladies are after." Dex lifted an eyebrow. "Would it work on you?" Tanner's arm came possessively around her waist and Dax swallowed a smirk. "Ah, don't worry . . . gotcha, bro."

"Tan doesn't need the accent. He's cashing in on the sympathy card," Reid chipped in carelessly, and Avery felt Tanner's flinch through the fingers that flexed on her hip just before he released her.

Henry seemed to spot it too, smoothly diverting their attention with an unexpected confession. "It worked when I met your mother."

"Henry Marler!" Cassidy narrowed her eyes at her partner. "I helped you get home because you told me you'd fallen off your bike and might have a concussion." She turned to Avery. "Ten months it took him to own up to the fact he'd come off his bike a week *before* we met. A week. Concussion, pah!"

Avery giggled. And Tanner relaxed again, smirking with his brothers, while Henry looked quite pleased with himself.

"I'm not often a quick thinker. That was some of my finest work," he said, pressing a kiss to the back of Cassidy's hand.

"People are taking their seats." Griff's dad nudged his wife. "Better not keep the happy couple waiting."

They all turned to look. He was right.

"Let's go." Tanner handed his empty glass to one of the waitstaff and Avery did the same. They followed his mom and Henry to the narrow wooden bridge stretching over a shallow section of river, with Dex and Reid behind them.

Bel waved from a row a few back from the front, where she'd saved a couple of seats for them. Sliding onto the chair next to her, Avery left Tanner the seat next to the aisle, so no one would jar his arm. He took up a lot of space as it was. Even once he'd shifted to try to give her a little more room, his shoulder still brushed hers, his thigh hot against the satin of her dress.

"Sorry," he whispered, although he didn't look sorry at all.

"It's OK," she replied, even though it absolutely wasn't.

His fingers gripped the Order of Service and Avery found herself swamped by the memory of them threading through her hair, stroking her skin, and dipping beneath her bikini bottoms. Despite the temperature climbing toward eighty degrees, a current traveled the length of her spine and she shivered.

Tanner dipped his chin to study her. "You alright?"

"I'm fine," Avery assured him, forcing herself to look ahead.

Johnnie stood at the front of the ceremony site with Griff, and he gave her a chin lift when she caught his eye, but she couldn't read his expression from this distance. As music began to play, heads turned, and Savannah started the short walk down the aisle, accompanied by her father. She took happy, confident strides, her dress a sleek and understated column of white stretch crepe. When Avery caught her breath at the sweetness of the moment, Tanner's hand crept from his own thigh to hers and he kept it there throughout the ceremony.

* * *

Hundreds of lights, strung between the beams, glowed like stars against the high vaulted roof as night set in. More LEDs encircled each supporting column and a central chandelier twinkled over the dance floor.

"It's like fairyland!" Gemma raised spread arms to the ceiling, swirling in her floaty floral jumpsuit. "I love it."

Avery agreed, tipping her chin to gaze upward. "It's magical."

"When I grow up, I'm going to have a wedding just like this one." Bel drained her glass decisively.

"Want another?" Avery asked.

"Mm, please."

"Gem?"

"I'd love one. Need a hand?" Gemma offered.

"I've got it. Back in a minute." Avery headed for the bar, skirting the group of guys chatting in a huddle.

Catching Tanner's eye, she gestured with the empty glasses to show she was taking a trip to the bar. He looked like he might offer to help but quickly realized his carrying power was limited, and a flash of frustration darkened his eyes.

His gaze followed her across the barn; Avery felt it like a heated brand on the back of her neck.

"Can I have a word?" Johnnie's voice near her ear was unexpected.

She startled, then laughed. "God, sorry! I didn't see you there."

"Maybe outside? If you don't mind?" He was already taking the empty glasses from her hand. "It's a bit loud in here."

Avery couldn't think of a reason why not. "OK."

It was a balmy evening, summer at its best. A smattering of people mingled in the softly lit space—mainly guests who wanted to hold a conversation without raising their voices, and a few others who were having a smoke. Avery spotted Cassidy and Henry sitting at a table with Savannah's mom and dad and a handful of older couples. Merriment drifted on threads of dusk.

Johnnie smiled. He stood closer than strictly necessary and she took a few steps back until it felt more comfortable.

"We haven't had a chance to catch up since the Bach Bash."

Avery blinked at the statement. "No, we haven't. How's things?"

"Yeah, not bad. You?"

Oh, you know. A tree fell on my workshop and I had the best sex of my life with a guy who's no good for me.

"Same. All OK." Avery played with the charm around her neck, restless with the sticky conversation. "And Mia? How's she? You two still seeing each other?"

"Yeah, she's fine. It's all good." Johnnie gazed around at the nearby guests before turning back. His mouth lifted in an expression she recognized. "Just maybe a bit . . . mainstream."

Studying Johnnie's face, Avery marveled at how ordinary he looked compared to Tanner. How much less he sparkled, despite his apparent efforts to charm.

"I miss you, Ave. I liked it when we hooked up."

Wow, what an accolade. She almost rolled her eyes out loud. It was time to shut him down.

"Look, it's cool to catch up and I'm glad things aren't awkward between us." *Lies.* This was the epitome of awkwardness. Avery wrapped her arms across her body as a slight breeze drifted in. "But we've both moved on now. I'm not looking to rekindle anything, so it would be better for you to concentrate on your relationship with Mia. Things you don't have often seem shinier than the things you do."

Johnnie's eyes narrowed at her well-meant words. "Sure you're not just blinded by all the shiny parts of Tanner Stone, Ave? The money, the house, the lifestyle? He looks pretty damn golden from where I stand."

You don't know the half of it. He is utterly golden.

"That's unwarranted. And not a pretty look on you," she said coolly, taking a step away. "I'm a free agent, Johnnie. I don't have to answer to you."

"Drink, Stretch?"

Tanner stood a couple yards away. He held a wine glass carefully in his right hand, a bottle of beer dangling from his left.

"It's a free bar. I could have got you a drink," Johnnie muttered under his breath.

"You didn't, though. Tanner did. Don't be a dick." Avery turned her back on him and headed for the man who called to her like an oasis in the desert.

Away from Johnnie, who was just another sand dune.

Chapter 30
Tanner

Yeah, the bar was free. Because he'd put a fuck-ton of money behind it as his wedding present to Savannah and Griff. But that wasn't something Tanner planned to announce to this prick. To anyone, in fact.

"Thank you." Avery smiled at him as she took the glass, and he thought he might stage a heist at a vineyard to bring her wine for the rest of her life if she'd curve her lips like that every time.

He'd shed his jacket inside the barn—glad of a momentary reprieve from the damn sling before he'd put it back on—and rolled up his sleeves, loosened his tie, undone the top button of his shirt. And his skin still sizzled. He was hot under the collar just from being near her.

As they rejoined the others, Tanner felt the zap of electricity from Avery's bare arm even though they weren't touching. Knowing how she tasted, how she felt, had flipped a switch inside him and he couldn't find a breaker for it. When he'd watched her walk outside with Johnnie, the churn of his stomach had blindsided him. Catching her comment about being a free agent, he could have thrown up. What the hell had she done to him?

While Avery collected drinks for Bel and Gemma, Tanner took in her softened shoulders, the ease of her lips. If the conversation with Johnnie had bothered her, it wasn't showing on her face now.

"You look relaxed," he murmured near her ear, the scent of her perfume in his nose. He wanted to duck his head and nibble her neck; she tempted his taste buds whenever he was within touching distance.

Avery's mouth lifted at the corners. "Left my phone in Drew's car. I didn't want to look at it today and I like being without it. My mom knows I'm at the wedding so she shouldn't call."

"You didn't want to take any photos?"

She shrugged. "Bel's been snapping away all day. I'll get her to send me a few."

Maybe he'd get Bel to send him some, too.

Avery's daily presence in the outbuilding and her brief forays into his house were killing him; the past ten days had been a wake-up call. He'd thought he could back off and accept that maybe they weren't meant to be. But the distance he'd put between them had only shown him the opposite.

Her presence close by teased him with everything Tanner wanted for real and couldn't have. He'd grown to love the sound of Avery's sneakers on the tiled floor of his kitchen, her hoodie draped over the back of a chair, her music drifting in the air outside while she worked. It unwound parts of him that he had thought would always be strung tight, and he wanted more of it. More of her.

If she'd take a chance on a guy whose career hung in the balance.

He'd overheard Johnnie's snarky comments and they echoed in Tanner's head. On the off-chance Avery did want shiny, he'd shiny the fuck out of her. Because she deserved it and because he wanted her to know he was serious. It was time to double down on his persuasive skills.

"You found her!" Gemma squealed from behind them.

"Dying of thirst over here, girl." Bel swooped in to relieve Avery of their drinks, thrusting one at Gemma and looping an arm around Avery's waist.

"How was Milwaukee?" Tanner asked Bel, since Drew had told him she'd had an overnight work trip at the back end of the week.

"Interesting." She sipped her drink. "I was called 'little lady' twice in the first half hour. I let the initial one go because I am little and I am a lady."

"Fifty percent right . . ." Avery murmured.

Sniggering into her wine, Gemma chipped in, "Second time around, she told the guy he wasn't passing her vibe check and to come back when he'd had a rethink."

"I have too much shit to do to spend time re-educating sexists." Bel's smile was steely.

Drew pressed a kiss to the top of her head. "I'd have fucking kicked his ass but your take is better."

"No one got my Stefan versus Damon references either. It was painful," Bel complained.

"Do you shoehorn *The Vampire Diaries* into many liability discussions?" Leo asked from where he leaned against a light-bedecked wooden post.

"More than you'd imagine," Bel admitted after a thoughtful pause. "I link to sources whenever it's practical."

"And sometimes when it's not," added Avery.

In the far corner of the barn, the band returned from a break and jumped straight into an upbeat cover. A rolling wave of wedding guests headed for the dance floor. Turning to place his empty beer bottle on a nearby table, Tanner cleared his throat.

"Want to dance, Ave?" Dammit if Leo hadn't beaten him to it.

Avery's smile creased the bridge of her nose. She'd swapped out the hoop for a tiny crystal stud today; it glittered as she turned and held out her hand. "I'd love to."

Watching Leo lead her away hurt more than finding out Lily had slept with the goalie. Without a drink, Tanner had nothing to occupy his hands and his fingers went to his watch strap. Unclipping and clipping it a handful of times in quick succession, he imagined body-checking Leo in a way that would get him a very long stint in the penalty box and probably screw up his shoulder for good.

He honestly did his best not to stare, but Tanner couldn't tear his eyes from them. The creamy tones of Avery's skin, her long, lean outline and the delicate curve of those goddamn lips—they had him running a finger along the edge of his shirt collar.

"Tanner Stone?"

He didn't recognize the female wedding guest in front of him. "Yes?"

"I'm a huge fan! I wondered if you'd sign this for me." The woman held out one of the Order of Service cards.

"Of course—although it won't be my neatest work." He gestured to the sling. "And I don't have a pen."

She pushed one forward. "I've come prepared!"

Tanner smiled automatically as he scrawled a messy autograph and handed it back.

"What did you do?" she asked, wide-eyed and eager to chat.

"It's nothing. Just an old injury." Tanner brushed her off, keeping his reply on the polite side of brusque.

"I couldn't believe it when Savannah told me she's your cousin. Like, no way could I be lucky enough to come to her wedding and meet you! And now I have, and I hope you don't mind me bothering you." The woman reached out to touch his forearm and, as always, it felt weird and inappropriate. He'd had worse though—an arm petting was nothing. Bethany Jenner's face floated into Tanner's mind, tightening the muscles in his neck.

Fuck. At some point, I should really take the leap and talk to Avery about that particular shitshow.

Tanner took a step back, his smile dialing down a notch. "Not at all. It's fine."

"Well, thanks for this." Sav's friend waved the Order of Service and looked as if she wanted to prolong the conversation, but he didn't help her out. "Good luck with the Rapids!"

Before she'd taken a half dozen steps, the woman turned back, tearing a strip off the lower half of the card in her hand. She scrawled something across the blank surface, leaning on the nearest table. Folding the scrap in half, she stepped forward and tucked it swiftly into the pocket of Tanner's pants before he could move away, a flush running high across her cheekbones.

"My number," she stuttered, her teeth flashing briefly. "If you wanted it. Just because I'll always wish I'd given it to you if I don't."

She turned and fled before he could respond.

Drew chuckled. "Not gonna lie, I'm surprised you haven't had more of a line forming."

Tanner fished the piece of card from his pocket with grimace. "I'm pretty sure Sav had a hand in that."

If his cousin had told her guests to keep it chill, he was grateful. Maybe in a previous life, he'd have enjoyed the attention of her friend, even kept and used the phone number. Who was he kidding? He'd have definitely called her. But these days, he had no interest in anyone who wasn't Avery.

Sliding the scrap of paper surreptitiously onto the table and covering it with an empty beer bottle, he turned back to the dance floor.

Avery and Leo danced well as a couple. For all his long arms and legs, Leo had musicality in spades. He moved naturally to the rhythm and Avery's dress shimmered with each fluid twist of her body. A hot restlessness swelled inside Tanner's chest.

"They look good together, don't they?" Gemma muttered dispiritedly.

Bel rubbed her arm. "Avery and Leo have only ever been friends. You know that." She raised an eyebrow at Tanner. "Leo says she used to watch you all the time in school."

Tanner grunted. If she had, he'd never caught her. "I hadn't done anything to deserve her attention then."

"You're a celebrity now though," Gemma said. "A household name and a famous face. It's so romantic."

A household name for how long? He refused to listen to the nagging voice inside his head.

Bel's eyes were pools of warm chocolate. "And you're the one looking at her like she's a celebrity."

"She is to me." Tanner watched Avery for another ten seconds. Then he cracked his neck with a practiced roll, easing the tension in his shoulders, and moved purposefully toward her.

Enough was enough.

Chapter 31
Avery

The music swept any restraint from Avery's body that the alcohol hadn't already diluted, the joy of the occasion and the easy pleasure of being surrounded by friends washing over her as she danced with Leo. Safe, secure, and relaxed, she let herself go. When she spun to find Tanner stalking onto the dance floor, an anticipatory tingle spread beneath her breastbone and a thread pulled taut from her belly to her throat. Every inch of her skin began to fizz.

"Mind if I cut in?" Tanner's easy smile was aimed at Leo but his eyes were on Avery as he reached for her hand.

Pulling her into a loose embrace, his left arm slid possessively around her waist and . . . fuck, it felt good.

"This isn't a slow dance." Her protest lacked any conviction even to her own ears.

Tanner's body pressed closer. One thigh sliding between hers, his fingers closed on her hip. When he lowered his head, Avery felt his reply against the shell of her ear. "I think you owe it to everyone else to make sure it is. I'm a liability with anything faster."

She looked up into his face and there was the smile again that she'd missed this past week. It was edible. However much she warned herself off, she wanted to lick it from his lips. The scent of him, his heat and his bulk made her stomach pitch and tremble. Avery's arms stretched up to loop carefully around his neck without consulting her first. Her fingers curled into the hair that skimmed the back of his collar and Tanner pulled her even tighter against his body until they were plastered together from knee to chest, not so much dancing as undulating slowly and deliberately.

He was mouthwatering. Her kryptonite.

"Mind your arm," she cautioned. It was all she could manage.

"I told you, it's fine. I only wore the sling to keep Sam from pounding on me." His right hand rested lightly on her hip.

Avery lost track of the music, the time, the people around them. There was only Tanner and his warmth and his eyes on her face. And she found it hard to remember any of the reasons why this thing between them scared her so much when it felt so right to be close to him.

He'll chew you up and spit you out! her common sense tried to scream in her ear. *He'll turn your emotions into a weakness, fold your feelings into a paper airplane and toss them aside. The only person you can trust is yourself . . .*

But, for once, the voice was muffled, drowned out by Tanner's proximity and the thunder of her heart.

"You're killing me, you know that?" His growl raised the hairs on her arms. "I dream about your body and the gorgeous fucking feel of you. I wake up every morning rock hard. I have to jerk off in the shower just so I can function. I only have to smell you and I can't concentrate on anything else. You calm me and rile me, both at the same time. Knowing you're working outside at home and not seeing you is agony—I have to fight myself to stay out of your way. But the thought of you not working there, not coming in and out of the house, is worse. You're going to ruin me, Stretch."

The unfiltered need in his words went straight to Avery's knees and she sagged against him, her lips parting on a strangled breath. She couldn't answer.

Tanner lifted her chin with a rough finger. "If your intention is to torture me, it's working."

His body moved against hers, his shirt sliding over the silky material of her dress, and her nipples peaked. As his thumb traced her lower lip in a slow sweep from one corner of her mouth to the other, the gold light in his eyes was consuming.

"If it helps, I'm not finding it any easier," Avery admitted painfully, torn by the battle raging in her chest. "But I don't want to mess you around. You've got enough going on right now without me blowing hot and cold. I'm not trying to be a tease, Tanner. I just—"

His right hand flexed on her hip, shifting her even closer. His hardness was impossible to ignore, and Tanner groaned. "You made yourself very clear upfront. I haven't been misled, Stretch." His smile was wicked, encouraging, daring. "You can tease me whenever you like. I'll take casual. I'll take anything you have to give me."

Dipping his head, Tanner drew her lip between his teeth and sucked on it gently. His fingers twined in her hair. She opened up to him, greedy for more, her hands at the back of his neck tugging him down. He tasted of beer and lime, refreshing and addictive.

Her rules, her fears, her parents and all the ways in which they'd screwed her up, had no real substance in this moment. Those binds weren't broken, but their hold was loosened enough to send a temporary rush of freedom to Avery's brain.

She was just her. And he was just him. And today wasn't tomorrow.

"But for Chrissake, decide quickly, because there's every chance we're about to cause a public display of indecency." Tanner breathed the unashamed disclosure against her temple and Avery felt the thrill of it right through to her center.

Take a chance. The voice had lowered to a tempting hum inside her head and she wanted so badly to listen to it. *One more night isn't the same as a relationship.*

"Wedding sex doesn't really count, does it?" She grasped desperately at straws. "Like drunk texts or holiday calories. That's a thing, right?"

"Pretty sure I read something like that somewhere." Tanner's voice was weighted with grit, gravel, and hope.

"Must be true then." They both knew the reasoning was weak but Avery's resolve had cracked down the middle, leaving a fissure that wouldn't be mended tonight. "Tell me you have a room to yourself."

Tanner's sharp intake of air whistled by her mouth. His grip on her hair was the best kind of pain.

"You'll have to walk in front of me," he rasped and spun her 180 degrees, steering her off the dance floor, his left hand curled around her waist.

They whisked past Bel and Drew, Leo and Gemma. "See you at breakfast!" called Bel, laughter rippling in her voice.

Tanner pushed Avery faster and faster toward the doorway of the barn until they burst out onto the pathway leading to the lodge. He grasped her hand, tugging her into a run, and she laughed breathlessly as she struggled to keep up with him on unfamiliar high heels.

"I'm going to break an ankle!"

"I won't let you, Stretch. I've got you." Tanner clamped her to his side, eyes sparkling as he grinned down at her, his muscular legs eating up the ground.

They pulled open the main entrance to the lodge, spilling into a lobby that was quiet and classy, wall lights dimmed to a relaxing glow.

"I left my keycard at reception," Tanner said as he made a beeline for the desk manned by a smiling gentleman in an immaculate suit.

Watching from a distance, Avery scrubbed at the goosebumps racing over her arms, smiling at the way Tanner crackled with energy, his feet shifting throughout the miniscule amount of time he was forced to wait. Perpetual motion in human form.

When he spun from the desk, pocketing the card, and grabbed for her hand again, she laughed.

This was madness.

The brakes were off and she was freewheeling out of control.

"My room. Now."

Fortunately, the elevator door opened instantly. Pushing Avery inside, Tanner backed her up against the mirrored wall, his desperation matched by her own as she twisted her fingers into his shirt front to drag him closer. His mouth was on hers before the door slid shut.

"It's only one floor up," he said between kisses, stabbing at the elevator button.

His chest pinned Avery to the wall as he teased her with the hot swipe of his tongue and small bites to her lips. Tugging the hem of his shirt free from his pants, she curled her fingers into the waistband where his taut muscles jumped at her touch.

The elevator pinged and the doors opened.

Spinning on his heel, Tanner dragged her out into the corridor. They reached his room in moments and fell in through the door. Inside, Avery caught of a glimpse of a tidy and unfussy space. He hadn't even unpacked the small overnight case which sat by the bed.

"Do you want a drink?" Tanner asked, his breath coming hard and fast.

She turned back to him and shook her head.

"Good." His eyes never shifting from her face as he prowled toward her like a big cat, Tanner unfastened the strap of his sling and threw it aside. His hands moved to the buttons on his shirt, unfastening each one so slowly that Avery's mouth dried. Slipping the cufflinks from his sleeves, he shrugged the crisp cotton from his shoulders until it slid to the floor in a heap.

His uncovered tattoos were like old friends that she'd missed. With a sweeping gaze, Avery traced the three words on his collarbone, the tumbling Icarus on his ribs that rippled when Tanner bent to undo his shoes, strip off his socks. She ran her tongue over parched lips, curling her hands into fists as his fingers went to his zipper. She couldn't move. Watching him undress was mesmerizing. Each soft sound echoed in the still room, fueling the expectancy pulsing between them.

Pushing at his pants to send them pooling around his ankles, Tanner kicked them impatiently to one side and Avery's center flushed with warmth, her thighs clenched and quivered. She couldn't look away from his tented shorts, his ripped stomach, his thick quads.

Crossing the room, Tanner bent to pull his wallet from his bag and drew a foil packet out from its folds.

"On the bed, Stretch." His voice was guttural, his smile rakish, as he threw the condom onto the covers.

"Can you undo the back of my dress?" she asked. It came out in a whisper.

"No."

Avery blinked. She frowned and opened her mouth but he cut across her.

"Get on the bed." His eyes burned like liquid gold.

Biting her lip, she kicked off her shoes and crawled onto the sheets.

"Nearer the edge." The ragged instruction was raw.

When Avery shifted obediently, Tanner expelled a pained breath as he knelt on the floor between her ankles. Dragging them apart, he drew the silky hem of her dress slowly up her legs. It slithered over her shins, past her knees and up to her hips, his hands brushing a path across her skin as the satin traveled higher and higher.

Avery fell back onto her elbows, unable to tear her eyes from Tanner's face as he followed the movement of his fingers.

"You . . . are . . . beautiful," he murmured. "Stroking you feels like the glide of my skates on the ice." His hair fell across his forehead as he propped her heels on the very edge of the bed, lifting her dress higher, baring the white lace of her panties. Tanner's teeth caught on his lower lip with a hiss of breath. "So fucking delicious."

He dipped his chin and Avery arched with a gasp as he kissed the inside of one thigh, then the other. There was a moment of anticipation so intense she couldn't move before Tanner's head lowered again and the heat of his mouth burned through cotton and lace. He lapped at the outside of her underwear, humming his approval—of her scent? Her panties? She didn't know. She didn't care.

He teased her by refusing to remove her clothes in an exact contrast to how he'd teased her with the steady stripping of his own. Oh, the gorgeous, infuriating irony. Avery begged and twisted and still he kept the barrier between them. The material, already damp with her need, grew even wetter from his mouth. It chafed her delicate skin until she craved the soft, soothing drag of his tongue.

"Please, Tanner. Please . . ." Avery threw her hands above her head, her heels sliding over the bed sheets as he pushed her legs wider apart.

"What do you want?"

"I need—"

"What do you need, Stretch?"

Curse him and his iron control. "Your mouth. I need your mouth on me. I need you."

Finally.

Tanner pushed her underwear to one side and the first hot, moist sweep brought a stream of swear words from Avery's mouth, which made him chuckle, deep and low. He tasted her again with another long stroke. Then another. And another. Each strung her tighter and tighter, the tension creeping through her limbs, building slowly, powerfully, relentlessly. He swirled his tongue over her clit and she trembled. The muscles in her thighs quivered. All Avery needed was the two fingers he slid inside her, the sensation of fullness at her core, and she clenched around him, coming with a shallow cry, the small of her back lifting from the mattress. He sucked at her, drawing out the pleasure while her body wracked with tremor upon tremor beneath him.

"Who needs wedding cake or champagne when I can eat you?" Tanner licked his fingers as he straightened, finally sliding her panties down her legs. "And white underwear is my favorite. If I'd known you were wearing these, they'd have been in my pocket before the speeches."

Avery opened her eyes, still trying to catch her breath. "You can keep them now—I don't need them."

"Bold of you to think I was giving them back." Tanner rose to his feet, stripped off his underwear, and moved to kneel on the bed, his eyes smoldering with an amber flame as he loomed above her. Wiping her moisture from his mouth, he reached for the condom. She ached with emptiness, needing more from him immediately, and the evidence of his desire, as he sheathed himself in the most fluent of maneuvers, clutched at Avery's belly. Settling himself in a seated position against the headboard, Tanner linked their hands and tugged. "Take pity on a poor, battered body and come sit on me? I promise I'll make it worth your while."

The laugh huffed from her lips as Avery sat up. There was nothing poor or battered about him. His stomach rippled with more muscle mass than she suspected she had in total. His chest was a tactile rockface of temptation, his arms corded in a way that made her mouth water.

When Avery slid her leg over his broad thighs, their eyes caught and held in a shared groundswell of desperate eagerness. His hands on her waist, Tanner pulled her steadily down until she felt the tip of his cock at her slick center and a gasp escaped her lips. With one long, slow drag and a fractured growl, he lodged himself inside her, rolling his hips until she was seated as deep as it was possible to go. It felt blissful.

The teasing, the touching, the waiting, all leading to this.

"Yes," Avery whispered, her eyes fluttering closed, her hands pressed to his chest. "I love the way you feel inside me." The admission slipped from her tongue on a breathy moan.

"That's convenient," Tanner rasped, his lips moving against her neck, "because I love the way I feel inside you, too." His hands slid over the silky material still covering her hips. "But I should have fucking stripped you. This dress is in my way—I want more of your skin."

He tugged the satin neckline down, pulled the delicate bra cup aside and closed his mouth around one nipple. Avery shuddered. He sucked harder, raising her hips then dragging them down again. He threw back his head, groaning aloud at her tightness as uncontrollable tremors rippled through her muscles. She drew her tongue along the scar that bisected his lip and took over the rise and fall of their movements to save his shoulder, sinking down on him again and again. The heavenly slide was too much and not enough. Avery urged him deeper, craving the possession and reveling in the thick stretch of him as he thrust upward at the perfect angle.

"Fucking yes! Holy fucking fuck . . ." Tanner muttered the obscene litany into her hair.

Her nails dug into his biceps as her breath hitched. The way he filled her was inimitable.

She rocked her pelvis, chasing the orgasm building rapidly from the friction between their bodies and panting out her needs. "I want . . . more, Tanner. That's so good. I'm nearly there—"

As the repetitive shift provided the perfect stimulation against her sensitive clit, another ruinous high wracked Avery's body in relentless waves. And Tanner came hard at the same time, his thighs shaking as he spilled his pleasure with surge after forceful surge. Savoring the dirty adoration that tumbled from his lips, she slumped against his chest with her fingers in the sweaty strands of his hair.

"I fucking love your body, Stretch. You make me explode." Tanner closed his mouth on the salty cords of her neck, dragging shuddering breaths in and out of his lungs. "There's no way I can play it cool when you only have to look at me and I'm desperate for you." He rubbed his thumb over the crumpled folds of silky material at her waist. "Also, you're probably gonna have to dry-clean this dress. I don't mind if you send me the bill—it was worth it."

Swallowing against a sudden tightness in her throat, Avery let out a winded giggle and held him closer. She didn't know how he could make her laugh so easily, even as her terror at wanting him this much threatened the blissful calm of the moment.

But with Tanner's ragged breath in her ear and the feel of his smile close to her temple, the fear couldn't take a proper hold just yet. And his sunshine began to seep perilously into the chilled and dusty corners of Avery's heart.

"It was perfect," she whispered, but there was a hollow edge to the words and they both heard it.

Chapter 32

Tanner

He couldn't persuade her to stay. Although Tanner had suspected it would happen, it still felt like she'd taken a cheese grater to his heart when Avery pulled away again, gathering her shoes to creep back to her shared room in the early hours of the morning with a stilted goodbye and flushed cheeks.

He knew he'd pushed too hard, said too much, both on the dance floor and in bed. But even if this thing between them was only ever one-sided, he couldn't bring himself to regret it.

Hiding the matching ache in his chest and his shoulder throughout the journey home, Tanner fended off the nosy comments and teasing from Dex and a concerned avalanche of questions about the upcoming surgery from his mom. Wanting nothing more than some time alone to brood when they dropped him off at home, he was thwarted by both his brother's request to take a look around and the appearance of his own G-Wagon on the driveway.

The latter wasn't entirely unexpected, given that Tanner had supplied Mats with the code to the gates and the alarm. Hidden a key for him, too. Appreciating that his old Boston teammate had given up his time to deliver the car—and that Dex had recently put him up for an entire month in the UK—Tanner resigned himself to being a good host.

What he didn't expect was to find Arlo in the pool.

"Dude, I can see why you like it here." Lifting his shades, Arlo squinted at him from the crocodile pool float. "It's not so bad for the middle of nowhere."

Mats rose to his feet. "He said you wouldn't mind him tagging along. Didn't leave me much choice and your phone went to voicemail."

"Nah, it's fine. He said he'd come visit soon." Tanner made the introductions. "Mats—this is my brother, Dex."

"Hi." Mats gave his brother a measured smile that didn't do much to lighten his serious face. His hand casually covered the fresh, puckered scar on his neck under the guise of rubbing at his jaw—a gesture Tanner had seen him make many times since the accident.

When Arlo raised a glass of something chilled in a jaunty salute, his teeth flashing white against his tanned face, Dex nodded a friendly greeting. The two had crossed paths a handful of times over the years.

"Thanks for bringing my car, man," Tanner said gratefully to Mats. "How's your off-season going?"

The heavyweight grunted. "Not bad so far. Spent three weeks with one of my sisters back home in Sweden—got to catch up with my nieces. Still want to fit in a golf trip to Arizona, if I can."

"Ten weeks before training camp starts, so you've got time." Shielding his eyes against the sun, Tanner battled the sinking sensation in his gut. "Looks like I've had all the golf I'm gonna get this summer."

"Sorry about your shoulder." Mats wasn't one to mince words.

Replying with a shrug, Tanner caught Dex's look of sympathy. "I was fooling myself that the strengthening exercises would solve the issue."

Arlo paddled to the edge of the pool. "That's why I'm here. We need to make sure we've considered all the options before you commit to anything rash."

Yeah, as if he hadn't done that already. "I wouldn't be opting for the surgical stabilization if I thought there was an alternative," Tanner grunted. "Six months off isn't ideal at this point." *Or any point.*

"You'll be back before you know it." Mats made the statement with an unswerving faith that Tanner appreciated more than the big guy would ever know.

"We still need to discuss it," Arlo pushed. "Wouldn't hurt to have a plan B up our sleeves. Although slacking on full pay doesn't exactly blow, I guess. Good job you signed the contract before this happened. Some of us have to slog it out for our money."

"Your life doesn't suck so much that you can't take the time to freeload on my hospitality." Struck by the paralyzing thought that plan B might involve a whole other fucking career, Tanner scooped up a bright yellow ball from the ground and lobbed it in Arlo's direction with his left hand. "How long are you staying?"

Arlo just dodged and smirked. The ball bobbed away from him on a ripple of water. "Haven't decided yet. But I can work from anywhere."

"And you, man?" he asked Mats.

"Until next weekend, if it's OK with you."

"Sounds great."

Tanner left them to it for quarter of an hour or so, taking Dex inside to show him around. When they were done, they made coffee for everyone and took it back onto the patio, pulling up a chair each and stretching out.

"It's a great house. D'you think you'll buy it?" his brother asked. "Or are you still looking around?"

Releasing the strap on the sling and dropping it beside him, Tanner rubbed at his neck. "Can't imagine anything else suiting me better."

"Still makes more sense to rent given the circumstances," Arlo interjected. "Gives you more options."

If they'd been alone, Tanner would have grilled him about money. The need to know more about his current financial position itched like prickly heat beneath his skin. Instead, he shelved that discussion for later and said, "Fisher's a cool coach. I'm lucky they're still willing to give me a chance."

"You'll be bored here as soon as you're back on the ice." With a laugh, Arlo sent a handful of water in a sweeping arc over Tanner's legs before heaving himself out of the pool to flop onto one of the chairs. He reached for his mug of coffee. "And then you'll be begging me to push for a trade to a bigger team."

Tanner found his eyes traveling to Avery's temporary workshop and his knee bounced. "Don't count on it."

"How was the wedding?" Mats asked, as if he could sense a change of conversation would be welcome.

"It was cool. Good fun," drawled Dex with an easy smile. "They did their first dance to 'Sexy and I Know It.'"

"Savannah was happy, which is the main thing." Tanner knew his cousin had looked gorgeous but he couldn't have described her dress to save his life. Avery's, on the other hand, was seared into his memory. Especially how it had looked bunched around her waist.

To hide a sudden surge of hunger that threatened to make itself embarrassingly obvious, he pushed to his feet and wandered over to the edge of the pool, kneeling to read the floating thermometer.

"Give it a year and she'll be moaning about him stacking the dishwasher wrong," Arlo grinned.

Tanner made a noise of disagreement. Dragging his t-shirt over his head, he lowered himself onto the pool edge and dangled his feet in the water. "You haven't met my cousin—she's a gremlin. It'll be Griff moaning about the dishwasher and Savannah won't give two shits. Neither will he, to be fair. He knows he's lucky to have her."

"Saw Lily out last week."

"Yeah?"

"She asked after you." Arlo's mouth kicked up at the corner.

With a noncommittal grunt, Tanner smothered a yawn. He had no interest in his ex-girlfriend.

"She's single again. The quarterback is history. Oh, and rumor has it, Bethany Jenner has called time on her marriage." Arlo carried on running his mouth off and this one hit a nerve.

His shoulders hunching, Tanner's fingers gripped the edge of the pool. The news was hardly a fucking surprise. Hitting on your husband's players wasn't the best sign of a healthy marriage.

"Shut up, dude." Mats's intervention was uncharacteristic. He stretched out a beefy leg and kicked Arlo's chair. "He doesn't want to know. Read the room."

Scooping up his phone instead, Arlo started talking asset management as he scrolled, expounding on short-term versus long-term benefits. He wanted Tanner to buy a boat. He could be pretty liberal with cash flow for a financial advisor.

"It'll be a good investment. You can offset some of the expenses—"

Tanner's brother cut across him. "Boats are never a good investment."

"I didn't know you had one." Arlo arched an eyebrow.

"I don't own a racehorse either," Dex said with a lazy shrug, "but I know I'd probably be poorer for buying one."

"Around a third of people in Sweden own a boat." Mats, the voice of reason, added his input. "They're fun but they don't make money."

Tanner rotated shoulder muscles pleasantly warmed by the sun and was relieved to find it felt OK. "I'm not that bothered, anyway. I doubt I'd use it enough to be worth the slip rental and upkeep. I'm not gonna splash out on anything I don't have to until the surgery's done and I've decided if I want to buy this place."

Arlo pulled a face. "There's nothing happening in Pine Springs, man," he groused. "Think of the fun we had in Boston. And Dallas. I don't want to settle somewhere I'm outnumbered by trees."

"No one's asking you to settle here," Tanner pointed out. "We don't need to live in each other's pockets."

"Don't give me that. You know you can't manage without me." Arlo leaned over to swing a punch at Tanner's ribs which was easy enough to dodge. "I'm the brains to your muscles. We make the perfect team."

They talked movies, travel, and sports for the next couple hours as the afternoon whiled away into a balmy early evening. Dex offered to cook and no one opposed the idea. From the scant contents of the fridge, he produced a pasta concoction that was devoured with no leftovers and they took a bottle of bourbon back outside.

Opening the banking app on his phone for a quick once-over, Tanner was just trying to remember why he might have made a hefty withdrawal of cash toward the beginning of the month when Arlo brought up Avery.

"I can't believe I finally get to meet the Scholarship Savior in person after all this time. Unless she's blown you off again already."

Arlo had been privy to the weeks of confusion and disappointment when Tanner's texts and calls went unanswered during that first semester at college. He'd offloaded on his roommate numerous times while he tried to work out why Avery wasn't replying, and it hadn't made Arlo much of a fan. His snarky jibe caught Tanner off-guard, skating as it did a little too close to the truth.

Tanner pocketed his phone with a frown, his chest tight with the doubt over whether those few wonderful hours last night had changed anything between him and Avery. "You'll see her tomorrow. She's using the outbuilding as her workshop at the moment."

"I hope you're charging her rent," Arlo said, tipping his head back to gaze up at the sky.

"As if," snorted Dex, nudging the side of Tanner's sneaker with a grin. "Ya boy's got it bad. They were all over each other at the wedding."

The combination of his brother's teasing and the memories of exactly how "all over" each other he and Avery had been sent a flush of heat to Tanner's groin. He felt like a goddamn teenager.

"So you're actually together now?" Arlo side-eyed him curiously.

"Not exactly," Tanner admitted, drumming fidgety fingers on the arm of his chair. "It's complicated."

"Always fucking complicated with that one," Arlo murmured under his breath, tapping away on his phone at the same time with a scowl on his face. "Couldn't you at least play the field for a bit? Have yourself some fun."

Dex huffed out a laugh. "Oh, he's having fun, don't you worry. And Avery's great. She's just gonna make him work for it."

"No bad thing," said Mats succinctly. "Easy is overrated."

"I like easy," Arlo objected.

Fiddling with his watch strap, Tanner flashed him a grin. "That's because you're always looking for a shortcut. Some of us understand that the end result is sweeter for putting in the hours."

And, as the others continued to drop dubious pearls of wisdom about women and dating, Tanner tuned them all out. While he was helpless to do anything about his shoulder and the upcoming surgery, devising a plan to win Avery's trust had to be within his capabilities.

She needed someone on her side. Someone to take care of her the way she looked after her mom. The hours they'd spent in his hotel room at the wedding had been so exceptional he knew he'd be replaying them tonight in the solitude of his own bed.

Somehow, he needed to show her that every night could be just as good if she'd only give him a chance.

Chapter 33
Avery

It was a morning of ups and downs.

Kneeling on the floor of the workshop with a feel-good playlist to boost her mood and four tacks between her lips, Avery had to turn her music down when Jackson Hale called. She spat the nails into the palm of one hand so she could speak.

"I've been offered three antique bed frames with upholstered ends, but they're damaged," he said without preamble. "Does that sound like something you can help with?"

They talked details for a few minutes, agreed a price for the labor, and Jackson promised to let her know when he could arrange delivery.

"Might see you soon anyway," he grunted just before hanging up. "Sam's been whining about getting everyone together for a game of softball or something. I swear he needs more exercise than a damn toddler."

She couldn't stop a small squeal escaping her lips as she bounced to her feet. Jackson had already commissioned a three-seater couch and an eight-piece dining chair set. With the work she already had on her books, she hadn't been this busy since she'd started her business. Avery sent up a quick prayer that maybe her shifts at the Rusty Barrel might be coming to an end.

She'd be on cloud nine if only *anything* else was running as smoothly.

The trolling on her online work accounts had continued to balloon. The vicious comments left a horrible taste in Avery's mouth, taking the edge off her satisfaction at the growing list of commissions but leaving her all the more determined to keep uploading her "how to" tutorials and makeover videos regardless.

"I guess there will always be haters," she murmured to herself as she worked. "Even if all you're doing is restuffing a recliner."

And it wasn't only the trolling that continued to be an issue.

She'd had a further three anonymous texts since the wedding, each one pointless and nasty. Bel said she should report them but it seemed like an overreaction to Avery. Their discussion—and disagreement—at home that morning had been interrupted by a delivery.

Assuming the box would contain the piping cord and heading tape she'd ordered, Avery opened it to find a giant tub of live mealworms instead. The company who'd sent it were unconcerned about the mix-up when she rang and, since the order had been paid for, they weren't interested in having it returned.

"Scatter it in your garden for the birds," the woman on the other end had suggested.

"I've got enough here to feed a family of pterodactyls," Avery pointed out, but she was already talking to dead air.

Her mom's call came swiftly after Jackson's. Having already had an hour-long chat yesterday as soon as Avery got home from the wedding, there was precious little left to say now it was less than twenty-four hours later. Avery listened with half an ear to her mother on loudspeaker as she continued to work.

She tuned back in when her mom brought up her father.

"No, I haven't seen him for a few weeks. He doesn't call me a whole bunch," she said, cringing when her mind leaped to the fateful confrontation with Paige in the bar. It wasn't something she'd shared with her mother. "Yeah, they seemed fine the last time we got together. But I don't—" Avery broke off when her mom interrupted. "Sure. I know it still hurts. But he's moved on and so have you. Don't give him any more power over you. Let it go now." She listened for a little while longer, then said firmly, "Let's not go over this again. *I'll* sort the gutters out—pretty sure they're all just full of leaves. And I looked at the downspout when I was there last. I can bring a stepladder over and push the joint back together. I'll do it before we get any rain. Promise."

With a few more platitudes, she brought the conversation to a close, hanging up with a stifled groan and raising her eyes to the ceiling.

"Problems?" Tanner startled her with his question from the doorway; she hadn't heard him arrive.

"Nothing I can't handle." Avery eyed him warily, fighting a traitorous roll of pleasure at seeing him. And memories of clever fingers and breathless sighs blended with the dust motes in the air between them, stealing her breath with their clarity.

"Happy to help if you need it." His voice was husky before he cleared it. "Mats and Arlo arrived yesterday. I brought them over to introduce you. As long as you're not too busy?"

"No, that's fine," she said, dragging her focus from Tanner to the two guys who trailed behind him into the workshop. Avery offered them a smile as Tanner made the introductions.

"Arlo and I were at college together—I told you that, right? He looks after all my business stuff. Arlo, this is Avery."

"Always good to put a face to a name, Boo." The glint in Arlo's dark eyes matched his toothy smile.

"Mats and I played together in Boston, as you know," Tanner continued and Avery looked up and up again at the monster of a guy who towered over them all.

"Pleased to meet you," said Mats, his voice low and soft, his face so much less outwardly friendly than Arlo's and yet somehow more appealing.

"Thought you might want a cold drink." Tanner handed her a can of Coke and leaned a hip against her workbench, twisting the silver chain at his neck. Masculine warmth and light sweat mingled in the air around him and the heady scent twisted something low in her belly. Avery's pulse gave a little hike as she popped the top of the can and took a grateful swig.

"What's this?" Mats asked as he bent to study a bulky item of furniture that was due to be packaged up for shipping.

"It's a four-fold screen." Avery crossed the workshop to stand next to him. "Originally people had them for privacy or to stop drafts. Sometimes they were used as a dressing screen for ladies. Now they're more often wanted for decoration or dividing up spaces."

"I like the fabric you've chosen." She noticed he positioned himself automatically so the long, livid scar that ran from his ear down his neck was facing away from her, and her heart went out to him. "It's interesting to look at."

"It's called 'toile de Jouy' and you can buy it with hunting scenes, rural landscapes, trees, and flowers—that kind of thing. This one has mythological characters. It was ordered by a photographer who wants to use it as a prop."

"She's going to find me a couch and cover it in this." Tanner wandered over to her shelves of plastic-wrapped fabric bolts and Mats followed him.

"Well played, sister." With a sideways glance, Arlo held up one hand for a fist bump.

"What do you mean?" Avery frowned, ignoring the gesture until she understood what he was getting at.

"New workshop, free services, custom-built space. You've done well here." Tanner's friend smiled. "I take it this is a level-up on your old place."

She opened a fresh box of staples. "It's only temporary. I'll be back at home as soon as I can get my own workshop rebuilt." Avery resented having to explain the situation to Arlo. There was something about him that was already rubbing her the wrong way.

"Sure." He winked. "It looks temporary."

Running her eyes over the set-up, Avery realized with a jolt that he wasn't wrong—she had settled herself in, filling the extra space and laying it all out exactly how she liked it. The new sewing machine she'd originally begrudged Tanner buying had become her pride and joy. The lighting was perfect, the ceiling fans made the working conditions blissfully comfortable, and the shelving unit was so much better than her secondhand one at home, which she'd salvaged from an estate sale and had never really been big enough. Everything she needed was here. Tanner had made sure of it.

It didn't look temporary. And suddenly Avery didn't know how to breathe. The feeling of being reliant on someone else gripped her by the throat like the main character in a dark romance novel—and it wasn't sexy.

"This is what Tanner does." Arlo gave an easy shrug. "He buys shit for people because he knows how lucky he is to earn the big bucks."

Gritting her teeth, Avery shoved her anxiety deep inside to examine later, at home, alone. She might be drowning in conflicted misgivings about her own relationship with Tanner but she couldn't let Arlo's comment go uncontested.

"It's not luck. He worked hard for his success. He's earned it."

Arlo eyed her shrewdly. "We both know that's not true. He wouldn't have gotten into college without your help. You deserve to get something out of it."

He made it sound like she'd had a long-term plan to ride on Tanner's coattails. "He'd have done it on his own, one way or the other. He's talented and driven."

Fiddling with some of the instruments on her workbench, Arlo just laughed. "Yeah, we all blow smoke, don't we? If that's what it takes to ride the train, Boo."

"Why do you call me that?" Avery itched with discomfort at his sly digs and shallow friendliness.

"You've always been Boo to me. Seemed like a good name for a girl who would ghost someone like you ghosted Tanner. It was cold, the way you left him hanging." The smile stayed on Arlo's lips but the look in his eyes was biting.

Avery stepped closer. "Don't judge me until you know what you're talking about," she said through pinched lips. Struggling to keep herself in check, she swallowed the anger clawing at her throat; she didn't need anyone else lining up to take a shot at her. Especially someone who knew nothing about her.

Tanner and Mats interrupted their standoff, but Avery caught the speculative look Mats gave them as Tanner said, "Sam messaged earlier. He's fixed up a softball game tomorrow night and he's after more people. Drew and Bel are in. Jackson and Leah, too. He mentioned others as well. Want to ask Gemma and Leo to join us?"

"I might give it a miss. I need to see my mom." She stonewalled the appealing suggestion, distracted by her irritation with Arlo and the reluctant determination to rebuild the barriers between herself and Tanner.

"I could ask if we can make it another night if you'd rather. Or you could see your mom after?" The corner of Tanner's mouth hitched as he studied her and Avery wished it didn't tempt her to raise onto her tiptoes and kiss it. Whole wars had been raging in her body since the wedding, with her need to protect herself fighting a losing battle with the ache, the yearning, that gripped her whenever Tanner was close. "You OK, Stretch?"

Another nickname. This one overflowing with humor and shared memories. Sinking into her skin like butter. If she wasn't careful, it would rust the barbed wire she'd wrapped around her heart.

"I'm fine, thanks. I just have things I should get on with."

Tanner studied her for another few seconds, then nodded. He began to steer the other two out of the workshop. "We'll leave you in peace. Don't work too hard."

Avery caved before he reached the door. "Tomorrow is fine. I'll come—and I'll ask Gemma and Leo, too."

Her reward was that smile of his that she'd come to miss when he wasn't around. He always seemed genuinely delighted to spend time in her company, consistently and patiently letting her call all the shots. The lack of pushing was eating away at her resistance.

But behind Tanner's shoulder, Avery caught a smirk on Arlo's face and instantly regretted her change of heart.

Turning her music back up once they'd gone, she returned to the job of attaching the new material to an old chair frame. When her phone pinged on the workbench, she swiped it open with only half her attention on the message that had come through.

Unknown:

Keep your hands off, Delgado. He's mine.

For fuck's sake. Now she was being hated on by anonymous Tanner fans?

And they weren't even actually dating.

This was getting ridiculous.

As Avery's day took another nosedive, any leftover shine from Savannah's wedding cracked and flaked away like a layer of old varnish on one of her restorations.

* * *

No one answered the buzz at the gates when the Jeep was delivered at the end of the afternoon. Since Tanner's car was missing from the driveway, Avery broke away from her work to wander over.

"You must have the wrong address," she told the guy driving the truck.

What is it with people who can't send stuff to the right place? And can't I be the one getting mistaken Jeep Wranglers fresh off the conveyor belt delivered instead of mealworms . . .

He checked his clipboard again. "Avery Delgado. This address. Looks right to me. You just need to sign here." Pointing to a broken line at the base of his docket, he offered her his pen.

Be careful what you wish for.

"I didn't order a car," she said wearily.

"Name on the details is Tanner Stone." He glanced up. "Wait—is that Tanner Stone, the hockey player?"

Avery flashed a reserved smile but ignored his question. Maybe Tanner had given her name in case he wasn't around—like now. So she signed the docket and let the guy unload his cargo. It seemed an odd choice for Tanner when he already had the G-Wagon. The new, shiny blue-gray Jeep and Avery's rusty old Honda (with its *serious* oil leak that she was running out of time to sort) made an incongruous duo in front of the house.

The truck passed Tanner and Mats as it was pulling out of the gates. They parked up on the driveway and a wide smile was already growing on Tanner's face as he climbed out of his car.

"Where've you been?" Avery asked, but when he dragged the hem of his tee up to scrub the sweat from his brow, the sheen of his abs splintered the question on her lips and her voice sounded hoarse. "I thought you were supposed to be resting your shoulder until the surgery."

He shot her a wink that was cocky and irresistible in equal damn proportions. "Legs take work, too, Stretch. Especially when they're as fine as mine."

Mats threw an eye roll that matched Avery's to perfection and they shared a muted smile.

"What d'you think?" Tanner asked, leaning in to peer through the passenger window of the Jeep. "Do you like it?"

"It's great. Nice color." It was tough to concentrate on the car with Tanner wandering back and forth in front of her, his hair dark and damp and his shirt plastered to his chest. When it came to admiring bodywork, the Jeep took second place.

Avery held the keys and signed paperwork out to Tanner as Arlo sauntered out of the front door to join them. "You'll need these."

Tanner reached for the docket. "I'll take this but you'll want to keep the keys."

They dangled from Avery's fingers as her eyebrows raised. "Why would I need them?"

"It's your car, Stretch." He rubbed his hands together. "Open it up so we can see inside."

A cold swirl of misgiving began to grow in her gut and Avery heard Arlo let out a snort behind her.

"Don't be ridiculous." Confusion sharpened the glare that she sent Tanner's way. "I have a car. I don't need another one."

"No, you have a heap of junk." Tanner eyed the Honda. "It might have been a car once—now it's just an assortment of parts. And that oil leak's staining my drive."

Avery couldn't bring herself even to glance at Arlo—the indignation, the tension, the outright dismay, built steadily layer on layer until she could barely contain the storm. Biting down on it all, she struggled to keep her voice calm. "It serves a purpose. I don't need anything newer."

"It's not always about the need. Sometimes it's fun to have new stuff." His grin dimmed a little. "If you're emotionally attached to your old one, you don't have to get rid of it. We can . . . um, store it somewhere? Or—"

"Turn it into a garden sculpture?" Arlo suggested.

"It's not that." Avery wished they weren't having this conversation in front of an audience; she wasn't sure how long she'd be able to keep this under control. "Look, Tanner. We've talked about this. I don't want you to spend your money on me. I don't need expensive gifts—I can take care of myself. A hoodie is one thing. I even let the purse go. But this . . ."

Tanner's grin flashed huge again. "Be honest, Stretch. You love that purse."

She floundered a little then because, yes, she loved her purse. But a purse wasn't a car.

Avery dragged in a shaky breath because she didn't want to crush him, but she needed to put a stop to this now, once and for all. "You can't just buy someone a car on a whim."

"Think you'll find you can when you're a super-successful and somewhat hot professional sports player," Tanner smirked. "It was pretty easy really."

"I have money myself—I could buy a new car if I needed one." She made another stab at getting him to see sense.

"You did need one and didn't buy it, so I've done it for you." He wasn't even pretending to be apologetic. "As long as you like it and wouldn't prefer a different one, it's all done now."

Avery had regrets over telling him about her damn car troubles at the wedding. "But you—"

"Oh, give it a rest, you two, for Chrissake," Arlo grumbled. "If you don't want the Jeep, Boo, I'll have it."

Tanner just laughed. "You chose the Tesla. I'd have bought you a Jeep if you wanted one." He turned to head for the house, throwing one last comment over his shoulder as he went. "Call it an early birthday present or a late Christmas gift—whatever you like. I've missed a few. Sorry I didn't wrap it."

Mats gave her a sympathetic look of understanding and followed Tanner inside. Avery turned her back on whatever expression she might have found on Arlo's face—she didn't want to see it. Her hands clenching and releasing by her sides, she stared blindly at the Jeep with her emotions in freefall, wondering why she ached so much for the things that money couldn't buy.

And in the heat of the sun, with an unfamiliar set of keys in her hand, the years fell away and Avery was once again the pampered high school princess with everything she could have wanted and nothing she needed.

Chapter 34
Tanner

"We've met before," said Sam, giving Arlo a chin lift when they all pulled up by the park at the same time. His grin was as broad and easy as ever but it didn't linger as he gripped Mats's hand instead and tumbled straight into conversation with the big guy.

A group had already gathered over the far side of the large open space, and Tanner spotted Avery chatting with Bel, Drew, Leo, and Gemma as they got nearer. She glanced over but made no move to stand up. He'd been so excited to get the Jeep delivered but he already knew from the cold shoulder she was giving him that he'd made another misstep. Driven half by the fear that his days of extravagant spending could be limited and half by Johnnie's overheard words at the wedding, he'd forgotten what his mom had told him.

"It's not love if you have to buy it."

Maybe she had a point. It was certainly proving difficult to spoil his friends and family these days. Sam seemed more delighted that he'd agreed to the game of softball than he was at having any of his bar bills paid, and Avery had shown a quieter pleasure in his offer to come pick up some furniture with her than she had at the arrival of the Jeep. When would he fucking learn?

"So, about this boat—" Arlo prompted, slumping onto the grass.

OK, so maybe not all his friends . . .

Sam snorted behind a hand. "You're thinking of buying a boat? Have you forgotten you get sick as a dog on anything bigger than a surfboard?"

Tanner pulled a face. "Dude, when you throw up solidly for seven hours on a deep-sea fishing trip *someone* booked as a special treat, you don't forget that shit easily."

"None of us who were there have forgotten it either," Kash admitted with a wince. It had been his twenty-fifth birthday present from Sam—and no one could say it wasn't at least a memorable way to celebrate.

"Just because you two have the stomachs of Vikings, there's no need to pick on us sensitive types," Tanner said, rubbing his hand over a phantom cramp in his abdomen.

"So, no boat then, huh?" Arlo scowled.

"It's not sounding likely." Lips quirking briefly, Mats ran his gaze over their surroundings.

Another small group of ten sat close by, laughing together with the ease of old friends. Covering the formalities for anyone who hadn't yet met, Kash stepped forward to introduce Roman and Elenie Martinez, Milo and Caitlyn Walker, Dougie Taggart and his fiancée Summer, Thea and Luke, and Jackson and Leah. Tanner greeted the police chief and his wife with particular interest.

"Hey, Sunshine!" Sam swept Leah into an extravagant hug.

"I've told you not to call me that," grunted Jackson, dragging his girlfriend away with a muscled forearm and the barest glimmer of a smile.

Leah pushed a dark curl out of her face. "How's work, Avery? Have you settled in at the farmhouse now?"

"Feet right under the table, aren't they, Boo?" Arlo said lightly.

"Don't be a dick," Tanner muttered, elbowing him none too gently in the side.

"It's going well—thanks to all the pieces Jackson's asked for!" Avery ignored them both, her face brightening as she wrapped her arms around bent knees. "And the workshop is perfect for what I need, although I'm hoping Luke will be able to start my rebuild soon."

As much as that thought unsettled Tanner, he was thrilled for her that Jackson was steering work in Avery's direction.

"The farmhouse was a state when they bought it but Jax saw the potential. I could only smell the damp! The difference between then and now is amazing." Leah rested her cheek against Jackson's arm and Tanner saw his fingers flex on her waist.

"It was a fun project," was all Jackson said in response, although he looked pleased.

"Decided what you're going to do about renting or buying?" Sam asked Tanner with the quirk of an eyebrow.

"I'm seriously tempted to buy it. I'll talk the finances over with Arlo while he's here." It would give him another reason to get up to speed on his financial position.

"Why don't we all sit down together?" Sam suggested. "That way I can answer any questions that crop up."

"Great idea. Let's do it." Tanner found his attention wandering as he spotted the opportunity to tease Bel out from the group while Avery chatted with Leah about her digital art.

"I need your advice because I keep fucking up," he admitted quietly, close to Bel's ear, and she heard him out as he explained his misjudgment with the Jeep. "I wasn't trying to be flash. I didn't think it'd come off like I was being high-handed. But her car's on its last legs and I want her to be safe."

Bel's eyes glittered when Tanner finished. "You haven't fucked up—yet. You're just not playing the right game for Avery. She's not interested in your money, Ace Face."

He was finally beginning to realize that. "I just want her to have nice things. Everyone likes nice things."

"They do—and by all means keep on with the expensive gifts. Avery needs to learn to accept stuff that's freely given as much as you need to remember that gift-giving is a love language best backed up with something else." Bel squeezed his arm. "She's had nice things before and they didn't mean squat. Her dad will still throw money at a problem if she catches him at the right moment, but the one thing he's never given her is his time." The no-nonsense look in her eyes told Tanner he needed to listen up. "What Ave needs most is someone who's there. Someone to lean on. Her parents let her down over and over. She needs a partner who'll put her first, even if she tells herself she doesn't want one."

His throat felt thick. "I can do that."

"I don't doubt it, pumpkin." Bel bumped his shoulder with hers. "In fact, I'm counting on it. The problem will be getting Avery to believe it, too."

They were interrupted by Tanner's phone vibrating in his pocket, and when he fished it out, the caller ID had a kink settling between his eyebrows. He shot a quick sideways glance toward Avery and said to Bel, "Back in a minute—I'm just going to take this."

The mystery of what his old coach might be ringing for was solved as soon as he swiped to answer.

"Hello, gorgeous."

It wasn't his ex-coach.

"Mrs. Jenner." Tanner found himself stuttering over the name. "Why—uh, what a surprise."

Why the fuck are you ringing me? was what he had been about to say. *And why ring me from your husband's phone?*

There was a throaty chuckle from the other end. "*Mrs. Jenner*—really? You're still going with that?"

"Um . . ." Christ, this was awkward. He'd never have answered if he'd thought it was her. "What do you want?" Tanner avoided her question, turning away from the gathering of people and rubbing the back of his neck as he spoke into his cell.

"Maybe I just missed your voice," she offered, and the inappropriate suggestion made his toes curl with discomfort.

"I'm with friends so I can't talk," he said gruffly, making one hundred percent sure not to say "I can't talk now." He didn't want to leave her any reason to call again.

Bethany Jenner acted as if she hadn't heard him. "I don't know if you've heard but my husband and I are separating."

Not fucking fast enough that you couldn't borrow his phone! Tanner broke out in a sweat to think of his number being the last one dialed on the handset.

"Perhaps I could come and visit you sometime soon?" she pressed. "I'd like to see where you're based now."

Her willful ignorance of his lack of interest pissed him off. Filled with relief to finally be able to speak freely without risk of reprisals, Tanner cleared his throat. "No, I don't think so. And I'd rather you didn't call me again. I don't want this. Not now, not at all, Mrs. Jenner. Please respect that."

Hanging up without waiting for a reply, he blew out a breath which tremored at the edges. His skin itching like he'd brushed through poison ivy, his shoulders hunched, Tanner rejoined the group to find everyone in the middle of a friendly argument.

"We're not playing softball," Bel said with unshakable conviction. "You've got the Pine Springs High golden boy of baseball over there"—she jabbed a finger in the direction of Roman Martinez—"and the hand-eye coordination king right here." This time Bel's elbow hit Tanner in the gut, before she fixed Mats with a steely eye. "And Bigfoot doesn't look like he'd be too shabby with a bat either. I'm not spending my afternoon watching a ball soar seventy feet over my head while I stand in the outfield like a vertically challenged goof."

Shoving Bethany Jenner and her unwelcome persistence to the back of his mind, Tanner summoned an empty smile. Bel's point was valid, although she'd overestimated his current threat. "You're forgetting I'd have to play left-handed," he pointed out. "I'll be more of a hindrance than a help to anyone."

When Avery gave him a keen look as she lifted her hair from the back of her neck and pulled it into a ponytail, Tanner wondered what she could read on his face.

"Just like our early college days before you cut and ran," said Arlo, lying back on the grass with a grin. "Rooming together was like majoring in distractions, with a minor in keeping you out of trouble."

Already agitated, his words needled Tanner. The way Arlo reminisced sometimes, he felt like they'd lived different realities. He'd bust his gut to get noticed by the right people in his first year of college. Already bruised from his near miss with the high school accident and feeling unworthy enough, he'd kept his head down and his nose clean. There'd been no trouble.

On edge and rattled, Tanner popped his knuckles one at a time and wished he could have five minutes in Avery's company to recalibrate. Even with all their ups and downs, *she* was the place of calm that he craved. Despite Bel and Sam still talking across her, she continued to study him and Tanner knew some of that desperation showed on his face. Avery's chin tilted upward, her blue eyes widening as their temperature slowly changed from spring lake coolness to the warmth of summer rain. And that was all it took.

As he met her gaze, Tanner dragged in a long, deep breath, then let it escape, and every word that Bethany Jenner—and Arlo—had spoken became as insignificant as a singular blade of grass beneath his feet.

Chapter 35
Avery

In the end, they settled on kickball, roped in some nearby teenagers who were happy to lend their soccer ball, divided up the teams, and the match got started.

Tanner, on the opposing team and fielding way out by the fence, seemed to have recovered his equilibrium. He'd been thrown off his stride earlier and, although Avery was still brooding, the ruffled self-doubt in his eyes had disturbed her. He was usually better at hiding his insecurities; it was an uncomfortable reminder that he still had them.

Although he'd swiftly buried them again.

Bouncing on his toes with a grin, he caught Avery's gaze, pointing at her with double index fingers and executing a pantomime slash across his own throat as Kash stepped up to the plate.

"Charming," said Bel next to her, and mimed stabbing Tanner in the heart, making him throw back his head and laugh.

Leo appeared on Avery's other side. "How're things?" he asked.

"Well, I was doing alright until some stupid kids egged my car last night," Avery grumbled, sliding her arm around his waist and resting her head on his shoulder.

"Tell him about the texts," Bel prompted, keeping her eyes focused on Kash with steely concentration.

Intercepting the mournful look Gemma sent them from center field, Avery stepped away from Leo with a sigh and unlocked her phone. "Yeah, it's been a great week in general. I've had some more shitty messages." She showed Leo her screen, pulling up the last text she'd received.

Unknown:

If people saw you how I see you, they'd run a mile.

Bel's mouth set in a hard line. "Gutless asswipe."

"That's fucked up." Leo's eyes went to Tanner. "Have you shown him yet?"

Avery shrugged, keeping her voice low. "Haven't really had the chance."

"You should—he'd want to know. And maybe talk to Chief Martinez," Leo suggested with a jerk of his head toward the rangy form of the police chief.

"I think that's overkill at the moment," she said, trying to downplay how much it was bothering her. She'd grown to loathe the sound of her notifications, would have left her phone in a drawer if it weren't for her mom.

Bel scowled. "I don't. I've told you to take screenshots and block the number. But any more messages and I agree with Leo."

"In other news, Tanner bought me a Jeep." Avery attempted to change the subject. "It turned up at his house yesterday and he just handed me the keys." The car was still parked on his drive at the moment because she couldn't bring herself to take ownership of it.

Bel's attention flicked back to the game. "What a jerk."

Avery nearly agreed, until she noticed Bel was laughing.

Leo sniggered. "I guess when you're paid as much as he is, a car is small change. It's not the huge gesture it would be to someone else. Money and fame can switch people up, Ave."

"I mean, yes, I get that. And Tanner deserves his success. In some ways, it's changed him for the better. Being able to provide for his mom was huge for him. And he seems solid, despite the celebrity lifestyle. Reliable, even. Maybe . . ." Her voice trailed away. She wasn't sure she could describe how Tanner made her feel. And she definitely wasn't sure she could trust it.

"He might be solid, but he never looks that steady," Leo huffed. "His fidgeting drives me nuts."

Bel's gaze was penetrating. "I think the steadiness is there when you know where to look for it. Not everyone in the public eye behaves like a jerk, Ave. I get the impression he'd be there for you if you needed it."

The thought sparked a resistant protest in the back of Avery's mind. "Maybe," she said again, the word weighted with doubt.

Poised on the edge of raw vulnerability, she wanted so badly to trust Tanner, liked him way too much to fall out with him. But the car was ridiculous. He had to see that! She wasn't some hanger-on who would settle for crumbs in a relationship as long as she was given a credit card to max out and a pat on the head. Avery told herself it didn't matter anyway. He wasn't offering her what she needed and she'd left the car keys on the table in his foyer, so that was that.

A trickle of sweat ran down her chest. Like most of the girls, Avery had chosen to play in her shorts and a bikini top. Half of the field lay in shade, the other half baked in the sun. Every now and then, the lightest thread of a breeze tugged on the highest branches of the trees, but closer to the ground it was still and heavy. The muggy air felt oppressive and a band of dark cloud was gathering in the distance.

Shit. She'd forgotten to check the weather. Avery hoped any summer storm would hold off until after she'd gotten to her mom's house. She hadn't had time to deal with the gutters yet.

Across the field, Tanner stripped off his damp tee and tucked it into the waistband of his shorts. His tattoos were a blend of ink at this distance, his muscles a single, undefined slab. He'd pulled on a baseball cap to shield his eyes. She imagined the ends of his hair were stuck in a sweaty mess against the pillar of his neck, and her stomach swooped. It was frustrating that she couldn't see for sure.

Thea Martinez, also on the fielding team, caught her watching him. She followed Avery's gaze, then swung back to her with a grin and made a big show of wiping her brow. Leah intercepted the action and giggled. Flushing, Avery turned to watch Sam take his kick and then it was her turn.

"Hold up, Boo," yelled Arlo from second base. "I'm just gonna switch with One-Armed Waldo to give him a break. We need to look after our weakest links."

"I could out-throw you if I still had the sling." Tanner flipped him off. "Stay where you are and take notes, asshole."

It was satisfying when she got her foot behind a poor delivery from Drew and managed to boot the ball into left field. Scudding once over the crispy grass, it was scooped up in the outfield by Tanner as Avery rounded first base and took a chance on second with Arlo tracking her moves. Sam, on third, headed for home just as Tanner released the ball like a rocket with his left hand. It hit Arlo so hard between the shoulder blades that he pitched forward, face first, into the dirt.

"Damn, maybe you were right—I was aiming for Sam!" Tanner shouted from the outfield. "I'll do better next time."

Arlo clambered to his hands and knees as he fought to get his breath back. A smear of dirt spread across his chin; his shirt was filthy. Kash jogged over to check he was OK.

When Sam dropped down to retie his laces, Avery could see his shoulders shaking. Tanner took off his cap to ruffle his hair and replaced it, facing backward. He was whistling as he sauntered back out toward the fence.

The game halted until Arlo was upright again. He held up his hand when he was ready to play on and one of the teenagers stepped up to the plate. His kick flew straight at Drew, who snatched it easily out of the air, leaving Avery only able to jog to third. It was the closest she'd been to Tanner since the game started. When their eyes met, a sinful smile spread over his lips.

"Serves him right for talking so much shit," he said, giving her a slow wink that she felt in her midriff.

And Avery couldn't stop the laugh that bubbled in her throat.

* * *

They were finishing up when the first drops of rain fell. Avery gave another quick glance up at the sky.

"I'm gonna cut and run, guys," she said to no one in particular, since Bel had already told her she was going home with Drew. "I need to get going."

Tanner threw his car keys at Mats. "I'll come help, Stretch."

That stopped her in her tracks. "You'll what?" Avery blinked at him.

"You're going to your mom's house to sort out her gutters, right?" Tanner said, dragging his t-shirt on over his head. "I'll give you a hand."

"With the gutters?"

"If that's what you need." He smiled softly and fell into place by her side.

"Because you know all about the issues with mulch." She was struggling even more to deconstruct this offer than his purchase of the damn Jeep.

"No, Stretch." And the patience in Tanner's voice took a grip on her throat. "Because you might want another pair of hands and I'd like to provide them."

The rain was coming harder already and Bel gave her a shove. "Take the help, Avery. You don't have to do everything on your own."

Tanner jerked his chin. "What she said."

So, with a last searching look to check he wasn't going to change his mind, Avery nodded. "OK. Let's go."

And the heavens opened as they jogged to her car.

Her mom rang Avery's cellphone twice on their drive to her house. The first time, Avery let it go to voicemail, but when it rang again, Tanner plucked her phone from the center console.

"May I?" he asked.

"Sure."

"Mrs. Delgado?" His voice was reassuringly steady as the rain battered against the windshield. "I'm Tanner and I'm answering Avery's phone for her because she's driving. We're on our way over to you right now." He paused to listen to her mom's reply. "We'll check it out as soon as we get there. I'm sure it'll be an easy fix, so don't worry. And a bit of rain will be good for your yard—we haven't had much recently, have we?"

He chatted freely with her for the next five minutes, telling her about their game in the park and somehow managing to avoid any of the pitfalls that usually triggered her mom into a full-on meltdown—mentions of the past, non-existent friends, or plans for going out anywhere.

"Thank you," Avery said when he eventually hung up.

Tanner just shrugged. "It was a phone call, Stretch. I've done more impressive things."

Pulling up outside her mom's house, the gutter issue was immediately obvious and Avery kicked herself for not making it a priority before now. With the rain already filling them to the brim at various points along the front of the house, mini cascades of water tumbled over the vinyl edges, splashing onto the stoop and cutting muddy rivers through the flower beds on either side.

They had to dodge a waterfall above the front door to even get inside.

Avery's mom waited for them with wringing hands, dredging up turbulent memories of other times when she had been this close to spiraling.

"The damp's going to come into the house, I know it is," her mother said breathlessly. "Then there'll be mold and mildew and I don't know how to get rid of it."

"It's not been long enough for that." Avery kept her voice calm, burying the worry and guilt that twisted in her stomach. "And I won't let the gutters get this bad again."

"We'll take care of it, Mrs. Delgado," Tanner added with a smile that was all radiance in the darkened kitchen.

"Maybe you could make us some coffee for when we're done?" Avery prompted, knowing her mom would be better with something to keep her busy. "It shouldn't take too long."

There was a ladder out back in the shed and they gathered gloves, a bucket, and a bamboo stake—"For the bits we can't reach easily," suggested Tanner.

"At least it's only this side that's blocked," he said as he propped the ladder up at the front of the house. "Good job there aren't any trees at the back."

The rain continued to pound down, water dripping from the end of Avery's ponytail and running in rivulets beneath the collar of the shirt she'd pulled on. Tanner's t-shirt was saturated, his hair plastered to his head, but he chatted as if they were on their way to Diner 43 for breakfast—casual and unconcerned. Right up until she went to climb the ladder.

"Not happening, Stretch. Move aside," he growled.

"Absolutely not. Your doctor would kill you."

"I'm not planning to hang by my arm." He refused to give way. "I'm just hooking out leaves and my legs'll take most of the strain."

"That makes no sense," she argued. "You hate heights and I don't mind them. Plus if I foot the ladder with you up top, the weight balance is out of whack. It's not as safe."

"So who would have steadied it for you if you came on your own?" Tanner raised an eyebrow. "I can't see your mom offering."

He'd got her there. And he used Avery's momentary struggle for a reply to nudge her out of the way.

"I've done a crate stack challenge," Tanner muttered to himself as he climbed. "I'm a sporting god with nerves of steel. I've got this."

"Is it true if you have to tell yourself you have?" Even under the circumstances, she had to smile as she handed him the bucket and positioned herself on the lowest rung of the ladder.

The muscles of his arms were corded and taut—very distracting, in fact. But there was also a tremor in Tanner's beefy thighs and his eyebrows formed a solid ridge. With rain slicking his legs and muddy water running from the bend of his elbow, he began to pull great fistfuls of sodden leaves from the vinyl piping.

"Nowhere I'd rather be, Stretch." Tanner forced the words out through gritted teeth. "Just a regular weekday evening for me. I'm always climbing ladders. The higher the better, I say." His knuckles on the top rung were white.

Thunder rolled in the distance and Avery blinked droplets from her lashes, her stomach flip-flopping like a boat pitching on a wave, as Tanner's outline blurred.

He could buy anything he wanted, hire anyone he needed to do a job like this. But Tanner Stone, NHL star, was balanced at the top of a ladder in the middle of a fucking rainstorm—hating every single second of it because he was scared of heights—all because he wanted to help her. Because he didn't want her to have to manage alone.

Her ribs felt like they were squeezing her lungs.

"You still there?" he called down. "Just checking you haven't gone off and left me."

"I'm here," Avery said and her voice was husky. "Right here. I've got you."

They moved the ladder in steady increments, clearing the gutters and tipping out the waste into a pile that she could dispose of in better weather. The collected water began to flow freely the further they went and the cascade above the front door trickled to a halt as Tanner managed to reconnect the downspout.

By the time they'd finished, there wasn't an inch of either of them that wasn't filthy or drenched. Mostly, they were both. It was impossible to believe they'd been playing kickball in the park just over an hour ago.

Avery's mom had a pot of coffee ready in the kitchen once they'd cleared up, with folded towels on the chairs for them to sit on and more to wrap around their shoulders. She beamed at Tanner like he was a visiting deity, despite the unpleasant aroma of stale debris wafting from his clothes. Avery secretly suspected she was looking at him the same way.

And throughout the twenty minutes they sat and chatted, before the cold finally got to them both and they couldn't stay any longer, Avery's mom didn't mention her father once.

Chapter 36
Tanner

"There are some benefits to driving a heap of junk," Avery said, and she had to force the joke out through chattering teeth as they pulled up in front of Tanner's house. "We'd have ruined your seats and you'd never get the stink out."

He acknowledged the truth of that with a low laugh. "A shower wouldn't hurt, that's for sure." She gave him a long look and there was something in her eyes that had Tanner's heart rate kicking up. A hesitant softness that pressed down on his chest and left him cupping a delicate handful of hope as he said, "Want to come in, Stretch?"

The moment unfolded into a lifetime, then finally, as another shudder gripped her, Avery nodded. "I guess hot water sounds pretty good right now."

Before she could change her mind, Tanner jogged around to her side of the car, pulling open the door just as she undid her seatbelt. They headed into the house and straight up the stairs to his room; there was no sign of Arlo or Mats. He'd take a guess that they'd ended up at the Barrel after the kickball game and, as Tanner turned on the shower in his en suite, he was grateful for the privacy.

"Get your clothes off and climb in," he told Avery, who was hugging the doorway, the hem of her shirt dripping onto the tiles. The blue of her eyes was luminous, even through the sodden strands of her bangs which were plastered to her brow, and he found it hard to look away.

She tugged her lower lip between her teeth and Tanner stifled a groan.

"Should be hot enough now," he rasped and left her to it. Stepping back into his bedroom, he braced his arms on the dresser and hung his head.

How did she do this to him every time? His whole body ached for her; his chest burned beneath icy skin. She had him twisted in so many knots that he was stretched taut. Something had to give.

Dragging his t-shirt over his head and peeling his shorts and boxers off his legs, Tanner dropped the whole grungy, stinking armful into a heap on the floor.

When he returned to the bathroom and slid open the glass door, Avery let out a muffled gasp.

"Tell me to get out if you don't want this," he said huskily as he stepped inside. The instant warmth was blissful but he held himself tense and kept his distance. "I will stick to any rules you like, do anything you want me to do—you only have to say the word." Tanner swallowed roughly. "But if there's a chance to be near you, I won't turn it down."

His knees went weak with relief at the greedy gaze that Avery traced over his jaw, his shoulders, his abdomen—and lower. It stoked the lick of heat that was just beginning to overcome the chill in his belly and spread like molten gold through his bones.

"The whole 'one night' thing has been working pretty well for us." He clenched his hands by his thighs. "How do you feel about seeing if 'rainy day sex' can beat 'wedding sex'?"

His breath strangled in his throat as he waited for her answer.

A multitude of thoughts spun behind Avery's eyes and he couldn't read a single damn one of them until desire reduced all the others to ash. Snared by the flames, Tanner let himself burn as she parted her lips and breathed, "I guess that . . . could . . . work."

The shower was a huge one so he took a step closer. Water ran in steaming rivers down her neck and over her breasts, her hair clinging like copper seaweed to her collarbones. He brushed it off one shoulder with his thumb.

"So fucking pretty." He was talking to himself more than her.

"Yes," Avery agreed. "So fucking pretty." She laid her hand over the center of his chest and Tanner's heart thumped extra hard beneath her touch.

"You take that back, Stretch," he grumbled, less than half his attention on what he was saying—all of the rest on the tantalizing movement of her fingers. "I'm a stud. Handsome, hunky, hot. A snack. I've got the DMs to prove it."

"A snack?" Avery's hand traveled lower. Her eyelashes were damp semicircles, her freckles glistening under the spray.

"A snack." His voice grated and broke as she followed the happy trail from his navel to his dick and closed her fingers around him. Tanner dragged in a tortured breath. "Fuck . . ."

"Good enough to eat?" Her eyes flicked up to his face and down again. The question had the muscles feathering on either side of his jaw. When Avery slid her grip along the length of his erection, he felt the pull throughout his body.

Tanner grunted, his weight rocking on his heels until his back was pressed to the tiles. She pumped him again, her gaze intently fixed on the movement of her fingers. He ached in her grasp, his hips moving of their own volition. Heat rose so sharply through his breastbone, he expected the falling water to evaporate on his skin.

"Come here." Reaching for Avery, he bit off a fractured curse when she lowered herself to her knees instead. For one mortifying moment, Tanner thought he might blow immediately. He reached above her hand to grip the head of his cock and squeezed for a couple of seconds to regain control. Her eyes, flicking up to his, nearly had him losing it all over again. He ground his teeth. "Fuck, baby."

Parting her lips, Avery ran her tongue along the underside of his shaft, her lashes fluttering as the water streamed down the sides of her face. He jerked in her grasp and groaned. When she closed her mouth around him, Tanner reached blindly for her hair, winding his fingers into the drenched strands and clasping them tight. The vibrations of her moan buzzed against his dick.

Avery braced a pale hand on one of his thighs and took him deeper. Between her mouth and her grip, she had him losing his mind. The look of her on her knees in front of him made his legs shake, his heart pound. He wanted to drop to his own knees and worship her instead, but Tanner couldn't bring himself to pull away from her touch.

He hit the back of her throat and swore. She only picked up the pace, torturing him on and on, winding him tighter and tighter. A shiver sparked in his groin, building steadily and spreading to the base of his spine. Hanging on by a thread, he lasted until she raised her eyes to his face again, holding his burning gaze with her own. Color and light painted the insides of his eyelids when he exploded in blissful streams on Avery's tongue. The universe collapsed in on itself, leaving only her touch and her warmth to hold him steady.

Tanner wasn't sure he could speak.

He pulled her to her feet with trembling hands beneath her armpits and tugged her to his chest. Kissing her temple over and over, he closed his eyes against the falling spray. They stood like that for several long minutes while his heart steadied.

"I need to wash my hair." Avery was the one to draw back in the end. She smiled up at him and it was still a struggle to form words.

When she reached for the shampoo bottle, Tanner took it from her fingers, squeezing a small swirl into the palm of one hand. Guiding her around 180 degrees, he soaped her hair into a lather with silent reverence, washed it off, and repeated with conditioner. That she stood so still and let him take care of her had a prickle starting up behind Tanner's nose, like a sneeze building that never came.

After a quick wash of his own hair, he shut off the shower and slid open the door. Wrapping Avery up in a huge towel first, he grabbed another one for himself.

"Will you stay?" Tanner asked and his voice didn't sound like his own. "Please don't go."

Avery studied his reflection in the mirror for a few seconds. Maybe it would make it easier for her to let him down gently if she wasn't looking directly at him. Tanner flexed his fingers.

"OK," she said at last, and he might have picked her up and spun her around if there had been space to do it.

Not trusting himself to speak, he found her a clean t-shirt and a new toothbrush instead. They brushed their teeth side by side in silence before he collected their clothes and ran them down to the washer, taking the stairs in twos back up to his bedroom, as if he were on a bungee cord.

When he still hadn't said anything more by the time he threw back the covers and crawled into bed, Avery's smile was slipping.

"Is something wrong?" She ran jerky fingers through her damp hair, the hem of his t-shirt dancing against her thighs.

"Babe . . . no." How could she think that? Tanner sat upright, forearms on bent knees. "I just—" He cleared his throat. "I'm feeling pretty lucky right now."

Avery smiled then, and there was relief in the curve of her lips as she chose to take his words as a general statement. "You've worked hard for all your luck. You deserve it."

With a lazy grin to hide how much her words mauled at his chest, he tried to keep the atmosphere light. "You wanna see if some of that luck could rub off on you?"

She sniggered. "Maybe I will, hotshot. Let me find a band and do something with my hair first." Avery looked around for her shorts before realizing he'd taken them.

"Try my nightstand. There are some in there." Happy just to watch her, Tanner flopped onto his back, folding his arms behind his head.

She tugged open the drawer and her hand paused halfway to reaching inside. "Why do you have so many? There's like a hundred in here."

He rolled over to snake his fingers past hers into the far corner. "The most important one is here." When Tanner drew his hand back, he was holding a faded and frayed single strand of elastic in his palm. "The real source of all my good fortune. This is my lucky talisman."

"Is that—?" Avery poked at the dangling scrap.

"Yeah. The last hair tie you gave me when I left Pine Springs." Tanner curled his hand around it. "I lost the first two. They shredded and broke on my sneakers so I never put this one on my shoe. I wore it around my wrist for years. It kept me calm and more focused when I fiddled with it. I was devastated when it snapped, but I carried it in my pocket instead and bought myself a dozen more packs—as similar to yours as I could find. I still have phases when I like to wear one for a while." Tanner ran his fingers through the damp strands of his hair. "During the season, I keep your broken one in my locker. It's my most prized possession because, however much money I earn, it's irreplaceable."

Avery's lips had parted. Her eyes fixed on the broken elastic.

"Turns out, you were irreplaceable too, Stretch. I couldn't find anyone else who makes me feel the way you do." He reached for her hand and chose to take the leap he'd cautioned himself against. There was no hiding it for him anymore. "It's always been you for me."

She looked at him then, terror battling disbelief in the searing blue of her irises. Tanner swallowed, his grip tightening as he prayed she wouldn't run for the hills.

"You're probably not ready to hear it, but I love you so fucking much. I'll give you everything, if you'll let me." The words spilled from him, unexpected, unplanned, and his heart pounded like he'd just finished a bag skate. "I want us for real. For good. And I know you don't do relationships. I know you find it hard to trust. But I've wanted you for fifteen years now so I'm all in, and I swear I won't hurt you. Just give me a chance, please. Don't leave me with only a hair tie this time."

He couldn't breathe as he waited for her to say something. Anything.

Chapter 37
Avery

He'd kept her hairband for all these years. Worn one around his wrist to remind him of her. Avery knew it was true because how many times had she seen Tanner's fingers go to his wrist, as if drawn there by habit? Over and over, she'd seen him pluck at something nonexistent but never wondered why.

The intangible bond had remained in place even when she'd been left behind. It meant more than she could explain.

Could she trust him, though? Would her heart be safe if she handed it over? Avery didn't know and it scared her to death.

But for the first time ever, she wanted to try.

Summoning all her courage to take a step forward, she climbed onto the mattress and slid her arms around Tanner's neck. Her damp hair was forgotten. Everything outside of this room, this bed, had ceased to exist.

"I love that a small part of me shared your journey." Avery pressed her forehead to his, and the words had to force their way out of her narrowed throat. "I didn't expect any of this and I don't know what to do about it but you're a really hard person to resist, Ace Face."

She dipped her finger into the crater of his dimple, ran her thumb over the wide sweep of his smile. If she could have licked the joy from his face without looking like a freak, she'd have done it in a heartbeat. Tanner's delight was a tangible, tactile presence and it wrapped her in its protective warmth, making her believe that this could all be OK.

"Come here." The command was a growl and he lifted her bodily to sit astride his lap, torso to torso. His arms were steel bands, his thighs taut beneath her butt as he fisted his hands in the t-shirt he'd given her. "And get this off. I need to thank my girlfriend for her shower services. I'm competitive like that."

"Well, *girlfriend* might be a bit presumptuous . . ." Panic threatened to overtake the steady rising of desire in Avery's belly as she felt the word cleave its way into her chest.

"I heard something about me being hard to resist." Tanner leaned in the minute he had her naked, his mouth dipping to one breast as he dragged her nipple between his lips and rolled it with his tongue. "Maybe we could give it a try."

He bit lightly, soothed, and bit again. Sucking on her until Avery felt the tug right through to her core, her muscles clenching, stomach tight. Tanner pulled away with a pop and she groaned at the loss of contact, reaching to draw him back again and losing track of what he was saying.

". . . if it feels like less pressure, we could treat this as a trial run. Just an extended period of one nights." He murmured his contentment against her skin as his mouth swept to her other breast and began to repeat the torture.

"You're very persuasive," Avery breathed, gripping his hair hard enough that it forced a groan from his lips. There was no way she could muster an argument right now with his erection twitching beneath her, pressing upward in search of her center.

But Tanner made no move to shift her. His teasing continued as if he was unaffected by the way she ground against his hardness while his chest exposed the lie, rising and falling with increased ferocity.

"I've already come in your mouth and I need you again," he admitted. "I want to feel you around my dick but I'm gonna take my time and taste you first. It's only fair."

The hitch in his voice sent tremors tingling through Avery's veins, and her fingers, a stark contrast to his dark ink, bit into the taut, smooth skin of his biceps.

"Get yourself up here." Tanner tugged on her thighs.

"Up where?"

"I think you know." His smile was rakish, his grip bruising as he lay back and slid her toward his chest. "I want you over my face."

Fuck.

Everything tightened inside her at that. Avery wanted it, too. Needed his mouth on her, his tongue in her. Fingers, too.

She crawled further up his body and gripped the headboard. With a groan she felt right in her sternum, Tanner dragged her into position, his huge hands cradling her hips. And he ate her as if he was starved. Knees quivering, knuckles white, Avery closed her eyes against the rasp of his tongue and the heat of his lips.

There was no vanilla in this intimacy. It was raw and basic and . . . so . . . damn . . . good.

She was his plaything. He, her tormentor. She felt like a queen being cherished and adored. The power balance worked every way around.

Avery found herself hoping his fingers bruised her thighs, wanted Tanner's mark on her to match how he'd inked her onto his skin. She was a breathless, pleading mess as he teased and tasted, bathing her with his tongue.

"No more," she begged him eventually. "I swear I can't—" Her body shuddered, tumbling toward a finish line he kept moving.

When Tanner's thumb slid past his mouth and over her clit, the pressure sent her flying over the edge. He slipped his fingers deep inside her, his satisfaction rumbling from his chest, and Avery clenched around him as she came, her orgasm submerging her like a breaking wave.

Slumped against the headboard, she laid her forehead on folded arms. Tanner lifted her off his face as easily as if she were made of feathers, gliding her back down his body until she was level with the fierce grin on his lips.

"You're my favorite flavor. My favorite everything." His erection pressed like steel between her legs but he just held her to his chest.

Counting the beats of his heart beneath her ear as her breathing began to steady, Avery considered the terrifying, wonderful possibility of seeing if she could love Tanner Stone.

Chapter 38
Tanner

He stirred in the middle of the night. The covers were on the floor, pushed away by overheated legs—either his or hers. When he felt for her and couldn't find her, Tanner cracked open one eye, his chest hollowing at the thought that she'd left him again.

But she hadn't.

Avery lay sprawled, more than a foot away, her red hair a tangled mess on the pillow, his t-shirt bunched around her hips. Fuck, he loved her in his clothes.

He loved her more against his body.

Tanner reached out, slid one hand between her thighs to cup her ass and dragged her toward him. His other arm slipped beneath her neck to pull her head onto his shoulder.

Better. He grunted with satisfaction, caveman-contented now his woman was closer and everything in him thrilling at the rightness of having her there. Avery snuggled into the new position with a breathy murmur but didn't wake. Core to core, their legs entwined. Tanner's fingers crept under her top until his palm was spread across her bare back. The comfort of her skin tipped him back into sleep and he fell, surrounded by the scent of her in his nose and the feel of her everywhere.

* * *

"Jeez, tone it down a little, would ya?" groused Arlo, digging into a bowl of cornflakes. "Feeling a bit nauseated over here from the hyper vibes."

Tanner hung an arm around Arlo's shoulders and squeezed, happiness oozing from his pores. "Can't help it, bro. I told my girl I love her and she loves me back."

He was buzzing, bursting out of his skin, and he couldn't keep the grin off his face as he walked into the utility room to turn the dial on the dryer so that Avery would be able to put her clothes on from yesterday once it was done. Somehow, in the ten years without her, he'd missed her without properly knowing it. Felt her absence without recognizing it. Needed her, even when he thought he had it all.

"She said that, did she?" Arlo's mouth ticked up at one corner when Tanner returned to the kitchen. "She loves you?"

"Not quite those words. I think I surprised her."

"Hmm." Arlo made a dismissive noise in his throat.

"What?" Tanner laughed and stretched, running his hands through his hair. He wondered if Avery would like pancakes.

"Not used to hearing the L-word coming from your mouth, that's all. You're not usually one for big feelings." Arlo shoveled in another spoonful of cereal.

"This is different, man. Avery's not like anyone else. She's my endgame. This is it."

"And you're not worried she's too smart for you? Or she might just be after the free cars and the lifestyle?" Arlo eyed him with speculation.

"I'm not stupid. And I love that she's clever and capable and so fucking together." Tanner shoved his hands into the pockets of his jeans, smile sliding a little. "Avery couldn't be less impressed by my money—she's no gold digger."

"I'm sure you're right." Crossing to the sink, Arlo rinsed his empty bowl under the faucet. "I'm not trying to put doubts in your mind but I don't want you hurt either. Not so soon after Lily doing a number on you."

Tanner slouched against the kitchen counter. "Lily was different. I didn't have these kinds of feelings for her. And Avery isn't Lily. She couldn't be less about the trappings. Look how she was with the Jeep."

The sound of Avery and Mats talking in the foyer floated into the kitchen.

"Just be careful, man. That's all I'm saying." Arlo shrugged. "I've known you forever and I've got your back."

Avery's smile was tentative when she appeared in the doorway. Dressed in a pair of Tanner's sports shorts pulled tight at the waist and the same t-shirt she'd slept in, she hung back, glancing between him and Arlo, and looking as if she still wasn't quite sure how to play this. The novelty of her presence, fresh from his bed, was a strike to Tanner's windpipe and he wished they were alone.

Fuck Arlo. If she wanted it, he'd give her the world.

"Hungry?" he asked gruffly, crossing the kitchen to twist a red strand of her hair between finger and thumb. His heart thumped an almost painful beat beneath his ribs.

"D'you know what? I am." Avery's shoulders relaxed and she gave him a private smile.

They made pancakes together, taking it in turns with Mats to cook, flip, and eat so everyone got to eat them hot. Arlo brought his laptop to the table, logging in to check his emails. He managed to chat and work with a multi-tasking focus Tanner envied.

"What're you up to today?" Avery asked.

"Mats is joining me and the Rapids guys for a workout this morning," said Tanner. "I've got to see the team doc after that and then there's a meeting this afternoon. Couple of them might come back for a swim later. How about you?"

She swallowed a mouthful. "I need to push on with Jackson's chairs."

Arlo looked up from his screen. "Yeah, some of us have to put in the hours to earn the money, dude. We can't all be taking the summer to chill out."

Mats grunted. "I'll remember I'm supposed to be chilling when I'm sweating buckets in the gym."

"Let's treat ourselves tonight and get takeout," Tanner suggested, licking a smear of syrup from his thumb. "Whoever's still here can join us. We'll have an evening by the pool."

"It'll be like that party at the Colonnade in Boston when we all rocked up to the rooftop pool." Arlo's face took on an expression of wicked reminiscence. "Although I only remember the first part of it. The drink was flowing . . . and the ladies were—" Mats's elbow to the back of his head had him changing what he was going to say. "—lovely."

Tanner reached for Avery's fingers and gave her a quick apologetic squeeze, but any disclaimer he might have made was drowned out by the sound of someone buzzing the front gate.

It turned out to be a package for Avery—a white shallow box, capital letters scrawled on the side.

"You're getting mail here now?" Arlo's eyebrows lifted.

"Just a few work supplies. Makes more sense than carting the heavy ones from home, but I don't remember ordering anything this small," Avery said, frowning at the package in Tanner's hands. "Got any scissors?"

"Nope." He butchered the cardboard with a single rip and a printed card flew out, falling to the floor.

Scooping it up, Avery read aloud: "'Transform a loved one into a snuggly friend you can take anywhere.'"

They both eyed the gaping box with curiosity.

Nestled in a bed of packing peanuts was a soft toy. A doll or a pillow? Tanner wasn't sure. The plush figure-shaped item, just over a foot in length, wore a printed black corset and fishnet tights. Its oversized head, beneath a sweep of red hair, had been personalized with a photograph of Avery's face.

"Well, that's . . . weird." Tanner fought a laugh.

When Avery reached into the box to lift it out, the smile slid from his lips.

"What the fuck—" he said.

There was a torn piece of paper pinned to the doll's fabric chest, and on it were three scrawled words: "He's playing you."

Avery drew in a tight breath and Tanner didn't hear her release it. Her fingers pinched at her lower lip.

Peering over her shoulder, Arlo asked, "Who's 'he'? What does it mean?"

Her eyes, when she raised them to Tanner's, seemed to tumble with a thousand thoughts all vying for position. "I think it's you," she said.

"What? Why?" Tanner frowned, at a loss trying to make any sense of the weird delivery or its message.

"I don't know why." Avery shoved the doll back into the box. "I've had a bunch of really nasty text messages recently and my social media is getting trolled. There have been more nuisance deliveries, too, and my car got egged the other night. I thought it was just kids." She looked around at the three of them, blinking rapidly. "But there's no reason for kids to send something like this, right?"

Taking the package from her hands and throwing it onto the kitchen island, Tanner paced the kitchen floor. "Definitely not kids. This feels personal, Stretch. And I wish you'd told me about the other messages." It stuck in his throat that she hadn't.

"Man, that's messed up," said Mats, studying the written note.

"The postmark's illegible." Arlo squinted at the packaging and rubbed a finger over the ink.

"You should put the whole thing in a bag, just in case the police can lift any prints from it," Mats suggested.

"The police—really?" Arlo looked doubtful. "It could just be a prank."

Fury solidified like a ball of ice in Tanner's gut as he took in the pallor of Avery's face. "Prank or not, when someone sends you a creepy fucking doll in the post with an anonymous message, you take it to the police."

Chapter 39
Avery

Within the hour, she was pushing through the door of Pine Springs police station with that "creepy fucking doll" under her arm and a fuming wall of vibrating muscle beside her.

"Hey, Maggie." Avery summoned a smile for the woman at the reception desk. Another familiar face in town. "How's things?"

"All good, thanks honey. And you?" Maggie peered over the top of her glasses and nodded a silent greeting at Tanner.

"Not so bad." Her usual answer, even when she was sinking. "Is the chief in?"

"He is. Go on through, past the other desks. His office is in the back."

There was a full show of law enforcement bodies in the open-plan office as they threaded between the desks. Officers Kristina Forsberg and Liam Morgan, deep in conversation, were both reading something from the same monitor. Dougie Taggart, talking into his phone, had a mug of coffee by his elbow and what looked like a bowl of oatmeal in his hand. He gave them a friendly chin lift as they passed, waving them onward with his spoon.

Avery paused by a door that stood ajar and was about to knock when it opened.

"Oops, sorry." Elenie Dax—no, Elenie *Martinez* now—apologized as they came nose to nose. Her gray eyes flashed from Avery to Tanner and back again, a quick smile on her lips.

Although she no longer worked there, Elenie had been a fixture at Diner 43 for years before she'd met and married the chief. Avery thought she must have had the patience of a saint to put up with Aunt Delia for that long. She certainly looked happier these days.

"Kickball was fun yesterday!" Elenie said. "We should make it a regular thing."

Avery and Tanner made polite noises, both too preoccupied to chat freely, and Elenie quickly picked up on the vibe. She made a sideways step with a cheery "See you soon" and kept on walking.

This time Avery did tap on the door.

"Come in."

Roman Martinez stood up behind his desk with the unhurried grace of a panther, shadow-dark from his boots to his graphite gray tactical pants and polo shirt.

"Twice in two days," he said and his imperceptible smile drained none of the intensity from his eyes. "Is this a social call, or . . ." Martinez left the question hanging.

"This came in the mail for me today." Avery held out the box.

His feet shifting on the worn linoleum floor, Tanner added, "She's been getting nuisance deliveries recently, but this one is nasty."

The chief's gaze sharpened and he reached immediately to pluck a pair of latex gloves from a box on his desk, snapping them on before he took the package from her hands. His expression flickered when he opened the torn flap of the cardboard box and Avery winced. She hadn't looked at the doll again; it seemed even more disturbing at second glance.

The print of her face—a copy of a photo from her website—gazed vacuously upward, the corset and fishnets mortifyingly sleazy on the undersized body. Martinez lifted it out, carefully turned it over, and examined the rest of the packaging. He tapped a finger on the note pinned to the doll's chest.

"What does this mean?" he asked.

Clearing her throat, Avery perched on the edge of one of the chairs facing the chief's desk, taking in the mess of paperwork rather than meeting his stare. "I think it's referring to Tanner."

In her peripheral vision, she saw Tanner's hands clench into fists.

"You two are together now?" Pulling out his own chair, Martinez sat down again.

"Yes, we are," Tanner said firmly while Avery stumbled over the blunt question. She found his eyes on her when she turned her head and a disconcerted tingle fizzed beneath her skin.

He made everything seem so simple.

"How was it delivered?" Martinez asked as he studied the address label and smeared date stamp.

"Courier service," said Tanner. He gave the chief the details of the company. "To my house."

Martinez plucked the printed card from the packaging and read: "'Transform a loved one into a snuggly friend you can take anywhere.'" His eyebrows pinching in a "not on your life" kind of way, he examined both sides of the flyer intently. "Tell me about the other deliveries."

"I've had abusive text messages as well and online trolling. A fake Facebook account," Avery said once the chief had made a note of all the weird shit she'd received through the mail. "And my car was egged overnight before the kickball game, although that might not be related."

Tanner began to pace the small office, flicking the catch on his watch with barely restrained agitation.

"Show me the messages." When the chief held out his hand, she dragged her phone from her pocket. He flicked through the texts, his mouth tightening as he read them.

"There were more," she said. "I deleted the first few." As precisely as she could, Avery recited their content.

"You blocked the number?" Martinez asked.

She nodded. "They all seem to come from different numbers. I don't recognize any of them."

"Send me screenshots of these." The chief reeled off his email address without breaking eye contact and Avery wished she had something more, anything more, she could tell him. Roman Martinez made a person want to spill all their secrets.

"Have you posted anything about your relationship online?"

"No," they replied together.

"Yet the package was delivered to your house, Tanner? Not Avery's." The chief made it more of a statement than a question, but they both nodded anyway. Martinez tapped his fingers on the outside of the box. "Interesting."

Taking a large, clear bag from one of his desk drawers, the chief pushed the package inside and tugged off the gloves. He picked up a pen, the hint of a resolute smile transforming his serious face. Both comforting and threatening, it said: *I will help you deal with this and you'd better believe I'll kick some ass while I do it.*

A fraction of the tension eased from Avery's belly.

Elenie was a lucky woman.

"We will speak with the courier company and the makers of this horror"—Martinez eyed the doll with distaste—"and try to trace who placed the order. But first, let's start at the beginning and draw up a list of everyone who knows that the two of you are seeing each other and that you, Avery, are working from Tanner's house."

* * *

When they left the station, she insisted that Tanner stick to his schedule, saying she could easily make her own way home. He took some persuading but eventually peeled off with obvious reluctance to head for his car. Avery almost called him back before he reached it.

The overwhelming urge to lean on him scared her.

Instead, firing off a quick message to Leo, Avery walked down Main Street and opened the door of Diner 43.

There was only one free booth; every other seat in the place was full. Claiming it quickly, Avery threw a smile at Hazel and Otto sitting a few tables along and raised a hand to wave at Florence Martinez, who was having a late breakfast with her mother at the other end of the diner. The scent of bacon and coffee in the air was both familiar and comforting.

She took out her phone to double-check for messages from her mom, surprised to see there was nothing for once, and it went a little way toward settling some of the anxiety in her chest. Avery sent her a text to ask if all was well after the storm, checked her email, and was just marveling over the fact that there seemed to be not one but two teenagers serving customers—how the hell had Aunt Delia managed that?—when Leo walked in with Gemma.

"Hey, Ave. Look who I found on the way," he said, sliding into the booth opposite her.

Avery examined Gemma closely. "You OK, Gem? You look rough."

"Allergies." Gemma sniffled, rummaging in her purse for a Kleenex. "My eyes are itching like crazy. I've come out to pick up some drops."

They placed their order with one of the young waitresses.

"What's up, Ave?" Leo questioned with a shrewd glance. "You sounded weird on the phone."

Playing with the charm on her necklace, Avery sighed. "I'm not going to lie, it's been a lot so far. And it's not even lunchtime."

She told them about the doll and her visit to the police station. Both Gemma and Leo wore matching expressions of concern by the time she'd finished.

"That's insane!" Gemma said. "Why would someone do that?"

"I have no idea," Avery admitted.

"Who would want to warn you away from Tanner?" Leo frowned. "Has he got any suggestions?"

"He's clueless, too," she said. "And really pissed."

"Is he worth it, Ave?" Leo asked, his elbows on the table and a frown narrowing his eyes. "I mean, I like the guy—don't get me wrong—but my loyalty's with you. Do you trust that he *isn't* playing you?"

And that was the million-dollar question.

It'd been rolling around in Avery's head all morning.

"I trust him," she said finally, and the alien words shimmered with promise on her tongue. "I don't think he would hurt me."

"Wow." Leo sat back in his seat, a broad grin sliding over his lips. "Never thought I'd hear that coming from you. Look how you've grown."

"Shut up, Grandpa." Avery threw a packet of sugar at him but couldn't stop the answering smile that twitched at the corners of her mouth. "Or I'll find another friend who isn't such a smartass."

Feigning hurt, Leo clutched his chest. "I'm not just any friend. I'm your oldest, dearest friend from school. You'll never get rid of me. I'm irreplaceable."

Gemma sniffled into her Kleenex, her eyes stormy. "Get you, Avery, with the devotion of not one but two men to choose from. Must be nice."

"It's not like that," Leo said and his teasing ground to an awkward halt. Avery had to hold back another sigh.

Gemma was going to ruin their friendship if she didn't tread carefully. He'd been careful with her feelings so far, but Avery could tell Leo's patience was wearing thin. After the morning she'd had, her own was pretty nonexistent.

When the diner door opened and closed, she glanced over automatically, looking for a distraction from the sudden tension at their table. And she found it.

The new customer turned out to be the well-dressed but unexpected figure of the ex-mayor of Pine Springs.

Her father.

"I'll be right back." Sliding out from the booth, Avery spared a second to hope that Gemma and Leo might clear the air between them in her absence.

Her dad only noticed her when Avery touched his arm. "Hey. What are you doing here?" she asked.

"Avery." He bent to kiss her cheek with an affable smile, his "public persona" twinkle in his eyes. "Just stopped by for a matcha latte, if that's not expecting too much from Delia's little establishment."

"I meant in Pine Springs."

"I'm meeting up with some old council friends." Her father checked his watch. "Soon, in fact."

"We could have had breakfast." *If you'd told me you'd be in town*, she thought, with the familiar bristle of being not only unimportant, but practically invisible, too.

"I don't do breakfast." Her father patted his flat stomach with fake self-deprecation. "It takes resolve to stay toned when you reach my age. You'll see."

He was in amazing shape and he knew it. Maybe there *was* someone new in her dad's life who was currently appreciating his trim physique, but Avery found she just didn't care—if only he'd stop making other people deal with the collateral fallout of his lies.

"Yes, you prefer evening meetups, don't you?" she said sharply. "Only, last time, you forgot to warn me that I was providing your cover. How did that end up working out for you?"

Her father's eyebrows kinked in a perfect arc of surprise. "Sorry? I'm not sure—"

"Oh, please." With no patience or respect for his duplicity, Avery's temper began to fray at the edges. "I don't want details or explanations. Just leave me out of your messed-up games. I've paid enough and my life is complicated already—not that you'd care. I have a stalker to deal with. I don't need anything more on my plate."

A huff of air escaped from her dad's nostrils and a muscle jumped in his cheek. "You've always been a magnet for drama."

"What the hell . . . ?" Avery seethed at his dismissive tone. "I've just told you I have a stalker and your response is that I've brought it on myself?"

"I was just saying—"

"Well, don't!" she bit out. "Maybe try 'God, that must be awful' or 'Tell me more' or 'Are you OK?' Then I might think you give a shit."

"Look, I don't have time for this right now. You're obviously overwrought." Her father held up placating hands. "I want to hear more—of course I do. But I'm meeting people as I said, and I don't want to be late."

"Of course not," Avery said, stepping back, her fingernails digging into her palms. "Heaven forbid I hold you up."

"I'll settle your check when I pay for my drink." He moved toward the counter and placed his order with one of the teenagers.

"There's no need. I'm with Leo and Gemma. We've got it." She wanted absolutely nothing from him.

"I insist. Your breakfasts are on me." It was a standard Joseph Delgado gesture. Off-hand and lacking in depth. He was already turning away from Avery with an air of relief when he made the mistake of adding, "Shout if you need anything."

The steam hissed in her midriff, locked down tight under firm pressure but ready to blow.

"And you'll do what?" she asked coldly.

"Hmm?" Her father glanced over his shoulder with a quizzical frown.

"If I shout, what will you do?" After rephrasing her question with careful emphasis on each abrupt syllable, Avery didn't wait for his answer. "Only you have a habit of saying things that mean nothing, so it's hard to see how shouting would benefit me."

"Darling . . ." Her dad attempted to use the weary endearment as a sweetener. A beleaguered expression hovered on his face, as if he was bracing himself once more for her to make a mountain out of a molehill.

"I can't even count the number of times when I've called you over the years needing your help—a girl does need her dad now and then. But you've never actually come through for me." Avery realized it didn't even hurt anymore. She was just bitterly and blazingly angry. "Mom and I went through hell and you weren't there. You packed your bags and left us to it."

"That's what happens when you get divorced, Avery. Your mother had to learn to stand on her own two feet and so did you. You were nearly an adult."

"I was seventeen and you were selfish and unkind. You cauterized your marriage and moved on so fast that you left us floundering." The furious words spilled without thought, long overdue. "I needed you then and I've needed you since."

Her father tapped his foot, his eyes wandering around the diner rather than holding Avery's gaze. "This isn't really the place . . ."

"No, you're right. But you brought it on with your 'Shout if you need anything.'" She let out a snort of disdain. "You can't blame me for pointing out that I've learned not to waste my breath."

The waitress set her dad's drink on the counter and he closed his fingers around the takeout cup, his mouth a clamped line.

"I've been there for you," he contended. "You seem to forget it was my intervention that kept you in school after your spot of careless driving."

And there it was. The obligatory mention of the only time she'd ever gotten into trouble. She was surprised her father hadn't brought it up until now.

Avery took a step closer, more than ready to lay that particular ghost to rest. "It was your intervention that gave you the opportunity to scout out your next family."

Behind the counter, Delia rifled noisily through a selection of coffee syrups.

With an icy smile, Avery continued, "And it wasn't me, that night in the school parking lot. It was Tanner."

"I beg your pardon?" Her father stilled.

"Tanner hit the floodlight and smashed up the cars. It was a freak accident like I said, but his truck skidded in the rain, not mine. His scholarship was at risk because Ottoline had put him on his last chance, so I stepped in."

"He had drugs in his locker—"

"Tyson Dax put them there," Avery said, "because Tanner made him look stupid when he stood up for me."

He'd had her back then and he still had it now. The teenager who'd protected her honor at school had turned into the man scared of heights who'd climb a ladder in the rain with a fucked-up shoulder so she didn't have to. Because she needed help.

A frown pinched her father's forehead. "And you never told us any of this because . . . ?"

"I felt guilty. I thought the crash and my lie was the catalyst that turned our lives on their heads. But actually it was you. You and Ottoline. And it seems some things don't change."

Damn, it felt good to get it off her chest.

"Take a long, hard look at yourself, Dad—or you're going to end up alone, wishing someone was around to answer *your* calls."

Avery watched him through narrowed eyes as he smoothed his perfectly styled hair, opened his mouth and closed it again. It was rare to see Joseph Delgado lost for words, but she didn't wait for him to rally.

Reaching over to tap his watch, she said, "I'm glad we had this chat, but I guess you'd better run if you don't want to be late. And I need to get back to my friends."

Her father cleared his throat a couple times. "Yes, well, time is ticking so I'd better—" He gestured toward the door. "I'll call you." And he strode away just slow enough, she guessed, to convince himself he wasn't fleeing.

Avery jumped when Delia crashed a tray load of clean mugs down on the counter.

"I've been waiting a long time to hear you put that smarmy sonofabitch in his place," her aunt grunted. She eyed Avery with something that looked a little like respect. "All mouth and no trousers, he is. Your mom's better off without him. Tell her I'll be in touch."

"I will." With a shaky smile, Avery turned away to rejoin her friends.

"And he didn't settle your check so you still need to pay," Delia shouted after her.

Chapter 40
Tanner

His shoulder surgery was scheduled for ten days' time and Tanner felt the specter of potential retirement stalking his every move. He wasn't ready to hang up his skates just yet. But what if that choice was taken away?

He wanted to bask in the joy of finally making progress with Avery, but his current professional knife-edge and the ugliness of the personalized doll had temporarily taken the shine off things—although he was confident that Avery was in safe hands with Chief Martinez.

His mom rang as Tanner split from the Rapids' meeting and drove back to Pine Springs. Utterly unable to hold it all in and spin the positives as usual, he pulled over to the side of the road and offloaded his worries on her in a jumbled rush.

There was a pause on the other end of the line. "Why have you been keeping all this to yourself, sweetheart?" His mom's voice was coated in soft concern.

"It's up to me to look after you now. Not the other way around." Tanner closed gritty eyes and swallowed. "I don't want to let you down."

"You've never once let me down," his mother said firmly, "and I'm the parent here. You don't need to take care of me."

"But when Dad left and you were so ill—"

"You were a child, Tan! It was never your responsibility and I'm so sorry you felt it was." The warm sincerity in her words eased some of the pressure on his chest. "I'm so proud of everything you've done and everything you've achieved. We all are. But if you never pick up a hockey stick again, we'll be fine. What matters now is making sure that you're going to be fine, too."

He had to swallow hard before he could reply. "I love you, Mom."

"I love you too, honey. Always have, always will."

Tanner took a few moments after hanging up to collect himself and then continued on his way, a little steadier than before—a feeling that stayed with him until he strolled into Archer & Desai Realty Management almost an hour later with a renewed frown on his face.

"What happened to your window?" Tanner jerked his thumb at the ply boarding that covered one half of the shop frontage.

"Smashed overnight." Kash looked pissed but resigned. "Someone tried to jimmy open the back door too but they didn't get in. Hopefully something was caught on CCTV. Dougie Taggart's checking it out."

"There are better places to hit if you're after petty cash," grunted Sam. "We only ever keep the bare minimum for stamps or sugar."

"Not the first time, probably won't be the last." Kash gave a shrug and neither of them seemed keen to discuss it further.

"We've put together a financial proposal for the farmhouse." Sam pushed two sheets of paper across the desk. "I'll email them to you, but I thought you'd like to take a look. This one," he pointed, "is the rental agreement you've already signed, with add-on details for a short-term interest-free loan after three months for us to use as a down payment on another flip. The second sheet gives you the figures and fees for buying the house, if you decide to go that route."

Tanner dragged the paperwork nearer. "I'll talk it over with Arlo, but I've changed my mind about renting. I want to buy the place if my finances line up. I'll pin him down on the details while he's here."

He caught the glance Sam and Kash exchanged.

"What?" Tanner asked, turning his head from one to the other.

"Arlo told Kash you'd be better off saving your money." Sam eyed him shrewdly. "He said you got lucky in the early days, that you haven't got the focus or commitment to settle with the Rapids long term, and your surgery is going to tank your career anyway."

Tanner blinked, the information taking far longer than it should to hit him. It hurt like a kick to the gut when it did.

"I told him to fuck off," Kash added grimly.

Tanner cracked his knuckles and a spark began to smolder inside him as betrayal battled anger. "Look, I've not always made the best decisions, especially early on. I was immature. Maybe I didn't deserve the success."

But dammit, he'd worked hard. He'd never lacked commitment. Big cities had been a fun playground when he was younger and the money was a novelty, but at heart he'd stayed a small-town boy. He could turn his back on city life without a single regret—that was Arlo's preference, not his.

And his friend's lack of faith in Tanner's return to full strength was particularly painful while his own doubts ran rampant. Contrasting it with his mom's instant and unwavering support on the phone, Sam's solid friendship, and Avery's unshakable confidence in him, it was a shock to realize that Arlo had never had Tanner's back in the same way.

"Listen, bro." Sam leaned forward, elbows on the desk between them. His face was set in serious lines for once. "Not a single one of us makes sensible decisions when we're young, but you busted your ass to get where you are. And you've stayed loyal to that little punk since college because you're that kind of guy." His top lip curled. "It's not even him riding on your coattails I object to. But if he's going to talk shit about you while he does it, then I'm calling him out. And you need to open your eyes to what he's doing. The dude is a leech."

Sam's unapologetic honesty was a wake-up call. Tanner sat back as the memory of Arlo's actions over the last week cascaded through his mind, then even further back and further back . . . Arlo had always made him feel a little bit worse about himself. Less worthy. Less sure. Less everything. He'd been there in the background, telling Tanner how it was just pure fucking luck that had gotten him to where he was. And his words had tainted the endless hours Tanner had dedicated to practice, fitness, healthy eating.

It pissed him off that he'd listened.

"You thought you were lucky to have a friend like Arlo because Arlo told you so. But he's been the lucky one. Don't let him ruin this new start for you." Sam sat back and tapped his pen. "Avery thinks he's a dick, too. She'd have told you at some point if I didn't. I thought I'd save her this conversation."

Rubbing the back of his neck, Tanner reined in his scrambling thoughts. "Get the paperwork drawn up," he told Sam firmly. "I want that house and Arlo can go screw himself."

Fury dogged his footsteps back to the car and he slammed the door behind him as he climbed in.

He'd never doubted that Arlo had his best interests at heart. He felt stupid beyond belief to have put so much blind trust in him.

On impulse, Tanner leaned over to open the glovebox and pulled out the letter he'd received about the office rental space in

Boston. He'd shoved it there, meaning to either call them to check the details or ask Arlo for more information, but typically had done neither.

"Good morning, Pelham Property Services."

Tanner checked the name at the base of the letter. "I'd like to speak to Dan Woodley, please?"

"Mr. Woodley's out of the office right now," said the efficient-sounding woman on the other end of the line. "Can I help or take a message?"

"You might be able to help actually. I'm after some details on a rental contract."

"No problem at all. Who am I speaking with?"

He paused for a second. "Arlo Stebbings. I handle the finances for Tanner Stone and this letter has come through without the address of the business unit. I just wanted to double-check it for my records."

"Of course, Mr. Stebbings. I recognize your name. I know Dan's been handling your client's needs but that information will be easy to find." There was a pause which began to drag on for a while. Eventually, the woman came back, sounding less certain than before. "This is strange," she said slowly. "I might have to call you back after all. The letter and the contract don't seem to tie together—there must be an admin error on our part."

"What kind of error?" Tanner asked, drumming his fingers on the steering wheel.

"Well, the letter lists an office rental, but the contract details are for a new-build condo in Maine through our sister office. I don't know why that is without talking to Dan."

Tanner's nostrils flared and, in the rearview mirror, his eyes snapped with a dark intensity. He didn't want to set any alarm bells ringing just yet. "Ah, no, it's fine. Don't worry about it. Mr. Stone is investing in both, so it sounds like a clerical error. I'll call Dan on his cellphone. No need to pass on a message."

Ending the call, Tanner stared out through the windshield.

There was little sign of last night's storm. They'd woken to another stunning summer day that had gotten brighter and bluer as the hours ticked by. The clear, azure sky held the promise of a perfect poolside evening, in the company of good friends. But was it going to deliver? He wished he felt more confident.

Firing the engine, Tanner decided there was nothing for it but to end the day where it had begun and make one more stop on the way home.

Chapter 41

Avery

The first half of the evening was fun. Surrounded by music, mayhem, and laughter, Avery allowed herself to relax and embrace the madness. With Bel at her side and Tanner just across the room it was perfect.

Well, nearly perfect. Arlo was still being a dick whenever he was given the floorspace.

"I'll choose the tunes. Tanner's got the taste of a twelve-year-old girl. He's always liked crappy music." Arlo plugged his phone into a portable speaker and hit play.

Avery and Bel exchanged a shared look of distaste.

"That little shit is toxic." Mats moved pretty silently for such a big guy.

"So it's not just me who thinks so." Avery was relieved by that.

He grunted and took a swig from his beer bottle.

"You should talk to Tanner. He'd respect your opinion." Avery knew she'd have to if Mats didn't, and she was still struggling to manage her feelings when it came to the two of them. Torn between running in the opposite direction and wrapping herself around Tanner like ivy, she wasn't ready for any extra "girlfriend" responsibilities.

"Not my business," Mats said firmly.

"You're his friend."

The bulky giant gave her a soft smile. "They've been friends far longer."

Tilting her head up to meet his eye, Avery asked the question that had been troubling her ever since Arlo had swaggered into her temporary workshop. "Is he a friend though? I don't think so. Everything he says seems aimed at knocking Tanner down."

"There's definitely an unhealthy dynamic going on there," Bel said, shooting a glare across the room at Arlo. Avery knew that look—it was her "I see you" look.

And she agreed. Plus, there was something weird, as well as unhealthy, flashing between Tanner and Arlo tonight. The vibes were off. Tanner, in particular, seemed different. He was giving Arlo a wide berth where he could and Arlo had fixed him with more than one long, probing stare in return.

When Mats ran a blunt finger along the length of his scar, Avery felt quietly flattered that he was no longer hiding it from her. "I wouldn't be here if it wasn't for Tanner. He's my hero." He flushed as soon as the words left his mouth but he didn't take them back.

Avery's eyes heated as Tanner threw back his head across the room, laughing at something Sam had said. *Mine too*, she thought. And, for the first time that evening, she wished there were a few less people in the house. There were things she wanted to say to him.

The guys ordered Chinese takeout and had it delivered—so much food that when Tanner and Karl carried it into the kitchen Avery's jaw dropped.

"We're athletes." Cam, the Rapids defenseman, gave her a good-natured wink. "I can burn half of that off in my sleep."

"Where's the hot sauce?" asked Leo, opening and shutting kitchen cabinets. "I know for a fact that Ave won't have committed to takeout and not brought it with her."

"It's in my bag." Avery smiled at his accuracy.

"I'll grab it—your hands are full," offered Gemma, eying the pile of plates in Avery's hands.

It seemed oddly intimate knowing where everything was kept in this kitchen. Like they were showing their relationship off in front of his friends and her friends, dancing around each other as they reached for more plates, cutlery, and bowls. And Avery didn't know how she felt about that. There were so many things to get her head around. So little space to think.

In a wave of organized chaos, everyone helped themselves to the food.

"Is it socially acceptable to dive in face first?" Leo asked, rubbing his hands together.

"Only if someone records it for posterity," she answered dryly, bumping him out of the way to snag a serving spoon.

Glancing over, Avery found Tanner watching them. There was a flash of something hot and heavy in the twitch of his mouth, before the corners lifted into a smile.

"Got everything you need?" he asked her across the table. "There are spring rolls and spare ribs over here."

Avery held up her heaped plate with a grin. "Maybe later."

She drizzled a little hot sauce over her rice.

"What's with that?" Arlo jerked a thumb at the bottle, his mouth full. "Soy sauce not adventurous enough for you?"

"Try some!" urged Bel with a wicked look in her eye. "Avery's been addicted since her dad brought her a bottle back from a European trip."

Arlo read the label. "'Vampire Hunter.'"

"It's lethal," said Gemma, whipping it out of his hand. "I swear it's ninety percent garlic and the rest is all chilies. You won't like it."

"I'll pass. Sounds like you should keep your distance, too, dude," Arlo smirked at Tanner. "I think Boo's trying to give you a hint here."

"Luckily, I'm no vampire—I love garlic and chili. And I don't scare easy." Tanner turned his back on Arlo and caught Avery's eye with a grin as he reached to take the bottle from Gemma's fingers, ignoring her sound of protest. He attempted to pour a small amount on the side of his plate. "Damn—these things always come quicker than you think."

"Talking about your teenage love life again?" Arlo snickered.

"Nope," Tanner said over his shoulder as he wandered away, and he wasn't smiling anymore. "Your adult one."

Bel and Avery pulled a face at one another. It sounded like she might need to have the chat with him that Mats had suggested sooner rather than later. But not tonight. They both deserved to have a little fun—some time without anything heavy. She'd shelve this thing with Arlo—and the sinister doll, too—in the back of her mind for now.

When Bel and Drew settled at one end of the long table, Avery steered Gemma to the kitchen island. "Sit with me, Gem?"

"Oh, I was going to . . ." Gemma looked around for another chair nearer to Leo but came up empty.

"You feeling any better?" Avery asked.

She didn't look better. In fact, she looked rough. Gemma's eyes were strained and red-rimmed, and her plate held a meagre selection of food.

"Not really. I hate it when I get it this bad." Dropping onto a bar stool, Gemma nibbled half-heartedly on a spring roll. "Allergies are the pits."

As the boys joked raucously with each other, Gemma's eyes bounced back and forth around the table. Avery made a mental note to quiz Tanner on whether there were any single guys on the Rapids team. Gemma could do with a distraction—and unrequited love was no match for muscles and confidence . . .

"Sorry I made it all weird in the diner earlier," Gemma said, fidgeting on her stool. "Put it down to a rubbish night and painful sinuses. I was being a bitch."

"That's OK." Avery brushed it off but reached out to squeeze her arm. "You are going to have to lighten up on your Leo crush though. I know it sucks, but he's just not interested, Gem. He's been as kind about it as he can and you can't make him feel something he doesn't."

"I know. Bel said the same." They both watched Leo surreptitiously as he poured a light drizzle of Avery's sauce, dipped in an egg roll and bit it in half. With a flinch and a swallow, Gemma dragged her eyes away. "It's too late now though—I've already ruined things."

"You haven't. You'll see. Just give it time," Avery urged. "And Leo makes a great friend."

Blinking her itchy eyes, Gemma struggled against tears. With a sniff, she fixed a weak smile on her face and leaned in closer. "So, is it the real deal with you and Quadzilla?"

Avery snorted, relieved that Gemma was making an effort to shift her mood. "Please don't let him hear you call him that. He'll have it put on a t-shirt."

"Do you love him?"

The strip of crispy beef caught in Avery's throat and she had to take her time answering. Her eyes went straight to Tanner like mini homing devices. Sat between Mats and Cam, he was talking earnestly into Cam's ear, his shoulders twitching and jerking to emphasize whatever point he was making. A messy lock of sandy hair had flicked forward over one expressive eyebrow, his silver chain half in and half out of the neck of his tee.

Avery's cheeks flushed, and a pulse below her ear quivered. He could do that to her without even trying. And from the moment he'd climbed that ladder in the pouring rain to scoop the muck out of her mother's gutter just so she didn't have to, he'd stolen her heart, too.

She'd told herself that falling in love was the worst possible outcome. That love diminished you, made you too vulnerable. Handed over all the control to someone else. She'd expected it to feel scratchy, restrictive, suffocating. Like the end of the world.

And yet it didn't.

Somehow loving Tanner made everything better. It was amazing. She felt effervescent. Scared, but so alive. And it wasn't even a choice, just an inescapable truth. Avery could no sooner *not* love him than not breathe.

"I do," she said, after way too long a pause. "I do love him."

He caught her eye at that moment, his expression stilling like someone had pressed pause on his face. The room was both crowded and utterly empty. Avery was aware only of herself and Tanner and this knowledge they shared that she was his and he was hers. The unbreakable connection that had seeded in a school nurse's office and forged solid over a gifted hair tie.

Pushing to his feet, he skirted the table, a smile growing on his lips, that dimple deepening. When he reached the kitchen island, he looped his arms around Avery's waist and pulled her back against his solid chest, propping his chin on the top of her head. It was like being wrapped in the wings of a sexy angel: intimate, secure, safe. Yet terrifyingly risky.

Instead of pulling away, she concentrated on relaxing each muscle in turn, and her spine softened gradually against the heat of his body.

"Missed you over there," he rumbled in her ear, and a thrill rippled under Avery's skin.

Gemma slid off her stool. "D'you know what—I'm feeling awful," she said and her throat sounded hoarse. "I'm gonna go home and sleep it off."

"I'll keep my fingers crossed for lower pollen tomorrow," Avery called after her as Tanner pressed a kiss to her temple that held a world of promise for when they were alone again.

* * *

As it turned out, Gemma wasn't the only one who didn't feel right.

At first, Avery thought she might have eaten too much. As the evening rolled on and everyone took drinks out by the pool, she ignored the initial churn of her stomach because she was having far too good a time. Sam, Olli, and Arlo had challenged each other to a bellyflop competition and it was easy to put her discomfort down to sympathy pains to start with.

"You're nearly twice my weight. You can do better than that!" Arlo goaded as Olli climbed back out of the pool.

"You calling me fat?" The Rapids center clutched at his chest, feigning hurt.

Avery's giggle broke off as the first twisting cramp caught her by surprise.

"You OK?" Tanner's eyes swung to her face when he felt her fingers twitch in his hand.

"Yeah. Just a bit of stomach ache." She tried to work out if her period was due. "I'll be back in a minute."

As she reached the kitchen, her head started to spin and her eyes blurred. A clammy sweat broke out on the back of her neck. Swallowing against the nausea rising in her belly, Avery quickened her pace and she headed for the upstairs bathroom, wanting peace and privacy. Her knees hit the floor the moment she pushed through the doorway, and she was instantly and violently sick.

The retching felt like it lasted for ages though it probably didn't. She'd only just sat back, leaning against the shower screen, when Tanner appeared. His brows were tight with concern.

"You look rough." He ran a washcloth under the faucet and wrung it out. When he crouched before her and gently wiped her face, Avery frowned.

"You're a bit pale yourself." Her voice was croaky.

"Not sure I feel great either." He gave a pained smile. "And Leo says his stomach doesn't feel right. That damn restaurant is getting a one-star review."

A light sheen of sweat had broken out on his forehead.

"I'll be fine. I'm going to sit here a bit longer, but you should go sort yourself out." Avery's eyes tracked the moist swallow in Tanner's throat and his obvious discomfort kickstarted her own nausea.

He pushed to his feet. "I'll come check on you soon." He looked unwilling to leave for a moment but then grimaced, laying a hand over his abdomen. Ducking back out of the doorway, his footsteps sounded on the landing and faded as he disappeared into the en suite off his bedroom.

Thinking she'd message one of her friends to bring her up a glass of water, Avery tugged her phone from her pocket. The lock screen image was a picture of Bel with a jaunty pair of devil horns and flames added by a filter and an MMS notification covered her chin like a goatee. "6 photos," it read.

Avery opened the messages.

In the first photograph, she was coming out of the general store. In the second, she climbed from her car on the driveway at home. There was a shot of her pulling the curtains closed at night; one of her and Bel in the front yard; her and Leo coming out of

Diner 43. And the last photo showed Avery cleaning the egg from her car. Random movements of the past week cataloged in images.

A rush of blood pounded in her ears. The implicit threat behind the photographs pumped adrenaline into her poor, drained body like water through a sluice gate.

What the actual fuck?

Dizziness overcame Avery again and she dropped her phone to the floor with a groan. As chills crept up the back of her neck like ghostly fingers and her stomach cramped, she realized the sickness wasn't done with her yet.

The next hour was no fun at all. Sore and exhausted, she vomited until she had no more to bring up. Then she struggled to her feet and washed out her mouth.

She thought she'd had it rough, but when Avery finally felt up to checking on Tanner, propping herself up, jelly-legged, against the doorjamb, she found him so much worse.

"Can't stop . . . being . . . sick," he ground out, arms folded over the toilet bowl. "And I can't breathe . . . properly. Something's not right." And then his stomach emptied again, his shoulders shaking with vicious tremors. Laying a hand between his shoulder blades, Avery found his t-shirt wringing wet.

Alarm bells rang when Tanner heaved again and she realized his lips were blue around the edges.

"I'm getting Drew," she declared uneasily.

His only reply was another painful retch.

After that, things moved fast. Drew, switching from carefree guest to eagle-eyed medic with instant efficiency, was blunt and decisive.

"That's not your usual kind of food poisoning," he said grimly, reaching for his phone. "I think someone put something in the takeout. I'm calling an ambulance."

Chapter 42
Tanner

Tanner felt like crap. His stomach, scoured and empty, twisted and clenched like a wrung-out dish towel, but it was a slight improvement on the previous eighteen hours.

"I'm fine. I just want to get out of here now." He tried a winning smile, felt it come far less smoothly than usual, and the doctor's raised eyebrow showed her lack of conviction. Beneath the sheets, his right knee jiggled.

He was getting sick of these four walls already. His mom and Henry had visited at lunchtime while Avery got some rest, worry written large across their faces. Mats and Arlo had arrived shortly after. But it was Avery he wanted. Avery he needed. And Tanner hadn't drawn a proper breath until she'd returned and he could make sure she was OK. Now he wanted to take her home.

"You've been extremely lucky, Mr. Stone. You're fortunate you had a medic on hand who recognized the symptoms of poisoning and called for help."

At his bedside, Avery gripped his fingers tighter.

"Give me half an hour to write up the paperwork and you're good to go." The doctor glanced toward the doorway. "I'll send your friends through if you're feeling up to it."

When she left the room, Avery slumped on the edge of the bed, her cheek pressed to his biceps. The hot slide of a tear trickled over Tanner's skin and it wrecked him.

"Hey, you heard her. I'm fine. We were lucky."

"I was so scared," she whispered.

Bel peered around the door, Drew and Gemma following her into the room. She draped herself gently around Avery's neck.

"You OK, babe?" she asked.

Avery nodded and Tanner watched her throat bobble as she swallowed. She looked thoroughly shaken.

Dropping onto a small two-seater couch by the window, Drew crossed his feet at the ankle. "We thought you might need a ride home."

"Thanks, man. We're just waiting for the release." Tanner wasn't only grateful for the offer. "And thanks for the swift diagnosis. I owe you."

"All part of the job." Drew passed it off with a tight smile, far more serious than usual.

Bel's gaze took in the surroundings. "This is pretty swish but it's still a hospital. Let's get you out of here as soon as we can."

With just over a week until he'd be back for his shoulder surgery, Tanner had no desire to draw out the stay.

"I brought you this." Gemma handed him a huge, folded card with "Get Well Soon" emblazoned on the front, bedazzled with foil lettering, plastic gems, and glitter pen. She shrugged under everyone's scrutiny and scrubbed at puffy eyes. "When you teach five- and six-year-olds, there's always a lot of crafting stuff lying around."

"You look as rough as I do," said Tanner, and maybe it was a bit blunt, but she really did.

Gemma sniffed. "I've run out of eye drops."

"Didn't manage to get any yesterday?" Avery asked.

"I . . . No—" Gemma ducked her chin and searched her pockets for a Kleenex. "They were all out."

"How's Leo doing?" Tanner said, swinging his legs over the edge of the bed and stuffing his feet into his shoes.

"Bounced back, the little shit," Bel answered. "He thinks you're just making a big deal of it."

She was interrupted by the sudden arrival of Chief Martinez in the doorway. Gemma squeaked as he strode with lean grace into the room, nodding a general hello to everyone gathered inside.

"Thought I'd catch you before you left," he said. "Your blood and urine tests have come back and the toxin was identified as tetrahydrozoline." On the couch, Drew pulled himself upright. "We found it in the hot sauce, not the food. That's why only three of you were sick." Eyeing Tanner with sympathy, the chief's eyebrows formed solid ridges above charcoal-dark eyes. "You had it worst."

"Because the fucking stuff flooded my plate," he growled.

"Avery and Leo were a little more fortunate." Martinez grunted. "And I'm using that term in the loosest of senses. It was also a good thing the bottle was almost full—it made the contents more diluted."

"But it's my sauce, not Tanner's. That means someone we know got to it either in my house or in his." Avery's thoughts were turning slot-machine fast. Tanner could see it on her face as she picked up on the same thing that had screamed at him the moment the chief mentioned the hot sauce. Crackles of rage coursed through the nerves in Tanner's fingers and he clenched them tight.

Martinez ran a hand over the scruff on his jawline and the sliver of a fine scar moved beneath his fingers. "Yes. It was someone close to you."

"What is tetrahydro-doodah anyway?" asked Bel. "And where can you get it?"

Drew opened his mouth to answer, a fierce expression on his face that Tanner hadn't seen there before, but the chief beat him to it.

"It's not actually that difficult," he said, his mouth set in a hard line, "because it's commonly found in over-the-counter eye drops."

"I didn't mean it!" Wild-eyed and white as a sheet, Gemma wrung her hands as the words burst from her lips. "It was stupid and I didn't think it through. I just did it . . . and then it was too late to undo it!"

Tanner surged to his feet.

"Gem—?" The name was a broken question on Avery's lips. "I don't understand . . ."

"I didn't know it would make you that sick, I swear." Gemma shredded the Kleenex in her fist. "Google said—"

"Oh, yeah, it was definitely the fault of the search engine," snapped Bel, her tiny fists clenched as tight as her teeth. "What the fuck, Gem?!"

Letting the drama play out without intervention, Roman Martinez folded his arms across his chest, every inch of him alert as he made a subtle shift to block the door.

"Why would you do this?" Avery said, her freckles standing out in stark relief on her cheekbones, and Tanner instinctively reached for her hand.

"I was . . . jealous." Backing up against the window, Gemma clutched at the sill behind her back, her reddened eyes spilling with tears. "I watched Tanner at the Bach Bash and he was gone for you before we got to the second day. It was that easy. And you didn't even want a relationship!"

"I—" Avery gripped Tanner's fingers so tightly that her nails bit into his skin, her face gray with the same shock he felt in his battered and tender gut.

"All I wanted was Leo. I've wanted him for such a long time." Gemma's whisper held a desperate edge. "We have things in common. We're both teachers. We enjoy walking. We like music and dogs. And it still isn't enough."

"Can you not hear how screwed up that is?" Bel's eyes flashed, melanite dark. "You put Tanner in the hospital because Leo doesn't mind a hike and is a sucker for a spaniel. That's not the foundation for a relationship, Gemma. It's not even the bare bones of a Tinder profile!"

"You three are all so tight, so close together." Gemma sagged, her shoulders heaving as she wept. "I've always been the one tagging along behind, making out I don't mind being the afterthought."

"It's not like that." Avery's protest was baffled.

"You've read it all wrong." Bel backed her up.

With a slow shake of her head, Gemma pushed a stray curl off her damp cheek. "When it wasn't the Avery and Leo Show, it was you two, thick as thieves and completely exclusive."

"That's just not true," Bel said, frustration in the pinched clamp of her mouth.

Martinez intervened, authority coiling around him like wisps of smoke. "And the doll? Will we find you sent that too?" The chief's voice was encased in ice.

Tanner swore. *Fuck, he'd forgotten about the hooker doll!*

Everyone's gaze swung back to Gemma, like a joyless parody of a tennis match.

"No! That wasn't me—I swear! I only . . ." She trailed off into sobs.

"You only tried to poison us." Avery's completion of the sentence was hollow and Tanner tugged her against his chest in a fruitless attempt to take some of her pain. "Did you send the photographs?" she asked.

His eyes narrowed.

"What photographs?" He and Martinez spoke at the same time.

Gemma wrung her hands together. "I don't know anything about photographs!"

That makes two of us. Tanner ground his teeth.

"I'll email them to you," Avery told the chief, exhaustion coating her words. "I got them last night, when I was sick."

Martinez gave her a nod and stepped forward to take hold of Gemma's arm. "I'm going to have to ask you to come with me to the station."

"I'm sorry. I'm so sorry." It was almost impossible to make out the words as Gemma buried her face in her hands, rivers of snot running from her nose.

And the chief guided her firmly out of the door, leaving a devastated silence behind them in the hospital room.

Chapter 43

Avery

Things were quiet over the next couple of days. Too quiet. It gave Avery way too much time to think.

She was on edge, withdrawn. She couldn't focus. Couldn't stop her mind from running away with her as her trust took another hammering. She examined every conversation she'd had with Gemma over the years from multiple angles. Obsessing over whether she should have handled things differently. Spotted some kind of sign of her friend's jealousy.

It was driving her mad.

"You have to let it go. This is about Gemma, not you," Bel said, as they stood in their kitchen making coffee. "Real queens fix each other's crowns. They don't put eye drops in the hot sauce."

"Again with the bumper-sticker wisdom." Avery chuckled despite herself, but she wrapped her arms around Bel's waist and soaked in some of her strength. "I love you, babe. You're the realest queen I've ever seen."

"Takes one to know one." Bel planted a kiss on the side of her face.

And it helped a little. The advice and the kiss.

Work helped, too. With Jackson keen to have the commissions he'd requested as soon as she could turn them around, Avery didn't want to fall too far behind. So she got stuck in and kept herself busy, turning up her music and losing herself in the physical work of replacing the webbing on a vintage couch. A couple of phone calls with Luke helped to get the plans for her own workshop rolling.

When Mats packed up to head home, she took a brief break to give him a hug filled with genuine affection.

"You take care, you hear?" he said gruffly into her ear.

"Promise." Avery smiled in response. "And you come back soon."

If only Arlo would follow suit and go too, but he was staying for now, making noises about finding somewhere to rent in Pine Springs for a while, although things remained stilted between him and Tanner.

Even more concerning, Tanner wasn't himself. Avery knew he was stressed about the surgery—and they were both stressed about the unresolved stalking—but there seemed to be more going on, even though he never passed on an opportunity to touch or kiss her, and he'd listened patiently to her complicated mess of feelings over Gemma's betrayal. But there was definitely something guarded about him, something he wasn't saying, which was so unusual she didn't know how to break through his reserve. He was distracted. And it made Avery worry.

What if the note on the doll was right? What if Tanner was less invested now the thrill of the chase was over?

Giving herself a grim shake, Avery resolved to give this dating experiment more than a forty-eight-hour try. Especially considering the forty-eight hours in question.

She was just grabbing a cold drink from the fridge in the farmhouse kitchen when Tanner returned from taking Mats to the airport.

"All OK?" she asked.

"Yeah, I dropped him outside. He checked the flight on his phone and it's all running to time." Tanner flicked the switch on the coffee machine, fidgety fingers tapping instantly on the counter. "Want one?"

Shaking her head, Avery held up her glass of juice and his smile flashed briefly before disappearing. Her chest tightened. "Is something wrong?"

Turning to face her, his mouth tugged down at one corner. "Stretch—"

And then Arlo slouched into the kitchen with crappy timing and no cares, wrenching open the door of the freezer to peer inside. "Yes! Butter pecan. The Holy Grail of ice cream." He took his time rooting through the kitchen drawers in search of a spoon to dish up his unsuitable lunch, before looking from Tanner to Avery and back again. "Don't let me interrupt."

Tanner's eyes darkened but he said nothing, just turned back to the coffee machine and finished making his drink. It was a relief when Arlo's phone rang and he took it outside by the pool, just close enough to the doors that they could still hear the murmur of his half of the conversation.

"I'm just on edge, Ave." Tanner blew out a long breath. "I wish I had a guarantee of what's going to happen after the surgery. I haven't missed a training camp in almost ten years and I hate the idea of the season starting without me. I want to be involved, I want to get back on the ice. I'm not ready for it all to be over."

For once, it wasn't hard to be the one to go to him. Avery's feet took her across the kitchen before she'd even thought about it and she wrapped her arms around his waist. Setting his steaming coffee to one side, Tanner drew her closer. He smelled of body wash and fresh air.

"We never know what's around the corner," she said, looking up at him. "If you'd have told me before the Bach Bash I'd be here now, in your kitchen giving you a pep talk, I'd never have believed it." His dimple made an appearance and she felt a little of the tension leave his frame. "Whatever happens with your shoulder, you'll find something that lights you up. You're that kind of person. There'll be parts of training camp you can get involved with, so be a positive force while you bond with the team. Build relationships, support the other guys and stay focused while you recuperate. And if you want to get on the ice, well, there's always Ella-Jane's Stick & Puck sessions. Make yourself useful and give those kids a thrill."

Tanner laughed into her hair, squeezing her tightly. "Dammit, you're right, Stretch. I needed that. How come you know exactly what to say?"

Because I love you and I'm here for you, the way you're here for me.

He was the sparkle of raindrops in the sunshine. The warmth of summer sand on bare feet. He was feather pillows, hot cocoa, and unequivocal comfort. And she loved him.

But, as they shared the stolen moment in the quiet of the kitchen, knowing Arlo could rejoin them at any minute, she could almost see an array of unspoken thoughts and unfinished business glittering between them in the shards of sunlight.

And although Avery already knew she was willing to take a chance on Tanner—on them—she stumbled over the words that wanted to fall from her tongue and she held them back.

* * *

He talked her into joining him in the farmhouse for a late breakfast the following morning, saying he'd come out to the workshop to get her once he'd picked up some food. When he appeared in the doorway, Avery laid down her tools and turned off the music, more than ready to eat.

Catching hold of her hand, Tanner dragged her toward him until she hit his chest with a muffled laugh. His tongue slid between her lips. His palm at the base of her spine pulled her closer. That groan he made as their kiss deepened? It lit Avery up from the inside. Flames spread through her stomach as his mouth traced the curve of her jaw and he sucked at the sensitive skin beneath her ear. He was hot and solid and she wanted to keep him here and forget about food, even if her stomach complained.

"Damn, why do you always look so sexy with a hammer in your hand?" Tanner's question was a gravelly grumble. "Makes me want to take you straight upstairs, but we have guests for breakfast. My mom's in the kitchen."

Avery snickered into his neck, her hands fisting in the soft cotton of his baby blue tee. "Maybe if you behave yourself during breakfast, I could make it worth your while once she's gone."

He cocked his head, eyes instantly alive with possibilities. "You would do that, huh?"

She nodded.

"Will there be nudity?" Tanner's slow grin was brushed with hope and dipped in devilry.

"There will almost certainly be nudity," she confirmed, heat pooling in her stomach.

"My room, your tits, my cock?"

"I'll bring mine if you bring yours." Avery rolled her eyes but laughed despite herself, and his grin split even wider.

Tanner kissed one corner of her lips and then the other, the sweetness of the gesture at wonderful odds with his dirty mouth. "Sold to the guy who's going to have to deal with a boner at breakfast."

Pushing her purposefully out to arm's length, he kept his grip on her fingers and towed her across the patio to the open bifold doors. Unusually, at this time of the morning, he wasn't sweaty and maybe she was just a smidge disappointed. Sweaty Tanner was one of Avery's favorite Tanners. Although, to be fair, there was strong competition.

She liked Freshly Showered Tanner, too.

Dressed-Up Tanner.

Dressed-Down Tanner.

Undressed Tanner.

And Rumpled First Thing In The Morning Tanner was turning out to be pretty fucking hot as well.

Still debating the issue, it took Avery a few seconds to register that the person chatting hesitantly with Cassidy Stone by the kitchen island was her mother. Bravely uneasy, Violet had a fresh cup of coffee in her hands and the wide-eyed look of a creature who'd escaped captivity.

That her mom instantly wrapped her in a hug surprised Avery almost as much as her presence. She smelled of lilacs and hairspray, and the embrace was comforting in a way Avery hadn't known she needed.

"What are you doing here?" she asked with a stunned shake of her head. The only place she'd seen her mother outside of her own house since the divorce was finalized was the Family Fare Supermarket five minutes from her home.

"Cassie and Tanner invited me for breakfast. They came to pick me up and said it would be a nice surprise for you." Violet's mouth quivered just a little, as if she wasn't quite sure whether or not that might be true.

Avery, still at a loss for words, pulled herself together enough to reassure her. "It's the best surprise, Mom. I can't believe you're here."

"They're not an easy pair to say no to," her mother admitted in a whisper that only reached the two of them.

Avery's mouth tugged at the corner. "Tell me about it."

With a warm smile so similar to Tanner's that Avery couldn't help but return it, Cassie pressed a mug of coffee into Avery's hands and moved to open up a cake tin. "Hazel sent me with some of her tea cakes. You have to try them—they're the stuff of legend."

Catching Tanner's eye over her mother's head, Avery mouthed, "Thank you."

She had no idea how he'd managed this feat but, if she'd been able to speak the two simple syllables aloud, he would have heard all the gratitude, sincerity, and emotion she was feeling.

From his smile, Avery suspected he knew it anyway.

"I was so shocked when Tanner told me what happened with Gemma. Whatever was she thinking?" Her mom took a seat at the table, legs crossed neatly at the ankle, and Avery sank onto the chair beside her. "That girl has been in charge of five-year-olds for years!"

"Good job all the scissors were blunt-ended." Avery's weak joke drew a sympathetic look from Tanner's mom. She did not want to talk about Gemma.

Violet laid a hand on Avery's knee in an awkward fashion. "You should have told me." She darted a self-conscious look at Tanner and Cassidy. "I'm not so fragile that you need to keep things like that to yourself."

"I didn't want to bother you," Avery said, but the truth was she *had* grown used to hiding stuff from her mom. Always careful not to unsettle Violet's flimsy balance.

Tanner's hand cupped the back of her neck as he moved closer to stand behind Avery's chair, his warm thumb stroking her skin in soft, blunt sweeps as Cassie stepped smoothly into the momentary pause.

"Let's have some breakfast. We picked up fresh fruit on the way over, as a healthy side to the tea cakes, and Tanner insisted on my baked oatmeal, too." Cassidy's laugh was light. "It's a foolproof recipe—one of the few things I make."

"And it's the best," he said, tugging out a seat at the table and sitting down. His fingers drummed happily on the table. "Just wait until you try it."

"Where's Arlo?" Avery asked.

"I'm not sure. He borrowed the car—said he had errands to run." There was a caginess to Tanner's words, something in his eyes that seemed to slip away when she looked again.

While they all dug into the food, Cassidy entertained them with tales from her book club, which sounded like a chaotic mix of characters and the source of very little actual book talk.

"It was Marjorie's turn to choose this month—Hazel's friend Marjorie from the general store?" Cassie checked to see if they knew who she meant. Avery nodded with a smile, picturing the woman, a forthright loose cannon who could always be relied upon to come out with the unexpected. Her mom shook her head. "Anyway, she spotted this book at the library called *Power of the Gods*. She swore she only picked it up because she's a fan of Greek mythology, but it turns out it's a dark romance!"

Avery spluttered into her coffee. Bel was going to be so pissed that she'd missed out on this.

"Was it a good read?" Tanner asked keenly, around a mouthful of oatmeal.

"Oh, very enlightening. And Hazel's decided it's a crying shame you can't book a day trip to the Underworld." Cassidy carefully sliced a plump strawberry with a sharp knife.

Avery found herself sniggering as her mom murmured, "I suppose it would beat a visit to the Battle Creek Taxidermy Museum."

"You should come along, Violet." Tanner's mother issued the invitation with casual warmth. "To the book club, not the Underworld. It'll be safer this month because I'm choosing the book, so we could pick something out together. The meeting is at my house, too. I'm happy to come and collect you."

With the briefest hesitation, her mom agreed. As if Avery hadn't come up with a thousand other suggestions in the past that might have helped her dip her toe back into more social waters. As if her mother hadn't made excuses not to try every single one of them for the last ten years.

Cassidy was a goddamn genius.

And Tanner, well, he was her knight in shining armor disguised as a fidgety Adonis with a dimple to die for.

Avery found herself setting down her coffee cup with a lump in her throat that made it impossible to swallow.

Chapter 44
Tanner

When Avery's fingers crept to his thigh, Tanner captured them beneath his hand. Her blue eyes met his, glimmering like the sun on water, and he felt like he'd done something truly remarkable instead of just enlisting his mom's help to coax Violet Delgado out of her house.

He was jolted from this glow of achievement by the sound of the front door.

"I found us a special visitor at the gate!" Arlo's voice echoed from the foyer. "You're not going to *believe* this."

His reappearance grated like sandpaper, twisting the dial on the brightness of the morning, and Tanner pushed to his feet with a grimace of apology to everyone at the table. He could hardly bear to be around Arlo at the moment, was itching for the confrontation he knew was coming. There were just a few last details that needed to fall into place before he had all the ammunition he needed.

Though the farmhouse was beginning to feel more like a motel than his own home, Tanner couldn't regret his part in bringing Violet Delgado over for breakfast. Avery's delight was priceless, and making her smile was turning out to be one of his favorite things.

His mind on how soon he might be able to get her all to himself, his fingers tugging at the neck of his tee, Tanner came to a halt on the threshold of the foyer. A query died in his throat when the poorly disguised glee on Arlo's face gave him stark warning that he wasn't going to like this new development.

And he was right.

Because just inside the front door—casually dressed, with a red purse slung over one shoulder and brunette curls held back from her face by the oversized sunglasses perched on her head—stood Bethany Jenner.

His ex-coach's wife. (His ex-coach's ex-wife?)

Her mouth, painted a glossy shade of rose pink, curled into a smile and she parted her lips to speak.

Absolutely fucking not.

Tanner opened his own to cut across her.

But his mom, in the kitchen doorway, beat them both to it. "I think Violet would like to head home now, sweetheart. Since you're busy, Avery's going to drop us—"

"Arlo can take you." Tanner swallowed his panic as Avery appeared by his mother's shoulder. When her eyes swept over Bethany, his stomach clenched.

"Probably best if Avery does it," Arlo said with a yawn that showed all his teeth.

Violet joined them in the foyer, clutching her cardigan and purse to her body. She took in the strained air, looking from Tanner to Bethany and back again, and said, "Actually, I know my daughter has work she needs to get on with and I feel like I've taken up enough of her time already. I'd be very grateful for a ride, if you wouldn't mind."

"Dude . . ." Tanner made the single word a demand and Arlo gave in with a grunt.

"Sure. No problem," he said reluctantly, straightening from where he leaned against the newel post at the bottom of the stairs.

"Thanks for coming, Mom. It was wonderful to see you." Avery drew Violet into a hug as they moved toward the door.

His mother pressed a kiss to Tanner's cheek. "I'll call you tomorrow, honey."

"Thanks for your help, Mom." Though he could hardly bear to take his eyes off the trainwreck waiting to happen within arm's reach, Tanner gave her a squeeze.

Arlo snatched the keys up from the bowl on the hallway table, flicked Tanner a look that clearly expressed how disappointed he was to be missing out on the drama, and the trio disappeared through the door.

The sudden silence was crippling.

"Sorry to have interrupted when you had company." Bethany sashayed further into the foyer. "But I decided our messages and calls weren't really cutting it."

Damn, she's made it sound so bad, putting like that. Dread made Tanner's fingers feel icy. Why the hell had he not come clean about this whole mess? He should have known it would come back to bite him.

"One message. One phone call," he clarified quickly.

Shit. Tanner could have smacked his own forehead. *That didn't sound much better.*

Bethany's gaze swung from him to Avery and back again. "Perhaps we could talk somewhere in private," she suggested, removing the sunglasses from her head and slowly folding the arms.

"I'll leave you to it." A polite smile played on Avery's lips, and Tanner couldn't tell what she was thinking. This was everything he didn't need her and her trust issues to face without warning. "I'm just going to clear up in the kitchen and then I'll be outside."

No way was that happening!

"We'll join you and talk in the kitchen," Tanner said immediately, unwilling to have any distance between them while he dealt with this shitshow.

"Babe—" Though there was objection in Bethany's voice, it didn't stop Tanner walking away. She could protest all she liked, but she would have to follow him into the kitchen to do it.

"This is Bethany Jenner, my ex-coach's wife," he told Avery, even though she wouldn't look at him.

"Not anymore. I'm a free agent now." Bethany's laugh was a carefree tinkle. "At last."

"What are you doing here?" Tanner asked, praying for patience as he pinched the bridge of his nose.

Bethany hung her purse over one of the chair backs and took a seat as Avery began gathering up the breakfast remains from the table. Tanner would have helped if he had been remotely able to multitask, but this whole situation was frying his brain. Instead, he flicked the catch of his watch open and shut over and over again.

"I'd love a coffee, if it's not too much bother," Bethany said sweetly to Avery, and Tanner realized the woman had taken her for a housekeeper.

"I'll make it," he snapped, stalking over to the coffee machine. "You talk."

Yeah, so that was a mistake.

"I heard you were missing me," Bethany said. "That you regretted what you said and that a visit would be a good way to clear the air."

Fuck, no.

Wheeling around, Tanner's eyes shot to Avery, who had paused on her way to the kitchen sink with a pile of crockery in her hands. He threw the coffee pod to one side, not caring if Bethany fucking Jenner died of thirst before he cleared this up with Avery. "That's not true. This isn't what you think."

Avery set the plates down with careful precision. "Why don't you let her speak, Tanner? She's come all this way and it would be rude not to hear her out." Over her shoulder, she gave Bethany a calm smile. Too calm? Maybe. He had no idea. "Just pretend I'm not here, Bethany," she told the older woman, "and I'll try to keep the noise down."

Tanner opened his mouth to protest, caught the hitch of Avery's left eyebrow, and closed it again. Dragging his hand through his hair, he reached for a mug instead.

"We've never had the chance to get to know each other properly," Bethany continued after a long pause when it became clear he wasn't going to say anything. "I thought we could remedy that now, since I have the time to stay for a few days. We can explore this thing between us—"

She broke off, clearly uncomfortable with having this conversation in company, and there was a flicker of frustration in the look she directed at Avery's back. Tanner's breakfast churned in his stomach.

"I think you should leave," he growled desperately. "This isn't—"

"No, do continue," Avery interrupted, prompting the damn woman with a nod over her shoulder. "I'm fascinated."

"Let's go somewhere alone to sort this out, babe," Bethany said frostily, color painting her cheekbones as she rose to her feet.

Turning from the sink with soapy hands, Avery dried them deliberately on a dish towel and her poise was dangerous. He could feel the storm brewing, even though her face still sported a practiced smile. "How long have you known Tanner?"

"Nearly two years. We met when he came to play in Boston." Bethany's lips pursed and her eyes narrowed. Maybe she could sense the storm, too. "The circumstances weren't ideal then, but things change and, well, look at him—he's gorgeous, isn't he? What woman wouldn't want herself some of that."

It was possible Tanner had never felt so insanely uncomfortable in all of his life as when Avery's eyes burned into his own. "Mmm, true," was all she said, and he would have sold his soul to know what was going on inside her head.

"I just had to wait for the time to be right." Bethany stalked toward him, a sensuality oozing from her pores that left him cold. "I'm so glad you realized we have something special, too. I knew you would."

"Sounds like you know him pretty well." Avery's tone took on an even more ominous edge.

Frustration locked the muscles in his jaw. "She doesn't—"

"I do." Bethany talked over him, as pigheaded as ever in her self-confidence. Tanner was one step away from physically ejecting her from the house.

"And yet," continued Avery, "you haven't seemed to notice that he doesn't want you here."

Tanner gave a ragged swallow, his eyes glued to her face.

"I don't think that's true," Bethany said tightly, turning back to Avery with a pugnacious tilt to her chin.

Avery leaned casually against the counter. "Oh, but it is. He's practically climbing out of his skin with embarrassment, and it's hardly surprising when you're talking about him like he's a thing you want to acquire because he's hot."

"I'm not sure what business this is of yours." There was a distinct bite to Bethany's voice now, but Tanner didn't spare her an ounce of attention.

It suddenly became the most important thing in the world to know what Avery was going to say next, without him explaining the whole fucked-up situation first.

"It's very much my business," she said with an icy smile and complete assurance. "Because I'm Tanner's girlfriend and, judging by the horror on his face when he saw you, it seems you've turned up here without an invitation."

She trusts me. She fucking trusts me. Tanner's knees shook with the realization and he grabbed the counter behind him in utter relief.

"He doesn't have a girlfriend," Bethany protested.

"You're wrong," he said, with every ounce of feeling he could inject into the words. "I have the most amazing girlfriend in the world."

"He does," Avery agreed, and her eyes burned a brilliant shade of blue. "It's been a wild ride but we've got there."

Bethany glared at them both. "But I was invited."

"Let me guess." Avery tipped her head and studied the woman shrewdly. "Arlo got in touch with you, didn't he? Did he spin you a line about how much Tanner was missing you?"

Tanner raised his eyes to the ceiling. "I should have fucking known," he groaned.

"You didn't ask him to call me?" All of a sudden, Bethany sounded a lot less sure of herself.

"No, he took it on himself to do that," he told her bluntly. "I made myself clear when you rang before. I'm not interested. I've never been interested. And whether you're married, separated, divorced, or just looking to screw around, I don't want anything to do with it. I'm with Avery."

He could tell from Bethany's face that she'd finally gotten the message. "He wasn't like this in Boston," she said cattily to Avery, as mortification made her mean.

"Don't you dare . . ." Tanner clenched his teeth, hands closing into fists. *This fucking woman.*

Avery's eyes flashed. "I didn't know him in Boston but I know what he's like as a person, so there's nothing you can hint at that will make me doubt him. He's thoughtful and honorable and caring. He'll do anything for his friends and he's proved himself to be the first person there for me whenever I need him. Even before I know I need him sometimes. He has the biggest heart and I trust him more than anyone else. And none of that has anything to do with the absolutely gorgeous fucking packaging it comes with."

Tanner could hardly breathe as she came to the end of the prettiest speech he'd ever heard. He wanted to reach out and tangle his fingers into her hair, pull her toward him and kiss the sense out of her. Instead, he settled for laying one hand over his chest in an attempt to calm its pounding.

"You need to go now," Avery suggested. "Tanner's made himself very clear and he's been more polite than you deserve. You can book a Lyft from outside the gates or, if you're lucky, you'll catch Arlo on his way back and the two of you can fuck off together."

Tanner and Bethany didn't exchange another word as he opened the front door for her, buzzed her out of the gates and watched until she'd left his property.

Heading back to the kitchen, he paused in the doorway.

"Well, that was interesting," Avery said as he re-entered the kitchen, her arms folded across her chest in a barrier that he'd kidded himself had fallen. Her eyes held a world of measured regret and Tanner's heart dropped all over again.

"I can explain," he said.

"Maybe later." Avery shrugged. "But since it's a morning for getting stuff out in the open, I think it's my turn."

Taking in her angled brows and straight mouth, Tanner's gut twisted. He tried to distract himself with the dusting of freckles, the tiny gold ring, but it didn't work.

Then it hit him. She'd said she trusted him. Not that she loved him.

But she'd also said she was his girlfriend.

Did she want to keep it casual? *Fuck.*

Tanner braced himself, feeling like a punching bag left swinging between bouts. And just as Avery opened her mouth to deliver the next blow, that damn fucking buzzer sounded again for the front gate.

Chapter 45
Avery

It wasn't midday yet and Avery's head was reeling as Roman Martinez and Dougie Taggart stepped over the threshold. Maybe Tanner should get a sofa installed in the foyer if he was planning on doing this much entertaining just inside the front door.

She didn't know if she had the strength for Round Two.

Declining a coffee for the both of them, Martinez launched straight in.

"We have an update for you on the doll situation, although we ran into a few roadblocks to start with," he said. "The order was placed from a public server and payment was by Apple Pay, which doesn't share card numbers with the company taking the money. The doll was originally delivered to a rented PO Box that was paid for in cash and given up immediately afterward."

"If this was a TV detective show, the stalker would have left DNA evidence in the mailbox." Avery blamed her frustration for the ridiculous comment.

"And I'd be a reclusive alcoholic." Martinez's reply was razor-sharp. The quick smile he paired it with elevated him from dark and dangerous to charming in an instant. "Luckily, we didn't need DNA because the facility was monitored by CCTV."

Dougie grinned. "Sometimes people make it too easy for us."

"Who was it?" There was grim desperation in Tanner's voice.

"I've got one more question for you first," the chief said. "Where were you the night before the doll was delivered?"

Surprise lifted Tanner's eyebrows. "I was here. With Avery."

Martinez and Dougie exchanged a quick glance.

"Well, if that's true, your car was on Main Street at around 2 a.m. without you," Dougie told him. "We have grounds to suspect that the same person who sent the doll smashed the window of Sam and Kash's shop."

"Arlo." Tanner and Avery spoke at the same time. He looked as grimly gutted as she was stunned.

"When you came to see me the other day—for the second time—I made some basic inquiries." Martinez took over, addressing Tanner. "You'll need to bring in a forensic accountant to take a deeper look at your finances. I only scratched the surface, but the trail's sloppy. It's my best guess that Arlo's been skimming from your accounts for years. I found shares, pension payments, and personal expenses listed in his own name. And none of it's very well hidden. Seems he just assumed you wouldn't look too hard." The shrug Roman gave was sympathetic. "The office space he purchased on your behalf to work out of doesn't actually exist. The money trail leads back to a condo in Maine. Once we examine his electronics, it's possible we'll find more—and I, for one, will be interested to see if we can find a trace back to Avery's nuisance messages."

She threaded her fingers through Tanner's, her heart sick for him at the revelations. "I'm so sorry."

"You're sorry?" Tanner's expression was livid. "I brought him here and he hurt you. He targeted Sam and Kash. I'm going to fucking kill him."

"It might be best if we help with the retribution," Martinez suggested. "We're gonna want you on the Pine Springs baseball team before the year is out. I'd hate to ruin our chances because you're behind bars."

The sound of the front door opening at that moment couldn't have been better timed.

"Honey, I'm home!" called Arlo, as he stepped inside.

Avery just knew that he had every intention of talking his way out of any involvement in the deception of Bethany Jenner; she clenched her fists. At this rate there was going to be a line of people wanting to kill Arlo.

But, as Arlo took in a welcoming committee he hadn't expected, his greeting strangled in his throat. And one glance around at everyone's faces showed him exactly how screwed he was.

"Bro—" Arlo took a pace toward Tanner.

"Don't." The look Tanner gave him in return was pure disgust.

"We'll take it from here," said Martinez, and all humor had drained from his eyes. "Arlo Stebbings, you are under arrest for misdemeanor stalking and malicious destruction of a commercial property. You have the right to remain silent. Anything you say can and will be used against you in a court of law. You also have the right to an attorney. If you cannot afford an attorney, one will be appointed for you."

Beneath his tanned skin, Arlo's face took on a sickly pallor. Wisely, he held his tongue as Taggart led him from the house.

"I'll be in touch," promised Martinez, before following in their footsteps, and a deafening silence settled back over the foyer as Tanner closed the front door yet again.

* * *

They made more coffee that Avery guessed neither of them wanted and walked out onto the patio. With the sun beating down on their shoulders, they settled on the edge of the pool, legs dangling in the water, and when one strap of Avery's sundress slid off her shoulder, Tanner pushed it back up with a finger so gentle she barely felt it.

So many emotions crowded his face that she couldn't separate them. He didn't deserve any of this.

Avery tried to think of something comforting to say but her throat was tight and her heart heavy. Instead she pressed her arm up against his and they sat without talking for several long minutes as they processed the morning's events.

But the silence didn't help, even after the emotional hurricane they'd weathered since breakfast. With so much unspoken between them, it wasn't restful and they both reached that conclusion at the same time.

"So, here's the thing—" Tanner's knee bounced next to her thigh. His mouth formed a muted copy of his usual grin.

Avery interrupted him.

"I think it's my turn to talk," she said softly, bringing his fidgeting to a halt with her hand on his leg. The bulk of Tanner's thigh beneath her palm was tense. "You've laid it out for me already and you deserve the same."

It was too raw to talk about Arlo just yet but there was so much else that needed airing out.

"I wanted to say this earlier, but we got interrupted and, well . . . anyway." She took a deep breath, felt Tanner go impossibly still beside her. "I'm sorry I didn't tell you how I feel sooner. I'm sorry I held back. I spent so long trying to work it all out, and then as soon as I did, the whole Gemma thing happened."

Avery looked out across the water, watched the ripples undulating gently in the sunshine. A memory of how Tanner had pinned her to the side of the pool and turned her inside out with his kisses on the night of his housewarming party swirled like a mirage in the hazy heat, and she had to swallow before she could continue.

"All the lies in my life that have caused so much unhappiness, and I held back on telling you the one truth that matters most."

Tanner's hand closed over her own, his grip just shy of painful. She laid her cheek against his shoulder and decided it was far easier not to look at him. Bravery only went so far.

"I admired you so much at school for your energy and your drive and your passion. Everything buzzes around you. *I* buzz when I'm around you. It's like a shot of adrenaline on top of too much coffee and I can't get enough of it." Avery's skin felt raw, her voice was thick. "Holding back from dating so I would never be hurt like my mom seemed like a foolproof plan, but I'm sick of being capable and alone. It's more painful than taking the risk. And I can't keep my heart safe any longer because it already belongs to you. Whether we're together or not, it isn't my own anymore."

"Oh, thank fuck for that." Tanner sounded just as choked up as she felt. "Jesus Christ, you scared me, Stretch."

He turned to drag her onto his lap and the action was an awkward, scrambling fumble which had them both breathlessly snickering when her shoulder smacked him under the chin and her knee nearly did him a mischief. But eventually, Tanner held her chest to chest with hands that weren't entirely steady—and Avery found more courage.

She drew back to study his face, caught and captured by the hope in his eyes.

"I love you, Tanner. Right through to my bones." If he could wear his heart on his sleeve, then she would do the same. "It didn't take a purse or a car for me to realize. Just a storm, a ladder, and a ton of moldy leaves. I was falling before then but that had me all in." She swallowed a moist gulp. "I love the way you love me and I want more of it. I want to love you back the way you deserve."

His broad ribs expanding on a juddering breath, Tanner leaned forward to capture her lips in a kiss that bathed Avery's heart in warmth. His beautiful tawny eyes were suspiciously damp.

"I love you, Tanner Stone." Avery repeated the words against his jaw as he skimmed more kisses over her face.

His dimple flickered, his mouth lifted. "And I love you too, Stretch. Then. Now. Always." He curled his fingers around the back of her neck. "I knew there was something missing. I was poor and struggling, then successful and rich, but never fully happy even when I had everything I thought I wanted. I've been somewhere on the edge of it for years."

"You and me both." Her laugh broke in the middle.

Tanner pulled her closer. "Not anymore."

Avery's eyelashes fluttered as his mouth traced the line of her neck. "I don't want to move out of your workshop," she murmured. "Not that Luke's given me a final start date for rebuilding mine anyway."

"I told him there was no rush," Tanner admitted.

"You snake." Her eyes flew open and she pinched his biceps.

"But if you're going to continue using my property, we need to discuss rent." There was a teasing pitch to his voice.

"I have money."

"I don't need money," Tanner said, nibbling on her ear.

God, she loved it when he did that. "What do you need?" The question emerged as a whisper.

"Well, now. I'm not sure where to begin." His fingers slid the strap of her sundress back off her shoulder. "But I can think of one thing I was promised that you never delivered on."

Avery drew back with a frown. "What's that?"

"Nudity." Tanner's hand stroked the soft mound of her breast and she sighed as his thumb brushed her nipple over the cotton drape of her dress. "A long, long time ago, before breakfast, I distinctly remember being promised nudity."

"There must be something about this pool that makes you horny." Her lips split into a curve and the smile spilled over onto his. Avery shifted teasingly in his lap, relishing the earthy groan that rumbled in his throat.

Tanner took her mouth in a kiss that promised retribution.

"There's something about you that makes me horny," he said when their mouths parted. "But I'm willing to worship every single gorgeous fucking inch of you in a variety of locations and then we'll know for sure."

"But no heights, huh? You'd probably prefer it if we keep our feet on the ground." She threaded her fingers through the hair at the back of his neck, joy spreading through her bloodstream like caramel syrup in warm milk.

"Avery Delgado." Tanner pressed his forehead against hers. "I would abseil from the Willis Tower for you." He nuzzled her nose. "Go paragliding or cliff diving." Kiss. "Ride ziplines and rollercoasters." Kiss.

She narrowed her eyes. "You would?"

"That and more. Try me and you'll see." A steady assurance shone in his eyes, even as his mouth lifted at one corner. "But maybe we could start slow and work up to the abseiling? I feel like I do my best work at ground level."

Melting into the protective cage of Tanner's arms, his breath against her lips, Avery smiled. "Show me," she said.

After all, one big leap of faith was more than enough for now.

Epilogue

Pine Springs Observer

PINE SPRINGS, WELLER'S LAKE & SURROUNDING AREAS

JANUARY 22, 2026

MULTIPLE CHARGES FOR HOCKEY STAR'S MANAGER

TANNER STONE AND GIRLFRIEND ARE VICTIMS OF THEFT AND HARASSMENT

Arlo Stebbings, 28, manager and financial advisor to NHL player Tanner "Ace Face" Stone, has been charged with embezzlement, harassment, misdemeanor stalking, and malicious destruction of property.

Although full details haven't yet been released as to the extent of the funds or assets stolen, it is understood that the total amount was significant enough to qualify for a felony charge.

During the investigation, officers discovered the defendant had also registered "upwards of 20 fake social media accounts and multiple email addresses" in order to digitally stalk, harass, and threaten Avery Delgado, Stone's 27-year-old girlfriend.

Stebbings pleaded guilty and will be sentenced shortly. He can expect to receive a significant jail term and a fine of up to $50,000, plus a court order preventing him from contacting Delgado for at least three years.

Tanner Stone, 28, who recently left Boston to sign with Grand Rapids, was not available for comment at the time of going to press.

"Unfortunately, repeated or continuing harassment of another individual with the intent to intimidate, frighten, or threaten is not an unusual occurrence. In this and in all stalking cases, we will seek to prosecute to the full extent of the law," said Pine Springs Police Chief Roman Martinez.

Nearly 1 in 3 women and 1 in 6 men will report stalking victimization at some point in their lifetime, according to the National Intimate Partner and Sexual Violence Survey.

Those who feel they are in danger or fear a threat of harm should call 911.

Seven Months Later

Avery

Tanner's flight home had been delayed. She'd been desperate to pick him up from the airport but the bus was already laid on and his car waited for him at the Ludlow Heights Arena in Grand Rapids. Bel and Leo had talked Avery into meeting him at the bar instead.

"I never get to see you these days," Bel wheedled, and her pout could have won awards. "Drew won't watch *Gilmore Girls* with me, and he doesn't know all the quotes from *Brooklyn Nine-Nine*. I need Avery time."

Bel had been living with Drew for five months, and complaining about the whole *Gilmore Girls* thing for four and a half of them.

"This is not an argument you're going to win, Ave. You might as well give in graciously," Drew said while Leo suppressed a grin. "Although I'd like it to show in the records that I absolutely do know all the quotes from *Brooklyn Nine-Nine*."

"It's bad enough to be let down by Tan—the least you can do is show up for your friends." Bel was shameless.

"He's delayed, not giving you the finger," Avery reminded her. "He'll get here as soon as he can."

"Then there's no reason not to come with us!" said Bel.

There was a comfortable hum inside the Rusty Barrel. It still felt different to experience the evening on this side of the bar, but Avery had been more than happy to hand her shifts over to someone else. She didn't need them anymore with the upswing in upholstery orders after Jackson had put her in touch with a couple of antiques dealers he knew. She now had a satisfying waitlist for restorations and not enough hours in the day.

Avery's friends had meshed easily with the ones she and Tanner had made through Sam, the gap left by Gemma's absence now that she'd left town and moved away becoming less noticeable over time. She'd sent Avery a letter, three months after leaving Pine Springs—two pages of heartfelt apology that healed a little of the hurt. In a twisted kind of way, Avery's experience with her parents had given her some sympathy for Gemma's remorse; one-sided love had not been kind to her mom. It took two people to create a real love story.

"I still can't believe you landed a stalker. What with me nearly set on fire, that's a lot of action for a small town." Leah was always up for swapping trauma stories.

"Elenie was beaten up and arrested. Her entire family is a bunch of douche-waffles and most of them are in prison. If this is a competition, she definitely wins." There was a lot about Florence Martinez that reminded Avery of Bel.

"Great. Thanks for getting that out there. My favorite thing is airing my dirty laundry. Go, you." Elenie's low-key complaint lacked heat.

"I was at school with your stepbrother." Avery realized she hadn't mentioned it before.

"Ty or Dean?"

"Tyson."

"Same grade?" Elenie asked.

"Yes. He hit me in the face with a basketball once."

"My commiserations." When Elenie's face turned guarded, Roman folded an arm around her waist and squeezed.

Avery smiled. "I only had to avoid him at school. You had to live with him. Plus, it was how I met Tanner—we bonded over bloody noses, so it wasn't all bad."

"Remember that Delia is Avery's aunt. Skeletons in closets come in all shapes and sizes," said Bel.

"Oh my god, yes!" Leah twisted a silver ring around her thumb. "She scares the crap out of me."

Avery grinned. "Me too. But I have a secret weapon now."

"And that is?" Elenie sounded intrigued.

"Tanner." Avery rolled her eyes. "Aunt Delia *loves* Tanner."

"Fuck me running, is there no one that boy can't twist around his finger?" Sam muttered in disgust. "Sometimes I'm so disappointed in the female population of Pine Springs."

"I think you'll find it's not just this town," Leah laughed.

"Rein it in, Raven. You want to lech, you do it in my direction." When Jackson shot her a glare over the neck of his beer bottle, she leaned into him with such a sweet smile that his expression softened.

"How did you two meet?" Bel asked them.

Sam and Kash chuckled. "Now that's a fun story," said Sam, propping his elbow on the bar and getting comfortable.

"I was kind of foisted on Jax as a housemate." Leah jumped in to stop Sam telling his version. "Let's just say it took him a while to realize how lucky he was."

Jackson choked on a swallow of beer. "She was a royal pain in my ass. Still is." But his lips curved and he tugged Leah closer.

"And you and the chief?" Bel asked Elenie.

Roman draped an arm around his wife's shoulders when she turned to look up at him, the wedding band glinting on his finger.

Elenie's gray eyes were warm. "We met in the diner, got to know each other at the town fair, fake-dated and split up, then I went undercover as a CI. The usual."

Martinez gave a gruff laugh, a slow smile lighting the planes of his usually serious face. "Yeah, pretty standard stuff."

There were so many follow-up questions to that, even Bel didn't know where to begin. But just as she took a big breath and was about to dive in, the main door swung open and Tanner strode through it, still wearing the suit he'd traveled in and clutching a gift bag.

His eyes found their group immediately and the grin that split his face sparked a matching one on Avery's lips. Coffee and sunshine, sand and waves—he was everything addictive that was good for her soul.

She met him halfway across the bar and his arms opened for her to slide right in.

"Damn, I've missed you." Tanner breathed the words into her neck.

"It was only four days," she reminded him.

"Four long, lonely, bleak, and miserable days," he grumbled.

"But you won."

His dimple flashed. "Of course we fucking won."

"Shoulder OK?" she asked.

"Shoulder, teeth, good looks." Tanner ran through the usual checklist. "All perfect."

His recovery from the surgery had been even swifter than they'd hoped. With the weeks of physio and strength training progressing quickly to on-ice drills, the prospect of how his shoulder would hold up to full contact had terrified them both, but they needn't have worried. Within six months, he'd been back, stronger and more fierce a player than ever, determined to make the most of this second chance.

Avery loved seeing Tanner on the ice—his talent, his commitment, even the brutality, captivated her every time. Though she tried to travel with him as much as possible now they were well into the regular season, she'd had to pass on this away game in Minnesota because she had too much work on. Not a bad problem to have.

When his lips dropped to hers, there was ease and adoration in the heat of his mouth, and welcome and comfort in hers. Beneath the palms of Avery's hands, the tension leached from his muscles.

She understood exactly how he felt.

With everything right in her world now that she was back in Tanner's orbit, Avery leaned into his reassuring bulk. His broad hand circled the curve of her neck like a clay vase on a potter's wheel, and she swallowed against the faint pressure of his thumb, beating him to the words he was always so generous with.

"I love you so much." That flare of molten gold in his eyes thrilled her every time. "Everything is better when you're home, Ace Face."

Tanner

Those words on her lips. Fuck. That was all his dreams come true right there.

Cursing every minute of the delay that had kept the team grounded, Tanner hadn't drawn a relaxed breath until he passed the Pine Springs town limits. Though he was thrilled to be a fixture on the Rapids top line, he'd turned into a sap who hated being away from home. Unless Avery came, too.

Time without her was a big "no, thank you" these days. She was the center of his world and he was forged to be her satellite.

All he wanted was his arms around her and his nose in the curve of her neck. He needed Avery's touch to relax him.

As Tanner slipped seamlessly into the group of friends who gave no thought to his public persona or earning power, he couldn't stop touching her. Threading his fingers through Avery's, particles of electricity sputtering between them, he listened with half an ear to Sam's update on the purchase of their latest renovation, and Leah's description of the chaos Hazel had caused at a recent book club meeting.

"Talking of which—" Avery squeezed his hand. "Mom says she's going to move back into central Pine Springs. Now she's such a regular at book club, she wants to be even closer to her friends."

"That's cool." Avery's relationship with her mom had slowly taken on a healthier balance, with Violet's need to lean on her daughter becoming more diluted as she rebuilt her social life. She'd even taken to meeting up with Delia here and there over the past six months. "I'm sure Sam can find her something and we'll help her settle in. Must be something in the water around here—Mats is thinking of making the same move. He's talking about retiring."

"Really?"

He'd grown even closer to Mats, and the two of them were talking about setting up a rotational buddy program to work with local youth teams if Mats moved to Pine Springs. Several of the Rapids players had promised to sign up. Still helping out at Ella-Jane's Stick & Puck sessions when he wasn't traveling, Tanner found the idea of encouraging and coaching the next generation of players an exciting one. Mats said he had a skill for it.

"I think his accident has changed stuff for him," Tanner said, toying with Avery's fingers, "although it's hard to pry much out of him. It's easier to get him talking about our plans for the buddy program."

The big guy was like that—quietly motivational, reliably steady. He'd offered solid support during Tanner's recovery and the messy aftermath of Arlo's various deceptions.

As Martinez had already discovered, it turned out that Arlo's criminal expertise hadn't matched up to his self-confidence. He had indeed sent the messages and photos to Avery—something that still made Tanner sick to his stomach—and, although Arlo thought he'd covered his tracks by swapping out prepaid SIMs, he hadn't realized he had a phone with a hybrid slot. After seizing his handset, Martinez and his team had found a micro-SD memory card holding multiple deleted texts and images—and, when they managed to recover them, the evidence was damning.

Arlo's harassment of Avery and, to a lesser extent, Sam seemed to have been driven by his resentment of their influence over Tanner—not that he'd ever admitted it. With everything that came to light, Tanner had no doubt Arlo was protecting the money stream he'd grown to rely on.

In total, he'd defrauded Tanner's accounts of somewhere in the region of $265,000. It wasn't easy to work out an exact figure because Tanner had been both embarrassingly lax in his attention and carelessly generous over the years. It grated even more that he'd been so prepared to share his wealth with Arlo.

But then, as Avery and Sam—and his mom—reminded him regularly, real friends weren't in it for the money. And he knew that now.

Talking of which . . .

Avery's eyes fell on the bag he'd stored under one of the booth seats and the hint of a frown stole over her face. "Did you bring me another present?"

Tanner's mouth went dry and his eyes slid to Bel. Her grin was blinding.

"Maybe just a small one." There was a fine tremor to his hands as he reached for the bag and handed it over.

"Red Wing boots!" Avery's smile when she peered inside was reluctant but delighted. "Damn, Tanner—they're gorgeous."

He'd consulted with Bel on her memories of the conversation they'd had all those months ago about what they would buy if money were no object. If Avery wanted Red Wing boots, Tanner was going to make sure she had them.

Avery's eyes sparkled as she instantly slipped off her sneakers and tried one on. He'd chosen carefully and settled on an ankle boot in an olive suede finish, and they made her legs look incredible. If he hadn't been so fucking nervous, Tanner would have patted himself on the back for a great job.

"They fit perfectly." She turned her foot this way and that. "I'm never going to take them off."

Trying to remember how to swallow, he undid the top button of his shirt. Sam caught his eye and winked. "Pull the other one on, just to be sure."

"Talk among yourselves if your idea of a great night out isn't watching me model footwear," Avery suggested to the group, a pink flush to her cheeks. But she took the second boot out of the bag and tried to slip it on. "There's something in the toe."

The tip of her tongue poked between her lips as she delved into the boot with her fingers and pulled out a small square box. When she turned with confusion to Tanner, he took it gently from her hand.

"What—" Avery didn't finish the question.

Her eyes widened as he lowered himself to one knee and his heart clattered in his chest like a lumpy camshaft. Behind him, Leah squeaked.

"I can't remember why I thought it was a good idea to do this here but I just know I don't want to wait any longer." He'd been confident right up until the last five minutes, but now sweat rose between Tanner's shoulder blades and his voice was a husky rasp. "I used to wonder who I was without hockey and you helped me see that I will always have other options. But a far bigger question is who am I without you, Stretch? Because honestly, I never want to find out." He dragged a breath in through tight lungs. "And I can manage all the rest—injuries, pressure, what comes next—as long as we're together, because nothing matters more than being the guy who tries to match his strength to yours."

"Damn you for making me cry, Tanner Stone." Bel's soft growl wobbled at the edges but, for once, he was oblivious to any distractions.

Fingers trembling, Tanner opened the tiny box and held it out, looking up at Avery's stunned face with a shaky grin on his lips. "I love you more than I can say because I'm not smart with words. More than you could ever possibly understand, but I'm prepared to show you and tell you for the rest of our lives. So please help a guy out, because my heart is going like the clappers. Will you be my wife?"

Avery's mouth moved several times before any actual words emerged. "You know you're probably kneeling in something sticky right now?" She faltered, her hand pressed to her chest.

Tanner grimaced. "I think I can feel it," he said. But when Avery reached out unsteady fingers to take the ring, he held his breath and any momentary regret at not picking somewhere more aesthetic for this proposal melted away.

The blue topaz caught the light, an exact match for the blue of Avery's eyes. He'd tried to choose one that was just as pretty but Tanner wasn't sure it was possible. The tremulous curve of her mouth was all wonder and delight as she slipped the ring onto her finger and he felt the symbolic punch in his sternum.

"Answer him, you goof noodle!" Bel prompted. Tanner could have kissed her for the nudge.

Avery gave a soggy laugh, swiping at a tear with the back of her hand and leaving a wet smear over one cheekbone.

"Yes, I'll marry you. I can't think of anything I want more." She tugged him to his feet and cradled his face in her hands. "But you have to stop buying me stuff."

Slipping his arms around her waist, Tanner lifted her feet off the ground to the whistles and catcalls of their friends. Exhilaration and gratitude thrummed in his veins as he ducked his head to kiss her deep and long.

"Some things might change over the years, Stretch, but you're onto a loser there." Tanner's grin came from the center of his chest. "I want to be the one to give you everything you need."

Only now he knew that the majority of those things didn't involve money.

When Sam and Kash grabbed the champagne and glasses he'd arranged to have waiting behind the bar, Tanner popped the first cork, congratulations showering over them from all sides. Giddy with relief, he pushed a glass into Avery's hand.

"To us," he whispered. "The idiot who nearly threw away his scholarship and the girl who saved him."

"To us," she replied. "The girl who locked her heart in a box and the man who prized it open."

"I did, didn't I?" Satisfaction filled his lungs. Persistence and hard work had paid off in many areas of his life, but never had they proved more valuable than in the pursuit of Avery Delgado. Breathing in the scent of her perfume, Tanner moved his mouth to her ear. "On a scale of one to ten, how much favor do you think I've earned from Bel tonight?"

"Oh, you've done well—I'd say a nine, at least. Why?"

Tanner's satisfaction was a growl in his throat. "Because I try very hard not to piss her off, but if I can't have you to myself in the next ten minutes, there's going to be trouble."

"She's cooking for us tomorrow," Avery murmured, blue eyes dancing. "Leo has a date he's bringing, too. So I think we're good to go now."

"Thank fuck for that." He grabbed her wrist and backed them steadily away from the group. "Looking forward to dinner, Bel! Appreciate all the good wishes, guys. You're the best. See you soon!"

Avery waved, laughter bubbling in her throat. Then they turned on their heels and headed for the exit, bursting like Bonnie and Clyde out into the parking lot, where the first few drops of a light shower were just starting to fall.

"Seems fitting that we should end up here, on another rainy night in a parking lot." Tiny specks of water mingled with the freckles on Avery's face.

"Oh, this isn't the end, Stretch." His heart full, Tanner pinned her up against his car and kissed her until all they could hear was their own breath in the dark. "We've only just started."

ACKNOWLEDGEMENTS

The journey to publication is a truly collaborative one and I am so fortunate to have the support of my wonderful agent, Rebeka Finch, plus the rest of the amazing Darley Anderson team behind the scenes.

Thank you to Victoria Pepe and Victoria Oundjian for their expertise in fine-tuning Avery and Tanner's story and supporting the entire series so wholeheartedly, and to everyone else at Montlake Romance and Amazon Publishing who have worked on the third Pine Springs book.

Thank you to Malika Nekhla and Elaine Hastings for keeping me both sane and amused, and for putting up with a higher percentage of meltdowns with this book than any of us would have liked. I will never stop shouting about your achievements because you're both brilliant. What a year it's been for us all!

Thank you to Madison Myers for your infinite patience with my "If women in the US have bangs instead of fringes, what do men have?" type questions. Every day that includes a message from you is a good one. And to Kaymie Wuerfel, who continues to be a supportive joy on the other side of the world.

The lovely Courtney from Romance and Rosemary knew exactly what I was after for the character art on this one, and I'm in love with the Avery and Tanner she created straight from my imagination. As always, it's been a pleasure working with you, babe.

And an extra-special thanks to my Twitter/X friend Tanner Howsden for lending me his name!

Thank you to my family for all the fun we had growing up. At least once a day I think of something truly unhinged that only we would find amusing and I know it creeps through into my writing.

Thank you to my fabulous girls, Mads, Martha, and Ims. I'm so proud of you all—Marilla Cuthbert has nothing on me—and I love that spending time with each of you individually and all of you together only gets better and better as you grow older. (NOTE: this is NOT a time to cue up "Slipping Through My Fingers" . . .)

Thank you to Trevor, whose positivity and faith in me is endless, even when mine is a little shaky around the edges. You are the calm in every storm and I love you immensely.

I owe a debt of thanks to every single author whose books I've devoured over the years. They have enhanced my life in ways I can't even begin to describe, and just the thought of bringing that level of delight and escapism to another reader gives me goosebumps like you can't imagine.

Which leads me to my final thank you: to anyone who chooses to spend some time in Pine Springs. I really hope you enjoy it there and I'd love you to return x

If you loved *Edge of Falling* why not read another in the Pine Springs series, *More Than Nothing*.

Chapter 1
Elenie

"Best place in town for breakfast if you can put up with being served by scum." The bristles of Chief Roberts' porn-star mustache rippled with familiar contempt. It had an entity of its own which was often mesmerizing, but today it made barely a blip on Elenie's radar. She was too busy casting furtive glances at the hot stranger on the opposite side of the table.

Pulling the notepad from her apron pocket, she smoothed her face into a blank mask and hoped the spring on her hair clip would last to the end of her shift. She could feel it weakening; a few sun-lightened strands of hair tickled her neck where they'd escaped.

"Hello, gentlemen. D'you know what you'd like to order?" Her stomach pitched and flipped, and she objected on principle. Elenie couldn't afford to be a pitch-or-flip kind of person. Sweeping the stray curls behind one ear with the end of her pen, she waited.

All coiled energy and loose limbs, the chief's breakfast companion had an intense, angular face and espresso-dark hair. His graphite gray tactical pants and polo shirt were casual but immaculate—America's Next Top Model in the latest Police Issue Workwear catalogue. He was magnetic. Compelling. She could swear the air crackled around him. Something about the way he watched her made Elenie feel like she had been dropped into deep water from a great height.

And his forearms. Bronzed skin, corded muscles, strong, lean, capable. Don't start her on the forearms or she'd be fangirling like a sixteen-year-old.

She swallowed. Eager to keep as low a profile as possible, Elenie made sure her own appearance whispered, "Nothing to see here": bistro apron tied over knee-length skirt, burgundy short-sleeved shirt, scuffed sneakers. Uniform faded but clean, nude lips and minimal makeup. But however hard she tried, it was impossible to slide under the radar of the police chief's disdain.

"Elenie Dax." A mix of derision and disgust coated her name on his lips. Elenie resisted the urge to squirm, but it was tough. The diner's bustle and babble continued around her, mingling with the country music station she'd tuned into at opening time. "One fifth of Pine Springs' biggest vermin problem. As you'll find out."

Low on charm, light on team-playing skills and manners, Chief Roberts was a bullfrog of a man. Always curt, he usually stopped shy of blatant offense, but not today. Not in this company. Drumming stubby fingers on the table, his puffed-out chest pulling the buttons tight across the front of his shirt, Roberts was bursting to make some kind of an impression on his new buddy.

"I can give you a couple more minutes if you're not quite ready?" Elenie could feel her ears turning red and hot. Her eyes on her notepad, she channeled professional efficiency through every inch of her body, armor and shield clanking securely into place. She reminded herself that she dealt with people like the chief every day. She could write a thesis on jackasses.

"No need. I'll have the pancakes and black cherries, please." Mr. Sexy Forearms had a voice as rough as sand on marble. She felt it like fingertips down her spine.

"Same," growled Roberts. "With a side of bacon and coffee. And make sure it's hot. Don't leave our plates sitting on the counter."

"Of course. *Grozna si kato salata.*" To take the only petty revenge she could, Elenie fell back on her favorite form of stress relief, sliding in a foreign insult she hoped she'd get away with—unless the hot stranger was Bulgarian, of course, but it didn't look likely.

Roberts drew wiry eyebrows together. "No, just the pancakes. If I wanted salad, I'd have asked for it."

His companion made no comment.

Bulgarian for the win. So satisfying.

"Coffee for you too, sir?" It took everything she had not to stammer.

"I'll have a hot tea, please. With milk." One side of his mouth lifted in a half-smile. He should carry a license for that. She allowed herself to catch his eye for less than a second (no more, in case her notepad combusted) and met a shrewd and shuttered gaze.

Well, what do you know? Other people have armor too.

"Coming right up."

Tearing the order from her pad, Elenie clipped it beside the kitchen hatch and grabbed the next selection of plated breakfasts from the counter. Handing them out to a couple with two small children, she noticed another of the booths had filled while she was busy, and stifled a groan.

What fresh hell was this? Not only did she have Chief Roberts to deal with this morning but her stepbrothers too.

Tyson and Dean lounged bonelessly on the padded bench seats either side of a corner table. A brunette in a shaggy yellow jacket that made her look like Big Bird pressed up against Ty, and one of their more cretinous friends, Vince, made up the foursome. Watching Vince pretend to snort three crystal lines of white sugar through a straw, Elenie estimated he'd be behind bars within six months.

"Friends and relatives." She kept her voice flat and low. "What can I get you today?"

Tyson, eldest stepbrother, moron and bane of her life—twenty-five to Elenie's twenty-seven—was a mixture of stupid and nasty that often exploded into violence. A recent barbershop visit had left him with a severe buzz cut at odds with the facial hair he'd left to grow into a short, patchy beard. Elenie eyed the tattoo of a death moth which spread down one side of his neck and disappeared into the grubby collar of his t-shirt. More ink lay beneath it, some better crafted than others. She dreamed of the day he'd come home with a spelling mistake in his latest creation, which no one in their house would notice but her. Not as tall as he'd like to be, Tyson made up for it in attitude. He thought he was a ten. She'd give him a two and a half at best.

Wincing at his loud and guttural sniff, Elenie chewed on her pen, well aware Ty was keeping her waiting just to be a dick. The diner was busy; he knew she was under pressure.

"Get us a Coke float and three chocolate milkshakes," he grunted finally.

A quick sweep of the room told her no one was listening, and Elenie couldn't resist messing with him. "I'll need to see your ID to check you're old enough to order those."

Dean and Vince looked confused; the brunette frowned.

Wow, this table has the collective smarts of a chicken nugget.

Tyson's eyes flared. "Just do your fucking job, Elephant."

"I'll be right on that, Typhoid," she murmured, giving him the fakest of smiles as she turned from the table.

Same shit, different day.

Some shifts felt so much harder than others. It wasn't even mid-morning and Elenie wanted to throw up her hands and surrender. Every time a customer held their purse tighter and gave her a suspicious side-eye, stiffed her on a tip, ignored her, snapped at her, or even moved their small child closer, it chipped away another fragment of her self-worth. Four years of this job would be enough to break anyone's spirit.

One day, things would be different.

One day, she'd slide into a booth, in her own clothes and with well-rested feet. She'd place her order with another waitress. She'd sit with friends and a partner who looked at her like she lit up his world. Like he couldn't take a proper breath without her nearby. Like . . . well, like the heroes in her favorite romance books. Who didn't exist.

Simple dreams. Impossible dreams.

And if I'm going after the impossible, make it him, please. The sexy stranger. Cool, calm, and charcoal-wrapped in gray.

It was a particular form of torture to have him listen, missing nothing, while Chief Roberts talked to her like a diseased possum. Elenie squeezed the mugs, pancakes, and bacon onto a tray and dragged her attention back to the present, wondering for the millionth time if her miserable boss would ever convince a second waitress to last more than a week.

"Here we are, gentlemen."

Roberts didn't bother to acknowledge her. He continued his monologue—something riveting to do with budgets—around a mouthful of bacon, stuffed into his mouth the moment the plate was laid in front of him. Manners of a pig, potbelly of a wild boar.

Mr. Sexy Forearms was a different beast entirely, radiating powerful wild-panther vibes. Fluid, alert, and contained. When he leaned back from the table to give Elenie space to finish unloading the tray, her hand brushed so close to his arm that her pulse took a little jump shot.

"Thank you." His smile was another small lift of his lips, but it was friendly. Surprising enough to make her pause, handsome enough to make her stare. His eyes, so dark it was hard to make out the pupils, studied and evaluated until Elenie felt way too exposed.

His face wasn't perfect. It was a little too drawn, hollowed around the cheekbones. The fine line of a well-healed scar ran just below the curve of his jaw, yanking him by the collar out of "Aftershave Ad" territory and into "I've Seen Some Things In My Time." His nose wasn't quite straight either. Maybe he'd broken it at some point, maybe it had always been that way. Maybe she should stop staring at him now.

Elenie poured the chief's coffee and moved away. Going from table to table, order to order, she made herself focus on the work, her surroundings, the customers—and was successful, to a point.

At the counter, Brody McAlpine, owner of the local gun and rod shop, gossiped with Nathan Reyes from the liquor store. Neither looked her in the eye as she delivered their breakfast sandwiches; unsurprising, as both had little reason for a favorable opinion of Elenie's family. Peggy Winterburn held court at a table of older ladies, complaining about the unnecessary power of her neighbor's security light. And, just inside the door, a gaggle of teenagers with a free first period took on caffeine to fuel their day at Pine Springs High.

Diner 43 was, as the chief said, the best place in town for breakfast.

Ringing up another check, Elenie saw that someone from the local business guild had dropped off a small pile of flyers for their gala dinner, so she shuffled them into a neat stack by the cash register. Taking two from the top and grabbing some clear tape from beneath the counter, she fixed one to the wall next to the coffee machine and took the other to the entrance. Taping it to the inside of the glass, she pulled open the door to check it was straight.

Expertly dodging the foot that Dean stuck out to trip her on her way back, she elbowed him in the head without breaking her stride. Younger than Tyson, Dean was softer in looks than his brother and Elenie found him marginally less irritating. But he upheld the family tradition of making consistently bad choices because he was slow on the uptake, hadn't been taught any better, and had friends who were all losers.

As she cleared her stepbrothers' table, hoping to encourage them to leave, Tyson flicked out his hand, catching the underside of the tray. The four tall glasses rocked and tumbled, a spray of ice cream and chocolate milkshake remnants showering Elenie from chin to waist and soaking her shirt. The float glass rolled over the edge and smashed on the floor.

Delia's head popped through the serving hatch, habitual glare in place.

Thanks for the concern—I'm fine! Globby droplets of vanilla dripped from Elenie's forearm.

Ty studied the puddle by her feet. "That's a health and safety hazard, sis. I'd get onto that if I was you."

Her toes curling inside her sneakers, she fought the urge to hit him smack in the face with the tray, walk her sticky feet through the door of the diner, and never come back. Instead, face impassive but throat tight, Elenie fetched a dustpan and a cloth to clear up the mess, suffering a roomful of eyes on her back as she swept and wiped. When a pair of black lace-up boots appeared at the edge of the broken glass wasteland, her eyelids fluttered closed for a brief, strength-seeking moment.

"Can I help you?" Hands filled with the wreckage from the floor, she tilted her chin to look up at the hot stranger—a long, long way up, into a face of shadows and angles.

Lean, but muscular, his trim, strong frame filled out his uniform like it was bespoke. She had a ridiculous urge to poke her finger into his stomach just to test how much give there was. She would bet on meeting a solid wall of resistance.

Elenie kept her finger to herself.

"I'd like to pay when you have a minute."

"Of course. Let me just get rid of this glass."

He gave her a brief nod and swept eyes as tough as black granite over her stepbrothers and their friends. They fixed on Dean, who stared blankly back from under his beanie.

"You'll want to hand over the cash you took from the next table." Flat and uncompromising, the man's suggestion was not a request.

Elenie stood up, dumped the dustpan and its contents onto the tabletop, and thrust out her hand. Pulling a crumpled bill from his pocket, Dean slapped it into her palm with a shrug.

Behind the counter, she busied herself at the cash register. Mr. Sexy Forearms slid a card from his wallet, his stare never wavering from her face, and the dry tinder inside Elenie's chest threatened to smolder and burn.

Get a grip, girl. He's in uniform, therefore he's dangerous. Out of bounds. Not. For. You.

She wished with all her heart that she was someone else.

"Roman Martinez! I heard you were in town." Dragged back to earth, Elenie watched Nathan Reyes reach out and the two men clasped hands. "Where've you been working?"

"Detroit PD. Homicide division." The words sounded forced on the hot stranger's lips.

"You're not just visiting either, by the looks of it?" Eyes alight with interest, Nathan gestured to his uniform.

"I'll be taking over from Chief Roberts at the end of the week."

Oh, dear God. That was both the answer to Elenie's prayers and a huge complication, all rolled into one.

"This guy. Best cleanup hitter Pine Springs High ever had!" Nathan said, turning to fill in Brody McAlpine with a broad grin.

"No one could touch us when Martinez was on the baseball field. We all thought he was headed for the big leagues."

The new chief smiled but Elenie noticed his fingers had clenched around the credit card in his palm. Ignoring Nathan's comment, he gave Brody a polite chin lift. "Pretty sure I recognize your face, sir. It's good to see you again."

The three exchanged a few more words while Elenie rang up the check. Heart as heavy as a bowling ball, fingers slippery with milkshake on the buttons of the card reader, she tried to pretend she wasn't an unholy mess of chocolate flavoring and ice cream and just did her job.

So, she'd been humiliated in front of the mouthwatering Roman Martinez, former Golden Boy of Pine Springs High. What did that even matter?

He'd find out soon enough why the Daxes didn't feature on the Christmas card list of anyone from the local PD.

ABOUT THE AUTHOR

Sophie Hamilton is a diehard romance devotee. If a lifelong search for her own personal Happy Ever After has taught her anything, it's that the path to true love almost never runs smoothly—but it does make a great story.

A PR journalist for over twenty years, she writes from the Georgian home in West Sussex that she has been renovating with her husband. She is unnaturally obsessed with dinosaurs and quite fond of her children, too.

Edge of Falling is her third novel.

Follow the Author on Amazon

If you enjoyed this book, follow Sophie Hamilton on Amazon to be notified when the author releases a new book!
To do this, please follow these instructions:

Desktop:

1) Search for the author's name on Amazon or in the Amazon App.
2) Click on the author's name to arrive on their Amazon page.
3) Click the "Follow" button.

Mobile and Tablet:

1) Search for the author's name on Amazon or in the Amazon App.
2) Click on one of the author's books.
3) Click on the author's name to arrive on their Amazon page.
4) Click the "Follow" button.

Kindle eReader and Kindle App:

If you enjoyed this book on a Kindle eReader or in the Kindle App, you will find the author "Follow" button after the last page.